FAIR CATCH

BOOK ONE OF THE LOVE AND SPORTS SERIES

MEGHAN QUINN

ISBN: 1500250279
ISBN-13: 978-1500250270

CHAPTER ONE

Lexi

Lexi was bent over, hands on her knees, panting, trying to catch her breath when a large, strong hand touched her back.

"Lex, that was your best yet!"

She couldn't even gather her words to respond to her best friend and current human stopwatch because of the lack of oxygen running through her body. She just finished her last sprint in a series of sprints around the bases that she was randomly tested on by her coach. Her coach gives each girl on the team the chance to run the bases in under twelve and a half seconds at the beginning of each year. Lexi had been striving for eleven seconds and, with the look on Parker's face, it looked like she hit her goal.

She finally caught her breath and glanced up at Parker. "Did I get it? Did I hit eleven?"

Parker grinned and showed her the stopwatch in his hand. She wanted to jump up and down out of excitement, but she had absolutely no energy to do so. Instead, she flopped her body on the dirt as if she was going to make a snow angel and motioned for Parker to join her, which he easily did, since he wasn't the one sprinting.

"Thanks for the help today, bud."

He leaned over and gave her a high five, which she returned with a brisk snap of her hand to his. "No problem, shorty."

Ever since freshman orientation at California University, Parker and her had been glued at the hip and he had been making fun of her height ever since. She didn't blame him, though. She was a five foot three blonde with one hell of a bat and impeccable range in center field that would frustrate any heavy-hitting batter. She'd received a full-ride scholarship for softball at Cal U. and had taken the school's offer very seriously. She strived to be the best on the field and in the classroom, which she had accomplished in the past three years of her college career, but now that she was starting her senior season, there was something missing and she couldn't quite figure it out.

She looked over at Parker, who was now sucking down the last contents of the PowerAde they decided to share. He was the shortstop for the baseball team and had the same work ethic as she did. That was why they were such great friends and friendship was all that there was between them. They tried getting romantically involved once, but it was way more wrong than right. It felt like making out with each other's sibling, which was not something they ever wanted to do again. So, instead of becoming romantically involved, they became emotionally attached. They went to each other for everything and when the coming year was over, Lexi dreaded saying goodbye to her best friend, who was already being looked at by a bunch of different professional teams. There was no doubt in her mind that he was going to make it big one day.

Parker tossed the empty bottle in front of them and said, "What do you plan on doing tonight?"

Lexi shrugged. "Not sure. I think Margo is coming back tonight. So maybe I'll do something with her."

Margo was Lexi's roommate. They had a two-bedroom apartment in the villas, right near campus. Most of the athletes stayed in them. The villas were the best housing for students and they were closest to campus. They were mini apartments; each room had its own bathroom with a shared kitchen and common area. The best thing about the apartment was the common areas separated the bedrooms, giving ample space between her bedroom and Margo's. She loved her roommate and teammate, but Margo was quite loose with her men and Lexi liked to stay as far away from Margo's room as she could whenever Margo had someone over.

Parker was shaking his head. "Nope, not going to happen."

"What are you talking about?"

"You're not spending your senior year locked up in your apartment like you have the past three years."

She wrinkled her nose. "Hey! You make it seem like I'm some sort of hermit. I go out when I want to."

"Yeah, on Halloween when the baseball team has a party, but that's it. This year is going to be different. We have an easy course load and you know it; we pretty much are amazing at everything we do on the field, so we're going to learn to relax a little and have some fun."

She was about to interrupt him when he held up his hand. "I don't want to hear it. This is our last year and hell if I'm going to let you sit around your apartment, wearing your dingy sweats while watching romantic comedies."

"My sweats aren't dingy," she said, while Parker practically lifted her off the ground.

"They aren't sexy, that's for sure."

"Well, when I'm home alone, I'm not trying to be sexy for myself."

"When you have a nickname known throughout the school like 'Sexy Lexi,' then I think you need to hold some higher standards."

She rolled her eyes. "I hate that nickname. Whoever started that needs to be shot."

"Hmm, I wonder who that was?" he said with a sly grin.

They started walking toward the lockers to drop of their gear off when she punched him in the shoulder. "You started that?"

He rubbed his arm and said, "Hey watch the money maker."

"Park, did you seriously start that ridiculous nickname?"

He smiled. "How could I not? Look at you!"

Lexi always hated when people called her Sexy Lexi; it made her feel like some kind of prostitute, which was what she felt like most of the time anyway. Her body proportions were way out of whack. She had a very petite frame, which helped with her speed, but she had breasts that belonged to a Playboy bunny and they were all real, which was another reason she rarely went out, because guys were only capable of staring at her breasts. She also had naturally beach-blonde hair and light blue eyes. Basically, she was your stereotypical California girl.

Lexi punched him again in the same spot, hoping she left a bruise. "You're an ass."

He grinned at her. "But I'm your ass!"

"I sure hope to God not."

They got to a point in the events center where their paths would break, since the men's locker rooms were separate from the women's. They stopped in the center, staring at each other.

"So what do you say? Will you come out tonight? The football team is having a party tonight and I could really use my beer pong partner at my side. What do you say?"

"Football party? Ugh Park, you couldn't have chosen a different party? The football team is the most arrogant bunch of douchebags at the school."

"They kind of have a reason to be, with such a great winning record over the last decade."

She shrugged. "Still, just because you're good at your sport, doesn't mean you can be a bastard. Look at us, we're amazing, but you don't see us strutting the campus with our wangs out."

Parker looked down at her crotch and raised his eyebrow. "If you have a wang you want to let out, I might have to reconsider this friendship."

"Ugh, you are infuriating today."

Parker pulled her into a hug and kissed the top of her head like he always did when they parted. "I'll pick you up around eight. Wear something hot!" He gave her a quick a grin, smacked her ass, and walked away.

Lexi watched his arrogant ass walk away and thought about how he could pass as a football player. Parker was one of the best shortstops she had ever seen and was quite the looker too. He was the dark and dangerous type, but with a heart of gold. On the outside, he looked like he could rip you into shreds with his bare hands, being six foot something and muscular, thanks to the strength and conditioning program, but he was a softy deep down inside. Almost all the girls on her team begged her to set them up with Parker, but she never found any of them worthy enough.

She keyed in the code to get into the women's softball locker room and threw her cleats in the bottom of her locker. The softball team had an amazing new stadium, but their locker room was sub-par. They didn't have enough room to hang their bat bags in their actual lockers, so they all piled them up in the middle of the room. It was easy storage, but hard to grab your bag in a hurry when it was on the bottom of the heap.

She looked around the empty room at the different names that were displayed at the top of each locker and thought about how much she was going to miss this. Softball had been her life since she was in fifth grade and to not have it anymore was something she couldn't quite comprehend. She had given up dances, sleepovers, birthday parties and pretty much every social gathering to drive around the west coast and play tournament after tournament. In the end, it all paid off because she got to play her sport at the highest level of play and get a free education at the same time.

She thought about the last three years of her life and yes, she was well-known in the sports community at Cal U because of her ability to shatter almost every previous softball record, but no one really knew her. People said hi and that was pretty much it. The closest people to her were Margo and Parker, but that was it.

Maybe Parker was right, maybe she should relax a little this year and experience that social life she'd missed out on over the past decade of her life.

It wasn't that she didn't like being social; she was just trained to concentrate on her softball skills and education her whole life, so she really knew nothing else. She didn't really know what she was missing out on until she arrived at college and saw everyone interacting with each other.

When she was a freshman, she didn't want to get mixed up in any kind of social scene and lose focus on what was important, so she stuck to herself most of the time and occasionally hung out with Parker and Margo. Her sophomore year, she found that the method she had used to handle college the previous year had been successful, since she had a 4.0 and was the starting centerfielder over a senior so she decided to continue with her work ethic. By the time her junior year rolled around, she made a goal to break almost every record possible, which she accomplished. Now that she was a senior and was looking back at her college career, she had accomplished everything she wanted to. Instead of replaying the last three years of her college career, she should do something for herself. She wanted to see what it would be like to let loose and have fun, while still maintaining her education and athleticism.

She could do it, she knew she could and Parker was right, her workload was light this year, since she took a lot of summer classes in between each year to keep herself busy. By the time she graduated, she would have a major in Journalism and a minor in Communications, something she was damn proud of. What she was going to do with that? She had no clue, but she had a year to think about it.

On her way back to her apartment, after dropping everything off in the locker room, she decided that she was going to take Parker up on his offer. It wasn't like he was going to let her get away with staying home, but at least she knew she was making the decision for herself.

She pulled into her apartment, took a quick shower and threw her hair up in a towel; she decided to let her natural waves take over tonight and let her long locks hang over her shoulders. If Parker wanted hot, she was going to give him hot.

An hour and a half later, she was dressed in her tightest black skinny jeans, deep purple tank blouse that hugged her figure and showed off a massive display of cleavage, and she put on her purple flats. She would have worn her heels, but knowing the party would be at the football house, the floors would be drenched with beer and she didn't want to slip on the frothy liquid. What a way to make an entrance, she thought. She wore a little bit more mascara and eye shadow than normal, but she kind of liked the way she looked…so mysterious.

There was a knock at her door, causing her to shove the rest of the peanut butter and jelly sandwich she was snacking on in her mouth as she went to open the door. Parker was standing at her door in a pair of worn jeans and a tight navy blue polo.

The look on his face was priceless when he saw her. She practically saw his mouth drop to the floor and his tongue hang out. Just the look she was going for. She thought to herself, eat your own words, Parker!

He shook his head and said, "Jesus Lexi, I can't remember that last time I saw you so dressed up. Damn girl, you look hot!"

She smiled and did a little turn for him. "So, you approve?" she asked, while holding her hands up.

"I definitely approve."

"Good, let me write a quick note to let Margo know I'll be out and then we can get going."

"Awesome. I hope you're ready to kick some beer pong ass tonight. I'm counting on you Lex. I want to own that table."

"Come on, if there is one social event I'm good at, it's beer pong. We'll own those football douchebags tonight!"

"Just the comment I wanted to hear."

CHAPTER TWO

Jake

The last thing Jake wanted to do right now was go to a party hosted at the football house. Last year, he would have been the one hosting the whole damn thing himself, but this year was different. This was his senior year and he needed to make sure he had one of the best seasons of his life. His plan was to move onto professional football and, so far, his plan was working out. There was buzz on the streets that he would be a first-round draft pick. He'd led his team the past two years to division championships and he planned on tacking on a third. Being the quarterback and one of the team captains for the very popular football team at Cal U was a ton of pressure, but it also had its perks.

He was friends with everyone, even the local patrons. He had every girl in the school throwing herself at him and he had possible future endorsements already lining up for when he graduated, but nothing set in stone, since it was illegal to take any kind of endorsement compensation while he was still playing in the NCAA.

He'd had one hell of a college career, his choice of girl, his choice of party, and his choice of what happened on and off the field with his teammates. The past three years he'd lived in the football house, goofed around when they didn't have practice or games, slept with almost the entire female athletic department, and drank his fair share of beers. They were good years, but now that he was moving on to his senior year and looking back on what he'd accomplished the last three years, he was disappointed in himself for not taking school more seriously.

Football only took athletes so far. What would he do if, heaven forbid, he wasn't drafted or if his career was short-lived? He needed to take his last year more seriously so he had an option when football was over for him. That was why he'd moved out of the football house and moved into the villas. He had his own place there; it was more expensive than splitting rent with five other guys, but his scholarship paid for it and he liked having his own place. The villas were mainly for athletes, which was nice because, even though he was living on his own, he was still surrounded by his peers.

He walked up the path to the house he'd spent three amazing years in and sighed. It was going to be a long night, especially since he was not in the mood for his senior year to start and the start of every new school year was shot off by the football team throwing one hell of a rager.

"Jake, over here man."

Jake's teammate, Mason, waved him over. Mason was also a captain on the team and Jake's best friend. They'd been scared freshmen together and made it through the past three years barely holding on by a thread from the pressure of popularity, football and school.

Jake grabbed Mason's hand and gave him a half hug.

"How was Hawaii, you lucky bastard?" Jake asked. Mason took the summer off with his steady girlfriend to explore the islands of Hawaii. His girlfriend's family was extremely well-off and Mason couldn't pass up the opportunity to visit the tropical islands.

"Amazing. Brooke looked so damn hot in her plethora of bikinis."

Brooke wasn't an athlete, but she was a sorority girl and was hotter than hell with her perky breasts, brown hair and green eyes. How Mason was able to score her, Jake would never know.

"I'm sure she did. Was her family cock-blocking you the whole time?"

Mason laughed, "No, we actually had our own hut looking over the ocean the whole time."

Jake shook his head. "You lucky, lucky bastard."

A freshman came up to them and handed Jake a beer. Jake nodded to the kid he didn't know, popped open the beer and took a long swig.

They were surveying the party when Mason asked, "Why are you so late? Everyone has been asking where you were. I was afraid you weren't going to show."

Jake shrugged. "I don't know man, this whole scene isn't really me anymore."

Mason snorted. "Who you kidding, bud? This scene is because of you. Are you going soft on me?"

Was he? How was Jake supposed to explain to his best friend that he wasn't really looking for the party scene anymore? He was more interested in becoming serious with his life. He was still young, but the fact that he was going to be going through some of the biggest changes in his life and he had no one to share it with, freaked him out. He'd lost his parents in a serious car accident right after he left for college, leaving him alone…completely and utterly alone. That was one of the reasons he lost himself in beer, parties and women; he was trying to fill an empty void. He was smart enough to pull off good grades to continue playing football, but he never actually applied himself. He would graduate with a major in English, but would have nothing, really, to show for it.

"Uh, hello, earth to Jake?"

Jake shook the thoughts out of his head. "Sorry, forget what I said." He gestured toward the beer pong table. "Competition good this year?"

"Oh man, this one team is on a roll…"

Jake didn't hear anything else Mason said because, in that instant, he laid eyes on the most gorgeous blonde he had ever seen and everything faded to black, except for a spotlight on her. She was gorgeous with her long blonde wavy locks, piercing blue eyes, so light they were almost white, and her tight body. Jake thought he was going to burst from the seams of his pants at the way his body was reacting to her.

He watched her every move as Mason rambled on about the tournament the football team hosted every year. Parker, who Jake recognized from the baseball team, came up behind the gorgeous blonde and scooped her up around her waist. Jake instantly wanted to send his linemen in for the kill to take out Parker, even though Jake didn't even know the girl. She laughed as Parker twirled her around. That was when he noticed they were the team Mason was talking about. The "Unstoppables" they called themselves.

Jake interrupted his friend. "Mason, who the hell is that?" He pointed at the beauty in front of him.

Mason gave him a puzzled look. "Have you been dead the last three years?"

"What are you talking about?"

Mason pointed at the girl, "That is the infamous Sexy Lexi, man."

Jake's jaw nearly hit the floor. "I thought that was some locker room myth bullshit that some lonely guy made up."

The guys always talked about "Sexy Lexi," but he never thought the image the guys built up in the locker room was an actual living, breathing human person. Now that he looked at her, what the guys said didn't even do her justice.

"No, she's the real deal."

"How come this is the first time I'm ever seeing her?"

Mason laughed, "Well, word on the street is that she hates the football team, calls us a bunch of douchebags, and she doesn't go out much."

"Well, we are douchebags, look at us."

They both looked around the party and took in all their

teammates; it was a conglomeration of idiotic asses parading around, showing off their muscles to the ladies, doing beer bongs and acting like adolescent morons by daring each other into stupid antics.

"Dear God," Mason said, "I hope we never acted like that."

Jake clinked his beer with Mason's and said, "I'm afraid we did."

"That's embarrassing to think about."

Jake chuckled. "Slightly. So tell me more about Lexi. She's a senior?"

Mason laughed at him. "Forget about it man. She is the type of girl you aren't used to. She's no one-night bang. There's no way you're getting in her pants."

Annoyed by his friend's assumption, which would have been accurate last year, he got up and headed into the kitchen to get another beer. Was he really looked at as a guy who just banged any girl he saw? Jake shook his head in disappointment; he was that guy and he only had himself to blame.

Mason caught up to him. "Dude, I didn't mean to insult you back there."

Jake shook him off. "No, don't worry about it. Something changed for me over the summer. It's hard to explain, but I don't want to be that guy anymore.

Mason grabbed them both another beer. "Any guy would want to be in your shoes, you know? And you just want to throw it away?"

"Out of everyone, I would think you would understand the most, being in a serious relationship and all."

Mason's face went sober. "I do understand. It gets lonely; I always wondered how you did it, man."

Jake shrugged Mason's comment off. "Well, I'm tired of being alone."

"You know you're not alone." Mason put his hand on Jake's shoulder.

Ever since Jake found out about his parent's accident, Mason had never left his side. Mason invited him to every holiday and made him a part of his family, something Jake will be forever grateful toward Mason for. Mason's family took him in when he had nowhere else to go.

"I know, thanks."

Mason shivered and said, "Alright, I need to get wasted now because we're looking like a bunch of pansy-ass fairies right now."

Jake laughed. "Before you get wasted and lose all ability to hold a decent conversation, I have one question."

"Shoot."

"Is Lexi dating Parker? They seem awfully chummy."

"Chummy? Really? Did you lose your balls this summer or something? You better clean up your act and get your bad-boy image going before we get back on the field. Lord knows, the guys won't let that kind of shit slip."

Jake rolled his eyes. "Just answer the damn question."

Mason smirked. "Not that I know of. She hasn't really had any kind of relationship, I don't think. She's been untouchable, but she has been starring in every male athlete's dream that lives and breathes near her."

Jake could imagine that easily. One look and he was hooked on her. He had an intense need to get to know her, to hold her, to touch her. He watched Lexi walk out on the deck after she and Parker won the last game in the tournament. Parker was trapped by one of the girl lacrosse players who wasn't actually too bad to look at, so Jake decided to take the opportunity to make his move with Lexi.

She was leaning against one of the pillars on the deck when he approached her from behind and what a fantastic behind she had. Her jeans fit her like a glove and glided over every single curve she had, as did the purple shirt she was wearing. Her hair was cascading over her shoulders, urging his hand to reach out and run his fingers through it. She wasn't wearing heels, like he normally preferred a girl to do, but the flats she was wearing made her seem oddly fragile, given the tough-girl exterior she displayed for the world.

"You've got a good shot," he said, startling her.

She turned around with her hand to her heart, her eyes wide with shock. They were the color of the sky on a bright sunny day and her mouth looked beyond kissable.

"Jesus, you scared the crap out of me."

He couldn't help but chuckle. "Sorry, I didn't mean to."

"So you think sneaking up on someone isn't going to startle them?" she asked, while crossing her arms over her ample chest. He averted his eyes so she didn't catch him staring at her breasts, but it was too late. Her forehead creased together in displeasure.

"You really are some player, like everyone says. You talk to me for two seconds and you're already staring at my breasts."

She sucked the air right out of his sails. She didn't even give him a chance to put on his charm before she started shooting him down. She shook her head in disgust and started to move past him. Never had a woman so instantly rejected him, without even giving him a chance to convince her not to. She almost got past him before he let go of the shock that took over his body and stood in front of her, so she couldn't move past him.

She looked up at him in horror. "Are you serious right now? You aren't going to let me through?"

He held up his hand to stop her from talking. "Listen, I think we got off on the wrong foot here." He held out his hand. "I'm Jake."

She looked at him with displeasure. "I know exactly who you are. I haven't been dead the last three years at this school. I'm just glad to see that you're living up to your reputation."

Now she was making him mad. She was judging him without even letting him get five words out of his mouth. If she wasn't so damn intriguing and beautiful, he would let her by, but he couldn't get himself to move.

"Wow, you're real quick to judge," he found himself saying.

"Do you blame me? I'm probably the only girl at this party you haven't banged."

Jake felt fire burning in his stomach. No one had ever talked to him like this and he didn't particularly care for her attitude, even though his instincts were telling him to rip her clothes off right now and take her to bed. What was wrong with him?"

"You're kind of a bitch, you know that?" The words slipped out of his mouth before he could stop himself.

She faked horror and waved a hand in front of her face. "Oh, how you hurt me with your words." She rolled her eyes and tried to move past him once again, but his stupid body stopped her again. He really wished his body and brain would reconnect because he wasn't happy with the miscommunication between the two of them.

"What's your deal?" he asked.

She crossed her hands over her chest again, but this time he made sure to keep his eyes locked on hers.

"I'm not going to be another notch on your belt."

"Don't flatter yourself, babe."

She snorted, "Oh please, I saw you drooling earlier when you were talking to your friend, Mason. I'm not an idiot. I know when I see a dog on the prowl."

"What if I just wanted to get to know you?"

His off-hand comment made her laugh out loud. It would have made him laugh, if he hadn't changed his perspective this year.

"That would be the day. You're just a ladies' man who has always gotten his way. Not this time!"

"That's not true," he objected. Then, all of a sudden, as if the dating gods were punishing him, two girls from the soccer team, twins to be exact, Judy and Julie, walked up on either side of him and rubbed their breasts against his arms as they surrounded him.

"Jake, you promised you would meet up with us after the summer was over. We've been waiting for you," they whined.

Perfect timing, Jake thought. He looked back at Lexi who rolled her eyes and finally escaped past him. He watched her walk away and sidle up right next to Parker, who put an arm around her shoulder and kissed her on the head. She whispered something in his ear, causing him to look back at Jake and then nod toward the door. They were gone in a matter of seconds and he was left with the soccer twins. That went well, he thought sarcastically, as the twins continued to press their bodies against his.

Fan-fucking-tastic.

CHAPTER THREE

Lexi

Lexi was still reeling from the party the night before and the audacity Jake had of coming up to her and just staring at her boobs. She knew she was way bigger than her body called for and she was wearing a low-cut shirt, but could he have been any more of a pig?

She thought about when he first told her she had a "good shot;" she was so startled he actually spoke to her that she failed to hate him for a second. When she turned around, she was even more startled by how ruggedly handsome he was. She cursed and hated herself for even thinking he was handsome, but how could she not? The guy was a freaking fantasy. No man should ever be that attractive. He was muscular beyond belief, had light brown hair that was styled just perfectly in a short do and he had the lightest green eyes she had ever seen. Plus, his dimples and chin cleft didn't help. She felt herself completely melting in his presence, which was why she acted like a complete bitch, which thankfully, he called her out on, because she didn't want anything to do with him. He was trouble with a capital "T."

"Hello, Lex, come on you have two more sets to go. I would

like to get out of here before my morning class starts."

Lexi snapped out of her thoughts. "Sorry Margo."

The team had morning strength and conditioning and Margo and Lexi were always partners. They were just finishing up on the bench press when Lexi got lost in her thoughts.

"What's going on, girl? Why are you so out of it today?"

Lexi finished up her last rep and helped Margo switch the weight. Margo always lifted more than she did.

Lexi blew out a breath, while Margo laid down on the bench and began her reps.

"Jake Taylor approached me at the party last night."

Margo placed the bar back on the rack. "Ooo, girl…You're lucky."

Lexi gave her friend a wrinkled look. "I want nothing to do with him. He is so full of himself and believes anyone who is in his presence should bow at his feet. He is so obnoxious and arrogant…"

Margo interrupted her, "Wow, slow down. If I didn't know any better, I'd say you like him."

Lexi huffed. "Didn't you hear anything I just said?"

"Loud and clear, you might as well go punch him on the playground. You're so crushing on him."

"I am not!"

Lexi felt her face starting to burn from anger…or was it embarrassment?

Margo set the weights down and looked at Lexi. "I can tell by the way your face is all red. You like him. Join the crowd, girl. Every girl who sets eyes on him can't help but fall under his charms."

They took the weights off and marked off their reps on the workout sheets provided by their trainer.

"I don't like him. If anything, I despise the guy. He just noticed me for the first time last night! We've been in the same class since we were freshman. That is just insulting."

"How is he supposed to notice you when you've been a

hermit your entire college career? Plus, he doesn't really have to notice girls when they're always throwing their bodies in front of his face."

Lexi flipped her friend off and went to return her training sheet back to her file where the trainer kept all of the athlete's workouts. Lexi was annoyed with Margo's accusations.

She did not like Jake Taylor, not even close. Yeah, he was attractive; she would give him that, but he was a player, he had his dick in almost every girl who was willing in the athletic department and he was completely and overly full of himself. Why would she want anything to do with him?

She was mad at Parker for dragging her to the stupid party in the first place. Yeah, she should be living up her senior year like he said, but she didn't need complications like Jake Taylor getting in her way. She still had to figure out what she was doing with her life after softball. Parker was lucky, he would be able to continue to play the sport that he loved and make millions by doing so, but Lexi, she had to actually go out into the real world and find what interested her.

She walked over to the water fountain to fill up her water bottle while she replayed her encounter with Cal U's one and only ladies' man over in her head. She cursed herself for envisioning his smile and remembering the little flutter that took place at the bottom of her stomach when he stopped her from walking away. No, she would not think about him, that was exactly what he would want.

She turned to grab Margo when she ran straight into a tall muscular mass. The impact caused her to fall back and stumble until she fell straight on her ass. Embarrassment laced through her body, as she looked up and made eye contact with those light green eyes hadn't been able to stop thinking about since last night.

"Whoa, sorry there, Lexi," Jake said, while reaching out a hand to help her up. She ignored his hand and got up herself. Margo caught up to her and the smirk on Margo's face made Lexi want to punch her best friend square in the boob.

"Hey Jake," Margo said. "Looks like you took down our little center fielder. No one ever knocks her down."

Lexi looked at Margo as if she was insane for talking to him. She grabbed her friend's arm and started walking away from the massive football player. Margo was mumbling something under her breath when Lexi was yanked back by the arm.

"Hold up," Jake said. "I want to talk to you."

Lexi looked at Margo and said, "Go ahead talk away. Margo, I'll catch up with you later."

Margo stopped her. "Dearie, he wants to talk to you, not me."

Lexi turned to Jake to confirm and he just smiled. Lexi folded her arms in front of her chest, putting off the most defensive stance she knew and asked, "What do you want? And why they hell are you up this early? The football team never has to work out this early."

"I wanted to catch you before you went to class."

Lexi shook her head. "How do you even know I have class this morning?" She held up her hand. "Wait, I don't care, just tell me what you want."

"Fine, I'll get right down to the point. I want you to be my date for the alumni dinner this Friday."

Lexi felt her mouth drop to the floor. He wants her to be his date? Want? He didn't even ask, he just stated his needs. She was about to open her mouth in protest when Margo beat her to it and said, "She would love to. What time?" Margo's interjection made Jake smile, causing Lexi to slightly melt, but then she realized what Margo had said and she was able to regain her senses.

"No, I would not love to. Where the hell do you get off going around demanding what you want people to do? You can find yourself another date. Lord knows any girl would trade her left tit to go on a date with you."

Her comment made Jake laugh, causing rage to take residence in Lexi's body. "What's so funny?" she asked.

"You, you're so stubborn."

"I'm stubborn? Because I don't want to go out with you?

That's not stubborn, that's just knowing what I don't want and I'm sorry to say it, but that's you."

Jake feigned an attack to his heart as he put his hands to his chest. "Your words kill me." She rolled her eyes. He straightened up and said, "I'll bet you for it."

Lexi wanted to take out whoever told him all about her. How the hell did he know she never turned down a bet? It was her one weakness, whenever someone said they would bet her, it was practically impossible for her to refuse. She looked at Jake and knew, no matter what he said, she wouldn't be able to refuse because she wanted to put him in his place and wipe that damn smirk off his gorgeous mug.

"What are you thinking about?" she asked. She saw Margo rub her hands together in excitement next to her.

Jake stepped closer so he was inches from her. She had to crank her head up to look him in the eyes because he was significantly taller than she was. He drew her in with those green eyes and his all-male scent pulled at her very core. Damn him.

"I challenge you to a race."

Margo laughed. "A race? How is that fair?"

Lexi wanted to shut her friend up, but she knew she might be right. Yes, Lexi was the fastest girl in her conference, but Jake was Jake Taylor, about to be a first-round draft pick. She didn't stand much of a chance.

"A race on the slide board," Jake finished.

Lexi couldn't help but smile. She owned the slide board; it was the one thing she could beat anybody at. When she was first introduced to the contraption, she was intimidated by it; now, she couldn't get enough of it.

"You're on! What are the rules?" Lexi was practically shaking with excitement.

"We slide for a minute. Whoever gets the most touches wins."

"Sounds fair enough. What are the so-called prizes?"

If it was possible, Jake got even cockier. "If you win, I'll leave you alone."

"Hallelujah!" Lexi shouted.

"And if I win," he interrupted her celebration, "you have to go to the Alumni dinner with me, on a date…dressed up and everything."

Lexi cocked an eyebrow. "What do you constitute as a date? I'm pretty sure we have very different opinions of what goes into a date."

"Just a date, maybe a casual touch here and there, but nothing else."

"No casual touches, you will keep your slimy hands to yourself."

"I would think that I would be allotted a couple of touches."

Lexi held up her hand to stop him. "Not that it matters anyway, because you're going down, Taylor."

"We will see about that, Knox."

They went back into the weight room and they each grabbed the plastic booties that helped them slide on the board and put them on their feet. Margo grabbed their trainer who had stop watches and Swiffer Dust to lube up the boards.

The board was a thick plastic surface with two rubber stops on each side. The point of the exercise was to work on explosive lateral movements, which Lexi mastered two years ago.

They each would have their own board and start on the same side. When they were told to go, they would have to slide from side to side and every time they returned to the side they started at, that counted as one.

Lexi grinned as she thought about how she had this in the bag. Not only was she the quickest at slide board, but she knew exactly how to work the dust polish to her advantage.

"Are you ready?" Margo asked.

She looked over at Jake who held out his hand, as a good luck gesture. She took his hand in hers and tried to ignore the zap of electricity that flowed between them. She chalked it up to the adrenaline of a challenge.

"Ready," Lexi said, as she pulled her hand away from Jake's

and rubbed it on her shorts, trying to erase the feeling of his skin on hers.

"Go!" Margo shouted.

Lexi took off and started bouncing back and forth, reveling in the fact that she was kicking Jake's ass. She didn't even bother looking over because she didn't want to feel sorry for the poor sap. Thank goodness Margo was counting for her because there was no way she could concentrate on counting how many times she hit the board. She was entirely focused on kicking Jake's ass.

Her legs were burning from pushing off the rubber and her breath was labored, but there was no way in hell she was going to lose to Jake Taylor, so she continued to push herself.

"Stop!"

Lexi slid one last time to one side and then hopped off. She put her hands on her knees as she bent over, trying to catch her breath. She stood up and put her hands over her head and looked over at Jake who was just standing there smirking at her. What was he so happy about? He didn't even break a sweat.

"What…is…the…count?" Lexi heaved.

"You got 50," Margo said, "I think that was your best."

Lexi did a mental fist pump, knowing she rocked it.

"What did Jake get?" Margo asked the Trainer.

"Sorry girls, Jake got 66."

Lexi nearly keeled over. "How the hell did he get 66?" She waved a hand at him. "He's not even breathing heavily. You're lying, he did not get 66."

"I'm afraid not, sweetie."

"How is that even possible? I'm the best at slide board."

"Until I came along," Jake said, while puffing out his chest. Lexi wished she could take a needle and pop all the air out of it.

Lexi sat down on a bench. "This doesn't make any sense."

"Sure it does, short stack," Jake said. "Look at your legs compared to mine. I have a wider range than you. Of course I would beat you."

Lexi almost choked on his words. Holy hell, he was right.

How come she never thought about that? He knew all along that he was going to win; even with her speed, there was no way she was going to beat him, all he had to do was lean over and his leg would touch the other rubber.

"You tricked me!" she shouted, while standing up and charging toward him. She laid a punch on his arm.

"Hey watch it," he said while rubbing his arm. "Don't be such a sore loser."

"I'm not being a sore loser. I just don't like being tricked."

"I didn't trick you. I just knew my strengths, that's all, something you failed to realize. Maybe if you weren't so caught up in yourself, you would have looked at the challenge logistically and realized that maybe that wasn't the safest bet you ever made."

"Caught up in myself? You have got to be kidding me!"

"Uh, can you two lovebirds take this little love spat somewhere else? You're distracting the other athletes," their trainer said.

"We are not lovebirds!" Lexi said over her shoulder, as Jake escorted her and Margo into the hallway.

He looked down at his watch and sighed. "As much as I would love to continue this little conversation, I have places to be. Margo it was nice seeing you. Short stack, I'll pick you up at 6 tomorrow night. It's formal attire, so wear something sexy."

He took off down the hallway and Lexi went to charge at him, but Margo stopped her. Lexi shouted over Margo's shoulder, "I'm wearing a turtleneck and slacks!"

Jake

Jake went to the football locker room and planted himself on the leather couch right next to Mason who was watching *SportsCenter* on the big screen TV they had in their locker room. Mason turned and looked at Jake with slight shock on his face.

"Wow, I didn't know you knew this morning hour existed."

Jake watched Mason take a bite of an apple. "I told you man,

I'm doing things differently this year."

"So, waking up early is how you're changing?"

"That and some other things."

Mason waved his hand in the air, silently telling Jake to carry on. "And what would those other things be?"

"Well, I just won a date with Lexi. I'm taking her to the Alumni dinner tomorrow."

Mason looked at Jake with honest surprise. "How the hell did you pull that off?"

"Won a bet against her, long story, but she's going. Not the ideal way I wanted to take her, but I guess I'll take what I can get."

"Wow, I'm impressed, man. I don't think anyone other than Parker has scored a date with her."

Jake thought about how beautiful she looked this morning. She didn't have any make up on, her hair was up in a ponytail and she had on gym shorts and a softball T-shirt, but he couldn't take his eyes off of her. She was beautiful, naturally beautiful. He had never felt like this before; he'd never felt such a strong attraction to another person. Ever since he laid eyes on Lexi, she was all he could think about. That was why he had talked to Parker and scored some valuable information about Lexi.

Jake was actually surprised about the amount of information Parker was willing to divulge about his best friend. Jake didn't care too much for the strong bond Parker and Lexi had, but if it was going to help him get some alone-time with Lexi, then he didn't mind too much.

"Earth to Jake," Mason interrupted his thoughts.

"Sorry."

"Man, you have it bad don't you? You really like her."

Jake shrugged and ran his hand over his face. "I don't know. All I know is that I can't stop thinking about her and I just want some time to get to know her. She's beautiful and sassy and an amazing athlete. For a second, I thought I was going to lose to her at slide board; she was good."

"You challenged her to the slide board? That was risky, she

owns that thing."

"I know; she was damn quick, but thanks to my long legs, I edged her out," Jake laughed. "And shit was she furious. I kind of get joy out of making her mad. She has quite the little temper."

Mason laughed. "Yeah, she's a firecracker. I've watched some of her games and, if she gets a call she doesn't like, she nearly flies off the deep end."

"I can imagine." Jake pulled out his phone and started typing out a text message.

"Who are you texting?" Mason asked, being nosy. He finished his apple and threw the core into the trash can. "Nothing but net. I should have gone out for basketball."

Jake looked up at the trashcan. "Because you can shoot an apple core into a giant trashcan from three feet away? Okay, keep dreaming, bud."

He sent a text to Lexi.

Jake: Had fun this morning, we should do it again sometime. See you tomorrow night.

Jake could all but hear Lexi gasp when she realized he had her phone number, another righteous score form Parker. He tried to give Parker something in return, but he wanted nothing. All he said was to not hurt Lexi. For some odd reason, Jake got the impression that Parker actually approved of Jake making a move on his best friend. Hey, that was one less boundary he had to cross to get closer to her. Winning the best friend's approval was always difficult, so he was glad Parker was so easygoing. Winning Margo over was no problem either. She seemed eager and willing to throw Lexi at him.

Mason and Jake were arguing about a highlight they saw on *SportsCenter when Jake's phone chimed with a text message. Not being able to contain a smile, knowing it was Lex*i, he looked down to read what she wrote.

Lexi: This is Professor Lyon. Lexi's phone has been confiscated, due to it going off in class. In order for her to get it back, you, whoever this is and Lexi better report to my office at two this afternoon to issue an apology and go over proper phone etiquette in the classroom.

"Oh shit," Jake muttered.

Mason turned toward Jake and asked, "What's wrong?"

Jake turned the phone so Mason could read the text message. Mason threw his head back and laughed. "Looks like you're starting off on the right foot."

Mason patted his back and took off for the weight room. Jake could feel his chest tighten. This was not the way he wanted to start things off with Lexi. He could see her little face fuming right now. The thought of it sort of made him smile. Yes, he might not be starting off on the right foot, but he got to see her again today, that was a plus in his book. Maybe not in hers, but he was going to win her over soon enough. He always did.

Margo

Margo was adjusting her bra when Parker Hill came up from behind and grabbed her waist, startling the crap out of her. She gathered herself before she turned around to look at those chocolate-brown eyes that starred in her dreams every night.

"Hey darlin'. How come it's okay for a woman to adjust her tits in public, but if a guy touches his junk, he is looked at with disgust?"

Margo lifted her head and made eye contact with the most gorgeous man she had ever seen. She'd had a crush on Parker ever since Lexi introduced him to her their freshman year. He was the perfect man: athletic, sensitive, handsome as hell and funny, but there was one thing wrong with him, he was untouchable. Lexi and he had a fling for a little bit and there was no way she would break the friend code of going after her best friend's ex, even though Lexi and Parker were best friends now. It would be too weird for everyone.

Margo thought about his question. "Maybe because men are dogs and love watching women touch themselves, while us ladies have class and know what's disgusting."

Parker seemed to weigh her answer and answered with a heartbreaking smile. "I think you're right about that. We are dogs. Do you have anywhere to be right now?"

"Nowhere at all," she said, even though she should be writing a paper that was just assigned to her, but due the next day. What teacher did that? Especially right after summer break. Margo thought there should be an understanding of easing students back into the swing of things, not bombarding them with useless educational material that they were not going to really apply in the real world.

"Great, let me buy you a drink and we can sit and chat."

Parker ordered them both smoothies from the kiosk in the middle of the campus square while she found a little bistro set to sit at. She watched Parker's behind shift back and forth while he waited for their drinks. God he was gorgeous, and he didn't even flaunt it like Jake, that made him even hotter.

When he turned around with their drinks and spotted her, he lifted his head in her direction to acknowledge he saw her and smiled. She sighed. She would never get tired of his smile. She dreaded their last year in college because she knew he was going to go off and do bigger and better things, while she was going to hopefully get her masters or get a job. She wouldn't have moments like this anymore and she most likely wouldn't see him very much, due to his soon-to-be very busy schedule.

A strawberry banana smoothie was placed in front of her as Parker asked, "Why the frown, sweet cheeks?"

Margo half-smiled at him. "Oh, just thinking about a stupid paper I have to write."

"Man, the blood-sucking professors already started attacking you?"

"Of course, I should have been smart like you and Lexi and

taken some summer classes, that way my senior year would be a breeze."

He tilted his drink toward her. "Yes, you should have. Haven't I always told you to follow my lead? Honestly Margo, when are you going to learn?" he said with a grin.

"I think I learned the first time I followed your lead and I ended up in a dumpster in the early morning with your jersey wrapped around me and the worst hangover known to man."

Parker threw his head back and laughed. "Ah, good times."

"No, not good times. That was the last time I ever followed your lead."

"At least you have a great story to tell your grandkids one day."

"In order to have grandkids you actually have to have sex and some kind of significant other."

The moment she said the words, she felt a flush of embarrassment rise from her toes to her cheeks. What would possess her to say something so candid, especially in front of Parker?

He looked her up and down and said, "Don't worry, there will be men knocking at your door when you're a teacher. They'll be begging for parent-teacher conferences."

"I don't even know if that's what I want to do, but I guess it's something to look forward to," she said with a halfhearted smile.

Parker probably realized how awkward the conversation had become and changed the subject quickly. "So, how about Jake and Lexi? I got a brief text from Lexi this morning about going to dinner with him tomorrow, but I don't know any details."

Margo leaned forward and put her hand on his arm. "I was there."

"What?!" Parker shouted. "And you've been holding out on me?"

Margo relayed all the details of her and Lexi's eventful morning. Margo specifically liked describing the way Lexi's face contorted into pure hatred when Jake said to wear something sexy.

She already liked the guy for giving her friend such a hard time.

Lexi could be so stubborn and such a hard-ass sometimes, it was refreshing to see someone push her buttons and make her do things she normally wouldn't even consider. Never in Margo's life would she have thought Lexi would go to a formal dinner, but Margo was proven wrong, thanks to Jake Taylor.

Parker leaned back in his chair and blew out a whistle. "Damn, I like Jake for Lexi."

Margo shoved his shoulder. "I was thinking the same thing. She is always on-guard and Jake is able to slowly pluck away at her walls she puts up and I like it. Plus, it's just great to watch her get all frazzled around him."

"I agree. You should have seen her at the football party after Jake approached her on the porch. She was practically dragging me out of there and she couldn't stop talking about how 'infuriating' he was. If I didn't know any better, I'd say she has a bit of a crush on him."

"I said the same thing to her this morning. Of course, pure denial spewed out of her mouth, but I can tell she likes him and is fighting it off."

"Only time will tell," Parker said, while sucking the rest of his smoothie down with his straw. He took her empty cup and tossed them in a trash can that was right next to them. "Well, I have to get going. Keep me updated on the Lexi and Jake situation. I want full details," he said with a wink.

"Don't you worry, I'll report later; we're going shopping after practice for a dress."

Parker laughed. "Ha, good luck with that. She will most likely want to buy some sort of peasant gown."

"Not if I have anything to say about it. She is going to show off every asset God gave her."

That comment made Parker frown, which caused Margo to think maybe Parker still had feelings for Lexi; he seemed awfully interested in her life, but then again he was her best friend. He was probably just looking out for her and, why would he be pushing

Lexi onto Jake if he had feelings for her? She was just imagining things.

Margo gave Parker a quick hug, which he returned, sending chills through her body. "I'll see you later. Keep me posted."

"I will." Margo waved goodbye and watched him jog toward the practice fields. Sighing once again, she picked up her bag and started walking toward the villas to start on her paper. But she knew she wouldn't be able to get anything done because all she would be able to think about was those chocolate-brown eyes that called to her in her dreams.

Lexi

Lexi paced back and forth in the hallway in front of her professor's office, occasionally looking at the clock on the wall.

"Where is he?" she muttered to herself. She had to go to practice and she didn't have time to wait for Jake to show up so she could get her phone.

The one day she forgot to turn her phone on vibrate, that egotistical maniac had to text her. And how did he even get her number in the first place? There were two suspects, Margo and Parker. She didn't feel like showing any mercy toward them next time they met up; no, she was going to kill them both with her bare hands. Because of them, she was going to be what she thought of as late to practice and she, once again, had to see Jake. Why was it that she went three years without even having a conversation with the man, but now, all of a sudden, she sees him three times in two days? Not that she was counting.

She paced back and forth some more when the elevator opened and Jake walked out with a smirk on his face. It took all the energy in the world not to smack the smirk right off his face.

"Finally!" she said, throwing her hands up in the air. "Let's get this over with."

"Am I missing something? He said two, right? It's ten till, so I don't know why you're acting like I'm thirty minutes late."

"Let's just get my phone and leave."

He shrugged as she turned and knocked on the professor's door.

"Come in," Professor Lyon called out.

Lexi pushed the door open and Jake leaned over her to push the door farther open for her so she could walk in. She caught a whiff of his cologne, which filled her senses with urges she shouldn't be having toward the man she considered to be the devil's child.

Lexi stepped into the professor's office and instantly started to apologize. "Professor Lyon, I'm so sorry, I completely…"

The professor held up his hand to stop her and got up from his chair. "Why Jake Taylor, I didn't know you were the culprit on the other end of that class disturbance." He sneered at Lexi. "How come you didn't tell me it was Jake who texted you."

Lexi was confused. "I didn't know it was…"

Jake interrupted her. "She doesn't like to flaunt our relationship around," he said, while wrapping an arm around her shoulder and pulling her in tight. She tried to free herself, but he was too strong for her, a move that should have made her incredibly mad, but instead, made her legs feel like Jell-O. She despised herself.

"Oh, I didn't know you were seeing someone," the professor said, "You're one lucky lady." He handed Lexi her phone back. "Just remember to put it on silent next time, sweetheart." He looked at Jake and put his hand out to shake Jake's. "Good luck this season, boy. I'm expecting another championship from your men."

"You can bet on it. Take care professor and thanks for being so understanding with my girl."

His girl? Lexi stared at the two men; Jake had the biggest grin on his face while Professor Lyon looked like he was star struck. Lexi wanted to puke from the attention Jake received, even from the staff, it was sickening.

They said their goodbyes and, next thing Lexi knew, she was

riding in a small elevator next to Jake wrapped up in his magnificent scent. He turned to say something to her when the elevator door dinged on the fifth floor and a pretty little brunette walked in. Lexi watched the brunette's eyes widen when she spotted Jake.

"Oh my God, Jake. It's been so long. I can't believe I've run into you."

"Bridget, hey how's it going?"

Bridget? Did he know every single girl on campus? Lexi rolled her eyes and crossed her arms over her chest, trying to act like the brunette's perky attitude toward Jake didn't bother her, but it did. All Lexi envisioned was yanking on the brunette's hair until she fell backwards on the floor. She thought about her little vehement daydream and decided, not only was Jake making her crazy, he was causing her to think more violently and she didn't like that, not one bit.

Lexi listened to their mundane banter while they rode to the first floor. Thankful for the distraction, Lexi slipped out of the elevator and started heading toward the practice fields. She was happy she only had a little interaction with Jake; she'd been dreading going to pick up her phone all day because she knew she would have to see the king of the campus.

What was that whole scene with the professor about anyway? Now that she thought about it, she wondered how the professor was going to treat her if the person who texted her hadn't been Jake? Would he have kicked her out of his class? He couldn't do that; he probably would have given her a good lecture and warning and then sent her on her way. Instead she was stamped as Jake's girl and sent on her way with a damn smile and a wave.

"Hey Lex, wait up."

Turning around, Lexi saw Jake jogging toward her. She let out a frustrated sound and kept walking, slightly quickening her pace, but clearly not fast enough because, of course, he caught up to her.

"Hey, sorry about that back there. Bridget is a family friend."

Lexi snorted. "Sure, is that what you're calling them now,

'family friends'?"

Jake turned her around so she was facing his extremely muscular chest. She had to practically tilt her whole head back to look him in the eyes.

"Jesus, what the hell is your problem?"

"Don't touch me," was all she could say and started walking toward the fields, again.

"Listen, I'm sorry about the text, but honestly, how was I supposed to know you were dumb enough to leave the volume up on your phone?"

"You think that was my fault?" She whirled around. "Maybe if you hadn't screwed with my head this morning, I would have been able to think straight and turn my phone off."

He smiled, causing her to think nasty thoughts of how to pluck every last inch of his gorgeous hair off his head. "You were thinking about me?"

"Oh. My. God! You're so full of yourself."

"Just stating the facts. But hey, I'm sorry about earlier. I just want you to know that. I'll see you tomorrow at six. Alright?"

She looked at him, searching his features for any kind of joke he might be playing on her. "You're serious? You actually think I'm going to that dinner with you tomorrow?"

"Uh, yeah, I won fair and square, so put on your fanciest dress because I'm taking you out tomorrow. I don't care what you say. You owe me."

"I owe you?"

"Yeah, I won, so you need to pay up. I would have held up my end of the bet if I lost."

"I doubt that." He just smiled at her. "Fine, I'll see you at six but don't expect anything magical from me. It is one night, one dinner, that is all and then you need to go back to ignoring me and hanging out with every other girl on campus."

"Ignoring you is not even an option for me. See you at six, babe."

Lexi turned around, not even whispering a goodbye because

his last sentence made her catch her breath. Why was he, all of a sudden, turning on the charm for her? He'd had three years to add her to his bang list, why now? She couldn't get distracted by him; she needed to figure out what the hell she was going to do with her life, not play dreamland with the hottest guy on campus.

CHAPTER FOUR

Lexi

"Margo, I'm not wearing that," Lexi said, while pointing at the barely-there dress her friend was holding up. "It doesn't even have a back."

"Duh, that's why it's so sexy."

Lexi kept searching through the racks to find something semi-presentable to wear to the damn dinner Jake conned her into going to. "That dress might be fine for you, but for a girl my size," Lexi lifted her breasts in her friend's direction, "Backless doesn't work for me, I need a bra and I know that doesn't have the support I need."

Margo looked her up and down. "You can go braless. Your boobs are still perky."

"I hope you're kidding."

"What about this one?" Margo held out a midnight blue dress with an asymmetrical neckline that would work well for Lexi's breasts. Lexi studied the beautiful midnight color carefully and liked what she saw.

"You know, I kind of like it. I could wear my glitter pumps with it."

"And you can borrow my silver clutch. Oh Lex, you have to try it on; it will probably look gorgeous on you."

A slight thrill of excitement took place in Lexi's stomach. A date with Jake was not what she wanted, but she couldn't help but feel excited. It wasn't very often a girl got to get all dressed up and go out to a nice dinner with an extremely good looking man.

Lexi had tried to get out of going shopping with Margo, but her friend wasn't letting her get away with missing the shopping trip and Lexi was a little grateful. She only wished Margo gave her a second to breathe before shoving her in Margo's car and driving to the mall. She barely had time to take a shower after practice before Margo whisked her away to Macy's before it closed.

The clothes that were hung up in Lexi's closet were less-than-desirable for a fancy dinner. Her usual "look" consisted of her hair up in a bun with a headband, sweats or gym shorts, depending on the weather and a T-shirt, so putting on such an elegant piece of clothing made her stomach flutter. She tried not to show her excitement to Margo, though, because Lexi knew Margo would make fun of her…and Lexi was not up for teasing. She was barely able to make herself think about going out with Jake; she didn't need the teasing to add to her anxiety.

They headed to the dressing room to try on the dress when Lexi's phone chimed with a text message. It was from Parker.

Parker: Hey kid, hope the shopping is going well.

"Is that Jake?" Margo asked, while carrying out the last letter of his name. Lexi rolled her eyes.

"No, it's Parker." Lexi noticed her friend perk up with more interest than if the text was actually from Jake.

"What did he say?" she asked, while smoothing her hair down that was, by no means, out of place. Lexi studied her friend's change of attitude. She was all-of-a sudden primping herself and incredibly intrigued by the message on her phone. Interesting, very interesting.

"He just wanted to see how the shopping was going."

"Oh. Well, go try that on; I need to see it on you."

Lexi walked into the dressing room and cringed at the lights they put in the rooms; they were extremely unflattering. How anyone bought anything under this lighting was a miracle. While she was taking off her clothes, she studied her body in the mirror.

She had to admit, she was extremely lucky in the genes department. She was blessed with a fast metabolism and a killer rack, which irritated her most of the time, but when she wanted to flaunt it, she was happy she had them. She was petite, but still able to hold her own, thanks to the strength and conditioning department. She had by no means bulked up like some of the girls on her team. Instead, she had toned, giving her a great body. Something she wished she had put to more use throughout her college years.

She sighed thinking about the last time she actually had a man admire her body, truly admire her…it had been years. Years! What was she doing with her life? Yes, she held practically every softball record at the school, but that was going to do her jack shit when she graduated. She had nothing to say for herself. No job opportunities or even career path in mind and no man to take care of her if she wanted one to. Not that she would ever want to be a woman who stood smiling by her man's side. That was her mother, not her. Lexi was a strong confident woman, who held her own. At least she thought she was.

She slipped the dress up her body and put the asymmetrical strap over her one arm. Thankfully, she was able to get the side zipper up by herself. She smoothed the dress down and looked up at her reflection. She nearly fell over from disbelief. That couldn't be her in the mirror, she looked too good.

The dress fit like a glove, hugging every curve and offering a very generous slip that cut to her upper right thigh, displaying her toned legs. Thank you squats!

"Come on Lex, I'm dying out here," Margo whined.

Lexi chuckled and walked out of the dressing room,

wishing her hair was not in a wet bun on top of her head.

Margo stared at her with her mouth open. "Oh my God, you're getting that dress and I don't care what you say. You look beyond amazing. I'm sending a picture to Parker."

Lexi did a quick pose for the camera and then looked at the mirror again that was in the middle of the dressing room. "I do kind of look good, don't I?"

"Kind of? Girl, you look hot. Jake is not going to know what hit him. Teach him to make a bet again."

Lexi's phone chimed, it was Parker.

Parker: Uh, you are not going out in that; you look too damn good.

Margo read the text message out loud and slightly frowned, but gathered herself when she looked back at Lexi. Very interesting, Lexi thought. If Margo kept razzing her about Jake, Lexi was going to have to return the favor with Parker. Although, it wasn't like Lexi's teasing would really affect her friend. Margo had her fair share of men throughout their years together. She probably had her share and Lexi's share; maybe that's where all the men went that were supposed to be paying attention to her; they were all over at Margo's. Not that she blamed them. Margo had the longest legs she had ever seen and the prettiest brown hair, a color you can't find in a box or at a salon and beautiful green eyes.

"Please tell me you're getting that."

Lexi played with her friend a little. "I don't know. It shows an awful lot of leg."

Margo blew out a frustrated breath. "You have got to be kidding me. I'm going to shoot you. If you can't realize that is the perfect dress for you…"

Lexi cut her friend off before she blew a gasket right in the middle of the department store. "Margo, I'm kidding; of course I'm going to get this dress. It's perfect."

"Thank God, I really wasn't in the mood for wrestling you to the ground and forcing you to buy the damn thing."

Lexi raised an eyebrow at her. "You really think you could take me?"

"We're not getting into this right now. Go get dressed; I'm starving and there's a piece of pizza at Sbarros that's calling my name."

Jake

Jake's palms were sweating, he was actually nervous. He had never in his life been nervous when it came to taking a girl out. What was his problem? He should probably blame Parker. Jake saw him in the weight room earlier that morning and all Parker could talk about was how amazing Lexi looked in the dress she picked out for the night. Jake thought about it and wondered, how amazing could a dress really be? Parker was probably just trying to fake Jake out, make him nervous.

Parker did give him a little man-to-man warning though, which Jake thought was odd. If Jake didn't know any better, he would have thought Parker had feelings for Lexi. How unlucky would that be for Jake if that really was the truth? Then, he would have absolutely no shot at getting to know Lexi. That's all he really wanted, he wanted to get to know her a little better, see what made her tick and if he happened to kiss her then, oops, so be it.

He wanted to do a lot more than kiss her, but he knew she was the type of girl you had to take your time with and he was ready to put in the time. Never in his life had he ever felt this strongly about a girl that came his way. It was kind of strange. He wondered if this was what growing up and turning into a man was like?

Completely out of place, Jake didn't know how he felt about his feelings because, if being a man meant sweating profusely before a date and getting nervous to the point of nausea, then he wanted nothing to do with being a man. He adjusted his tie before he knocked on the door of Lexi's villa. They, surprisingly, only lived a couple of buildings away from each other. It was an easy five minute walk to pick her up. He drove, though, so they could head straight to the dinner that was being held in one of the many gyms they had on campus.

Jake smoothed down his tailored pants and brushed off a piece of lint that was on his steel grey suit that he'd paired with a white shirt and black tie. The suit jacket fit him to a tee; he preferred a more tailored look, rather than a baggy suit like most of the guys on his team wore. He'd worked hard for his body and he liked to show it off when he could.

He knocked on the door again and put his hands in his pockets so he didn't look like a fool wringing his hands together, which would blatantly show off his nerves. Hell, he had to look as cool as a cucumber. He heard the door unlock and Margo opened the door.

Looking him up and down, she said, "Hey Jake, you look really good." Jake liked Margo, she was incredibly nice, easy on the eyes and she was Team Jake, which was refreshing, since Lexi seemed to be anti-Jake. "She'll be out in a minute. Can I get you a drink?"

At the mention of a drink, Jake felt his throat parch. "Uh, yeah, some water would be nice, thank you."

"Not a problem." Jake watched Margo's tall, lithe body slide behind the bar of the kitchen and grab a glass to fill for him. "Did you get to take a look at the gym this morning where the dinner is being held?"

"No, I didn't get a chance. Did you?"

"Yes," Margo sighed. "It's so dreamy. You would never know it was a gym."

"Yeah, the alumni go all out for this event. It's my second year being invited; it's kind of boring when it comes to all the networking you have to do, but the dinner and dancing is great."

"Well, Lexi is one lucky girl." At the mention of her name, Lexi walked out of her room and Jake almost choked on the water Margo had handed him. Margo patted him on the back, trying to help him regain his composure. She could do all the patting she wanted, but he didn't think he would ever recover from seeing Lexi.

"You okay there, big boy?" Margo asked, while grabbing the glass from him.

Jake could only nod because he had never seen anything as beautiful as Lexi. She wore a deep blue dress that made her sky-blue eyes sparkle, the slit in the dress made Jake's mouth water and the way her hair cascaded over her shoulders in soft waves begged for Jake's fingers to explore the depths of her blonde locks.

When he realized he was staring, he cleared his throat and tried to avert his eyes from the smug grin on Margo's face. "Wow, Lexi, you…uh you look gorgeous."

Lexi fidgeted in place and that was when he saw the glitter stilettos she was wearing. It took all the energy in Jake's body not to toss her against the wall and take what he so desperately wanted.

"Thanks, uh should we get going? We don't want to be late."

"Yes, let's get going." Jake felt so awkward; usually he was a lot smoother than this, but Lexi seemed to drive away all coherent thoughts from his brain. He was helpless around her.

Margo escorted them out the door and waved goodbye. "Now, you kids have fun, but not too much. I won't be waiting up," Margo said with a wink. Jake heard Lexi groan under her breath as she walked past him.

Jake led the way to his Jeep and opened the door for her. She hiked her dress up so she could get in the car, which was when he was able to notice a very delicate ankle bracelet that was wrapped around her slender leg. Jake shut the passenger door and begged God for some will power. He could do this; he could be a normal human being and not attack his date in the first five minutes of them being together. But if she kept surprising him with sexy little touches to her appearance, he was not going to be able to last the whole night without mauling her.

When he opened the door to his side, he was smacked in the face with the scent of her perfume, a very feminine scent that made his toes curl. He swore under his breath and started the car.

"What was that?" she asked.

"Uh, just saying how amazing you look." He tried to recover.

"Oh, thank you." She turned to look out the window, avoiding all eye contact with him.

Real smooth, Taylor.

Lexi

It was a suit, just a plain suit, which, of course, was tailored to fit every contour of his body. He was so damn hot, it hurt to look at him. How was that fair? Well, her dress was the same way so she guessed it was fair, but men shouldn't look that good.

Why was she doing this? She should fake a headache and have him drive her back to her apartment. She didn't want to stay out too late because she had practice early in the morning and she didn't really want to be seen publicly with Jake because she didn't want people getting the wrong impression. She didn't really know who was going to be at the event. All she knew was that there were going to be a lot of elite people and that was intimidating enough for her to come up with a fake get-a-way.

The alumni dinner was for the "celebrity" alumni to come back to the school and hob knob with the potential "celebrity" graduates. Of course Jake was invited, he was going to be drafted into the NFL in a couple of months; he was talked about nationwide and she was the one on a date with him. Well, a so-called date. What the hell was she thinking? She started to fidget in her seat and was about to open her mouth to complain about her head when Jake spoke first.

"You must be nervous."

Was she that obvious? "Uh, just a little. These dinners and events aren't really my thing."

"Well, they look like your thing. You'll fit in perfectly. Everyone is going to be staring at how gorgeous you are."

Great, just what she needed, all eyes on her and Jake. She wanted to crawl into a hole. She looked over at him and noticed his smile. That seemed sort of cheesy. Why was it so hard for her to believe him when he said she looked beautiful? Was it because he probably said it to every living thing walking on two legs with two breasts? Whatever it was, she didn't find him genuine and that bothered her.

She tried to strike up a conversation instead of being a wet rag. "So, do you know anyone who will be attending?"

"Just a couple of people, not too many. Coach is making me attend, more than anything. He said it would be good for my career. I don't necessary like doing these things."

That shocked her a little. Jake Taylor, not liking the spotlight? That seemed odd. The words slipped out of her mouth before she could stop them. "You? Not like that spotlight? That's hard to believe." Instantly, he frowned at her words. Damn, she didn't want to be a bitch, but it just happened whenever she was around him. "Sorry, I didn't mean for that to be insulting."

"Of course you did."

Mouth wide open in shock, she spun around in her chair to look at him. She apologized, he didn't have to be rude to her. He parked the car and got out fast enough so she couldn't confront him about his comment. He came around to her side and opened the door for her while grabbing her hand and helping her out.

"I didn't mean to be rude, it just slipped out."

"Exactly, that's what your subconscious thinks of me, that I'm some egotistical maniac."

She secretly agreed with him because that was how she saw him, but she didn't want him to know that. She squared her shoulders and met him face to face. "Maybe this wasn't such a good idea."

"Maybe it wasn't," he replied, shocking the hell out of her. She thought that she was just another hurdle to jump on his way to conquering the female athletic department, but if he was giving up this easily, maybe she wasn't. Was this some kind of sick game he was playing?

Someone called from across the parking lot. "Jake, hey man." They both looked over and saw Darren from the lacrosse team jogging over to them. Darren eyed Lexi up and down and blew out a whistle.

"Damn, Lexi, you clean up real good. I didn't even recognize you." He gave her a kiss on the cheek, causing Jake to squeeze her hand he was now holding tighter. The little jealous gesture confused her. She had no clue what Jake was up to, but whatever it was, she didn't care for it.

"Thanks Darren, you look pretty sexy yourself. I didn't know you knew what a tie was."

He laughed, "I had to have my roommate tie it for me."

They both laughed together, while Jake stood there and watched them interact with each other. Lexi knew Darren from an English class they took together previously, but hadn't seen him in a while. The only reason why they survived the incredibly boring and pompous class together was because they would play Hangman with each other throughout the entire class. They had a running score at one point.

"I still lead you in Hangman," she bragged.

"Ha, you wish, I owned you."

"Keep dreaming."

"I will now," he said with a wink, which caused Jake to barge into their little banter.

"Alright, we'll see you in there," Jake said dismissively.

Darren looked at Lexi and then at Jake's menacing face. He got the picture very quickly that Jake was painting for the world to see, which caused Lexi to blush with embarrassment. Darren waved goodbye and walked into the building, leaving Lexi and Jake alone once again.

"Was that really necessary?" she asked.

"Was what necessary?"

She poked him in his chest with her finger, his rock hard chest. "You know exactly what. You didn't have to be rude to him.

We were just joking around with each other."

"Yeah, and as much fun as that was for me, I would prefer that my girl wasn't flirting with other men while I was around."

That made her put her hands on her hips. "Your girl? Are you living on Mars? By no means am I your girl or will I ever be your girl."

She turned away from him and started walking toward her apartment. It would be a brisk evening walk in high heels, but it would be worth it, if it meant getting away from Jake Taylor. He was infuriating. If he wanted to see flirting, she could show him flirting. She was merely being polite to an old friend; there was nothing wrong with that.

She felt an arm grab her and spin her around.

"Lexi, stop, we have to go in there. You can't just walk away."

"We," she emphasized, "We don't have to go in there, you do!"

She saw him struggling to find words, but she frankly didn't care. She should teach him a lesson and just take off, leaving him to explain to everyone why his date didn't show, but then she saw a bit of a lost boy in his eyes when he looked at her. Groaning inwardly, she wanted to smack herself for feeling sorry for him.

"Please, Lexi, I'm sorry. Just come inside with me."

Big puppy-dog-eyes pleaded with her; how could anyone say no to that? She blew out a hefty, irritated breath, ripped her arm from his grasp and walked toward the building, trying to leave him in her dust. Unfortunately, he caught up and placed his hand on her lower back.

"Thank you."

She just nodded and allowed him to escort her into the building.

The party committee had transformed the gym into a beautiful dining area full of plants and twinkle lights; it was slightly magical, but also ridiculous, Lexi thought. The money they spent on this dinner probably could go to something more beneficial. She couldn't think of anything at the exact moment, but she did believe that all the pomp and circumstance she was currently experiencing wasn't entirely necessary.

Lexi silently thanked Margo for making her get the dress she was wearing. Everyone was dressed to the nines. All the women had their hair in up-dos and wore gorgeous dresses that made hers look like it was from a discount store. Lexi self-consciously stroked her hair, wondering if she should have put it up like everyone else.

She felt a hand brush against her neck and Jake's breath right next to her ear. "You look beyond amazing; don't let anyone make you think differently."

Startled, she looked into his eyes and saw that he was being truly genuine; he wasn't just throwing one of his smooth lines out for her benefit. For the first time since she had first interacted with him, he was actually showing a little piece of himself. It was marginally refreshing. The intimate gesture made her confidence slightly spike.

They grabbed their name cards and took their seats at one of the tables that was in the front of the room, right next to the podium. Jake must be an extremely VIP to have one of the nicest seats in the place. They sat down at their table that was already occupied by people she had never even seen before. All the women were practically perfect in their appearance and the men reveled in the arm candy they brought with them.

Was this what the real world was like? At least in the "celebrity" world, was this what it was like? Practically perfect women sitting next to their distinguished men; it was all too weird for Lexi to process. The whole picture just seemed so fake to her. This was so not the world she wanted to be a part of. Yes, they were rich and they were an exclusive gaggle of people, but that didn't matter to her; they seemed boring as hell, stingy little bastards.

The night was incredibly awkward for her. The tension between her and Jake was unmistakable. All she wanted to do was go home; even though he was putting in an effort to be interested in her when they had a chance to talk, it wasn't enough for her. Almost every five minutes someone came up to their table and shook hands with Jake. It was nauseating listening to all the people sucking up to him. He threw a damn sphere around a grassy field and everyone treated him as if he just took a fresh pile of shit and turned it into a new cure for cancer.

She studied her nails while Jake talked to some software billionaire that just donated enough money to the school to have his own wing in the lecture hall. He had donated an obscene amount of money to have his name plastered on the side of a building, how ridiculous was that?

Lexi's thoughts were interrupted when the billionaire spoke. "Jake you must meet my gorgeous daughter." Lexi's eye shot up from examining her nails and made eye contact with a leggy blonde. The blonde gave Lexi a menacing grin and then extended her hand out to Jake who took it in his. "This is Jessica, Jessica this is Jake."

Lexi watched the whole interaction play out in front of her, as if she was watching some sort of television show.

"Jessica, it's very nice to meet you. You must get your good looks from your mother because you didn't get anything from this old man," Jake said, while patting the billionaire on the arm and they all laughed together, except Lexi who was still staring in amazement at what was unfolding in front of her.

"You are right; her mother was an angel."

"Was?" Jake asked.

"Yes, we lost my dear Clarice when Jessica was a wee little one, I raised her myself." Lexi watched Jessica look Jake up and down and lick her lips. Good Lord, she was playing up the "I lost my mother when I was young" role. Jessica stuck out her bottom lip and pouted. Good grief.

"Jake, would you mind taking my daughter for a spin out on the dance floor?"

Jake didn't even hesitate, or look at Lexi. "I would be

honored, sir."

Sir? Who was he kidding? Could Jake's head go any further up the billionaire's ass? Lexi watched Jake place his hand at Jessica's lower back and escort her to the dance floor where they wrapped their limbs around each other and slow danced to some song Lexi thought she remembered from one of those popular vampire movies, not that she watched them or anything.

Absolutely in shock, Lexi just stared at them and thought about how ridiculous this night had turned out to be. What an ass! Jake was a giant, self-absorbed, unfortunately good looking, devil of an ass. She pulled her lip gloss out of her clutch, not knowing what else to do, and reapplied a sticky layer to her lips.

A lady from across the table tsked at Lexi. "Looks like you just lost your man."

Lexi looked at the lady's judgmental eyes and was about to respond with a snarky comment about her husband's poor choice of a toupee when Darren came up behind her and whispered in her ear.

"Care for a dance?"

"I thought you would never ask."

Lexi put her hand in Darren's as they swayed onto the dance floor. Darren was good looking, but nothing ever really transpired between them, just like Parker, Darren and she were friends.

"So what's with you and Jake?"

Lexi knew that question was coming, especially since Jake was currently dancing with someone other than the girl he brought to the stupid dinner. Not that she should really care. Jake wasn't hers to claim, but there were moral standards people should live up to, she thought. If a man brings a date to a dinner, that means he dances with his date and pays attention to his date; he shouldn't go off with another woman without even consulting with his date first. It was like, once Jessica, the leggy blonde, came along, Lexi vanished from Jake's thoughts.

Lexi answered Darren's question. "Nothing, absolutely

nothing."

"Didn't seem like nothing in the parking lot." Darren spun her so she got a glimpse of Jake and his dancing partner, who was practically drooling all over him and rubbing her body up and down his.

"It's nothing, trust me. I'm just another mountain for Jake to conquer. The only reason I'm here is because I lost a bet; frankly, I would rather be home in sweats eating some frozen yogurt."

"Well, let's go then. My treat."

Lexi looked at him. "Are you serious?"

"Yeah, why not? Jake clearly is occupied and I said my hellos to the people I needed to say hello to. I'm ready to go, are you?"

Lexi eyed the happy "couple" again; she watched them laugh in unison and decided right then that, yes, she did want to leave.

"Let me just grab my bag and we can get out of here."

"Perfect."

Lexi spent the rest of the evening in her fancy dress at the frozen yogurt store, playing Hangman with Darren on napkins and laughing harder than she had laughed in a while. Darren helped her forget the crappy night she started out with. Relief washed over her from knowing that the crazy, uncomfortable dance she had been doing with Jake the past couple of days was finally over. He found someone new to try to land in his bed and she was free to go back to her stress-free life.

Jake

Jake sat on a bench that was in front of Lexi's villa. It had been an hour since he left the stupid dinner and he figured since she left two hours ago, without a good bye, she would be home by now. Margo wasn't home either. She was probably out with a guy, like she always was.

He couldn't believe the nerve of Lexi to just leave him stranded at the dinner to fend for himself, especially after everyone noticed his date had disappeared; it was embarrassing. He figured her disappearance had to do with the Jessica interruption. That was a whole other frustrating situation. The billionaire, as he was known around campus, got in contact with Jake weeks ago and mentioned how he would be bringing his daughter to the dinner and hoped they would be able to meet. Jake completely forgot about the planned meeting until Jessica came up to him. He didn't want to piss the billionaire off, since he was a very influential person, so he went with the flow. Lexi had to understand that, right?

Jake ran a hand over his face and thought about the look of displeasure on Lexi's face when he turned around at one point as he was dancing with Jessica. She was not happy at all.

Shit, he blew it big time. He ended up dancing with Jessica for three songs until he was able to peel himself away, claiming he had to talk to other people in the room before the night was over. She didn't keep her intentions of their meeting a secret, though, when she slipped her number into his pocket.

Finally, a car pulled up to the front of the building which Jake recognized as Darren's. What the hell? Lexi slipped out with a huge smile on her face and walked arm and arm with Darren to her door. It wasn't until Jake made himself seen that her smile faded into a frown.

"What the hell are you doing here?" she asked, hatred falling from her mouth. Jake watched Darren look at both of them, like he previously had when they were in the parking lot earlier. Luckily for Darren, he backed off, but not before he placed a kiss on Lexi's cheek.

"Thanks for a great time Lex, I'll see you later."

"Thank you, Darren." Darren walked away and Lexi blew past Jake and headed straight to her door without saying another word to him.

He stopped her before she was able to unlock the door.

"Were you with him this entire time?"

Lexi faced him and looked him dead in the eyes. "You have some fucking nerve coming here, you know that?"

Wow, she was pissed. He knew she might not be happy, but she had fire spitting from her eyes and looked like she could do some real damage, if given the opportunity.

"Listen, I know the night was less than ideal…"

"Less than ideal? The best part of my night was when I left that dinner. Just leave me alone, Jake."

"You don't have to be jealous. I had to dance with Jessica; I didn't have a choice."

"I'm not jealous, I'm humiliated. The minute that leggy blonde came in and said hello to you, you practically spent the rest of the night drooling all over her. I could care less if you dance with someone else, but when you completely ignore me, it's insulting, especially since you dragged me to this stupid thing in the first place. Was that your intention the whole time? To make a fool of me? Well, congratulations Jake, you did it. You got what you wanted, so just leave me the fuck alone."

She unlocked her door with precision, slipped inside and shut the door in his face before he was even able to reply to her rant.

By no means did he bring her to the dinner to humiliate her. In fact, he actually wanted to get to know her better. He wanted to spend time with her. Never before in his life had he actually want to get to know a woman.

Shaking his head in disgust, he knew he blew it big time. He banged on her door and called for her to open up. He continued to get louder and louder with his pounding and shouting, knowing that she would open the door just to shut him up.

Almost exactly on cue, she threw the door open. "Will you please stop that? You're going to cause a scene."

"Let me explain."

"What is there to explain, Jake? What you did tonight

mortified me; there is no explaining it."

He saw the pain in her eyes and his stomach dropped to his shoes. His intention for tonight was to woo her, to make her see him for who he wanted to be. Instead, he gave her the impression that he was still the old Jake, the ladies' man Jake. Someone who he despised.

"Lexi, I'm sorry. Please, just let me in and we can talk about this."

"No, Jake, this is over and if you don't leave I'm going to call the cops and we all know what that would do to your precious little reputation."

He was about to open his mouth to protest when she slammed the door in his face.

Damn.

CHAPTER FIVE

**Jake*

Jake met up with Mason the next morning at an hour Jake didn't usually even know existed, but if he wanted to change, he needed to start changing his habits now, which meant no partying at all hours of the night and sleeping till noon. He enjoyed the morning workouts he and Mason did since the weight room didn't have anyone in it to bother him and the field house was completely empty. It was actually relaxing and peaceful. He wished he had woken up early all four years instead of just his last year of college. He wondered if, just maybe, he had worked even a tad bit harder throughout his college years, maybe he would have been even better than he was now. That thought was something he couldn't focus on. He was never a "what if" kind of guy and he didn't want to start now.

Jake and Mason went through a series of sprints in the field house, ladder workouts and footwork exercises. Jake threw a couple of passes to Mason, but saved his arm for practice. He could already feel his footwork starting to improve, which would help him when he was struggling to find an open receiver in the pocket during the games.

Jake threw a long ball to Mason, who dove and caught it in the end zone. Mason stood up and performed his signature wobbly-leg touchdown dance. That was one thing Jake was going to miss, his best friend and go-to receiver. He knew the reality of Mason and Jake ending up on the same NFL team was slim-to-none and their days of hanging out together every day were numbered. He tried not to concentrate too much on saying goodbye to Mason, since it was depressing as hell.

Jake and Mason had gone through practically everything together, from being scared freshmen their first hell week, to meeting girls, throwing parties and going through hardships that only a true brother would understand. Jake was getting nostalgic and he needed to snap out of it because it was only going to bring him anxiety and depression, which was something he didn't need going into his senior year.

One thing he couldn't stop thinking about was that, once he graduated, he was going to be alone, more alone than when his parents died. Mason had been the backbone Jake needed throughout his college career, but now that he was graduating, he would be on his own, which scared the hell out of him.

Mason was moving on too after graduation, but he wouldn't be alone like Jake. Jake was envious of the relationship Mason had with his long-term girlfriend, Brooke. Jake knew they were going to get married at some point and he would be Mason's best man, which was an honor Jake could only hope to reciprocate in the future.

Although, the thought of being able to reciprocate the honor of having Mason as his best man vanished pretty quickly last night in one bad move on Jake's part. Instead of dancing with Jessica, he should have introduced Lexi and let everyone know she was his date. What was wrong with him? Why didn't that clue in on him? He was hoping that if he gave the billionaire's daughter one dance, he could brush her off and spend the rest of the night with Lexi in his arms. Instead, he was stuck with Daddy's little princess whispering obscenities in his ear. The old Jake would have been turned on in two seconds and maybe even taken her to the bathroom to cash in on her promises, but all he could think about was Lexi and how he wished it was her whispering into his ear, rather than Jessica.

"Uh, hello Jake? I asked if we're done here?" Mason interrupted.

Jake grabbed the football from his friend and quickly looked at his watch; he still had time. "Yeah, thanks for the workout."

"Are you still thinking about what happened with Lexi?"

Jake had told Mason the entire story when they were warming up and all Mason did was shake his head at him. Mason didn't even have to say anything because Jake knew he messed up, messed up big time.

"I am. I can't believe I fucked up so bad."

Mason shrugged. "Hey, you're not used to treating women with respect." Mason grinned.

"Fuck off," Jake said in a teasing tone and pushed his friend. "I have to take a shower real quick and then head to the coffee kiosk before eight."

"What are you doing, man?"

"Trying to get back in Lexi's good graces." They headed back to the locker rooms to freshen up for the day.

"I don't know if that's a good idea. She made it quite clear yesterday she really wanted nothing to do with you. And, what if she's seeing Darren?"

The mention of Darren's name made Jake clench his teeth. If the bastard wasn't such a good guy, Jake might knock some teeth out of his pretty little smile. When Jake saw Darren walking arm in arm with Lexi last night, Jake almost lost it. He didn't even want to think about the jealous instincts he had for Lexi because that would open a box he wasn't ready to open. Damn it, he just wanted to get to know the girl. Was that too much to ask?

"They're not seeing each other," Jake said through gritted teeth.

Mason threw his hands up in mock defense. "Don't bite my

head off. I'm not the one who ditched my date for a billionaire's daughter, fuck stick."

When they entered the locker room, Jake threw the football into the corner and spun around to face Mason who looked a little shocked at Jake's erratic movements.

"I didn't have a choice. I had to dance with her. The guy could easily fuck me over in more ways than one."

"He's a billionaire, he doesn't own the NFL. What could he possibly do?"

"He practically owns the internet. He could destroy any image I have before I ever go public. I have to watch my back."

"Well then, how come you're trying to pursue Lexi when you should probably be kissing his daughter's ass?"

Jake thought about the phone number Jessica gave him last night that burned a hole through his pants pocket. He wanted nothing to do with her. Yes, she was pretty, but she was no Lexi and she was a little too wild for his liking, especially since he was trying to change his image.

"She'll be fine. I'm not concerned about her. I did what I had to do and danced with her, which was all her dad asked of me. He can't force me into a relationship with her."

Mason just shrugged his shoulders and peeled his sweaty shirt off, showing off his many tattoos.

"I don't know why you're so concerned with my life when you should really be concerned about those love handles you got going on there."

Mason snapped his face at Jake and flashed him the middle finger. "You wish I had love handles because then you wouldn't have to compete with my awesome body," Mason said, while caressing his sides.

"Keep dreaming, you know I'm more ripped than you will ever be."

Mason stepped in front of one of the mirrors and started flexing. "This, my friend, is what they call a bicep, something you might not be familiar with." Then Mason turned to the side and stuck his belly out and placed his hands on his lower back. "And this is a gut, something I know you are quite familiar with."

Jake whipped him in the back with a towel causing Mason to yelp and tackle Jake to the ground.

Lexi

Lexi dried off from her shower and slipped on a pair of yoga pants and a tight-fitting tank top. She threw her hair up in a massive messy bun and applied some mascara. She never went anywhere without a little bit of mascara; she felt naked without it.

Their workout this morning was awful, Lexi already felt sore from the conditioning workout they went through. Their coach was in a bitch of a mood; it must be her time of the month because she made them do pyramids, but at a fifty yard distance. Whenever they did pyramids, they always did them on the basketball court, but her coach thought she would turn into the devil this morning and torture the hell out of them. Most of the freshmen threw up, something Lexi remembered doing her first year, but since then, she'd worked out like crazy so she would never be the girl puking on the side again.

Looking back at the morning, she felt bad for her teammates because if Lexi was having a hard time functioning after their workout, then the other girls must be hurting in a bad way. Still, she couldn't figure out why she felt so slow this morning. Her coach even called her out on it, so then Lexi had to work even harder to prove that she was her normal self, even though she felt a million miles away from herself.

She was avoiding the real reason why she was tired and lethargic; she blamed it on the workout, or maybe not eating breakfast, but she would not blame it on the fact that it felt like Jake sucked the life out of her. She talked to Margo about the incident and she didn't have much to say; she couldn't explain the odd behavior and then apologized for encouraging Lexi to go out with him, when clearly Lexi wanted nothing to do with him.

She didn't blame Margo; there was only one person to blame and that was the guy with the green eyes. Lexi shook her head in disgust; never in her life had she ever been so mortified. The people at her table had given her the "I'm sorry for your life" look, which Lexi had a hard time tolerating. She couldn't stand getting pitied, especially when it was coming from pompous society folk.

"Are you coming?" Margo asked.

"I'll catch up with you later," Lexi replied.

Margo sat next to her on a bench while Lexi tied up her shoes. "Lex, you can't let him get to you. That's letting him win."

"I'm not letting him get to me; I'm not even thinking about him," she lied, "I'm just really worn out. I think I've been working too hard. Maybe I need to cut back on the workouts. I didn't appreciate Coach riding my ass this morning."

"No one enjoys Coach riding their ass, especially when the bitch is eating donuts while we sweat our asses off and puke on the sidelines."

Lexi thought about how their coach sat in a cushioned chair and blew her whistle while she munched down on her sugar-infested breakfast. If her coach wasn't so damn good at her job, Lexi would report the dumb bitch to the athletic director.

Completely annoyed with the morning, she was about to respond, when one of the freshman came into the locker room and said, "Uh, Lexi, someone is waiting outside for you."

Lexi looked at the freshman with confusion, but all she did was point her thumb to the door and then head into the bathroom that connected to all the girls' locker rooms. Maybe Parker was outside waiting for her, most likely he wanted to get all the juicy details about what happened last night. Lexi didn't feel like repeating all the gory details, but she knew Parker wasn't going to let her get away with being silent. Maybe she would blow Parker off for class and leave Margo to tell him the story. That way, she wouldn't have to relive it.

Looking over at Margo, Lexi said, "I have to go. I'll catch you later. Let me know about dinner tonight; I'm thinking tacos."

Margo agreed as Lexi grabbed her backpack and headed out the opposite door. Lexi stopped in her tracks when she saw Jake leaning against the wall wearing jeans and a "Property of Cal U Football" shirt. His hair was wet and tussled around and he was holding a drink carrier and a bag.

Lexi's mood went from annoyed to icy in a matter of seconds. "What the hell do you want?"

"Good morning to you too. How was your workout?"

"Like you care," she said, as she turned and started walking toward the door so she could walk up the hill to her class.

"I do care." He caught up to her. They were outside, starting to walk up the hill when he spoke again, this time getting ahead of her and stepping in front of her so she couldn't walk any further. "Can you please stop for one second and talk to me."

She put her hands on her hips. "And why would I want to do that? You had all night to talk to me last night, but instead you decided to dance with someone else."

Jake blew out an aggravated breath and said as quickly as possible, "I had to; her Dad had asked me to dance with her a while back and I couldn't say no. I should have handled the situation better, I know that now, but honestly, I was trying to get rid of her as quickly as possible so I could spend the rest of the night with you."

She put her hands to her heart. "Oh, how caring of you. I could tell that after two dances you were really trying to get rid of her on my behalf, thank you," Lexi said in a sarcastic tone.

"You can believe me or not, but what I'm telling you is the truth."

"Okay, Jake." She tried to walk again but he stopped her. She looked up at him and knew it was a mistake. She looked directly into his eyes and saw the slight insecurity clouding his sight, as if he was actually putting himself out in the world to be vulnerable. No, no, she was not going to melt before him. She needed to stay strong. "Is there a reason for this little morning meeting or can I get to my class?"

He held out a warm cup to her, reached in the bag he was holding and handed her a yogurt parfait, damn him for knowing what she liked.

"A peace offering. I know it doesn't make up for what I did to you last night, but I just wanted to say how sorry I really am. My intentions were not to ruin your night and fill it with embarrassment. I actually wanted nothing more than for you to be the one I held in my arms all night."

She looked away because, if she looked in his eyes, she was going to falter. His voice was sincere and sweet…A side of him she had never experienced. It was as if he actually cared. She had seen him operate on many different occasions while talking to women and this was the first time she ever saw this side of him.

Instead of being a grown up and looking him in the eyes to thank him, she tilted her cup at him and said, "Thanks, I better get to class."

He let her walk by, thankfully, because she was through with playing his little sidewalk tango. On her way up the hill, she thought about the words he said to her as she tried to block them out of her memory. He was an ass. People didn't change in the matter of a night. He treated her like crap once and he would do it again.

When she got to her classroom, she pulled her phone out to turn it on silent when she noticed she had a text message and, of course, it was from Jake.

Jake: By the way, I don't think I got the chance to thank you for being my date last night, even though I blew it, but thank you. It was a pleasure to have you on my arm. P.S. You look beautiful this morning.

Damn it all to hell…

Margo

"Taco time!" Margo sang out as she sat down at the table

with Lexi and Parker. Parker was looking sexy, as usual, Margo thought. Not even going out for a late-night date with a guy on the football team could cure her need for Parker.

"These look awesome ladies; thanks for having me over," Parker said, with a devilish grin. Margo felt her entire body sigh with content. Just being able to hang out with him was amazing.

Lexi had her elbow on the table and her hand holding her head up as she stared down at her food, not eating it, just pushing it around on her plate.

"You actually going to eat that, Lex?" Margo asked. Lexi just looked up and nodded. This was very unlike her friend, she loved tacos. She loved all meals. "What's wrong girl? Is Jake really getting to you?"

"Oh yeah, you never gave me the details of what exactly went down. I just got the abridged version from Margo," Parker said, while biting into the crunchy shell of his taco.

"I don't want to talk about it. I just want to forget Jake ever stepped into my life."

Thrown off by the snappy tone Lexi just used, Margo and Parker exchanged looks of concern. They shrugged at each other and dug into their tacos and forgot about the topic of Jake Taylor.

All three of them just sat there in silence. Lexi still didn't touch her food, which caused Margo to worry. Lexi worked out every day, sometimes more than twice a day. If anything, the girl needed more food to keep up with her burning metabolism.

Margo knew Lexi didn't want to talk about Jake, but she also didn't want her friend to go anorexic either because of some jackass. Margo stepped into the mother role. "Lexi, can you please eat? Don't let Jake bother you that much."

Lexi snapped her face up and stared down Margo. Margo actually felt fear creep across her body. In the three years Margo had known Lexi, she had never seen her friend so distraught and just flat-out angry about something…or someone, for that matter. Lexi pushed her food to the side and went to her room, slamming the door shut.

Margo blew out am agitated breath and stared down at her food. Parker reached across the table and squeezed her hand, sending chills all the way up her arm.

"Don't worry about her," he said. "Just keep being a friend like you are and she'll realize what a bitch she's being." He winked at her as he shoved a tortilla chip in his mouth.

That made Margo chuckle. She looked Parker in the eyes and he gave her another quick wink as he tore his hand away from hers to grab one of his tacos, which he so disgustingly shoved in his mouth, making a mess of his entire plate.

"You're disgusting, you know that?"

He talked with his mouth full. "Distracted you from the little girly drama that just took place, didn't I?"

"You're right about that, but for God's sake, can you stop talking with your mouth full? It's revolting."

Parker laughed, causing a chunk of ground beef to pop out of his mouth and hit the table. They stared at the browned meat for a couple of seconds before they both started to laugh hysterically.

"Oh my God, that was so disgusting."

Parker just smiled at her and shrugged while taking another bite of his taco. Margo sat back in her chair and enjoyed the chips and salsa that were on the table. Even though Parker had zero table manners, she enjoyed watching every little food particle fly out of his mouth. What was wrong with her?

Parker wiped his mouth with a napkin and asked, "So are you going to the mixer on Friday?"

"Possibly, there should be some really hot guys there," Margo said, trying to gauge Parker's interest in her.

"That's right, because I'll be there."

"Awfully full of yourself today, aren't you?"

"It's kind of hard not to be with a physique and face like this," Parker said, while motioning his whole body with his hands. Margo just rolled her eyes at him, but secretly agreed. He was practically a god. "Well if you plan on going, let me know. I can pick you up and we can ride together."

Margo tried to act cool, but her stomach was doing flips with the mere fact that Parker offered to pick her up. She knew it wasn't a date, but they were going to be able to spend some more time together, one on one. That was what she needed, just a little more Parker time before he went off to do bigger and better things.

"You're on," she said, trying to be cool, "But you better not be late, you know how I hate missing all the good beer."

Lexi

Lexi managed to get through the rest of the week without hearing from or running into Jake. She apologized to Margo and Parker for her childish outburst during taco night; they were more than understanding. Sometimes she wondered why they stuck around her. They were off to the mixer together, while she headed to the weight room. The last thing she wanted to do was interact with a bunch of drunken idiots and possibly run into Jake.

Not that he would really pursue her if they did see each other. Ever since his morning breakfast escapade, she had not heard from him, which was a good thing. She was able to get her life back on track. He really caused a big disturbance and she didn't care much for it.

Parker begged her to go out with him and Margo tonight, but she wanted nothing to do with the stupid mixer. Parker reminded her of their deal about going out and having the best senior year possible, sending guilt through her entire body, but she didn't cave. She promised him that, after this night, she would go to whatever party he wanted; she just needed a little more time to herself.

She didn't really know what was wrong with her. So what, a guy ignored her when she was his date. It shouldn't have bothered her that much, but for some reason, it did. It nagged at her day in and day out. It nagged her so much that, after the first couple of days after the horrible night, her coach called her into her office and reminded Lexi of her leadership role on the team. Her coach told her she better get her shit together before the season began or else she would be finding someone to replace her.

The fat, donut-eating bitch was right. When had Lexi ever let a man affect her like Jake had? The answer was never. She played the night over and over in her head and tried to think about why his actions bothered her to the point of not wanting to enjoy taco night. She came to the realization in one of her media classes. The night of the dinner, she was secretly living out a fantasy she never got to have. She never went to one of her proms or was asked to a dance, so when Jake asked her, it was like being able to step back in time and have that moment she never had.

It was so corny, but she couldn't help but feel let down, like some reject who sat on the bleachers and watched all the pretty girls dance with their dates while she sat alone. A flood of raw emotions attacked her in class and she had to leave early so she didn't embarrass herself. The night with Jake brought back all her insecurities growing up and she associated him with those insecurities.

She grabbed a towel from the equipment room and headed for the weight room. What she needed right now was to sweat and push herself to the limits. She went straight for the bench and racked up her weights. She pounded out a couple of reps and then just sat at the bench, staring at her lap, wondering if staying in tonight was the right choice.

"Hey."

Lexi nearly jumped out of her skin from the friendly hello. She thought she was the only one in the training facility. She looked up and found herself looking at two pools of light green eyes.

Jake.

Lexi didn't know what to do or how to react. What the hell was he doing here? It was a Friday night and there was a party full of willing and eager women to please him.

"Uh, hey. Why aren't you at the mixer?"

Jake pulled up to the bench next to her and started pumping out reps. The weight on his bar was significantly bigger than hers and she couldn't help but stare as his muscles rippled beneath his shirt when he pressed up and rested the bar on the holders.

"We have our first game tomorrow, so we're on twenty-four hour." Lexi didn't think the football team followed the twenty-four hour rule of no drinking before a game.

"I didn't know you football players followed that rule."

"We didn't until this year. I suggested it and we all agreed, well most of us agreed."

Completely shocked, Lexi nearly fell off her bench. Jake, the party man of the athletic department, enforced the twenty-four hour rule on his team. She better go look out a window because she would bet a million dollars she would be seeing a pig fly right now.

"Wow, that's a little shocking."

"Why's that?" he asked.

"Uh, because you're the biggest partier on campus and for you to suggest such a rule would be like Parker eating a jelly donut and not getting it all over his shirt."

Jake picked up his weight again and grunted out, "Not anymore."

Lexi decided to stop watching him. She took the weights off of her bar and went over to where the exercise balls were so she could work on her core, which she took great pride in. Not a lot of people knew that having a stable core could help any athlete become better in their sport. That was why Lexi spent extra time in the abs department and also because she liked looking good in her bikini, which she was able to wear often since she lived in southern California.

They both worked out in silence, aware of each other in the room, but never making eye contact. Jake actually was wearing ear phones, completely tuning Lexi out. Well, if she wasn't convinced before about Jake being able to forget about her, she was convinced now. He floated around the weight room, focusing on different parts of his body and flexing with every pump of iron.

It took all the energy in Lexi's body to ignore him and just focus on her workout, but after twenty minutes of pure torture, she decided to call it a night. She couldn't be in the same room alone with him anymore, especially when he was deliberately ignoring her. But wasn't that what she wanted? She wanted him to ignore her? She wanted to go back to her normal life before Jake took a tiny step into it.

She grabbed her towel, took one last look at him in the mirror and left the weight room. She filled up her water bottle and threw her towel in the dirty laundry bin. What a night. She thought it would be relaxing to work out, but instead, she had a tension-filled night that was cut short by her inability to act like a grown up and share a weight room with a member of the opposite sex.

Once in the locker room, Lexi grabbed her bag, located her keys from the front pocket and exited her locker room while sucking down her water. When she lowered her water bottle, she made eye contact with Jake, once again.

She placed her hand over her heart. "Jesus, you scared me. You can't be lurking around in hallways when it's late at night."

She could tell he was holding back a smile at scaring the crap out of her. "You startle easily."

"And you're a creep for waiting around in the dark by the girls' locker rooms."

"Point taken."

They stared at each other for a couple of seconds, not saying anything, so Lexi started walking toward the exit.

"Hey, are you coming tomorrow night?" Jake asked, when she was about to open the door to the warm night. She turned around and saw that he hadn't moved from where he was standing; instead, he was leaning against the hallway wall. He looked like a little lost boy, it was almost endearing…almost.

"I don't know, maybe."

"I hope you do."

"We'll see." She was about to walk out the door when he caught her before she shut the door.

"If you do decide to go, there will be field passes for you, Margo and Parker waiting at will call."

"Field passes?" Lexi asked in a shocked voice. If she told Parker she had field passes to the first football game of the season, Parker would make her go. The game was fun to watch from the stands, even she would admit that, but never had she experienced the game from the ground level where all the action was. Field passes were hard to come by, especially since they were given to all the VIP alumni or donors.

"Yeah, the first game is always the best to be on the field for. The excitement in the air is contagious."

"I can imagine."

"Alright, well, have a good night. Hopefully I'll see you tomorrow." He squeezed her shoulder and took off to the weight room. She watched him walk away and, right before he was about to put his ear buds back in his ears that were dangling on his well sculpted shoulders, she shouted down the hallway.

"Kick some ass tomorrow."

He spun around and smiled at her before walking into the weight room and disappearing for the night. He had field passes for her on reserve? Parker was going to pee his pants when he found out. Looks like she needed to bust out her Cal U football jersey she got for Halloween one year because she was going to need to look the part tomorrow night.

CHAPTER SIX

Lexi

"Wooo! Go Bears!!"

"Parker! Can you please not do that right in my ear?" Lexi asked, while holding her hand over her right ear, the one right next to Parker's megaphone of a mouth.

He nudged Lexi, "Oh come on, loosen up a little bit. How could you not let out a good old woot woot right now? We're killing the Cardinals, all thanks to your boy, Jake."

"He's not my boy."

Margo lifted her VIP pass and said, "These passes beg to differ."

The marching band started up their victory march again once the kicker made his field goal, dragging Lexi's attention to the field. They really were killing the Cardinals; it was almost kind of sad. Jake was right about the atmosphere; the energy in the stadium was contagious. If she wasn't trying to play it cool right now in front of her friends, she would be jumping up and down, cheering for her home team.

Jake was leading the team down the field with his precise throws to his receivers and quick foot work. Mason and he were really connecting tonight, she thought. Lexi watched the whole night in amazement at how accurately Jake threw the ball down the field while in the midst of angry linebackers trying to get a piece of him. It was actually quite impressive, now that she thought about it. When she was in centerfield, all she had to do was hop, skip and jump and hope the ball landed in the catcher's mitt when she was throwing home. She didn't have over-juiced men running at her with death glares, threatening her.

Last night in the weight room, Lexi saw a change in Jake. It was as if he traded bodies with Parker or something because, while Parker normally would have been in the weight room with Lexi, he was out partying. She would have bet a million dollars Jake would had been the one partying with women hanging all over him.

Lexi tried not to think about how genuine, kind and sexy Jake looked in the weight room. She tried to drive away the image of his green eyes bearing down on hers or the way his backside looked when he walked away. It was all too much for her. The man was infuriating at times, but then so kind and caring; it confused her. She didn't know what to think.

Of course, this would happen her senior year; she would be interested in a guy when she was trying to find herself. Was she really interested in him?

The team obtained possession of the ball and Lexi watched Jake put his helmet on as he jogged out to the field. Yup, she was interested. How could she not be? She would be dead if she wasn't interested. He was drop-dead gorgeous, athletic, sexy as hell and, at times, she could sense that he actually had a heart. Shouldn't that matter the most to her? That he was kind and caring, not just some hot piece of ass? She cursed herself for letting her libido take over her thoughts.

There were twenty seconds left in the game and, instead of absolutely humiliating the other team, Jake let the play clock run out of time. The crowd erupted when the game was over. It was a great start to what looked like another championship season.

"This has been one of the best games I've ever been to. Thanks, Lex, for hooking us up with these tickets, even though it pained you," Parker said with a grin.

"I actually had a lot of fun. Jake was right. It's much more fun down here. You get the feeling you're actually a part of the team."

"I agree," Margo said, while looping her arms in Lexi and Parker's arms as if they were about to skip down the yellow brick road. "What's next? Shall we go get some frozen yogurt?"

Lexi was about to say she wasn't hungry, when Parker stepped in before she could, "Oh yeah, that sounds great to me. Shall we ladies?" Parker started striding toward the exit with his ladies on his arms.

There was a lot of cheering coming from the crowd and it seemed like the noise was getting louder as they walked away. Lexi thought it was odd until she heard her name being called.

She turned around and saw Jake running up to her…sweaty, but, oh so handsome. "Lexi, wait up." His helmet was off and his hair was wet from sweat, but he still looked so good, so damn good. He was significantly taller than she was, but with his gear donning his body, he seemed like a giant.

"Hey, good game," Parker said, while giving Jake a high five. "You didn't even give those fools a chance."

Jake didn't even look at Parker when he said thanks, he just kept staring at Lexi. "Are you guys leaving?"

Not wanting to stammer, Lexi gathered her wits before she answered. "Yeah, we're going to get some frozen yogurt."

Margo pushed Lexi forward making her run right into Jake's chest. He steadied her with his arms on her shoulders. Margo yawned, "Actually, Parker was just going to take me home. We're so tired."

"We're not…" Margo elbowed Parker in the side causing him to cough. "Oh yeah," he fake yawned. "So tired. See you Lexi; good game Jake." And just like that, they left her alone with Jake. They melted into the crowd that was exiting the stadium, not even turning around to see if she was going to be okay.

What friends they were…they were her ride home. She looked at Jake who had hopeful eyes. Damn, she couldn't do this dance much longer. Her resolve was weakening with each passing moment she had with him. She was going to give in soon, but she didn't want to. She didn't just want to be another girl for him to check off on his list. She didn't think if she gave into Jake she was going to be able to say goodbye after one night. She would most likely want more and she knew that was not how he rolled.

"Were they your ride?" he asked, still holding onto her arms.

"Yeah, not a big deal though. I don't mind walking."

"You're not walking. Who knows what kind of sick fucks are waiting to attack you out there?"

"I'm a big girl, Jake. I can handle it."

"Please, Lexi. Let me give you a ride."

Lexi didn't really want to walk to her apartment since it was a good five miles, something she didn't want to tackle at ten at night, but did she want to be trapped in a vehicle with Jake? The more she thought about it, the more she knew Jake was right, there would be creeps out there waiting to take advantage of her. She'd always heard about those campus rapes that happened around the country and she definitely didn't want to be a part of that horrifying statistic.

She conceded. "Okay, thank you."

The smile that lit up Jake's face when she agreed to a ride from him was unforgettable. It was as if she just told him she got him a new puppy. It was such a charming little-boy smile that triggered her legs to start to melt. She needed to get ahold of herself before she did something completely embarrassing, like kiss his entire body from head to toe.

"Meet me outside the locker room. I'll be really quick, I promise."

Lexi nodded and watched him jog off toward the other players. He gave them high fives and pats on the back as they walked through the tunnel together. Even though he was egotistical and a player, she could tell that he truly cared about every single guy on his team and really saw their win as a team effort and not the Jake show. The thought made her shudder with anticipation about what other kind of team player he might be. She rolled her eyes at her thought and proceeded toward the locker rooms, despising herself.

Jake

"Great game, Jake," Mason said, while slipping on a pair of pants.

Jake took one of the quickest showers of his life after the game and was trying to dress as quickly as possible, so he didn't keep Lexi waiting outside. "Thanks, you had some amazing catches tonight."

"Have you realized that, ever since we've been doing our morning workouts together, it seems like we've been more in tune with each other?"

Jake agreed. "I thought the same thing, let's keep it up." Jake threw his wallet in his back pocket, tossed a shirt over his head and made sure to apply some deodorant.

"Hey where's the fire, man? Aren't you going out to McGirk's with us for some drinks?" Mason asked.

"No, Lexi is waiting for me outside. I'll see you later."

Mason stopped Jake by placing a hand on his chest. "Lexi? As in the girl who completely hates your guts, Lexi?"

"She doesn't hate my guts. At least, I don't think she does, but yes, that Lexi. I gave her and her friends field passes for tonight. I caught her right before she left. I'm giving her a ride back to her apartment."

Mason laughed, "Wow you must be crazy about her if you're willing to shower and change like a maniac to just give her a ride home."

Jake shrugged, "What if I am? It would do me some good to settle down."

Mason faked horror. "As I live and breathe, I never thought I would hear you say those words."

Jake playfully punched Mason in the shoulder. "Fuck off," Jake said with a smile. "I'll see you later. Have fun at the pub."

Mason took his towel and whipped Jake in the ass as he was on his way out. Normally, Jake would turn around and tackle his friend, but he had better things to do. When he exited the locker room, he looked around but didn't spot Lexi. His stomach dropped with a sickening feeling, thinking that she might have tried walking back to her place alone. He was going to kill her if some creep didn't before he could get to her.

He was about to exit the building, when he saw her leaning against the wall near the exit. She looked cute wearing her football jersey that was tight in all the right places and her short jean shorts. She looked up and their eyes met. He watched her fidget while he walked toward her and he relished the fact that, even though she gave off a tough persona, she could be human as well and show that, in fact, she could be vulnerable as well.

"Were you waiting long?" he asked.

She shook her head and her beautiful blonde locks shifted on and off her shoulders as her head turned. "No, I'm actually surprised at how fast you were."

"Well I cleaned all my orifices, if that's what you were wondering."

A little smiled appeared on her lips. "For your information, Jake, not every girl is thinking about your body and its orifices all times."

Jake playfully acted like she hurt him. "Oh, Lexi, how you hurt me with your words."

She just smiled at him and they walked to his Jeep. Jake opened the door and helped her in. He desperately wanted to keep talking to her, to not drop her off so suddenly, but he'd just started getting her to talk to him, so he didn't want to scare her away. He had to take what he could get for now.

They drove in silence to her apartment and Jake cursed himself the entire drive for not being able to come up with one single thing to say to her. What was wrong with him? He never had a problem talking to girls before, but whenever Lexi was around him, it was like his mind went completely blank.

They arrived at her apartment way too quickly and he listened to the deafening sounds of her unclicking her seatbelt. He begged and pleaded in his mind for her to ask him into her apartment, but knew that was not going to happen.

"Thanks for the ride. I appreciate it." She was getting out, when he placed his hand on her arm to stop her. She looked at him with those bright blue eyes that sent shivers down his spine. He didn't know what he was going to say, but he wanted to prolong their encounter a little bit longer. He wasn't ready to say goodbye yet.

"Uh, thank you for coming tonight. I'm glad you had a good time."

"No, thank you, we had a great time and you really played great tonight."

Jake wasn't going to mention the fact that he could feel her presence on the field which spurred him on to make every pass perfect and every play a gain of yards. It was a lot of pressure, but every time he succeeded, it took all the energy in his body not to look over at where she was standing to search for her approval. The fact that she complimented him on his level of play tonight meant the world to him.

"Thanks." He wanted to ask her out tonight, to go to the pub with him or get frozen yogurt like she was going to, or even just talk in his Jeep, but he didn't. He lost all his nerve. Instead, he let go of her arm and allowed her to get out of the car.

She waved to him and pulled her keys out of her purse to let herself into her apartment. Jake rested his head against the steering wheel. He hated that he didn't ask her to stay. He sensed a little hesitation in her step when she was shutting the door to his jeep but he was too much of a coward to do anything about it. What it came down to was, he didn't want to get turned down by her when he was so close to winning her over. No, he would take baby steps, because right now baby steps seemed to be working toward his goal of being with Lexi Knox.

He put his Jeep in drive and was about to press the gas pedal when he heard his phone chime with a text message. He looked at the screen and saw that it was from Lexi. Quickly, he opened the message and read it.

Lexi: Thanks again for a great night. I look forward to watching you play in your next game. Go Bears!

Jake felt his heart surge with happiness. He was making leeway with getting Lexi to be on his good side. Things were looking up for him, even though the timing was incredibly slow. The wait was worth it. Lexi was worth the wait.

Margo

"I hope Lexi doesn't hate us tomorrow," Parker said, while shoveling a spoonful of frozen yogurt into his mouth. After spending some time with him, Margo noticed that he was kind of a slob when it came to eating his food. It was also endearing; he was like a little boy who had quite the sweet tooth.

"Well, at least you don't have to deal with her when you get home. She's most likely going to have my head. Did you see the evil look she gave me when we left her there with Jake?"

Parker laughed and shook his head in agreement. "I do feel nervous for you. You have to promise to text me in the morning to let me know you're still alive."

Margo tried to be cool about his suggestion to contact him. She would text him anytime he wanted. Her feelings for Parker had gone past infatuation. Her feelings had turned into full-blown obsession now. She couldn't get enough of Parker; she felt like a borderline stalker. She kept reminding herself to cool her jets because she didn't want to scare him away.

"I'm surprised you didn't have a guy lined up for tonight," Parker said with a smile.

"What are you talking about? You're a guy."

Parker playfully flexed his arms. "Hey look at that! I am, aren't I? Who would have known?"

"It's kind of hard to miss."

Parker gave her a strange look and then started laughing. "Oh, no you don't, babe. I know what you're trying to do. You are trying to use your feminine wiles on me. Not going to work, I know your track record; you're like the female version of Jake."

Margo cringed at the thought of being compared to Jake, well what seemed like now as the old Jake. Yes, she'd had her fair share of men, but she was nothing like Jake. She could at least tell you who she had been with; Jake probably had no clue. She also didn't like that Parker recognized her wild ways. She didn't want him to think she was a slut. That would significantly lower her chances at ever being with Parker. Not that she was sure if she could be. She still wasn't sure how Lexi would feel about the feelings Margo had been harboring for her best guy friend.

She decided to laugh off his comment instead of becoming offended. "Oh, you caught me."

Parker tapped her on the nose with his finger. "I knew it. So, guess who talked to me today?"

Curious at the change in subject she asked, "Who?"

"Sierra from the basketball team."

Trying to hide the frown that formed at her brow, Margo tried to act supportive like a normal friend would do. Inside she was fuming, though. Why the hell would that bitch, Sierra, be talking to Parker? Oh, Margo knew why, Sierra was talking to Parker like any other woman with eyes would talk to him. Margo plastered on a fake smile.

"Oh?"

"Yeah, she suggested we go out sometime."

Margo was practically grinding her teeth together. She put down the rest of her frozen yogurt on the table she was sharing with Parker and pushed it away. She was no longer hungry. Parker scooped it up and started finishing her cup.

"Well…that should, uh…be fun," she said trying to be supportive. "Are you going to go out with her?"

He shrugged. "Don't really know. I don't want her to get the wrong impression. I'm really not looking for anything serious right now. I kind of want to live it up my senior year. Plus, who knows what next year will bring? I don't want to be attached to someone, especially if I might be travelling all the time."

The fantastic night Margo was having with Parker came to a grinding halt. He didn't want anything serious. His words kept ringing through her head as she sat there staring at him. She felt like she was going to be sick to her stomach. She knew that having any kind of romantic involvement with Parker was a long shot, but she didn't know she had no shot at all. He wanted to have fun and that had been her motto all throughout college, but she knew she wouldn't be able to just have fun with Parker. She would get too attached.

There was only one thing she could do, forget about him…forget about having any kind of romantic involvement with him. That could be easy. She could just drown herself in the lacrosse team. There were plenty of extremely attractive guys on the team she could get lost in. Forgetting about Parker wasn't going to be a problem at all, she tried to convince herself.

Finally able to put some words together after her initial shock, Margo said, "Maybe she just wants a fling. Go for it."

It pained her to say those words, but she had to act as if what he just said didn't destroy all her hopes and dreams for her senior year, and her future.

Parker gave her a quizzical look. "You think?" He licked his spoon and wiped his mouth with a napkin. "Maybe I will."

Well that was it, Margo thought. The end of any kind of relationship with Parker. After tonight, she didn't plan on spending any kind of alone time with him because her heart wouldn't be able to take it. She had to cut herself off. It was the only way to get over Parker Hill..

CHAPTER SEVEN

Lexi

It had been two weeks since the night of the football game. Lexi had not seen or really heard from Jake since he dropped her off. His non-existence in her life could partially be because he'd been on the road for back-to-back away games. Not that she was keeping track or anything.

She had seen a real change in Jake and it killed her that he hadn't tried to pursue her again. She for sure thought that, after the game, he was going to ask her out. She wanted him to ask her out. When did that happen? Did she really want to go there? Yes, yes she did. He wasn't the same guy from the past three years, he was different…he was a guy she could see herself falling for.

Lexi constantly heard gossip from other girls on different teams that Jake wasn't his normal self this year and he had been keeping to himself instead of going out like he normally did. The girls were angry that he hadn't been at parties, but Lexi was secretly happy because it meant that he wasn't putting on some kind of act just for her to get in her pants. If she wasn't having such a bad week, maybe she would be actually excited about the fact that Jake was a changed man…well, hopefully a changed man.

Starting her terrible week off with a speeding ticket, which was her fault, of course, but she wished the officer had given her a break, just this once, her crappy week continued. Her dad, once again, fell off the wagon and the only reason she found out was because her mom called her from the bedroom crying and praying that he wouldn't find her. Lexi didn't understand why her mom stayed with her dad. He was an abusive asshole. A long time ago, she had good times with her dad when they were traveling around going to her softball games, but once she hit high school and was able to drive herself, her dad stopped going to Lexi's practices and games and started hitting up the bar more often.

Lexi never really talked about her dad to anyone besides Parker and Margo, but they weren't even around to talk to. Parker was too busy with Sierra, the new point guard on the basketball team, and Margo had been gone for nights on end. Lexi's only guess was she was at the lacrosse house. Sometimes, she worried about her friend and wondered if she was making the right decisions when it came to her sex life.

So, instead of talking about her problems with the two closest people in her life, she bottled it up to the point that it affected her play, once again. She wasn't hitting like she was supposed to and she made a few errors in the field at practice, causing the team to do thirty burpees for every error. Lexi's legs were sore as hell; she felt like she could barely walk, but she continued to work out in the morning and then attend the team's workout later on in the day. She pushed herself harder and harder each day, and she knew why. She was running away from the pain her dad brought to the family and the pain she heard in her mom's shrieking voice over the phone, as well as the pain from not hearing from Jake.

Dead silence filled the locker room as Lexi walked in. Usually, everyone was talking and joking around before practice, but when she walked in, it was as if someone had died. Lexi looked around and all the freshman had their heads down. This wasn't good. Lexi looked up at the whiteboard that hung in their locker room and saw her coach's handwriting.

Don't bother going to the field, basketball courts at five.

Shit.

"What's going on?" No one answered. "I asked what the hell is going on?"

One of the underclassmen walked past her and said, "You'll find out."

Lexi grabbed her running shoes, slipped them on quickly and headed up to the gym. Her stomach was twisting in knots. Whenever they were asked to go to the basketball courts, it was never a good sign. It meant something bad happened and they were about to pay for it.

Lexi walked into the gym and saw her coaches standing in a circle together, discussing something quietly. Her head coach was swinging a whistle around her hand.

Fuck. Definitely not a good sign. Lexi spotted Margo and sidled up next to her.

"Hey, what's going on?" she whispered.

Margo shrugged her shoulders and then stretched her quad. "You got me, but I'm assuming we're about to get our asses handed to us."

Lexi agreed with Margo's obvious observation. Lexi looked at the rest of her teammates and, once again, the freshmen looked guilty. This had to be their fault. What did they get into?

Her coach blew her whistle. "On the line!" she shouted. "Suicides, ten, go!"

Lexi groaned and took off. Suicides were torture and ten in a row was unbearable. This was going to be really bad.

Lexi made sure to hit every line with her hand and to sprint her ass off in between line touches because, if anyone needed to set an example, it was her. She was the team captain and, even though she had no clue what was happening, she needed to lead her team. Her legs felt like noodles; she didn't even feel like they were attached to her body as she sprinted up and down the basketball court. They felt like dangling muscles that, for some odd reason, were propelling her forward. If she knew she was going to be tortured at practice today, she wouldn't have done an extra set of lunges in the weight room.

They finally finished their ten suicides and looked back at their coach to see what was next. Everyone was trying to catch their breath, some girls were bent over, but Lexi made sure to stand up straight…even though she was sucking air.

"Freshmen, do you care to tell your team why you're all here getting your asses handed to you?" their coach said. No one spoke up, which made their coach even angrier. "Give me ten more suicides," their coach screamed, then blew her whistle.

This was going to be one long night. Lexi heard Margo groan next to her and she silently agreed with her friend. Lexi tried to push back all thoughts that were floating through her head, so she could slip into her blank space she visited when in these type of situations. She just let her body run on auto pilot. She felt numb; she had felt numb for a while now, but today, she truly had no feelings. She should be outraged, she would normally be screaming at her teammates by now to demand what was going on, but she couldn't, her emotions were checked at the door.

When they were done with another round of suicides, their coach looked at her. "Where have you been Lexi? You're supposed to be leading this team and right now, you couldn't lead a bunch of two year olds if you tried. Fifty burpees, go!" She blew her damn whistle again.

Lexi felt her face go blank. She really wasn't being a good leader; she could barely control her own life. How would she be able to take care of a team? Was it because she had no purpose? Was that why she was so empty? She would be saying goodbye to the sport she loved in less than a year and she had no clue what she was going to do with her life. She had no plans at all. Or was it because of her family's dirty secret? Or was it the fact that an extremely gorgeous man made her think he was interested in her, but kept ignoring her?

Lexi waited for the rest of the team to finish up their burpees while she caught her breath.

"Anyone want to speak up yet?" Still there was silence, what the hell? Lexi thought. "Ten suicides, and follow them up with fifty more burpees."

Their coach's whistle rang through Lexi's ears as she plowed through the physical demand their coach gave them. Some of the girls were falling over and picking themselves back up. Lexi thought she was sprinting, but when she looked up at where she was in the gym, she realized she was practically jogging, but her legs couldn't go any faster. It felt like cinder blocks were attached to her hips as she tried to trek her way down the court. She tried to go faster, but her legs wouldn't budge; they were fried.

"After your burpees, I want 20 down and back sprints, since you're all taking it so easy on your suicides."

Fuck!

No, Lexi could feel herself starting to get upset. She had to go back to her blank space, but there were too many emotions floating through her body.

Fury started to trickle through her body as she worked her way through the list of physical demands yelled out by her devil of a coach. Anger, a lot of anger, was rushing through her body now. Margo collapsed next to her and Lexi grabbed her by the arm, making sure her friend didn't get in any trouble.

"Come on, Margo," Lexi said, in between huffs.

Sweat trickled down her back as Lexi felt like she was separated from her body and was watching herself run up and down the court from the rafters. She looked pathetic, useless and pathetic. Never in her life had she despised herself so much. When had she ever let her personal life affect her this much? Screw her dad and his drinking, screw her lack of plans for the future, screw the prick of an officer that gave her a ticket, screw her friends who hadn't been there for her and screw Jake Taylor.

When they finally finished their coach's previous demand, Lexi put her hands on her knees to catch her breath.

"Let's hear it ladies, what do you have to say?" Still silence.

Lexi couldn't take it anymore. She stepped out on the court and looked at her freshmen. She pointed at them. "Tell Coach whatever the fuck you did because I don't want to be running on your sorry asses' behalf anymore! Damn!"

Silence enveloped her as her bitch of a coach clapped slowly. Lexi looked at her coach with confusion.

"Thank you freshmen; you were quite the actresses."

"What the hell is going on?" Lexi asked, spinning around to look at everyone.

"Looks like you owe your team an apology, Lexi. You see, it took, let's see how many suicides, burpees and down and ups to finally light a fire under your ass?" Her coach got right in her face. "That is what a captain is supposed to do, control her team, not sit back and make errors while she wallows in her own self-pity. I'm just sorry I had to use your teammates as an example to get you going. You ladies are dismissed." Her coach looked Lexi dead in the eyes and said, "Get your shit together, Knox or you'll be warming the bench all year."

Her coach turned on her heel and left Lexi in the gym all by herself.

This whole practice was because of Lexi? They just ran their asses off because of her? She had never been the one to cause the running and she just put her team through hell because she was letting her personal life get to her.

Feeling like pure shit, she leaned against the padded wall and slowly lowered herself to the ground. She pulled her knees into her chest, placed her head on her knees and cried. She let herself cry for a while. She let herself feel again and she let herself have one last pity party.

Jake

Jake looked all over his locker for his watch, but couldn't find it. Where did he put it? Practice wasn't too bad today; he knew his coach was taking it a little easy on the guys because the past couple of games they'd killed their opponents. Jake appreciated the break, but after practice, he went up to his coach and asked him to not let up on the guys anymore; they needed to continue to practice the way they had been so they could continue to play the way they were. Their coach agreed, but also stated he didn't want to run the guys ragged, which Jake could agree with.

The guys were all going to the sports bar after practice, but Jake decided to pass, since he was feeling tired and didn't want to push himself. The last thing he needed was to get sick.

He gathered his items and walked out of the locker room. He was about to leave, when he remembered he'd left his watch on the indoor track this morning when he was working out with Mason. Jake walked out onto the track, grabbed his watch, and was heading for his Jeep when he heard someone crying.

He looked around, but didn't see anyone. That was weird, he thought. He continued toward the exit when he heard another sob. He turned around and looked at the closed door to the gym. He heard there was a team in the gym that was getting their asses handed to him so he decided to take a peek to see if there were any stragglers.

When he looked around in the gym, he saw Lexi sitting on the floor with her head on her knees, crying. The only reason he knew the person on the floor was her was because she was wearing gym shorts with softball written on them and a massive amount of blonde hair was spilling over the girl's shoulders.

He jogged up to her and knelt down. He startled her when he put his hand on her shoulder, which caused her to frantically wipe away her tears and clear her throat. He hated how she always had to be so tough around him.

"Lexi, what's wrong? Are you okay?"

Lexi shot straight up from where she was sitting and then toppled over from being unbalanced. Jake caught her in his arms, trying to steady her.

She stared up at him with watery blue eyes that stole his

heart. He hated seeing her in pain. He wanted to be able to wipe away all the pain in her face and make everything better. She struggled to gain her balance, but continued to cry, so she wasn't having any success at holding herself up. Instead of helping her back down to the ground, Jake took charge. He escorted her out to his Jeep, buckled her up and drove her to his place. It was a little closer than hers and he didn't have a key to get into her apartment.

He pulled her out of the passenger seat, where she was curled up and carried her into his apartment. He placed her on the couch and got some water from his fridge for her.

Seeing Lexi so deflated made him nervous; he always saw her so strong and stubborn, never like the mess she currently was. He had never seen her so down before and it was crushing him. He sat next to her on the couch and pulled a pillow onto his lap. She rested her head on the pillow and cried.

"It's okay," he said, while stroking her head. He had no clue if it actually was okay or what "it" was, but he knew whatever happened, he was going to help her through it; he wanted to, he needed to.

Ever since he'd laid eyes on Lexi at the football party, he couldn't get her out of his head. Now that she was vulnerable and actually letting him take care of her, he wasn't going to go anywhere, no matter what her problem was.

At that moment, he finally realized what it was like to have someone to care about. Even though Lexi barely gave him the time of day, he cared about her.

When Mason first started dating Brooke, Jake thought his friend was a fool. He always wondered why Mason would give up his bachelor life to be with one girl. Now Jake understood. It was about taking care of someone, having someone to lean on, to laugh with and to share life with. Right now, he wanted to take care of Lexi; he wanted to wash her pain away.

Her cries settled down into sniffs and then her breathing turned heavy. Jake continued to stroke her hair and realized that she had fallen asleep. He pulled a blanket over her without disturbing the way she was sleeping and made himself comfortable. Thankfully, he had his phone with him because he was able to check ESPN for scores and updates while she slept.

Soon enough, Jake's eyes started to get heavy and he drifted off into sleep as well, a very deep sleep.

Lexi

A sharp pain radiated through Lexi's neck, causing her to wake up. She shifted from where she was laying and almost fell off her bed. She caught herself right before she tipped over. Her eyes flew open from the adrenaline rush of almost falling to the ground and that was when she realized she wasn't in her bed, she was on a couch. Her hand was on something hard. She looked over and saw that her hand was gripping a man's thigh. She shot up from where she was laying and saw the man whose thigh she was grazing.

Jake.

Instant mortification took over her body, as her whole body burned with heat. He found her at her worst moment and he didn't run away. Instead, he decided to take care of her. No, she told herself, she was not going to get into this with him. Wasn't the practice they just had a big enough push away from Jake? She lost sight of what was important for her team and she wasn't going to let it happen again. She couldn't let Jake get in the middle of things. She couldn't let him plant himself in her head again.

Her coach made it quite clear that Lexi needed to get her head out of her ass and focus on what was important. Lexi was able to succeed her entire college career because she never let a guy interfere with her goals. Jake was a distraction, a handsome distraction, but a distraction she couldn't afford. This was her last year, she needed to focus on figuring out what she was going to do with her life and she needed to focus on her team. She needed to give them her one hundred percent, not wonder whether or not the hunky quarterback was going to ask her out again.

Lexi was able to slip off the couch without waking Jake up.

She didn't see any of her belongings around his apartment, probably because they were still in her locker. She had her workout clothes still on, so she decided she would turn her trek back to the events center into a little workout, even though it felt like she'd pulled every muscle in her legs.

She looked at Jake one last time and then slipped out of his apartment. She stretched her back and started to jog over to the events center. The entire time she replayed what happened last night in her head. All she could remember was crying hysterically and Jake carrying her around. Her mouth went dry and her stomach ached. Life wasn't fair. Finally, she found a guy who was caring and sweet, yeah, he had a bit of a battered past, but he had changed before her eyes and it pained her that she couldn't do anything about it.

Lord knew that she couldn't handle being there for the team and having her own relationship, something had to give and that was Jake. Not that he wanted to be in a relationship with her, she didn't know that, but it did seem like he cared about her.

What was she doing? She cursed herself out and picked up the pace of her run. She reveled in the burn that was traveling the length of her legs from the asinine workout she put her team through.

She was supposed to be forgetting about Jake and putting him behind her. She wasn't supposed to be analyzing his feelings for her and whether he actually had any. This was never going to work.

She arrived at the events center and went to her locker room. As usual, she was the only one there. She pulled out her toothbrush and toothpaste she kept in locker and brushed her teeth at the sink in the bathroom. She hated having morning breath before a workout. She brushed her hair and threw it up into a messy bun, grabbed a towel, and headed for the weight room.

After waving good morning to the trainer, she started working out on an exercise ball. She hadn't done much ab work lately and, since she was incredibly sore from yesterday's practice, she didn't even want to attempt to do any squats or lunges.

Lexi worked out until she couldn't feel her abs anymore. It was the only way she knew how to erase her current pain, by causing new pain to focus on, so she did. She spent half on hour on the exercise ball doing all sorts of balancing and weighted ab work. She looked at the clock and realized she needed to get in the shower and get up to class.

After an extremely quick shower and brush of her hair, she threw on her spare clothes and headed out of the locker room for class.

"Hey."

Lexi stopped in her tracks and turned to find Jake waiting for her. He was leaning against the wall, once again, but he was wearing sweats and a T-shirt that showed off his amazing muscles. Lexi felt her voice get caught in her throat, so she just smiled at him.

"So, you're just going to walk out of my apartment without saying anything?"

There was hurt in his eyes when he said his words. Lexi felt extremely guilty. She was trying to figure out what was best for her when she left Jake's apartment, she didn't even consider what it would be like for Jake. She was an ass.

"I'm sorry. I was just, uh, embarrassed."

He walked closer so he was only a couple of inches away from her. "Why?"

She looked up into his green eyes and felt the walls she was trying to build this morning crumble to the ground; they were completely nonexistent now.

"Because Jake. I mean, who cries like that? It was embarrassing for you to see me like that."

"Why do you care how I see you?" He was even closer now as he placed his hands on her hips. His hands felt so strong, protective…safe.

She looked down, but he lifted her chin so she was looking at him. "I don't want you to look at me differently?" she said.

"And how would I look at you?"

Lexi blew out an exasperated breath. "Like a weakling."

"You have to know by now I don't see you as a weakling. I see you as a strong, confident, sexy woman."

"Well, I wasn't last night, especially the sexy part." Lexi felt herself turn bright red at the thought of what she might have looked like last night. She knew she didn't have a pretty cry face. She could only imagine the horror she might have caused Jake.

"You were human last night; it was charming. It made me like you even more."

"Like me?"

He smiled at her and brought his head down toward hers. Oh God, he was going to kiss her. She felt her body tense up and panic, while at the same time, her heart hammered against her chest. She wanted this, she wanted Jake. His lips were a breath away from touching hers as he cupped the nape of her neck.

"There you are! Thank…Oh, sorry I didn't know." Lexi shot away from Jake as if he was acid that was burning her skin off. She looked over at her grinning roommate and Lexi instantly hated herself. "I was worried about you, but if I knew you were with Jake…"

"I wasn't with him, well not the way you were thinking." Lexi looked at Jake who was sporting a deep frown and then she looked back a Margo who would not stop smirking. "I'm fine, I have to go. I'll see you at practice."

Lexi couldn't even turn to look at Jake to say goodbye because she couldn't stand to see the hurt in his eyes again. She knew she was blowing him off, but she couldn't do this right now, this, whatever it was with Jake. Even though her heart and her body were telling her to skip class and invite Jake to breakfast, her brain was actually working and telling her to get her ass in gear. She had things to do and she couldn't spend her day pining away over Jake.

Jake

Jake watched Lexi walk away without even acknowledging him. What the hell? He turned to Margo, who was still standing in the hallway, grinning like an idiot. "Thanks a lot, Margo."

She feigned shock. "Oh, was I interrupting something? Perhaps something that continued over from last night?"

Jake wished! "No, actually. I had to track her down here when she left my apartment after not saying anything."

He told Margo about how he found Lexi in the gym crying and Margo told him all about their practice from the night before. Jake could completely relate to what Lexi was going through. He got ripped by his coach last year for not performing as a leader. Being captain was difficult because you had to be the best at everything, while being a team leader. It was a tough spot to be in and if you were off your game for even one day, you were called out on it.

Jake shook his head. "I wish she would talk to me about it."

"And why would she do that?" Margo asked.

"Because I care, because I want to help her. I would have thought she got that impression from what I did for her last night."

Margo just shrugged. "Sometimes with Lexi, you have to voice what you're feeling. I'm not going to get into it, but she doesn't have the best family life and it takes a lot for her to trust someone, especially, no offense, someone with your kind of past."

"I would tell her how I feel if she gave me the time of day."

"You haven't even talked to her for the past couple of weeks. If you're interested in her, you have to make it known. Stop pussy-footing around and take what you want. Don't take no for an answer. Make her feel special Jake; she deserves it and, if you're not up for the challenge, then please just let her be. She can't take the distraction if you're not going to be all in."

All in, was he all in?

He thanked Margo for the advice and walked toward his locker room. He thought about last night and how great it felt to have Lexi so close to him, to take care of her, to run his hand through her hair and he thought about the moment they shared together right before Margo interrupted them. If being with Lexi meant having to be all in, then he was all in. He couldn't walk away now. He was so close to something he never thought he would ever want, he couldn't give up now. He had never been a quitter and he wouldn't start now.

He pulled out his phone and sent Lexi a text message.

Jake: Have dinner with me tonight, after practice. Please.

It didn't take her long to respond.

Lexi: I can't.

Jake: I know you have nothing planned, please let me take you out. Just something casual.

Lexi: I don't think that is a good idea, Jake. I appreciate what you did for me last night, but I think we should leave it at that.

Jake: I'm not taking no for an answer. I think, after last night, I at least deserve this.

Lexi: I'm sorry, you're right. I will meet you after practice.

Jake: Thank you. See you then and Lexi, have a great day. I will be thinking about you.

Lexi: You too.

Jake stuffed his phone in his locker after reading her last text message and put on his running shoes. He was going to let Lexi know how he felt at dinner; he was going to take what he wanted and show her how special she was.

Lexi

Lexi was a bundle of nerves while she was getting ready for her so-called date with Jake. Practice went much better today. Lexi felt like her old self again out on the field. She led the team every way possible, being the first on the field and the last to leave. She even got a brief nod from her coach, which she knew was her coach's way of showing her approval. Lexi might have let her guard down for a second, but she was back in the game again. She was able to shut her personal life off when she stepped on the field, something she recently forgot how to do.

Everyone was already gone, Lexi stayed behind to take a shower and try to make herself semi presentable. She put on a pair of navy blue yoga pants and a tight white T-shirt, along with her lime green Nikes. She knew it wasn't a dress and high heels, but she just got out of practice; she wasn't going to get much more out of herself in the fashion department. She made sure to throw her hair up in a messy bun with a headband and put on a generous amount of mascara to make her eyes pop.

Looking at herself in the mirror, she approved of her reflection. She wasn't sex on a stick, but she wasn't half bad either. She grabbed her backpack and headed for the door. She made her way to the half-wall that was just outside the events center to wait for Jake. It was a beautiful day and she might as well enjoy the weather while she waited for Jake. She knew Jake's practice ran a little later than hers, so she was prepared to wait. She sent a text to Jake to let him know where she was.

Nerves ran through her body as she couldn't believe she was actually going on a date with Jake…again. This morning she had sworn off of him. How was it that he was able to change her mind so quickly? Wait, her mind wasn't changed. She was just going out to dinner with him because she owed it to him, since he took care of her during one of her lowest points. She was going to hold true to what she told herself. She had no time or room for a guy in her life.

The side door to the events center opened up and Jake appeared wearing a pair of Cal U gym shorts and a dark grey football shirt. His hair was wet, most likely from a quick shower and he was wearing flip flops. She was glad she went super causal because she would have felt stupid in jeans and a nice shirt. She hopped off the half-wall and met him on the sidewalk.

He beamed at her with one of his kill-me-now smiles. "Hey gorgeous, are you ready?"

"Yup." They walked toward his Jeep while she asked, "How was practice?"

He rubbed his shoulder before he opened the door for her. "Oh, you know, painful as usual." He shut the door and jogged around to his side. She surveyed the interior of his Jeep and came to the realization of how much she loved his car. How stupid was that? It was a just a car, but it was so him, rugged on the outside but soft and safe on the inside. "How about you?"

She looked at him confused. "Huh?"

"How was your practice?"

"Oh, it was a hell of a lot better than yesterday. That's for sure. It's obviously our off-season right now, so we focus a lot on technique and drills. It can get really boring at times. I prefer to do situational plays and scrimmages."

"Doesn't everybody? Drills can be so monotonous at times."

Lexi agreed with him. Their conversation struck her as strange because the only other person besides her teammates that she talked about her sport with was Parker. No one else seemed to care, so it was refreshing to have another understanding ear to talk to. It didn't really dawn on her that Jake was going through the same thing as her. Trying to play the sport he loved at a high level, while also trying to earn a degree. No one really knew what they went through, unless they were actually in the same boat.

They continued with mindless chitchat until they pulled up to Panera. Lexi couldn't help but let out a little giggle.

"Something funny?" he asked.

She shook her head and exited the car. He met her in the parking lot. "I just never pictured you as a Panera guy. I expected a Mexican joint or, I don't know, a steak."

"What can I say? They have the best mac and cheese. Is this alright? We can go somewhere else."

"No, this is great. I love it here, but I'm sorry to say, I've never had their mac and cheese."

Jake stopped in his tracks and turned to face her. "You have never had the mac and cheese? That is crazy."

"I love the Fuji Apple Salad; I always get it."

Jake just shook his head. "Women and their salads."

When they got in Panera, they ordered, a salad for Lexi and mac and cheese and a sandwich for Jake. They both got drinks, picked up their food from the counter, and found a cozy little booth in the back corner, where no one could bother them. Lexi eyed Jake's mac and cheese and, she had to admit, she was jealous when she turned back to her salad.

They started eating and, at first, Lexi was self-conscious, but got rid of that feeling right away when Jake got sauce from his sandwich all over his face. He acted like nothing was on his face as he continued to tell her a story about Mason getting stuck in the bathroom at the football house their sophomore year. Jake had a huge glob of sauce on his cheek and Lexi knew he knew it was there, how could he not? She could feel it touching her own skin, it bothered her so much. Occasionally she would wipe the same side of her face hoping Jake would get the hint.

"So, Coach was on the field screaming about where the hell Mason was and why he was missing practice. None of the guys knew where he was and I started to get nervous Coach was going to have a heart attack because he was so mad." Jake took another bite of his sandwich, letting sauce hit his chin; Lexi cringed and he smiled.

"Are you trying to be disgusting on purpose?" she said with a laugh, while handing him a napkin.

"No, just trying to ease the tension." He wiped his face and continued with his story. "So, the other guys and I got back to the house, where Mason's car was, his phone was in the house along with his backpack. We started to get really nervous because it wasn't like Mason to miss practice. I started to get terrible thoughts in my head like he committed suicide or a jealous student shot him to death, you know the typical overreactions." Lexi nodded in agreement. "Well, after calling his name, we finally heard him yell out from upstairs. We all went running to his voice and followed it to the bathroom where the knob from the outside had fallen off, so he had no way of getting out. We got the door open and there he was with a towel wrapped around his waist and the shower curtain wrapped around his shoulders."

Lexi burst out in laughter. "Why did he have the shower curtain wrapped around him?"

"Apparently, the bathroom tiles were cold."

Lexi could not stop laughing. Picturing Mason in such a scenario was one of the funniest things she had heard in a while. "Did Mason tell your coach what happened?"

Jake took a sip of his drink. "Well, once we found Mason, we called Coach right away. Coach called an early meeting the next day and made us all do fifty yard sprints for half an hour."

"What? Why?" Lexi asked in outrage.

"As Coach put it, if Mason was dumb enough to get himself locked in a bathroom, then we should all pay the price as his teammates for having to put up with his stupidity."

"That makes absolutely no sense."

Jake shrugged his shoulders. "It really doesn't, but we did them together, the entire time trying to hold back chuckles. That year at the team Christmas party, Coach got Mason a nice floral shower curtain with a note attached that said 'to keep you warm on the bus.'"

Lexi burst out in laughter again. "Well, at least your coach can show a little bit of a sense of humor. I swear it's a prerequisite of a division one coach to be completely devoid of humor."

Lexi was almost done with her salad, but kept eyeing Jake's

mac and cheese and finally gained enough courage to dip her fork quickly into his bowl and snag a bite. She reveled in the taste of the melted cheese when it touched her tongue. Jake was right, that was the best mac and cheese she had ever tasted. She looked at him and saw a huge grin on his face.

"What are you smiling at?"

"It's funny how you so easily reached over and stole some of my dinner without even looking guilty. You know it's a dangerous thing to steal a sturdy football player's dinner, especially after a grueling practice."

"Oh please, what are you going to do, wrestle me to the ground?"

Jake started to get up and said, "Don't mind if I do."

"What are you doing? Sit down you oaf."

Jake chuckled, "You're all talk."

"What? You think you could beat me in a wrestling match?"

He looked Lexi up and down and laughed. "Uh, sorry to say it, short stack, but I would own you."

Lexi lifted her chin in defiance. "I might be short, but I'm quick and scrappy. I would have you down so fast, you wouldn't even know we started."

"I doubt that. I'm sorry to say it, but I probably have about one hundred pounds on you."

"I guess we'll never know."

"I'm willing to settle this challenge. You're the one backing down."

"I'm not backing down. I'm just saving myself the hassle of giving you a free grope session as you try to prove yourself as a man by taking down a girl half your size."

"So you admit I can take you?"

Lexi rolled her eyes. "You're infuriating."

"Yes, but you like it."

Lexi looked him in the eyes. They were done eating now and just sitting there enjoying each other's company. Lexi couldn't remember the last time she felt so relaxed and at ease. Her doubts about being with Jake left her brain completely and the walls she thought she put up this morning were once again in ruins. She was giving herself over to Jake and she was scared to her core, but she knew she couldn't avoid what he was doing to her anymore. She was giving in and, if she was going to give in, then she was going to do it on her own terms. She wasn't going to let him whisk her away so fast. She was going to take things slow, incredibly slow.

"I do like it." She must have shocked the hell out of him because his reaction was priceless, she rendered him speechless. The only response he was able to muster was a smile that stretched from ear to ear. She decided to cut the night short while she was ahead. "Thanks for dinner, but I have to get back to my place. I have a bunch of reading to do for a class and I don't want to fall behind."

"I understand." He threw their trash out and escorted her back to his Jeep. "Thank you for coming out with me tonight. I had a great time."

"Me too, thank you for asking."

They drove in silence back to her apartment. She didn't want the night to end, she didn't want to say good bye to him right away, but she didn't want to get in over her head. One step at a time, she kept telling herself.

They pulled up to her place and they both got out of Jake's Jeep. He met her at the front of his Jeep and grabbed her hand as he entwined his fingers with hers. Her stomach did flips and she felt the heat in her body rise a couple of notches. They walked hand-in-hand to her door and turned around to face each other. He looked so good, it was almost painful to look at him. How was it possible for one single human being to be so incredibly attractive? Wasn't it a crime?

He rubbed the back of her hand with his thumb. "Can we do this again, Lexi?"

He looked so vulnerable when he asked her. She wanted to ease his anxiety. "I would love that."

"Great. I'll call you."

He started to lean in and she knew he was going to kiss her, but she wasn't ready. So, instead of letting him make his move, she released his hand, gave him a quick hug, and went into her apartment. She was breathing heavily and not from her fast movements. She almost kissed Jake Taylor. Was she crazy? She leaned her head against the door and thought about their evening. It was amazing; it was something that she felt had been missing from her life and that something was fun, pure fun.

Her phone chimed and the noise brought her back down to earth from her thoughts. She looked at the screen and surprise, surprise, it was from Jake.

Jake: I had an amazing time with you tonight, short stack. Thanks for coming out. Sweet dreams, oh and P.S. Don't think you can avoid that kiss every time. It's going to happen.

Lexi felt her face flush at reading his text. He totally called her out, but she couldn't help but giggle like a little school girl. She sent him a quick text good night and went to go brush her teeth. She stared at herself in the mirror and wondered what life would be like if she was actually in a relationship with Jake Taylor.

CHAPTER EIGHT

Jake

"You're killing me this morning," Mason said, while he tried to catch his breath. "Where are you getting all this energy from?"

Jake was feeling great; he had felt great since his dinner with Lexi. They hadn't been able to get together again in a week and, even though it was driving him crazy to not see her, he knew he had a plan this morning to see her and he was excited. He had never felt so alive before, it was like Lexi had awakened something in him he never knew was missing.

"Well, we should stop because I don't want to tire you out for tonight."

"Are you not even tired?" Mason asked, while leaning his hands on his knees and breathing heavily.

"No, I feel great," Jake said nonchalantly, while Mason flipped him off.

They both grabbed their towels and walked out of the gym toward the locker rooms. Jake stopped him and said, "I have to make a detour, I'll see you a little later."

"Let me guess, checking to see if a certain blonde is in the weight room?"

"What's it to you?"

"It's not. It just amazes me to see you like this."

"Like what?"

Mason looked Jake up and down and said, "Not a dickhead."

Jake playfully punched him. "I'll see you later; ice those knees. I expect a big score tonight."

They parted their ways and Jake walked toward the weight room like Mason predicted. He wanted to be able to catch Lexi before she left. It was a Saturday, so he wasn't even sure she would be there, but knowing her work ethic, she most likely would be in there getting a workout in before practice. He admired her for her hard work. No wonder she was so good at her sport, she put more time in the gym than anyone else he knew, even more than him.

While he walked down the hall toward the weight room, he thought about how he was going to miss walking the halls of the event center. There were pictures of past athletes hung on the walls, displaying the amount of athleticism that had graced the halls. There was a picture of Jake hanging near the football locker, it was an honor to be on the wall and he didn't take it for granted.

He walked up to the weight room and peeked in. Lexi was by the free weights doing lunges in the shortest pair of spandex shorts he had ever seen and a tight tank top with a neon sports bra peeking out. She had ear buds in her ears with her iPod attached to her bicep. Her hair was pulled back in her classic messy bun that stood high off her head because of the massive amount of hair she had. Jake stood in the doorway admiring her from afar, trying not to drool over her luscious ass. Lunges had done her well.

"Hey peeping Tom, are you going to work out or what?"

The head trainer scared the crap out of him. Jake didn't even know the guy was in the weight room. Jake felt a flush creep over his body at being caught staring at Lexi.

"Uh, no I just need to talk to Lexi and I didn't want to disturb her." He walked past the trainer to avoid any more embarrassment and walked up behind Lexi who was looking at herself in the mirror while doing bicep curls. When their eyes met, he watched hers widen in surprise. She quickly set her weights down, pulled out her ear buds and asked, "Hey, what are you doing here?"

"I came looking for you." Jake looked at their trainer who was eyeing them. Jake tilted his head toward the hallway and said, "Uh, could we talk without an audience?"

Lexi looked at the trainer, smiled and nodded. They walked out into the hallway and hovered by the water fountain. Lexi's eyes were sparkling this morning and Jake hoped it had something to do with him.

"What time is practice today?"

"Ten, I wanted to get in a quick workout beforehand."

"I figured as much."

They stood there for an awkward moment before Lexi said, "What's up, Jake?"

He hated that he got so nervous around her. He never lost his cool before, but he so easily did around her. It was as if he was back in grade school and he was asking out a girl for the first time. He felt his hands start to get sweaty, so he casually wiped them off on his shorts. He was leaning against the wall, trying to be as casual as possible.

"What are you doing tonight?"

"Not sure," she said with a shrug.

"Really? You aren't going anywhere tonight?"

"Nope, I think I'm going to just hang out at my place. Maybe watch some mushy romantic comedy starring Tom Hanks."

"So you didn't plan on going to one of the biggest games of the season?" Jake asked, almost hurt.

"Oh, is that tonight?" She waved her hand in dismissal. "Well, I had no clue and since I already made plans with my couch…I guess I'll have to pass."

Jake just realized she was pulling his leg when she flashed her gorgeous smile at him. Jake rubbed his hand over his face.

"Good Lord, woman. If you traded tonight's game in for Tom Hanks, we were going to have to have a serious chat."

She laughed and grabbed his hand. She mingled her fingers with his and said, "Of course I'll be there. Parker got us some seats on the fifty yard line. I don't know how he managed such great seats since students usually sit in the end zone, but I'll take them."

He played with her hand and felt their palms come together, it was comforting, supportive. The little gesture of her taking his hand sent his heart rate to a sprinting pace. She was leaning against the wall now, so he positioned himself in front of her so her back was up against the wall and his hand that was not mingling with hers was supporting him on the wall right next to her head. He watched her breath quicken and her pulse in her neck take off.

"When we kick the Tiger's asses tonight, will you go to the football house's party afterwards with me?"

Her free hand played with the collar of his shirt as she stared at him with her crystal blue eyes. It took all the energy in his body not to lean down and kiss her, even though they were already inches apart.

"You want to go to the football house together? Won't that be sending everyone a message if we show up together, possibly hand in hand?" She took that moment to stroke the back of his hand with her thumb. Her little touches all over his body sky rocketed his senses. He didn't know how much more he could take.

"That is a message I don't mind sending. What about you?"

Lexi ran her hand up his arm, as if she was secretly exploring his body. "I think it would be okay."

Jake wanted to skip down the hallway like a leprechaun because she agreed to accompany him to the party tonight. By her saying yes, she was giving him permission to claim her as his. He had never felt so amazing.

"So you don't mind people knowing we're an item?"

"Is that what we are? We only went out to dinner once, you know," she said with a smile.

"Believe me. I want people to know we're an item. I don't need guys thinking you're available. Sorry to say it, babe but you're kind of attached to me now."

"Oh, is that right? Is that so you can stare at me from the doorway of the weight room and not get caught?"

Jake felt another rush of heat flow through his body. "I thought you didn't know I was there."

"I'm a good actress."

Jake laughed and then changed the subject quickly. "I'm not sure if we settled this or not. Are you going to the party with me tonight?"

Lexi acted like she was weighing her options. "I don't know, Tom Hanks or football?" She held her hands out as if she was Lady Justice, balancing her scales. Jake went in for the kill and tickled her. Her hands flew to his chest to stop him. They were inches apart and the feel of her hands on his chest was like an addiction he didn't think he could ever bounce. She slid her hands up his body and wrapped them around his neck. He placed both of his hands on either side of her head as he stared down at her gorgeous face.

She spoke first. "Of course, I'll go with you." Her thumbs rubbed the back of his neck where her hands were. He leaned forward, even closer. He wanted to kiss her so badly, but he wasn't going to be the one who made the first move; he wanted her to take charge.

The side door to the outside opened and Margo came into view. "Ugh, get a room." Jake rested his forehead on Lexi's in disappointment at Margo's impeccable timing. He was so close, yet so far. "We have to get going Lex, see you in the locker room." Lexi nodded toward Margo and then looked at Jake.

"Well, I have to get going. Good luck tonight."

He smiled down at her. "Thanks."

She removed her hands and maneuvered out of his stance that pinned her against the wall. Jake let out an exasperated sigh as he turned around to face her. He leaned against the wall and let her take his hand in hers again.

"Meet you outside by the half-wall after the game? Or do you want to go separately?"

"Oh, we will be going together. By the fence sounds good. Have a good practice."

"I will, kick some ass Taylor."

She gave his hand one last rub with her thumb and took off down the hallway. He watched her walk away and admired her sweet little ass as it swayed back and forth.

Jake ran both of his hands through his hair and leaned his head against the wall. He wasn't sure how much more he could take. He felt so close to Lexi, yet there was still a huge distance between them. He took a quick sip from the water fountain and then walked back to his locker room. When he got there, he checked his phone to see what time it was and noticed he'd received a text message from Lexi. He smiled and read it as he thought about the little tradition they were starting with text messaging.

Lexi: Good luck tonight, big guy. I will be cheering for you from the fifty yard line. And don't worry, you will get that kiss soon, maybe it will be your prize if you win.

Jake smiled when he read her text message. If getting a kiss from Sexy Lexi wasn't incentive enough to win a game, then he didn't know what was.

Lexi

"Why are you so jittery?" Margo asked Lexi.

Lexi didn't know why she was so jittery tonight. She was nervous about the game because she desperately wanted Jake to win. It was a huge rivalry game and she knew if the team lost tonight, the Tigers would never let them live it down. Now she knew how her parents felt when, that is when they cared, when they were watching her play. It was so nerve-racking to be in the stands. If she had to admit it, she was also nervous about the party tonight. She was going to be seen publicly with Jake and that was a big deal. She was going to be measured up by every girl at the party and, most likely, deemed unworthy of Jake's arm, something she wasn't looking forward to.

It would be the first time they went out together since their little date at Panera. They had talked on the phone and texted throughout the week, but both of their busy schedules didn't allow for them to make plans for any dates. Lexi looked forward to their phone calls at night because the sexy tone of Jake's voice over the phone sent chills through her body, making for a very peaceful sleep.

Instead of confessing her fears to Margo about her date, she just said, "Uh, just a little cold."

Margo looked Lexi up and down, just the way Lexi feared the girls at the party would do. "Maybe if you didn't dress like a hooker, you wouldn't be so cold."

Lexi took offense at Margo's comment. After practice, Lexi was able to take her time getting ready for tonight. She painted her nails and toenails, took a nice long shower, scrubbed every inch, as well as made sure to shave everywhere on her body. Lotion was strategically slathered everywhere to give her skin a smooth glow, just in case her body was touched by Jake. She curled her hair in long flowy waves that cascaded down her slender shoulders. She applied some make-up, but kept it natural and dressed in her jean mini skirt, navy blue tank top to show off her school colors, and put on a pair of her brown sandals. She was casual, but cute, she thought.

"I don't look like a hooker."

Margo laughed. "God, you need to loosen up a bit Lex, can't you take a joke?"

Lexi rolled her eyes at her friend and then nudged Parker. "You're not even watching the game. What are you looking around for?"

"Sierra said she was coming to the game."

Lexi heard Margo make a disapproving tone, but the unladylike noise fortunately didn't reach Parker.

Margo was more on edge lately and not as fun as usual; Lexi wondered if it had to do with Sierra. Lexi wasn't stupid, she knew Margo had a giant crush on Parker and when she had her eyes set on something, Margo just had to have it. Parker was her new target and she wasn't able to obtain him like she normally would any other man.

"I thought you weren't going to settle down with any girl this year."

"He's not," Margo said with an attitude. "They're just fuck buddies." Margo grabbed her purse and said, "I'm out of here. Clearly, we're going to win; we're killing them. I'll see you later. Have a good night with Jake."

Lexi grabbed her friend's arm to prevent her from leaving. "Are you not coming to the party tonight?"

"No, I have a date with one of the lacrosse guys."

"Shocker!" Parker said a little more snidely than expected.

Margo rolled her eyes and left. What was that all about?

"Why were you just rude to Margo?" Lexi asked, concerned that she was so far gone on Jake that she failed to see things falling apart around her.

Parker rolled out some kinks in his shoulders. "She's been a bitch to me for weeks now and I have no clue why."

Men, they could be so clueless sometimes, Lexi thought. It wasn't her place to blow up Margo's spot, especially since she hadn't even confided in Lexi about her feelings, so Lexi just had to play dumb.

"Maybe she's going through a tough time; cut her some slack."

"I hope she uses protection. Who knows what kind of virus she could catch from those idiots. Doesn't she realize they're some of the grossest guys in the athletic department? The things they talk about make me feel ashamed to be a guy."

"She uses protection, don't worry about that. Who would you like to see her with?"

"Why do I care?"

The Bears scored another touchdown. The score was not even close now. Lexi watched Jake and Mason chest bump in the air and then walk off the field together. Jake took his helmet off and put it on a helmet rest while he looked toward her direction. He smiled at her when they made eye contact. She smiled back, trying not to melt on the spot. Trying to act like a normal human, she turned her attention back to Parker.

"It kind of seems like you do care if you're making such a big deal out of this."

Parker ignored her. "Oh there's Sierra, I'll catch you later."

And just like that, Lexi was left alone in the stands. Thankfully, there were only a couple of minutes left in the game so she didn't have to feel like a complete loser all by herself.

Lexi pulled out her Chap Stick and applied a decent amount, as she thought about the text she sent to Jake earlier in the day. If they won, she did say she would let him kiss her. And if she knew Jake like she thought she did, he would be cashing in on his prize the moment he saw her.

She was just putting her Chap Stick back in her purse when she heard two girls behind her talking.

"Are you going to the football house later tonight?" one of them asked.

The other girl replied with a higher pitched voice that resembled Adelaide's from *Guys and Dolls*, the musical. "I wouldn't miss it. I plan on congratulating Jake on his victory the only way I know how."

Lexi cringed. She had been so caught up in herself and Jake that she forgot there was a world outside of them, a world where women used to throw themselves at Jake and he used to happily accept their advances.

"Not if I get to him first. Plus, you already had a piece of him."

Lexi felt like throwing up. Jake had changed so much this semester that she almost forgot about his sordid past. It was hard to forget all the women he had relations with, all the drunk nights that he couldn't even remember who he had been with. Was she really about to get involved with someone who she would randomly hear stories about that would tear her gut apart, like she was right now?

"It was just a small piece, or should I say big piece." Both the girls laughed as the horn buzzed for the end of the game. Lexi shot out of her seat and walked quickly in between cheering fans. She had to get out of there. She felt like she couldn't breathe.

Lexi made the brisk walk to the half-wall where she was supposed to meet Jake. She sat down on the edge and thought about what she was going to do. Was she strong enough, brave enough to dabble in a possible relationship with a man who dabbled with almost every girl in the athletic department? Every time she was working out in the weight room, or was at a party, or in class she could risk running into someone who had possibly been with Jake. Then there was the fact that he was extremely experienced and she had only been with one other person.

Not that she was ready to jump his bones right away. She would be putting that off for a while. She wasn't going to give her entire body up to Jake until she knew for sure his intentions. She once gave her body to someone who didn't appreciate her. She didn't want to go down that road again. Given Jake's track record, she was going to make him earn the privilege of sleeping with her, of owning her body.

She felt like she was going to hyperventilate from thinking about what a risk it was for her to get involved with someone like Jake. She didn't have the typical support system one usually received from their family, so what if something did happen to her? What if Jake ended up breaking her heart? It wasn't like Margo and Parker were there for her right now. They couldn't look past their own noses to notice anyone else in the world.

Worrying thoughts of Jake scattered through her mind as she waited for the man in question and she must have been thinking for quite some time because she almost didn't notice his strong presence walking toward her. She looked up and saw Jake smiling as he got closer to where she was sitting. His hair was wet from a shower, causing Lexi's hand to want to run her hand through the wet strands. He was wearing jeans and a light blue polo shirt. He looked good, and he smelled good.

"Hey babe, you look hot." He straddled her against the half wall and placed both his hands on her waist. "What a game huh?" She had a hard time responding because all she could think about were the girls behind her planning their moves on Jake right in front of her, or behind her. Jake was too in tune with her because he noticed her sour mood. "Hey, what's wrong?" he said, while lifting her chin so she had to look him in the eyes, his beautiful light green eyes.

She shook her head. She felt so embarrassed to tell him, but if she was going to give their relationship a shot, which she didn't think she could walk away from, she had to express her concerns.

"I'm sorry, I'm being rude. You were amazing tonight."

"I don't care about the game. What's wrong Lex?"

"I, uh, I don't know if I can go to the party tonight."

"Why? I thought you wanted to." He looked as if she just broke his heart, she felt terrible.

"I do, it's just. Ugh, at the game, there were two girls behind me bragging about how they were going to approach you tonight, and you know, offer themselves up."

Jake laughed, prompting her to swat him in the chest. "It's not funny."

He chuckled a little more before he answered her. "So, since these girls said they were going to 'offer themselves' up to me," he said, while making quotation marks with his fingers, "Then I'm automatically going to sleep with them?"

Well, when he put it like that, he made her feel stupid. "It's not just that Jake; almost every girl around here has a story about being with you and, if you want this to work between us, you have to think about how hard it's going to be for me to hear all those different stories."

Jake pulled her in tight and wrapped his warmth around her. She rested her head on his chest and breathed in his scent. She reveled in the fact that she felt so safe, even with all the doubts in her head as to why being with him wouldn't work, she still felt so safe with him, like he was home.

He kissed the top of her head. "I'm sorry that my idiotic past is going to haunt you. If I could take it back, I would, but I can't. You're just going to have to trust me, trust that you're the only girl I'm interested in. Can you do that? Can you put your faith in me?"

She looked up at his pleading eyes and she thought about how, yes, she could trust him. Even though he'd treated women like crap in the past, she believed Jake and she believed his intentions were pure. She truly believed that he had changed…for the better.

"Yes, I can trust you."

He squeezed her harder and kissed her on the head again. "You don't know how happy that makes me feel." He lifted her up so she was positioned better on the cement half-wall, making her almost face-to-face with him. "Now, I just have to tell you how hot you look tonight."

Lexi felt her skirt hike up to an almost inappropriate level, but for some odd reason, she didn't care. She wrapped her arms around Jake's neck and brought him in closer. He placed his hands on her hips once again, sending chills down her legs.

"You look pretty good yourself. Now, about that game, you really were amazing. You and Mason make such a good team."

"Thanks. I can't tell you how great it feels to have you cheering me on in the stands. I haven't had a little cheering section since my parents died. To have you there, watching, means the world to me."

Lexi had heard about Jake's parents dying in a horrific car accident his freshman year, but never thought he would ever really talk about it, at least not so soon. She caressed his neck with her thumb and said, "I'm glad I was there to support you."

He changed the subject quickly. "So, you ready to go?"

"Yes, but I need to do something before we go" Jake nodded and pulled away to let her down, but she wrapped her legs around him and pulled him back in. She brought her lips to his and kissed him. At first, she felt him stiffen up from her boldness, but then he wrapped his arms around her and brought her in closer.

Her entire body lit on fire and she felt her toes start to tingle. She slightly opened her mouth, granting him more access into her mouth and he took advantage of it. He worked her lips until she didn't think she could take it anymore without bursting with joy. He didn't let up though, he kept diving in for more. Her hands found his chest while one of his hands was on the back of her neck and the other one was working dangerously up her leg. At that moment, she decided to pull away.

They both were breathing heavily and, when she finally opened her eyes to look at him, his eye lids were heavy and he looked almost dazed. Lexi took her hand and brushed her thumb against his cheek. "Congratulations on your win, big guy." She hopped down from the half-wall and started walking toward his Jeep.

He finally caught up to her, twisted her around and caught her in his arms. He lifted her head up and kissed her again. This time, he was more frantic, as if he couldn't get enough of her. She matched his desperate need to be closer and wrapped her arms around him. She opened her lips allowing him to slip his tongue in to meet hers and explore every surface of her mouth. A dull thud started to pound in her body and she could feel the excitement taking place all the way down to her toes. This was getting out of hand. If she didn't stop him now, she could foresee herself having an orgasm in the middle of the parking lot.

She pulled away and swatted him on the arm. He rubbed the attacked spot and said, "What was that for?"

She pointed at him and said, "Don't get fresh." Then she chased her sentence with a smile over her shoulder and waited for him to unlock the door to his Jeep.

He gently pushed her up against the Jeep and said, "You are slowly going to be the death of me, babe." He gave her a quick peck and opened the door for her. She was smiling and more pleased with herself than she should be.

Jake

Jake was still reeling from Lexi's surprise attack on his lips when they arrived at the football house. The last thing he wanted to do after Lexi kissed him was go to a football party. Instead, he wanted to take her back to his place and practice their make-out skills some more. The moment her lips hit his, he knew he wasn't going to ever let Lexi go. She was it for him. It was like their kiss sealed the deal for his future. He couldn't say that to her, though, because she still was very skittish around him, but what he did notice was that she had started to give in and warm up toward him. The way she touched him, looked at him, and of course kissed him, he knew she had feelings for him.

"Are you just going to stare out the windshield, or are we actually going to go in?"

Jake chuckled. "Sorry, I was just thinking about earlier. You know, we don't have to go the party."

Lexi gave him a skeptical look. "Nice try, big shot, you just want to go back to your place and make out."

"You read my mind."

Lexi rolled her eyes and got out of his Jeep. Well, a guy could try, he thought. He met her at the front of his Jeep and looked down at her beautiful blue eyes.

"You ready for this, babe?"

"More ready than I ever will be."

He took her hand in his and led her into the house. Almost everyone was already drunk and having a good time. Jake was confused about how all the guys got to the party before him, but then again, he was kissing Lexi out in the parking lot for a little bit.

He went to the back of the house, out to the patio where he knew he could find Mason and Brooke. On their way back in, he made sure to grab two beers from the fridge.

A drunk freshman stopped them and said, "Jake, you were the fucking man tonight."

"Thanks," Jake said, as a whiff of the freshman's intoxicated breath smacked Jake right in the face. "Maybe you should lay off the beers for a little bit."

The freshman didn't acknowledge Jake. Instead, he was eyeing Lexi, which was starting to make Jake's blood boil.

"What do we have here?" The freshman started toward Lexi and Jake couldn't take it any longer; the guy needed to be taught to look a girl in the eyes, not her breasts. Jake pinned the freshman up against the wall with his forearm resting against his neck.

Lexi screeched and put her hands over her mouth. "Don't you dare look at her like that. You hear me?" Jake tightened his grip and the freshman nodded his head. Jake let him go and said, "Call a taxi and get back to the dorm before I let Coach know you're a drunken idiot; he'll have you running fifties until your legs fall off." The freshman nodded and scurried away like a dog with his tail between his legs.

He turned to see if Lexi was alright. "You okay, baby?"

She had her fists on her waist. "Was that necessary?"

"Yeah, he was eyeing you like you were a piece of meat he was about to bite into."

"I can handle myself, Jake. I don't need you slamming poor freshmen against the wall for me."

Jake could tell she was mad at him, but he didn't care, he would do it again. That was what he was there for, to protect her. He wasn't going to let some drunken idiot go up to her and stare at her like she was his personal prize to look at.

Jake grabbed Lexi's hands. "I'm sorry that I stepped in; I know you can handle yourself, but I want to take care of you."

Jake saw understanding in Lexi's eyes, but she still tried to sound tough. "Fine, but for God's sake, don't take it out on the freshmen. You practically made the poor guy pee his pants."

Jake chuckled and brought Lexi into his embrace. "Well, that taught him not to stare at my woman."

"We're back at that? Your woman?"

Jake kissed the top of her head. "Like it or not, babe, you're mine now. Once you kissed me, you signed up to be stuck with me."

"That was a pity kiss," she said, while playing with his shirt collar.

"Didn't feel like pity."

"What little you know. Wait until you see the real thing," she said with a wink and then dragged him out to the patio.

Jake thought if her kisses in the parking lot were pity, the real thing would send him to an early grave. He walked behind Lexi, holding her hand and admiring her short skirt. He was acting just like the freshman ogling her, but this was different, he had permission.

They got out to the patio that was lit with string lights and, thankfully, was not as crowded as the inside of the house. The rule of the football house was the patio was for the more laid back crowd. If you wanted to be rowdy, then you could go in the house; the outside was to chill. That's why Mason and Jake always found themselves out on the patio lately.

Mason and Brooke were sitting at a teak table that was surrounded by tiki torches, another reason why the rowdy crowd had to stay inside. They didn't want drunk morons setting the house on fire by knocking into one of the tiki torches.

Brooke looked as amazing as usual. Mason sure was one lucky son of a bitch, but then again, Jake was even luckier since he had Lexi at his side. Mason tipped his beer at them and waved them over.

"Hey, there's my boy. Where have you been?" Mason asked.

"Oh, just settling some stuff before we came over." He gave Lexi a wink which caused her cute little button face to blush. Jake thought how endearing it was. "Lex, this is Brooke, Brooke this is Lexi."

"Hey Lexi, Mason has told me all about Jake's failed attempts to win you over." Lexi laughed and Jake glared at Mason.

Mason held his hands up in defense. "Sorry man, there are no secrets between us. Although, since there are no secrets, one of us could at least keep our big mouths shut." He looked at Brooke who just laughed.

"They act so tough, don't they? Really they're a bunch of babies."

Jake sat down in one of the wooden chairs next to Mason and Brooke and when Lexi went to go grab a chair, Jake said, "Where do you think you're going?"

"To get a chair, you don't expect me to stand do you?"

"Ooo, she has sass, I like her," Brooke commented.

"Your seat is right here." Jake patted his lap. Lexi looked at him skeptically.

"Seriously, you want me to be like every other bimbo who has sat on your lap?"

"That's my girl." Brooke tipped her beer at Lexi and took a swig. Mason grabbed the beer from her and gave Brooke a kiss on the lips.

"I think that's enough beer for now, sweetheart. Or else we might have to stick you with the rowdy crowd."

Brooke grabbed her beer from Mason and slammed the rest of it. She got up from the table and grabbed her purse and Lexi's arm. "Come on Lexi, we're going to the bathroom for some girl time."

Before Jake could even protest, Brooke had swept her away without even a chance of stopping her. Jake looked over at Mason. "That can't be good for me."

Mason chuckled, "It can't be good for either of us. Whenever women get together, it's always a bad thing." He took another swig of his beer. "So seriously, where have you been?"

Jake couldn't help but smirk. "Oh, you know, just making out in the parking lot."

Mason punched Jake in the shoulder. "Man, I didn't even think you were actually going to get her to come tonight, but you also snaked a kiss? I guess you haven't lost your touch after all. How was it?"

"What are we, women now, sharing our feelings?"

"Fuck off dude, just tell me how it was."

Jake's mind went back to the moment when his lips met Lexi's, when he knew it was the beginning of the end for him, the end of his search. He didn't even realize he was searching, until he saw her.

"Fucking amazing."

Mason laughed. "That good, huh?"

Jake nodded. "I think that's it for me man, I think she is it."

Mason sat up straighter and set his beer down on the table. "Are you serious? It's only been a couple of weeks since the first time you saw her. Don't you think you're moving a little fast?"

"I don't think so, but she would tell you that I'm moving too fast. That is why you have to swear you won't say anything to Brooke. I don't need her telling Lexi and then scaring Lexi away. I'm having a hard enough time trying to get her to go out with me."

"So, she's giving you a run for your money?"

Jake guffawed. "You could say that."

Lexi

Brooke whisked Lexi away before she could protest. She had never even met Brooke before tonight and she was acting like they were best friends, which Lexi didn't mind, she just found it odd. Brooke was actually really sweet, even though she was halfway in the bag.

Inside the house was tight, but Brooke took charge. She pushed past a couple of gossiping girls that were standing right outside the bathroom and locked them both in the room. Lexi looked around and realized she was in the most disgusting bathroom she had ever seen in her life. Clearly, a bunch of boys lived in the house because she didn't think the bathroom had seen an ounce of cleaning spray…ever. Since Lexi didn't have to go to the bathroom, she leaned against the door, which seemed like the only safe place to stand.

Even though Brooke was drunk, she was smart enough to hover over the toilet while she peed instead of sitting directly on the seat. Lexi silently gave her props for being able to hold herself so steady over the toilet and not make contact with the contaminated porcelain bowl.

"So, you really like Jake?" Brooke was smiling up at Lexi from the toilet and Lexi, to be kind, averted her eyes.

"Yeah, I was nervous at first, given his reputation, but he has changed."

"You can say that again." Brooke was wiping now, another thing Lexi averted her eyes from. "I have never seen him act like this before. It's as if you gave him a tranquilizer."

Not knowing what to say to that, Lexi stayed quiet. She did wonder why Jake calmed down his bad boy attitude for her. It was something that had bothered her because men never changed that fast and they never really changed for a woman. Her dad was proof of that statement. She'd spent hours on the phone with him, begging and pleading for him to stop drinking, but her cries and her mom's cries weren't good enough. He wasn't going to do what they asked of him, he was only going to do what he wanted to do and that meant drinking and beating the crap out of her mom.

Brooke washed her hands and patted them dry on her jeans, thanks to no towels in the bathroom. "These boys are pigs. I'm so glad Mason doesn't live here anymore. The first couple of years we were dating were terrible when I would visit him here. Let's just say, we spent more time at my place."

"Where does he live now?"

"Oh we have a place together in the villas, same building as Jake. I heard you live there too. We should go tanning together."

What an odd thing to do together, Lexi thought. How would that be an activity they could do together? Unless they shared a tanning bed, which was not going to happen, not that Lexi actually went tanning in the first place.

"Or we can get coffee," Lexi suggested with a smile.

"Or that."

They walked out of the bathroom and ran into a bunch of girls. "Are you the girl with Jake?" A scary-looking brunette asked.

Lexi looked at Brooke and tentatively said, "Yes, why?"

"Well I would get back to your man if I were you, you can't leave fresh meat like that unattended when there are a bunch of prowling lionesses waiting to get a bite in." The girls giggled and walked away.

"What was that about?" Lexi asked.

Brooke looked concerned. "Those were a bunch of Alpha Sigma bitches. Basically, in order to be in that sorority, you have to be a whore. Let's get back to our men."

Brooke led the way, almost being slammed into a wall by a drunken guy, then they finally made their way out to the patio where Lexi stopped in her tracks. Sitting in a wooden chair was Jake and, on his lap, was some blonde with tattoos. Jake instantly stood up and then locked eyes with Lexi. She didn't stay to see what happened next. Instead, she walked past everyone in the house and stormed out to the road, where she started walking at a quick pace and ducked out of sight so Jake couldn't see her. She dialed a cab's number and told him to meet her at the curb.

She was breathing heavily and knew this whole thing with Jake was a mistake. She couldn't handle all the girls throwing themselves at him. What was wrong with women anyway? She would never do that to a guy, just walk up and sit on his lap. She was glad she never received that gene because those girls were labeled as extremely desperate and she never wanted to be labeled like that.

Her phone started ringing, she looked down and saw it was Jake. Yeah, she wouldn't be answering that.

Her cab pulled up to the curb; she got in and told the driver her address. Eight calls and twenty bucks later, she was back at her place with the door locked and putting on her pajamas. Her phone chimed with a text message.

Lexi grabbed her phone and thought, "This will be interesting." Of course it was from Jake.

Jake: Lexi, where are you? I can't find you. We need to talk about this.

Lexi laughed, talk about this, yeah right. She brushed her teeth and made sure to floss with extra detail. Her phone chimed again.

Jake: Babe, I'm scared. Where are you? Please answer me.

Babe? Was he kidding? She was not his babe, although earlier she thought the way the term of endearment rolled off his tongue was like music to her ears. Now, it made her want to gag the guy uttering the words. She was so mad at him. What possessed him to let another woman sit on his lap? Just like she thought in the semen-infested bathroom at the football house, men didn't change. Another chime.

Jake: Lexi, baby please. Answer your phone. I need to know you're okay.

Lexi turned her phone off. She didn't want to hear any more from Jake. She washed her face and made sure all her make-up was off before she lotioned up and turned out her bathroom light. Lexi plugged her phone into its charger, got into bed and turned off the light. She was done for the night.

She laid in the dark of her room as she fought back the tears that were starting to prickle her eyes. Why was she going to cry? It's not like she and Jake were anything serious, right? It's not like they actually made a commitment to each other. So, why did it matter to her? In the back of her mind, she knew why. Jake was the one guy that had stolen her heart and too quickly. So quickly that Lexi didn't even know it was happening until she kissed him in the parking lot.

They had the same goals and aspirations for their sports. He gave her something to look forward to, especially since the life she knew was coming to an end in a couple of months. Jake was something to look forward to and kept her moving forward. He made her want to work harder, even when he was incredibly annoying.

Her bedroom door busted open and Lexi nearly flew out of her bed at the shock.

"Jesus, there you are! Thank God." Jake was standing in her doorway running his hand through his hair. Mason and Brooke followed right behind him.

"How the hell did you get in here?"

Margo peeked her head around the corner, of course Margo would let him in. "Hey, don't be mad at me, you're the one who turned off your phone."

"Well, I'm fine, so you all can take your little party somewhere else."

Mason stepped forward. "Lexi, Jake didn't do anything." Lexi threw her hand up to silence him.

"Mason, I appreciate you coming here to check on me, but frankly, I don't want to hear your story. Please leave."

Mason nodded and grabbed Brooke's hand who gave Lexi a sympathetic look and waved goodbye. Margo slipped out of the room as well, leaving her with Jake, who looked like he had seen a ghost.

"That includes you too."

He closed her door and came to her bed. "I'm not going anywhere."

"Jake, I don't know what you're trying to prove here with trying to go out with me, but it's not going to work. Tonight at the football game, those girls talking, I let that go because it was all talk, but when girls take it to the next level and throw themselves at you. I can't take that. I'm not strong enough and, frankly, I just don't want to deal with it."

Jake shook his head as he looked at his hands. "Lexi, you have to believe me that I didn't do anything."

"Even if you did Jake, it's not like it matters, we aren't exclusive or anything. We only went out once. That doesn't mean anything."

"That's where you're wrong, it means everything to me. I

haven't thought about another girl since I laid eyes on you. Lex, you're all I want." He took her hand, but she pulled it away.

"I believe you that you didn't do anything, but that's beside the point. What I'm talking about is girls throwing themselves at you."

"I can't do anything about that, except to fight them off. I don't know what you want me to do."

"Exactly, there is nothing you can do."

"So what are you saying?"

Lexi let out a breath. "I'm saying this isn't going to work. You're a great guy and all, but I don't know if you're worth the heartache."

Jake looked shocked and hurt at her words. Damn, her words came out harsher than she wanted them to, but she had to get her feelings off her chest. There was no way in hell she would be able to deal with all the Jake-fantasizing whores; she wasn't strong enough.

He got up and started walking toward her door. He turned around before he opened it and looked at her like she just ran over his puppy. She had never seen him look so dejected and it was killing her inside. She wanted to run up to him and pull him into her arms, but she wasn't going to do that.

"You know Lexi, if it was the other way around. You can bet your ass, you would be worth the heartache to me."

With that, he left, leaving Lexi feeling like a leftover pile of crap on the football house's floor. She spent the night crying herself to sleep and wondering what possessed her to say such awful things to the guy who had stolen her heart.

CHAPTER NINE

Lexi

It had been a week, a week since she last saw Jake. She didn't know why she was counting, since she was the one who had ended whatever they had, which was not much. Still, she felt herself lazing about her apartment when she wasn't at practice or in class. She'd skipped out on her morning workouts in the weight room, due to fear of running into Jake and, instead, she did her own workouts in her apartment, which was proving not to cut it. Lifting cans of beans and doing stairs on two steps was not a sufficient way of keeping her up to her own workout standards.

At least she had an exercise ball in her apartment, which made her workouts a little bit better, that was until Margo walked in and said it looked like Lexi swallowed her gum and farted out a huge bubble. Ever since then, Lexi couldn't look at an exercise ball the same way.

She was just putting away her cans of beans when there was a knock at the door. Lexi fixed her messy bun and answered it. Mason was standing in her doorway holding two smoothie cups from Jamba Juice. He gave her a tentative smile and handed her a smoothie.

"Can I come in for a second?" Lexi couldn't turn him down since he brought her a smoothie, so she let him in.

Mason looked around at Lexi's sad attempt at a gym and asked, "Is this where you've been working out in the morning?"

Lexi felt embarrassed because it was obvious that she was avoiding the weight room in fear of seeing Jake. She lied, "Uh, yeah, you know…just needed a change of scenery."

Mason didn't buy it. "Uh, huh." He sat down on her couch and pushed aside a workout band. "What are you doing, Lexi?"

She sat down in a chair across from him and took a sip of her smoothie. It was strawberry banana, her favorite. "What do you mean?"

"Why are you torturing you and Jake?"

"I would not say I'm torturing myself; I'm fine thank you," Lexi said with an indignant tone.

Mason looked around her apartment and gave her a "yeah right" look. "Lexi, he misses you. He has been moping around, not working out like he had been. He's been terrible at practice and is not even close to prepared for the game tomorrow."

"How does that have to do with me?"

Mason blew out air and ran his hand over his face. "God, you really are stubborn." His voice turned sterner. "Look, Jake is trying hard to change. I know he has a fucked-up past that might cause issues for whoever he dates, but he's trying, he likes you, he wants you. Why can't you give the guy a chance? He is throwing himself out there and you are too stubborn to realize it. He is making a change, a change to be with you, why can't you sacrifice a little and try to be with him as well? You guys are meant for each other. You need to get that through your thick skull."

Lexi couldn't even believe the things Mason had said. She was speechless. She didn't even know where to start. She was just about to blow up at him when Mason interrupted her.

"Do you know what he said to me while you and Brooke were in the bathroom?" Mason didn't give her a chance to answer. "He told me you were the most beautiful girl he had ever laid eyes on and, not only were you beautiful, but you made him feel whole again, since his parents died. He said you made him feel alive again.

Don't tell me you're just going to walk away from him because you're not strong enough to stand up to a couple of bitches. I've seen what you can lift in the weight room. You can take out any of those noodle-armed whores. You're just too chicken to face the fact that you actually like Jake and he might be the one for you."

Mason got up and walked toward her door. "Call him, Lexi. He really needs to hear your voice, especially if we want to win tomorrow." Mason slammed the door shut before she could even say anything. She buried her head in a couch pillow and screamed.

Mason was right; she was being a chicken. She was too much of a coward to throw her heart in the wrestling ring of love in fear of her heart being wrung out to dry. But which was worse, not giving in and keeping herself semi-safe from any kind of heart break or throwing everything she had into a relationship with Jake? Well, right now she felt like crap and, when she was with Jake, yeah it was stressful, but it was also amazing. She missed the way she felt in his arms, the way he smiled at her, and the way he would lean against a wall and wait for her like he had nowhere better to be.

She was an idiot and it took Mason to help her figure it out. Lexi looked at her watch, tore her clothes off and headed to her bathroom for a quick shower. Thirty minutes later, she was in her car headed down to the events center parking lot. She had thrown on a pair of jean shorts, a white T-shirt and her brown flip flops. Her hair was in a messy bun on top of her head and she was able to throw on a little bit of make-up before she headed out. She pulled up next to Jake's Jeep and looked at the clock. He would be done with his morning workout and out to his Jeep in a couple of minutes. She got out of her car and decided to sit on the hood of his Jeep.

Just like clockwork, Jake exited out of the side door of the events center and walked toward the parking lot. He was looking at his phone, so he didn't see her until he was a couple of feet away. When he looked up, he stopped in his tracks.

Jake

Jake felt like crap, he had felt like crap for a week and there was one word for it; Lexi. He promised himself he wouldn't call her or bother her. He wanted to give her space and time to think about what they had, what they briefly shared together. Yes, she was right, they only went out one time, but there was much more to them than just the one date. They had a connection he had never experienced with anyone else before and, once he lost that connection, he found it quite hard to function.

He was finally able to drag his carcass out of bed for a morning workout, since he had missed the rest of his workouts all week. Mason didn't even show up this morning, probably because Jake had stood him up every other day of the week. Jake didn't mind working out on his own though; he was able to abuse his body without Mason telling him to take it easy.

Practices had been awful. He had been playing like hell all week, so he decided to punish himself, even though he had a game the next day. He needed to get his head back in the game, but it was hard since his head was somewhere else. He had a meeting with his coach yesterday about his piss poor behavior and Jake had to lie, saying he thought he was coming down with something. He didn't think his coach bought it, but he let Jake go, slightly unscathed. Jake left the meeting with his coach telling him to pull his shit together because Saturday night was a big game.

Jake exhaled and headed towards his Jeep; he'd been checking the football rankings on his phone when he looked up and saw the most beautiful sight in the world. He stopped a couple of feet away, not believing what he was seeing. He blinked a couple of times to make sure he wasn't making things up in his mind.

"Hey, big guy."

Her voice confirmed that she was, in fact, sitting on his Jeep. He adjusted the strap of his messenger bag that was hugging his chest and walked closer to her so she was only a couple of feet away.

"What are you doing here?" he asked, still shocked that she

was near him.

She turned so she was facing him and put out her hand for him to take. He reached out and she clasped her hand around his, pulling him into her. She wrapped her legs around his waist and kept him close, while she stroked his hair with the hand that was not holding his.

"I'm sorry," she said. "I'm sorry I scared you the night of the party, I'm sorry for the things I said that I didn't mean, and I'm sorry for letting you walk out the door when I should have gone after you."

Jake couldn't believe what he was hearing. Was this the stubborn Sexy Lexi he was talking to? She bent her head down and kissed him on the forehead. It was such a tender gesture that melted his heart.

"Do you forgive me?"

Jake looked into her pleading eyes, her crystal blue eyes. How could he not forgive her? She was all he ever wanted. "Of course. I'm sorry I put you in that position at the party." He kissed the palm of her hand that was caressing his cheek. "I don't want to upset you and I promise, I will do whatever it takes to show you how much I truly care for you and want to be with you."

She shook her head. "You don't have to prove anything to me Jake, I believe you. But there have to be some ground rules if we're going to make this happen."

He kissed her hand again. "Lay it on me babe, I'm all ears."

She smiled. "Well, first off, keep calling me babe, I love it."

"Easy enough."

"Secondly, if I'm going to be with you, I'm only going to be with you. It has to be exclusive."

"Done." His quick response brought out her gorgeous smile.

"Thirdly, I want to hear of every girl who throws herself at you because I'm going to have to personally kick their asses and let them know that you belong to me now. Maybe then girls will start getting the hint?"

He laughed out loud. "I can do that. I promise if a girl does try to get my attention, I will make it quite clear that I'm off the market and they can take it up with my bad-ass girlfriend.

She brought him in closer, her lips were mere inches from his. "That's what I like to hear." Then she pulled him in the last couple of inches and kissed him while she sat on the hood of his Jeep as he rested between her legs, leaning in, trying to get as much Lexi as he could.

Her lips were so soft and molded precisely into his, as if they were meant to be together. She wrapped her hands around his neck and rubbed his cheek as they kissed. Her small touches sent him off to the moon with no return in sight. She made a little moaning sound, which caused him to bury himself deeper into her little body.

She pulled away and rested her forehead on his. They both stared each other in the eyes.

"God, I missed you," Jake finally said. "I could barely function. I didn't work out in the mornings until today."

She laughed. "I made a really pathetic gym in my apartment to avoid you in the mornings; if I knew you were going to be a lazy-ass, I could have spared myself and gone to the weight room."

Jake squeezed the ticklish spot right above her knee, causing her to jerk and slide off the Jeep right into his arms.

"Do you have dinner plans?" she asked, while studying his face.

"No, I would love to have dinner with you."

"You're buying," she said with a devilish grin.

"Oh, is that how it's going to be?"

"That's what you get for making me work out with cans of beans."

Jake threw his head back and laughed. "You don't even have your own weight set?"

She scrunched her nose. "Beans worked out just fine."

He chuckled and opened the Jeep door for her. "You're cute, babe." He kissed her on the nose and practically skipped to the driver's side. When he got in, he noticed she had thrown on his aviators.

She shrugged. "It's sunny out."

"You look fucking hot."

That brought out another smile of hers. "Alright, big guy. Let's get a move on. I have some things to get done today. Pick me up after practice?"

"You got it, hot stuff."

Lexi

Lexi sat on a bench outside the lecture hall, studying before her next class. She was having a difficult time focusing because images of Jake kept popping into her head. She knew it was going to be a difficult road, but she was ready to face it head-on with him. She hadn't felt this good in a while. She actually felt like a weight had been lifted off her shoulders, especially with everything that had been going on with her parents lately. It was nice to have something else to keep her thoughts busy.

Images of Jake kept running through her head, preventing her from internalizing any studying materials, so when Lexi spotted Parker walking toward her, she was grateful for the break from her books. She shut her books and tucked them away in her bag. She stood up and greeted her friend she hadn't seen in a while with a big hug.

"Hey stranger," she said.

"Hey Lex, how's it going?"

Lexi couldn't help but smile. "Great."

Parker sat down next to her and pointed at her face. "I know what that smile is. That's an I-have-a-hot-man-in-my-life smile." Lexi nodded her head, letting him know he was right. He clapped her on the back, almost sending her to the floor. "That's my girl. It's about time. He was moping around the men's locker room area all week. Just in time for game day tomorrow as well."

"Yeah, I needed a little help getting my head out of my ass, no thanks to you."

"Hey, I've been busy."

"How's Sierra?"

Parker stared out into the quad, like he was thinking about all the different experiences he had with Sierra. "She's amazing, what can I say? I can't get enough of her."

Lexi scrunched her nose. "Really?" Lexi didn't see what all the hype was about with Sierra. Yes, the girl was attractive, but she was also kind of an idiot. She said some of the dumbest shit Lexi had ever heard. She never thought Parker would go out with a dumb blonde.

"What's that look for?"

Lexi shrugged and tried to pass her look off as nothing, but he knew better; he just stared at her until she answered him. She let out a longwinded breath and said, "I don't know Parker, she doesn't really seem like she's your type. She's kind of…you know, ditzy."

Parker waved his hand at her, dismissing her comment. "That doesn't bother me, since she's hotter than hell in bed."

A swift intake of water got stuck in Lexi's throat, when Parker caught her off-guard with his comment. She started coughing frantically while Parker patted her on the back. She wiped her mouth and looked at him. He had the devil's smirk on his face.

"Jesus, Parker."

He laughed. "Don't be such a prude."

"Don't be such a pig." Lexi surveyed her friend who had been like a brother to her and realized that he had changed this year, and not in a good way. It was like he didn't care about the people around him and didn't treat women with respect. It nagged at her. This wasn't the Parker she knew. In the past, he would never go out with a girl if she wasn't able to hold some sort of intellectual conversation.

Instead of getting into a long drawn-out and uncomfortable conversation, she changed the subject. "Have you talked to Margo lately?"

"Nah, she's been weird lately and she's always at the lacrosse house."

"That's not true. She's been home a lot lately."

Jake shrugged and took a sip of his drink. "Not what I heard, apparently she's been making her rounds again."

Lexi got defensive. "No, she's been home."

"Whatever, not my problem."

"Parker, what is wrong with you? Margo is our friend; if people are spreading rumors about her, you should set them straight."

"How am I supposed to know they're rumors; the girl gets around."

Lexi didn't care for Parker right now and, before they got in a huge fight, she decided to leave the situation before it blew up. She stood up and gathered her items.

"Hey, where are you going?" he asked.

"I should get to class." He stood up with her and grabbed her arm before she could walk away. He pulled her in close and wrapped his arms around her, planting a kiss on her head, like always.

"Listen, I'm sorry. I didn't mean to upset you and I'm sorry I haven't been there for you lately."

Lexi could feel herself start to crumble, she hated when Parker got all emotional on her. "It's fine."

"No, it's not. I haven't even asked you how your parents are. I know this is always a bad time for your dad."

Damn him for bringing up her family. Parker and Margo were the only ones who knew about her shitty family situation and she planned on keeping it that way. She didn't want Jake knowing about her dad and his issues, Jake would only judge her. Lexi fought back the tears that tickled her eyes.

"They're not good. My dad had another episode yesterday. Luckily my mom was out with my aunt, so she didn't get caught up in his destructive tornado. When she got home, she found my dad passed out drunk on the floor, surrounded by a broken coffee table." Lexi shook her head in disgust. "I don't know why she just doesn't leave him. It would be easier on me if they just got a divorce, rather than hearing the horrid stories about how much of an ass my dad is."

Parker squeezed her tighter. "She is going to have to make that decision on her own, no matter how much you beg her. She is never going to leave until she is ready. You just need to keep being supportive and encouraging her. Maybe if you talk to her about your relationship with Jake and how happy you are, it will give her an idea of what a healthy relationship is like."

Parker was right; he had a valid point. Maybe if she did talk to her mom about Jake, it could open her mom's eyes to what an abusive drunk her father was. Lexi tried reporting her dad once, but when the cops came, her mother denied everything. Ever since then, Lexi never went home and only communicated with her mom over the phone, trying to convince her to move on with her life. With the way things were going, Lexi didn't ever think her mom was going to leave.

"I might just do that, thanks Parker."

"You're welcome. I'm sorry I dropped the ball on our friendship. I'll talk to Margo too. I was having such a nice time with her earlier. I don't know what happened."

Lexi knew what the problem was and it was blonde, leggy and ditzy. Margo would never confess to it, but Lexi knew her friend. She just felt bad for Margo and wished there was something she could do to help her. She didn't like it when Margo turned to sex with random men to cover up her feelings. She wished she would talk about them like a normal human being would.

"That might be a good idea. You guys were really hitting it off; I felt like the third wheel for a little bit there."

Parker laughed. "Hey since I'm being such a good guy right now, do you think Jake could score us some more field passes for next week's home game?"

Lexi shook her head at her friend's attempt to leverage her relationship with her guy for his own betterment. "You have no morals, do you?"

"Not if field passes are involved."

She laughed, "I'll see what I can do. Meanwhile, stay on your best behavior, mister."

He crossed his heart and gave her the scout's honor hand signal. "Promise."

They said their goodbyes and Lexi walked off to class, thinking about what she might wear on her date with Jake tonight.

Jake

Jake couldn't believe how fast the evening went by with Lexi. It felt like two minutes ago he was knocking on her door and waiting for her to answer. When she opened the door, he felt his stomach flutter at how good she looked. She wore extremely tight dark jeans, a green tank top and black heels. Her hair was down and wavy, just the way he liked it. She was perfect.

They had a great night at a local restaurant he loved going to because they didn't treat him like the top dog at school. They treated him like any other normal patron and he appreciated it. Plus, the restaurant was very private, which was good because he wanted some serious alone time with Lexi.

After their romantic and quiet date, Jake walked Lexi back to her apartment. He didn't want to say goodnight to her so soon, but he had an early morning the next day because they were traveling and she had an early practice. If only they didn't have their sports for a week or so, just so he could spend every waking hour with Lexi to get to know her more.

They stopped in front of her door and turned toward each other. God, she was beautiful. He would never get tired of looking her in the eyes, her expressive, gorgeous eyes. She wrapped her hands in his and pulled him in closer.

"Thank you for dinner." She looked up at him with a smile.

He felt himself sigh. "You're welcome, babe."

Her nose slightly crinkled. "How come you guys didn't drive out tonight? We always go the night before a game to get settled."

Jake shrugged. "Coach didn't think it would be a big deal this go-around and he was trying to save money. It's only a two hour trip, so no use wasting money."

"That's true and it's not like you guys play a three-game series like we do."

"Yeah, we could never do that."

Lexi twisted her foot while she stared at the ground. It looked like she wanted to say something, but was too shy. He encouraged her. "What is it, Lex?"

She stabbed him in the heart with her blue-eyed gaze once again. "I'm just going to say it. I'm not ready to have sex with you."

Jake felt like she'd pushed him back in the bushes without a warning. Where the hell did that come from? He felt like the wind was knocked out of him; he didn't even know what to say, but she searched him for some kind of comment, so he gathered his wits and answered her.

"Uh, where is this coming from?"

She didn't look at him when she answered. "I know how you are Jake, I'm just not ready."

Tension soared through his body at her judgmental sentence. He thought she understood him, but maybe he was wrong. He tried to stay calm, but he could hear the anger in his voice.

"And how am I Lexi?" he gritted through his teeth.

Her eyes shot up to him, realizing she'd made him angry. She put her hand over her mouth and shook her head. "I'm so sorry, that came out wrong." She started to try to dig herself out of the hole she put herself in and it was kind of charming to watch, even though he was still angry. "You know how guys are, they're all about sex and I just wanted to let you know I'm not ready."

They weren't holding each other now, instead it felt like they were a million miles away. He missed her warmth. He wished she'd never said anything about sleeping together. They were having such a good night.

"I'm sorry. I didn't realize I was putting out the vibe that I was pressuring you to sleep with me." He knew sarcasm wasn't the way to communicate, but he couldn't help himself. She'd made a snap judgment and it hurt him, especially after all the changes he had made in his life.

"You're not! Oh, this is coming out all wrong," Lexi said, while holding her head and shaking it.

"What are you trying to say?" he asked, as he folded his arms across his chest. She looked up at him and separated his arms, making him circle her waist. She put her arms around his neck and pulled him close, so they were mere inches from each other.

"Jake, I'm sorry. What I was trying to say was, I'm not ready to have sex, but I don't want to leave you just yet. I was going to ask you if you wanted to spend the night, but without the sex."

She made a cute wrinkle in her forehead and Jake kissed it away. "You want to spoon, is that what you're asking?"

She buried her head in his chest and nodded. "I should have just said that. Will you stay, even though I insulted you?"

"Of course, babe." She unlocked the door and brought him inside. "Just so you know. I'm never going to pressure you, okay? When you're ready, you're ready. You are worth the wait."

She smiled up at him and pulled him down for a kiss, just what he was looking for. She led him into her bedroom and he took instant comfort in her personal surroundings, as if he was meant to be in her room. She shut her door and dug around in her bag that was on the floor. She pulled out a brand new blue tooth brush and smiled.

"This is for you."

"You planned on whisking me away to your bed, didn't you?"

She smiled, "Let's not get carried away there, big guy. I just like to plan ahead."

He tipped the tooth brush at her. "Good planning."

"I'm going to get changed real fast and then you can brush your teeth."

Jake wanted to laugh at her because she was acting like this was some sleepover with her friend, not her boyfriend. Was he her boyfriend? They talked about being exclusive, but did that make her his girlfriend? If he had anything to say about it, she would be.

He scoped out her room while she was in her bathroom. She had a bunch of pictures of her team and friends. She was the prettiest in every picture. She had one of the best smiles he had ever seen. She was so full of energy, it was infectious. He noticed a couple of odd knick knacks placed on flat surfaces throughout her room. There was a little gerbil-looking thing that had heart boxers on, Jake wondered what the hell that was about. She had all the seasons of "Friends" stacked next to her little TV and DVD player. Jake thought about the size of his TV compared to hers, it was almost comical.

Drawings by children scattered the surfaces of her walls, thanking her for her help out on the softball field. She must have helped them out at a clinic, which was something the football team did as well. It was one of his favorite parts of the summer, helping the kids out with different skills related to football and teaching them how to stay active. She must enjoy it as well, he thought, since she kept the thank you notes from the kids she helped.

He was studying a picture that looked like it might be her parents when she stepped out of the bathroom. He turned around to head for the sink with his toothbrush when he stopped in his tracks. She was wearing just her boy-short underpants and a tight black tank top with no bra. He felt his mouth start to water. Was she trying to kill him?

"What the hell are you doing?" he asked. "Are you trying to be a cock tease?"

She looked down at herself. "What? This is what I wear to bed."

He swallowed hard. This was not going to be easy. He huffed past her and went into the bathroom, closing the door a little harder than he wanted to. He pulled out his tooth brush and brushed his teeth till his blood levels returned to normal.

Lexi

Giggling to herself inside, Lexi smiled at her sleepwear. The look on Jake's face was priceless. She wasn't going to have sex with him, but she thought might as well throw the guy a bone. That was why she chose her tightest tank top and cutest boy shorts that showed off a good portion of her ass. She knew she was being a tease, but she couldn't help herself. The reaction her outfit warranted was perfect.

She knew she was bold stating she didn't want to have sex with Jake and saying she wanted to cuddle instead, but she wasn't ready to say good night to him and she definitely wasn't ready to give herself over to him either.

Climbing into bed, she made sure only her bedside lamp was on. She heard the toilet flush and the water turn on, indicating that he was almost done in the bathroom. She gave him points for washing his hands, not many men thought it was necessary to wash their hands after using the bathroom, which disgusted her. She was happy she didn't have to teach Jake good personal hygiene.

He popped out of the bathroom and smiled at her. "Thanks for the toothbrush, babe."

"Of course." He stopped right before the foot of her bed and took his shirt off, revealing the most impressive muscular chest she had ever seen. Her mouth went dry and she felt heat spread throughout her body. He was beyond ripped from his chest down to his abs, to the little "v" in his sides that pointed to his unmentionable. The contours of his muscles were so defined, she couldn't help but stare. Finally tearing her gaze away from the Adonis in front of her, she looked him in the eyes where she noticed he was smirking like a fool.

Then he started taking off his pants and she snapped out of the muscle-induced daydream she was in. She held out her hand to stop him. "What do you think you're doing?"

"You're not the only person who sleeps in their under-roos," he said with a grin.

She laughed. "Touché."

He shed his socks too and climbed into bed with her.

Thankfully, she had a full-sized bed, so there was enough room for the both of them. Although, she did notice how much smaller her bed was with Jake in it. He let himself under the covers and grabbed the ticklish spot above her knee.

She shrieked, "Jake!"

He laughed. "That's for being a cock tease. I brushed my teeth extra-long to calm myself down."

They turned toward each other and she stroked his cheek. "Oh, poor baby."

He grabbed her at the waist and pulled her in closer. Her heart felt like it was beating out of her chest from the close proximity of their bodies and the heat that was pouring off of him. She felt so safe. She never wanted to leave this moment as their legs tangled together and their foreheads pressed against each other.

"I don't think we hammered out one detail this morning," he said, while making tiny circles on her hip with his fingers, causing heat to flee to places she hadn't felt in a while, or maybe ever.

"What's that?"

"We didn't establish titles. Am I allowed to call you my girlfriend?"

Lexi's heart melted, he looked like a little boy in grade school, trying to ask out his first girl. It was so charming.

"Do you want to call me that?" He gave her a quick kiss on the lips and nodded. "Well then, I guess it's settled."

"Perfect, now tell me about your family." He nodded toward the picture of her and her parents at her graduation. "Are they your parents?"

Lexi tensed up immediately. She didn't want to ruin this moment with talking about her crappy family life. Jake didn't need to know her personal problems and Lexi wasn't ready for him to know. So she tried to be as evasive as possible

"Yup, those are my parents, they're back home. I don't have any brothers or sisters. What about you?"

"You know my parents passed when I was a freshman and I don't have any brothers or sisters either."

"Do you miss them?" She stroked his face to help encourage him to talk. She could tell the subject was difficult for him to talk about. She wished she could be as strong as Jake. Instead, she hid all her problems and tried not to bring them up.

"Every day. They were the couple that would have made it to fifty years plus together. I only hope I'm able to have a marriage someday like theirs." He shook his head and she placed a kiss on his cheek. "I wish they could see me where I am today. They always believed I would be playing in the NFL; I just wish I could share that with them."

Lexi stroked his cheeks with her thumbs and kissed him on the lips. She didn't know what to say, so she kissed him with all the love she had in her body. He pulled her even closer so their bare stomachs touched, he pushed her shirt up even more than it was and he rested his hand on her ribcage and stoked right under her breast. She felt herself go weak. If she was standing, she wouldn't be able to hold herself up.

She opened her mouth and he kissed her even deeper. She felt his erection against her body and was turned on even more from the thought that she could turn on a guy as hot as Jake. She shifted her body to get closer and, when she did, his hand slid up her body, slightly making contact with her breast. She moaned into his mouth and wrapped her leg around his waist so their groins matched up together. His hand slid up a little bit higher so now his thumb was stroking the underside of her bare breast, causing her to lose control.

Not being able to hold back, she drove her tongue into Jake's mouth and he met every stroke with hers. Her body tingled from his touch and burned where his thumb stroked her. She moved her body lower so he was almost caressing her nipple. She moaned again which gave Jake the go ahead to fully cup her breast. She threw her head back in pure enjoyment at the way his strong hand gripped one of her most tender spots. The moans and cries coming from her mouth sent Jake into a mad frenzy to find her mouth again, while he squeezed her breast.

"Jesus," he breathed out heavily. "You're so damn hot."

She couldn't even respond, since he was kissing every single sensitive spot on her throat. Things were getting out of control and she needed to stop him before they hit the point of no return, which was coming at an alarming rate. She felt heat starting to pool between her legs, thanks to his touches and the prodding of his stiff cock against her groin. She felt here entire body go numb with pleasure as he ground his hips into her and continued to squeeze her breast. She realized that she was seconds away from a powerful orgasm.

She moved her hips so they were rubbing against his stiff rod and gave him better access to her breasts and neck. He pushed up her shirt so that there was nothing between her breast and his mouth. She guided his head down and watched as he sucked gently on her nipple and thrust his groin into her once again, which sent her over the edge. She threw her head back and ground her hips onto Jake while tremors of ecstasy took over her body. She rode the pleasure he gave her until there was nothing left in her body.

She looked up at Jake and instant mortification took over her body. She covered her face with her hands, trying to avoid eye contact with the man she had so furiously dry-humped.

"Oh my God, I can't believe that just happened."

He removed her hands and kissed her lips. "That was fucking hot, babe."

She looked at him as if he was crazy. "I just got off from dry humping."

He laughed, "There was nothing dry about that."

She swatted his arm. "Don't be disgusting. I clearly have no self-control. The minute I get you in bed, I attack you" She looked down at his lap and saw how excited he was "I'm sorry." She reached down to stroke him, so they would be even on the pleasure score, but he stopped her.

"Don't even think about it," he said.

"Why not?"

"Because, I didn't do that to you so I could get pleasure

too. Just because you got off doesn't mean you have to return the favor." He turned her so her back was nestled into his chest. She still felt him poking her from behind, but that was natural after such an intense moment of passion.

"I just feel bad. What you must think of me right now." She shook her head in disgust.

"Don't," he said, while kissing her ear, sending chills up her leg. "I enjoyed myself just as much as you did. By the way, you have the most amazing tits I have ever felt in my life." She booty-blasted him, causing him to groan. "Watch it baby, it's a little sensitive down there."

She turned around so she could face him, quickly put her hand on his crotch and almost gasped from what she felt. He pulled her hand away quickly.

"Seriously, Lex, I don't need that. I just want you in my arms." He kissed her on the lips ever so gently, twisted her around and pulled her in close. He buried his head in her hair and sighed. "Now go to sleep."

"You're no fun," she joked. She scooted backward until she didn't think they could get any closer and relished how safe she felt in his arms. If she wasn't careful, she was going to wind up falling very hard and vary fast for Jake Taylor.

"Jake?"

"Hmm?" he said into her hair.

"I really like you."

He squeezed her tighter. "I really like you too. You're everything I never thought I wanted."

She laughed. "I guess that's a good thing."

"It's a really good thing. Now shush those luscious lips and close those beautiful eyes of yours."

She sighed and relaxed into his embrace. "Good night, Jake."

He kissed the back of her head. "Good night, baby."

Jake

Jake settled into his favorite bed on the bus that they took to away trips. The football team had their own private bus that had beds lining the sides and in the middle were tables with benches on either side so guys could do their work, or play cards. Jake always got the bed in the back where no one could disturb him. He usually watched game tapes or just slept while listening to music. After last night, he would be sleeping so he could dream about Lexi.

Last night was the best night's sleep he'd had in a while. It felt so natural to have Lexi in his arms, sleeping next to him. When she asked if he wanted to spend the night, he didn't think he could get any more excited until she walked out in what she claimed was her bedtime gear. If she wore that to bed every night, she was doing the male race an injustice by keeping to herself for so long. He loved lingerie and the way it looked on a woman, but all Lexi had to do was wear a tight shirt and boy shorts and she had him begging for more.

It took all of his will power last night to not let her return the favor of the pleasure they briefly shared. If it was anybody else, he would have gladly obliged, but he wanted to prove to Lexi that he wasn't the selfish asshole she'd heard about and seen the last three years. He wanted to give her pleasure and give her all the attention.

When they started kissing last night, never did he think they were going to end up where they did, but he was glad they did. When she moved her body down so his hand slid next to her breast, he picked up on the permission she gave him. When she groaned in his mouth and he fully grasped her amazing breast in his hand, he almost threw all his inhibitions to the wind and fully attacked her.

He was proud of himself for staying in the northern region of her body and what an amazing northern region it was. It was funny to Jake how damn sexy she was, even though she didn't really even play it up. Any other girl with her tight body and heavy chest would be showing off her goods every day, but not Lexi. She didn't have to.

Man, was he lucky. When he thought about his college career, he never thought it was going to end up like this in the end. He tried not to think about what was going to happen after they graduated, but he liked where his life was heading. He was hopefully going to be drafted, but what about Lexi? If he had anything to say about it, he was going to take her with him. He couldn't imagine being away from her. He hated that he had to go on a road trip right now and would be away from her for a night.

"Taylor!" his coach screamed. Jake grunted, got out of his bed, and headed for the front of the bus.

"Yeah, Coach?"

"Someone is here for you. Make it quick."

Jake instantly panicked. Occasionally, random fans of the female nature would come wish him good luck before a game. In the past, he'd gladly accepted the "luck" they'd dispensed to him, but now that he had a girlfriend, now that he had Lexi, he wanted nothing to do with the blood-sucking leeches.

"Uh, is it one of those girls again, Coach?"

"Yeah, she brought snacks for everyone though, so you need to at least say thank you," his coach said, while biting into a cookie. Jake rolled his eyes and got off the bus to thank the girl.

"Took you long enough, big guy."

Jake turned around and saw Lexi leaning against the bus with her arms crossed over her chest. She was wearing sweats, a softball shirt, and her hair was up. She was about to go to practice, but she still looked as good as last night.

He sauntered over to her and pulled her in for a hug. "What are you doing here?"

She gave him a kiss on the lips and wrapped her arms around his neck. "Just wanted to drop off some treats for my man and his men."

"That was sweet of you. Coach has already started in on them."

"Figures," she said, "He was more than willing to take them off my hands."

Jake chuckled. "That's Coach for you. He's got quite the appetite." Jake kissed Lexi again and this time, lingered on her lips. He didn't want to let her go. "Thank you for letting me stay last night. I had the best night's sleep ever."

She rubbed his face with her thumbs, something he had grown accustomed to…he found comfort in her touches. "So did I. We should do that more often."

"Agreed." He pushed Lexi up against the bus and kissed her, like it was the first time he ever kissed her. He couldn't get enough of this sweet and amazing woman. Her lips were so soft and so full, he felt like he was in heaven whenever their lips met.

"Get a room, Taylor," Mason said, as he walked by and shoved Jake with his bag, causing Jake to ram Lexi into the bus.

"Hey, watch it, dickhead."

Mason got on the bus and shouted over his shoulder. "They make rooms for a reason."

Jake shook his head. "He's just jealous his girlfriend doesn't come down here to say good bye."

Lexi pushed on his chest with her fingers and then she sighed. "Ugh, why do you have to be so damn good looking and fit?"

"Sorry about that, I'll start working on my beer gut when I get back."

"Alright, I'll work on my muffin top."

Jake laughed. "Please don't." He squeezed her waist. "You don't want to mess with perfection."

Lexi started making gagging noises and moved away from him. "Honestly Jake, could you be any cheesier?"

"What? I thought that was good."

"It was lame and, because of that, I'm leaving you to your cheesiness. I can't be late for practice."

He pulled her in close again and gave her a big hug. "I'm going to miss you, babe."

"I'm going to miss you too, big guy. Good luck, you're going to be amazing. I know it. Bring home a win and I might give you another reward."

Jake wagged his eyebrows at her. "Fans should pay homage to you for being the best motivator for me to win."

"I'm thinking about making a website so people can pay me to reward you."

"Wouldn't that be whoring yourself out?"

Lexi shrugged her shoulders. "Hey, support your Bears, is what I say."

Jake chuckled and kissed her on the lips. "I'll call you later."

"Sounds good." She winked at him. "Don't think of me too much," she said, as she walked away.

"Thanks for the treats, baby."

"Anytime," she said, while spinning around and then headed toward the locker rooms. Man he had it bad.

Jake got back on the bus and noticed there were only three cookies left. Apparently, the team heard there were treats on the bus and took advantage of the homemade confections. His coach stopped him before he could head to the back of the bus.

"Is that the centerfielder on the softball team?" Jake nodded cautiously, wondering where his coach was going with this. "She's good for you, Taylor. I'm glad to see someone has wrangled you in."

Jake was shocked at his coach's admission. First of all, his coach's mouth was usually dripping with saliva while he screamed his head off and secondly, he never talked about personal things, so hearing him say he thought a girl was good for Jake was like seeing a blizzard in Cuba.

"Uh, thanks Coach."

His coach pointed his finger at Jake and said sternly, "Don't screw it up, Taylor. She's a good girl and you're lucky as shit she's hanging around with the likes of you."

Jake got the point, but tried to lighten up the mood. "Jeeze, Coach, if I would have known some cookies could win you over, I would have brought you cookies my first day on the field."

"Get your ass seated Taylor before I sit your ass for you."

Jake saluted his coach and went to the back of the bus where

Mason was settling in his bed. He punched his friend in the arm. Mason rubbed his arm and said, "What was that for?"

"That was for shoving Lexi into the bus."

"Well, if you weren't mauling her, she wouldn't have been shoved into the bus."

"Don't get jealous, green is a fucked-up shade on you."

"Fuck off."

Jake smiled at their playful banter, something he would miss when they graduated. Jake got in his bunk, pulled out a picture that Lexi gave him and stuffed it in the ceiling above him so he could look at it. He put his ear phones in and played his music so he could drift off and think about how amazing his life had turned out to be.

CHAPTER TEN

Margo

The last thing Margo wanted to do right now was sit through a meeting with her coach, she would rather be lying in her bed with a pint of ice cream nursing her state of depression. What was Parker thinking, going out with Sierra? What happened to his statement of not wanting to start up a relationship his senior year? Margo was an attractive girl, why wasn't she good enough for Parker? Yeah, her hair was a chestnut brown to Sierra's blonde and Margo's eyes were green compared to Sierra's blues, but Margo thought she had more substance to her body then Sierra. Sierra was a bean pole and Margo had some Latina flavor in her. She got her Latin heritage and her dark green eyes from her dad, a lethal combination in Margo's book.

Didn't all guys like a little spice in their life? Margo sighed as she waited for her coach to return to her office. Her coach had every medal, honor and award hanging in her office, along with a retired jersey from when she played. She was a bitch, but she was a smart bitch. Most of the time, the team hated her, but she was good at what she did, leading them to many conference championship games which they finally won last year.

They had a lot of expectations to live up to this year. Margo felt the pressure, so she could only imagine how Lexi must feel, being the team captain. Speak of the devil, Margo thought, as Lexi came strolling into the office with a stupid grin on her face. She must have just seen Jake. Their whole relationship made Margo want to stab her eyes out with rusty cleats. They were sickening, but, unfortunately, sweet at the same time.

Lexi looked at Margo. "What are you doing here?"

Margo shrugged. "I don't know; Coach called me in."

"Me too." Lexi sat down and checked her phone. Clearly, she'd received a text message from Jake because she was smiling while she sent a text message back. Margo decided enough was enough.

"Interesting noises coming from your room last night."

Turning her phone over, Lexi sat up straight and stared at Margo with her mouth open. "Margo!"

"What? Just pointing out the obvious."

"Well, can you keep your observations to yourself? Good Lord, and it wasn't what you thought it was."

Margo snorted. "Okay, Lex."

"It wasn't, we didn't do anything…technically."

"Yeah, technically."

"Good morning, ladies." Their coach walked in and Margo turned to look at her friend who was bright red from the conversation they were just having. Margo could only imagine what was going through Lexi's mind right now. Their coach continued, "I'm just going to get right down to business." Her coach turned and looked Margo in the eyes. "What is this I hear about you spending every night in the lacrosse house, being passed around by every guy and getting yourself into trouble?"

Margo nearly fell out of her seat. "What?!"

"I got wind from one of the assistant coaches for the lacrosse team that you've been the team, how did he put it, uh 'gang bang.'"

"Oh my God!" Margo felt tears starting to form in her eyes and she couldn't do anything about it. Crying in front of their coach was a big mistake because she took it as weakness, but Margo couldn't help it; she was completely humiliated. Who would start such an awful rumor?

Thinking about who might say such awful things about her, Margo thought it was a stupid question to ask herself. She knew exactly who started that rumor.

Lexi stepped in before Margo could say anything. "Coach, I assure you, Margo has been home alone every night. She hasn't gone out in a while."

Their coach looked at Margo. "Is that right?"

"Yes, Coach, I've been home. I swear."

"Then why would the lacrosse team be telling people otherwise?" Their coach raised a questionable eyebrow at them, which so desperately needed to be plucked because it looked like a grizzly bear's ass was plastered across her forehead.

Margo put her head in her hands and felt Lexi rub her back like any good friend would. "This is so humiliating. I shouldn't have to be talking to my coach about this."

"You're right," she said. "This is shit I don't want to deal with, so tell me right now what the fuck is going on, Margo."

Pulling herself together, Margo sat up straight and explained. "A week ago, after the football game, a guy on the lacrosse team brought me back to his place and he tried to have sex with me, but I didn't want to. When I kept refusing his attempts and walked away, he said he would tell everyone we did it anyway, so might as well make it a reality. I left without looking back. I haven't been there since. I most likely bruised his ego so, in retaliation, he started running his mouth."

Lexi continued to rub her back. "Oh, Margo. I'm so sorry."

Margo just nodded at her friend. Her coach spoke up. "I'm going to need a name."

"Coach, I would rather not. Can't we just move on?"

Her coach slapped the desk with her hand. "Not when one of my players is being dragged through the mud. Now you give me a name or I will sit your ass for the rest of the season and you can enjoy your senior season picking splinters from your butt cheeks."

Well, when she put it like that. "Doug Yolk."

Lexi twisted her face and raised an eyebrow at her friend. "Doug, really?"

"I was in a bad place. You can understand my refusal to sleep with him."

"Uh, yeah. Gross, I think he showers like once a month."

"Ladies!" Their coach shouted to stop them from talking. "I don't need to know the hygiene rituals for the horny lacrosse team. Margo, I will take care of this. If you're having a problem with something that drives you to a man who apparently doesn't shower, I expect you to talk to your captain about them and your friend."

Margo nodded at her coach and then they were dismissed, just like that. Lexi and Margo walked to their locker room together so they could grab their stuff for practice.

"What do you think Coach is going to do?" Margo asked, trying not to sound completely paranoid.

"I don't know, probably talk to their coach and bring the lying rumors to his attention. What their coach does with it is up to him. It doesn't seem like Doug would be the only one who gets in trouble. I talked to Parker the other day and he was telling me how he heard the rumors about you from other guys."

Fucking rich! Margo wanted to slam her head against the concrete walls. That was the last thing she wanted, for Parker to think she was out whoring around town, while he was tucked away at home with Sierra.

"Great, glad to hear the whole athletic department sees me as some used up taco."

Lexi shivered. "That's disgusting."

They got to their locker room door, but Lexi stopped Margo from going inside. "Margo, what's bothering you?"

Yeah right, like Margo was going to tell Lexi that she has a massive crush on Parker. Lexi was with Jake now, but still, friends didn't go out with each other's exes. Instead of telling Lexi the truth, she lied. She lied to Lexi for the first time since their freshman year when they met.

"Just upset about this being our final year. I'll get over it."

Lexi eyed her skeptically but continued into the locker room. Thank God, Margo thought. The last thing she wanted to do was get into a long discussion with Lexi about her inappropriate crush on Parker.

Lexi

Nervous flutters flowed through Lexi's body as she made sure her room was straightened up and devoid of all clutter. She had lit a candle and was playing some Adele on her computer for a sensual atmosphere. Jake was supposed to be back from his away trip any moment and he was coming over right after he got off the bus.

The football team continued their undefeated season by narrowly squeaking by with a three-point win. The game was televised, so Lexi was able to watch part of it. Towards the end of the game, she was biting her nails; thankfully, they won. She was happy they continued their winning streak, but she also was excited because she really wanted to reward Jake. She was planning on giving him a massage, mainly to relax him, but also so she could feel up his glorious body. She even got special lotion to use.

Lexi made sure to stock up on Jake's favorite PowerAde and snacks, so he didn't have to go anywhere; he could just stay with her in her room. She asked what he liked when they were talking on the phone the other night. They talked for over an hour and finally hung up because the guys were ragging on him for being on the phone too long.

She didn't think she had ever been this happy before. She looked at herself in the mirror for the tenth time and adjusted her top so her ladies looked a little perkier. She wore an extremely low cut shirt that she wouldn't normally wear, but it was for Jake and she paired the shirt with her favorite pair of yoga pants that made her ass look amazing.

There was a knock at her door and Lexi went flying to open it, expecting to see Jake, but instead came face-to-face with what looked like her mother, but Lexi was having a hard time telling because the lady's face was bruised beyond belief.

"Mom?"

"Hi, honey. I'm sorry to stop in like this, I just needed a place to stay tonight." Her mom shuffled around on her feet, looking extremely nervous.

Lexi ushered her mom inside and sat her on the couch while she got some ice from the freezer for her mom's face. Her mom's battered face was something Lexi, unfortunately, was not shocked by, but this time the abuse was worse than she had ever seen it.

"Mom, what happened?"

"Your father was upset about a bet he lost and I got in his way."

"You got in his way?" Lexi asked incredulously.

"Yes, I knew he was upset and I should have just steered clear of him. But instead, I tried to make him feel better. I should have known that wasn't the right thing to do."

Lexi just stood there, in shock, listening to her mom and how weak she was…how pathetic she sounded. Lexi loved her mom, but she didn't respect her. What woman stayed with a man who beat the living hell out of them? The whole situation made her completely sick to her stomach, causing Lexi to think enough was enough and she went to grab her camera. She brought it out to the living room and turned it on.

"What do you think you're doing?" her mom asked, while covering her face.

"I'm taking evidence to show to the cops. He needs to be stopped, Mom, and if you're not going to do it, then I am."

Her mom ripped the camera out of Lexi's hand and threw it against the wall, smashing it into pieces. Not knowing how to react, Lexi just stared at the broken camera on the ground.

"Don't even bother taking pictures with your phone because I will do the same thing. I came here to get a good night's sleep, not to be chastised by my own daughter, who should be helping me out. If you don't think you can handle doing that this one night, then I guess I'll just have to go back home and face your father."

Lexi just stared at her mom; she couldn't believe her. All Lexi wanted to do was help her mom, but her mom wanted nothing to do with setting the record straight, setting her dad straight, for once. Not having much of a choice because Lexi didn't want her mom going back to the wrath that was her father tonight, she decided to let her mom stay.

"You can take my bed, Mom. I can sleep with Margo."

A loud knock on the front door shook Lexi out of the situation with her mom and reminded her of the night she had previously planned. Lexi's heart dropped; it was Jake and the last thing she wanted was for him to see her mom for the first time like this, let alone know about her parents.

"Mom, go wash up and throw on a pair of my pajamas. I'll be in to help you in a second."

Her mom left the room and Lexi went to grab the door. She wiped at her eyes to make sure she didn't have any tears showing; she didn't need Jake wondering why she was so upset. She flung the door open and her heart sped up from just the mere sight of Jake. She quickly scooted herself outside, so he couldn't see the inside of her apartment. He greeted her with a confused look.

"Hey babe, what's going on?"

She couldn't believe she was about to lie to Jake; she didn't want to, but she had to, she had no other option. She knew this wasn't the way to conduct a relationship, but she didn't want him knowing about her despicable family history, not yet anyway.

"Uh, tonight's not a good night. I have a headache and uh, just don't feel good."

Jake brought her into a hug. "Let me take care of you, then."

Lexi pushed away. "I don't think that's a good idea." She pretended to yawn. "I'm tired anyway." She gave him a quick peck on the check and said, "I'll call you tomorrow, night."

With that, she shut the door on him and cursed herself.

She could have handled that situation way better, but she panicked instead. She was so nervous that her mom was going to come out of the bathroom and ask her a question that she tried to hurry Jake out of her apartment as quickly as possible.

Regret rushed through her body, making her question whether she had done the right thing. She couldn't forget the hurt look on Jake's face when she brushed him off. If only he knew how excited she was to see him, to have him spend the night, to spoil him rotten with a massage. Instead, she was stuck staring at her mom, who didn't even seem like the woman Lexi once knew. Instead of the strong confident woman Lexi once knew, there was a ghost in her place. Her mom fell to her dad's abuse and based her life around him, something Lexi swore she would never do. She would never rely on a man so much that he became her world, because that was when you got in situations like her mom.

Lexi settled her mom into her bed and went over to Margo's room, where she would be shacking up for the night. Margo was still out with a couple of the girls, so Lexi wrote a note on the door so when Margo came back to the apartment she wasn't scared shitless when she found someone sleeping in her bed.

Lexi was just snuggling into the covers when her phone chimed with a text message. She knew it was from Jake without even having to look.

Jake: Look, babe. I don't know what that was all about back there, but you're scaring me. Is everything alright between us?

Yup, Lexi felt like complete shit. She definitely should have handled Jake better tonight. Instead of comforting him and sending him on his way, making sure to show him that everything was okay, she'd made him think there was something wrong between the two of them, when, in fact, that was farthest from the truth. Lexi cursed out her dad for putting them all in this position. She wrote back to Jake.

Lexi: Everything is fine, I promise. I just needed to take care of something. I'm sorry.

Jake: So you don't have a headache?

Shit, this was why she didn't lie, she wasn't good at it. She was digging herself quite a hole where Jake was concerned. She was going to lie again to fix her slip-up, but decided not to. She was already in too deep. She wish she'd never lied in the first place, but that would have meant letting Jake see her mom and there was no way in hell she was going to expose Jake to her mom's battered face.

Lexi: No, but something important came up. I promise I will make it up to you.

Jake: I don't want you to make it up to me, I just want to help. Let me help you and be a part of your life.

Why did her life have to be so fucked up? Tears started to prick at her eyes, but she refused to give in to the pain her dad caused. That would mean he would win and there was no way she was going to let that happen. He didn't deserve the satisfaction of ruining her life and her mom's.

Why was Jake such a good guy? Why did he want to help? Couldn't he be like every other guy and give two shits about what was going on? She wished he was obsessed with video games or something mind-numbing like that, so he was distracted rather than so attentive. Why did she have to be dating the one guy who actually paid attention to what was going on in their relationship?

Lexi: I appreciate it Jake, but I can take care of it. I will talk to you tomorrow. Good night. XOXO

She decided to end the conversation before it got any worse.

She knew she should have just told him the truth, but what would he have thought? Some people just don't understand the situation her family was in; hell, Lexi barely understood it. She didn't want to subject Jake to her family issues, especially when everything was perfect and new between them. No, she would wait. Her phone chimed again.

Jake: Okay. Good night, baby.

Lexi's heart melted and wept at the same time. She so desperately wanted Jake with her, she needed him with her. He had become her safe haven and, right now, she needed that haven more than ever. She wanted to get lost in his arms so she could forget the sick reality that her father was an abusive dick and her mom was a spineless victim. Instead of leaning on Jake, she had to get lost in Margo's sheets, which didn't even come close to measuring up.

Jake

It felt like the weight of the world was resting on his chest. Jake could feel the tension he was carrying around in his shoulders and it was starting to cause him some serious stress. He hadn't seen Lexi in a couple of days and it bothered him. They talked on the phone, but that wasn't enough for him, especially since they only lived a couple of buildings away. She hadn't let him in her apartment the night he came back from his away trip, or any other night since he'd been home. He missed her. Every time he tried to get together with her, she was always busy. Jake didn't see her in the gym either, he wondered if she'd reverted back to lifting cans of beans in her apartment to avoid seeing him.

He didn't think the reason she was being elusive was because of another guy, at least he didn't want to think that. He couldn't. She was very adamant about being exclusive when they started their relationship. Although, he found it incredibly odd that she wouldn't let him in her apartment. What was she hiding? And why wouldn't she tell him? He wasn't an expert on relationships, but one thing he knew for sure was, couples didn't keep secrets from each other; instead, they leaned on each other for support.

Annoying music bumped through the training room, which only raked on Jake's nerves even more. He blew out a frustrated breath and set the dumbbells he was lifting back on the rack. He didn't know how many reps he did, all he knew was his biceps were on fire and he had zoned out a while ago.

"Finally," Mason said. "I was getting worried about you over there. I didn't know if you were going for some kind of record or if you'd turned into a moron and forgot how to count."

Jake ran his hands over his face. "Does Brooke keep things from you?"

"What do you mean?"

Jake went into story mode right in the middle of the weight room and told Mason everything that happened after he got off the bus the other night. Jake wasn't much for sharing, but he had to get the heavy weight Lexi put there off his chest. He told Mason how it made him feel and his fears of there being a possible other man in the mix. Mason chewed on Jake's information for a second before he answered.

"I don't think it's a guy."

Jake felt his spirits perk up. "You don't? Why?"

"Because of the way she looks at you man, I don't think she could look at you like that if there was another guy."

"You're basing your theory off of a look? That doesn't mean much."

Mason shrugged. "Could mean everything, man"

Mason tossed an elastic band at Jake so he could work on his rotator cuff. They both put the end of their band under one of the squatting rack barbells and turned around to work their rotator cuff muscles.

Thoughts of the other night kept running through Jake's head as he went through his rotator cuff exercises, which were required for every quarterback, since shoulder injuries were a big concern in his position.

When Jake finished his last rep, he looked up and spotted Lexi walking into the weight room. She was a sight for sore eyes and looked amazing, as usual. She was wearing her little spandex shorts, a workout tank top and her hair was up in a messy bun. She wore neon colored shoes that offset the tan on her legs.

Jake's heart hammered heavily in his chest from just knowing she was in the same room as him. She hadn't spotted him yet, so he was able to observe her from a decent distance. She was talking to the trainer and laughing about something on the bulletin board that hung up in the weight room…usually showing off poor-humored jokes. She was so gorgeous it almost hurt Jake's heart to see her so happy when clearly he wasn't the reason why.

She grabbed her workout file and turned toward the center of the room, which was when they made eye contact for the first time in a couple of days. She stopped mid-stride and smiled at him. He smiled back, unsure of what else to do. He knew she needed space, but all he wanted to do was run up to her and take her away from everyone so he could have her to himself.

She walked toward him, more like sashayed, Jake thought. It wasn't fair that she had such a sexy walk too, amongst other things. She was right in front of him as he finished up his exercises. She reached up and brushed his cheek with her thumb and planted a gentle kiss on his lips. Every bad feeling he had toward her melted away and he felt himself falling all over again for Lexi Knox.

"Hey, big guy."

"Hey, short stack."

She nodded toward Mason. "Hey Mase. Good game the other night."

"Thanks." Mason took his band and put it away, giving them their space.

"How's it going?" Jake asked, suddenly feeling awkward. He wished she would kiss him again because, when they were touching, it felt so right.

"Good. Are you done with your workout?"

"Yeah, this was my last thing. Haven't seen you in these parts lately. Have you been hanging out with your cans of beans again?"

She chuckled and peered at him with her sky-blue eyes. "No, just haven't had time, so I better get going with this workout because I have some catching up to do." She started to walk away, but Jake pulled her back. Her hands rested on his chest and he reveled in the way her small hands felt against his body.

"Can we have dinner tonight? I miss you, babe."

She looked away and shook her head. "I'm sorry. I have some things to take care of tonight and I have to write a paper."

Jake's heart sank to the floor. "You do know I leave tomorrow for another away game, right? I haven't seen you all week." He tilted her chin up so she was looking him in the eyes. "Are we okay, Lexi?"

"Of course," she said with a half-hearted smile. He knew it wasn't her genuine smile because her genuine smile lit up a room; it lit up his heart "I just have a lot to do. I will talk to you tonight on the phone. Alright?"

Jake ran his hand through his hair, frustrated and angry, but also sad because whatever was going on with her, she didn't want to include him and that hurt more than anything. Unless she was actually seeing someone behind his back, then of course she would keep him out of the loop. Why would she want him finding out about her affair with someone else?

"I guess," he said. He removed her hands and gave her a quick goodbye before heading out toward his locker room. He couldn't be around her anymore, especially when she was acting so strangely. He felt like his heart was being ripped out of his chest and he didn't even know why.

"Jake."

He spun around and saw her running after him. She wrapped her arms around his neck and pulled him in for a long luscious kiss. He wrapped his arms around her and brought her in closer. He felt her breasts press against his chest as she took control of his mouth.

He let her do all the work. He let her be in charge because he wanted to see if she was kissing him with true passion or if it was just a pity kiss. When she deepened their kiss further, he knew she was kissing with passion.

She pulled away and said, "I'm sorry." Then she walked away without another word.

What the hell? Jake stood in the hallway completely shocked, as she walked back into the weight room. What was she sorry for? For being weird? Or for something worse, like cheating on him?

Cheers erupted down the hall, but Jake didn't even bother to see what it was about; he was way too confused and scared to worry about anything else. Jake walked back to his locker room, more annoyed than ever. She was so good at making him ride a damn emotional roller coaster, which he wished he could get off of. It was frustrating to have to keep up with her varying emotions and deciphering what everything meant. Why couldn't women just come with a manual? It would be so much easier to deal with them if they did, Jake thought.

CHAPTER ELEVEN

Lexi

Finally, her apartment consisted of two residents, rather than three. Lexi was able to get her mom to go to her aunt's house instead of back home to her dad. At least that was what Lexi hoped her mom was doing. She knew when her mom first showed up at Lexi's doorstep she was staying for the night, but Lexi softened up toward her mom and asked her to stay a couple more days, even though it put a strain on her relationship with Jake. But now, her mom was gone and things could go back to normal. She only wished her mom went back a night sooner so she could have spent the night with her man. Now Jake was away and, instead of being with him, she was watching him on TV.

She wished she could have given him a proper sendoff, but when she wasn't in class or practice, her mom demanded Lexi's attention, claiming they never did anything together anymore. So the past week, they spent a lot of mother-daughter time together, too much time, Lexi thought. She loved her mom, but her mom was weak, not a strong woman like Lexi desired to be and felt it hard to be around her.

A special piece about Jake possibly going to play in the NFL came on the TV. Lexi couldn't help but smile at the screen, thinking about how lucky she was to have him in her life. When he got back from his away trip, she was going to make it up to him, big time. She finally felt ready to be with him. She knew he wasn't going after her just to cross her off his fuck list, he actually cared about her. He actually wanted to be in a solid, committed relationship with her. And she was ready to reciprocate his feelings.

The campus was more than happy to receive them as a couple, which shocked Lexi; she for sure thought she would get some backlash from some of Jake's most admiring fans. They obviously didn't make a public statement about their relationship, but when they were together, they didn't keep it a secret that they were with each other. Because of Jake, Lexi became more of a celebrity around campus, not that she cared about those things, but people would come up to her and tell her how much they loved Jake and how great he was. She would thank them, she didn't know why, but she thought it seemed appropriate.

The cameras zoomed in on Jake while he was stretching. He looked different, he looked off. He didn't have his normal game-face on and he wasn't joking around with the other guys like he usually did. She hoped it wasn't because of the stress she put him through the past week. Lexi cursed herself for not having the nerve to tell him about her mom. She was just too ashamed. She thought if she could get rid of her mom, Jake would never have to know about her abusive asshole of a father and weakling of a mother. If things went further down the road with Jake, maybe she would tell him, but right now she didn't want any negative light shone on her, especially since their relationship was so rocky.

She thought about the conversation they had last night and wondered if there was already a negative light on her because Jake knew something was up. He was short with her on the phone after she turned him down again about meeting up and he barely texted her today, even though she sent a bunch of messages to him, wishing him luck and telling him how much she missed him. Lexi started to feel sweat trickle down her back as she thought about the strange way Jake was acting. Was Jake going to break up with her? Did she make the wrong decision by not telling Jake about her sordid family?

She looked at the camera again; he definitely didn't look like himself and the fact that he barely talked to her today skated across her nerves.

"Oh no," she said out loud. Could she have driven him away from her?

She looked back at her text messages from today and the last one he sent said, "Thanks, baby." She wished him luck, hoping that even though he couldn't take her calls right before the game, her text messages would show how much she cared. Lexi thought it was good that he called her baby in his last text message. That settled her nerves a little, at least for the time being. If he was going to break up with her, he definitely wouldn't have called her baby.

Lexi grabbed a pint of ice cream from her fridge and sat down on the couch to watch the game. Margo and Parker were both busy tonight, so she was all by herself, which she didn't mind. Since she had been crowded by her mom for a while, she enjoyed the peace and quiet. Margo actually was visiting her parents this past week, which was good because that gave Lexi a full bed to herself while her mom had been visiting. Coach gave Margo a little break to go back home and gather herself after the horrible rumors that were spread about her.

All hell broke loose when Coach approached the Lacrosse coach about his players' careless way of treating one of her players. Needless to say, the lacrosse guys got their asses handed to them and then the whole athletic department had to sit through a lecture about spreading rumors and bullying. Lexi felt like she was back in middle school, but as long as Margo's name was cleared, Lexi didn't mind.

She talked to Margo on the phone earlier to see how she was doing. It was refreshing because Margo sounded full of energy and ready to come back. Lexi was happy for her friend that she was bouncing back from the hell she was put through. Margo was bouncing back faster than Lexi thought she could if she was ever thrown into Margo's situation.

The Bears returned the ball to the forty yard line after the first kickoff; what a great start, she thought. She settled into the couch and watched Jake work his magic. He was so fluid with his movements and bounced around in the pocket as if there weren't three hundred pound men coming after him. Jake threw the ball to Mason for a gain of twenty. So close to the end zone, Lexi thought. They were going to score a touchdown within the first minute of the game. Lexi sat on pins and needles waiting to jump up in celebration.

Jake yelled out a play and then the ball was hiked. He fake handed it off to their running back and then looked for Mason in the end zone. All of a sudden, it was like someone pressed the slow motion button on the remote. Jake had his back turned and his gaze fixed on his receivers instead of floating around like he usually did in the pocket. Out of the corner of the screen came a huge linebacker and Lexi just sat there and screamed when Jake was pummeled from behind and flattened to the ground. She could feel the impact of the hit as if she was the one eating grass instead of Jake. She sat on the edge of her seat while Jake lay motionless on the ground.

Tears formed in her eyes as she shook her head in disbelief. He wasn't getting up. Why wasn't he getting up? The trainers went running up to Jake as the refs tried to clear the way and get the players out of the area so Jake could be properly tended to.

A phone rang through the silence that was encompassing her apartment, startling her out of her negative thoughts. She looked down at the caller ID and saw that it was Margo. She picked up instantly, knowing Margo would be the only one she would want to talk to at the moment.

"Hello?" she practically said in a whisper.

"Are you watching the game?" Margo asked in a panic.

Lexi brushed away a tear that slid down her face. "Yes, how come he's not getting up, Margo?"

"I don't know, sweetie."

The insensitive reporters kept showing the collision in slow motion so Lexi got to continuously watch Jake's head fly back in an odd way as he got hit from behind over and over again. Lexi thought she was going to throw up from the gruesome replays.

"Can they please stop showing how he got hit?!" Lexi shouted to nobody in particular.

"Lex, he's going to be okay, he's built like an ox."

"Yeah, and the guy who hit him is built like a steam train. Oh my God Margo, what if something serious happened to him? I could never forgive myself for how I treated him this past week."

"You can't think like that." They both watched in silence when the on-field stretcher and medics came out and started attending to him.

The announcers started talking. "Wow, this could be a career-ending injury. What do you think, Bob?"

"Well Mike, I couldn't agree more; a hit like that when you're caught off-guard isn't easy to recover from, especially since he hasn't moved since he landed on the ground. We might have just watched Jake Taylor's last play on the football field. Let's take a break; we will be right back."

Lexi was crying as she barely held the phone to her ear. She heard Margo from a far distance talking to her. "Don't you listen to them, Lexi, those guys will say pretty much anything. Jake is going to be just fine."

"I have to go, Margo. I'm going to try to contact him. At least let him know I'm watching and I care about him."

"Good idea. Please let me know if you need anything."

"I will." Lexi hung up the phone and pulled up her text messages. She clicked on one she recently sent to Jake and started typing frantically.

Lexi: I know you can't look at your phone right now, but I just want you to know I was watching the game and you are going to be okay, I just know it. Hang in there big guy.

She knew he wouldn't get the message for a while, but as she sent the message to him, it felt like she was silently communicating with him. She sat on her couch and waited for the commercials to end as she rocked back and forth, hoping and praying that Jake was going to be okay. She couldn't imagine how it would be if his career was over; he was so brilliant on the field…it would be such a waste.

Graphics for the game came back on and the announcers started talking.

"If you just missed the last five minutes of the game, here is a replay of what happened." They showed the clip again and Lexi cringed as Jake once again fell to the ground. "We are getting news from the locker room now that Jake Taylor is, in fact…" The announcer pressed on his ear, probably trying to hear whatever the little guy in his ear was trying to say. "Yes, he is awake now in the locker room and most likely suffering from a concussion. He is moving around…"

That was all Lexi needed to hear; he was moving around. She cried into her hands as they held her head up. She was so grateful that he was okay. She tuned out the rest of the game as their backup quarterback took over and threw a handful of interceptions costing the Bears their first loss of the season. Lexi didn't care though; all she cared about was that Jake was going to be okay.

She spent the rest of the night waiting by her phone, waiting to hear something from him, any kind of information that he was doing alright, but she never heard a word. She decided that she was going to meet him in front of the events center when their bus returned from the airport. She wanted to see him more than anything…and as soon as possible.

Jake

Jake rolled his head to the side and cringed; he was sore as hell thanks to the semi-truck that hit him from behind on the field. Not to mention that the bus bed wasn't the most comfortable bed he had ever stayed on. Thankfully, it was a semi-short trip from the airport. Jake replayed the moment he got hit over and over in his head. He had been thinking about Lexi, not about what was going on around him, which cost his team the game. He'd never let his personal life creep into his game before, but he did this time and he got burned because of it.

He could easily blame Lexi, since she had been so evasive the whole week, but he didn't. He was the one who brought his problems on the field and that was ultimately why he got hurt. The doctor in the locker room kept telling him how lucky he was that he walked away with just a concussion. His first-ever concussion. He didn't care for it too much. He didn't think he was going to get any concussions until he was at least in the pros, but now he could add one to his football resume.

He swore at himself for losing focus during the game. He would never let that happen again. James, one of his linebackers, felt awful for not defending the steam engine that charged at Jake, but Jake knew it wasn't fully James' fault. It was a combination of everything, especially a lack of focus. Jake was supposed to relax the rest of the week and do some easy workouts if he wanted to play in next week's game, which Jake was determined to do. He was livid that the team lost. He was going for a perfect season and that wasn't going to happen now.

Mason came up to Jake's bed. "You feeling better, man?"

Jake rubbed his neck. "Yeah, just a little sore, that's all."

"Why don't you get out of that bed? We're about five minutes from campus; you should stretch out a bit."

Jake agreed with Mason, gathered his stuff and got out of the bed to head to the front of the bus. The guys gave him the night to recover from the injury, but after that, they started ribbing him for having a concussion. Jake knew it was all in good fun, but he had the hardest time laughing along with his teammates.

"What are you doing tonight?" Mason asked.

"I don't know. Hopefully Lexi will want to hang out. I haven't talked to her since the hit."

"Why not?" Mason asked, looking worried. "Everything okay between you two?"

"I don't really know. I wanted to talk to her; she was the first person I thought about, but I didn't want her pity. I got a text from her after I got hit saying I was going to be okay, but I can't help but wonder if it was a pity text. She's been so weird lately. I guess I just wanted to see her reaction when I got back into town. I didn't want to hear it on the phone. Does that make sense?"

"I guess so. Go to her place when we get back and don't take no for an answer."

"I don't think that's going to happen," one of the freshmen piped up from the front of the bus.

Jake and Mason both looked at him as if he'd lost his mind. "Excuse me?" Jake said.

The freshman pointed toward the events center and said, "Looks like Lexi has moved on, man."

Jake and Mason scrambled to the front of the bus to see what the idiot was talking about. When Jake focused in on what he was pointing at, Jake almost fell to the floor. Standing in front of the event's center was Lexi wrapped up in Parker's arm and he was kissing her head.

"What the fuck?" Jake yelled.

Mason put his hand on his shoulder. "Dude, calm down; they're just friends. You know that."

Jake did know that, but with everything that had been going on between them and the way Parker was holding her made Jake think something was going on. His teammates decided to continue the ribbing from earlier and started to push his buttons even further.

"Looks like you can't hold a woman down, Taylor."

"Can't blame her, I would have dumped his sorry ass after getting scared like that too."

"Parker is the man!"

Jake turned to Mason for support, but Mason just shrugged his shoulders as if Jake was on his own. Good friend he was. Jake peered out the window again and saw Lexi spot the bus. She shook Parker off quickly and watched him walk away. Nothing was going on, Jake's ass. She was busted and he was going to make sure she knew it. Jake turned to Mason.

"Can you take care of my gear for me?"

"Jake, don't do it."

Jake got in Mason's face. "I didn't ask for your fucking opinion; just take care of my damn gear, please."

Mason held his hands up in defense. "Fine, but don't say I didn't warn you."

Jake was seething mad and could feel his body tense up more than it was before as the bus got closer and closer to its designated spot. He tried to calm himself, but once the bus stopped and the doors flew open, he jumped off the bus and headed straight toward Lexi, who now moved to her car and was standing in front of it, waiting for him.

She held her arms open. "Hey, there you are…What's wrong?" She asked with a confused expression. Jake grabbed her by the shoulder and moved her to the side of her car, so they had a little bit of privacy. She ripped her arm way from his grasp. "Ouch Jake, that hurt."

"What the fuck was that all about?"

She searched his eyes, as if she didn't know what he was talking about, but he wasn't going to fall for it.

"What was what about?"

He got inches from her face and pushed her up against the car. "You know exactly what I'm talking about. Is Parker the reason why you refused to be with me this past week?"

She tried to push him away, but he didn't budge. "Jake, you're scaring me."

"Just tell me the truth."

"About what?"

He pushed her against the car again, not realizing that he might be hurting her; he was just so mad, mad about the game, mad about her neglecting him, and mad about the guys on the bus.

"Don't fuck with me Lexi, are you fucking Parker behind my back?"

Her mouth dropped open in shock and she slapped him across the face, sending a sting through his head. He grabbed her wrists and put them by her side. She squirmed, telling him to let go, but he wouldn't.

"What's going on over here?" Jake's coach stepped in. Jake backed off of Lexi just enough so she could give him a swift kick to the shin.

"Son of a bitch!" he screamed, while clenching his leg.

Lexi shouted over to his coach. "Control your men, Coach." She got in her car and drove off, leaving Jake in the parking lot, hobbling on one leg.

"Taylor, what the hell has gotten into you? I told you not to fuck around with that girl; she's too good for you. You better treat her with respect next time I see you two together or I will make it my personal mission to see that you never see a minute of playing time in the pros. Do you hear me?"

Jake nodded his head and said, "Yes, Sir."

His coach walked off and Jake hobbled over to Mason's car to wait for a ride. He was going straight to Lexi's. Thankfully, he had her emergency key, so he could get in what he knew was going to be a locked door.

Lexi

Flinging herself on her bed, Lexi buried her head in the pillow and started crying like a fool. Did Jake really think she was cheating on him with Parker? Jake knew Parker and she were close; he accepted that, so why now? Why the questioning? Lexi shifted in bed and felt the rough lace lingerie she was wearing rub against her body.

She'd planned on picking Jake up after he got off the bus and taking him back to her place to finally let him fully have her, mind, body and soul. To think that she was going to finally have sex with that Neanderthal. He treated her just like her dad would have treated her mom, well maybe in a more subdued way, but still, it scared the hell out of her.

Why did he freak out so much? She ran into Parker when she was waiting for the bus. He asked how her mom was and how Jake was doing after his big hit. Parker was just leaving and giving her a hug good bye when the bus pulled up. He was going out with Sierra, which was another thing. Jake knew Parker and Sierra were an item, so what would possess him to think she and Parker were together?

Was that why he never contacted her yesterday after his injury? She couldn't believe he never texted her or called her, especially after she had tried to contact him for hours. She for sure thought she would hear from him, at least this morning, to let her know he would be home soon. It hurt that he didn't contact her, more than she thought it would hurt. Even though he caused her pain, she still wanted to make up with him and reconnect with him in a way they hadn't yet, hence the lacy lingerie.

Lexi sat up in her bed and decided to get into her pajamas because she had no use for the uncomfortable lingerie anymore. She pulled off her T-shirt and jeans and put them in her hamper. She was about to take off the lacy push-up bra that extended a little past her rib cage and opened in the front when she heard her front door slam. She froze in her tracks. Margo wasn't due back until Monday, so that could only mean one thing.

Jake.

Jake

Jake tore through Lexi's apartment and headed straight for her bedroom; he stopped abruptly when he saw what she was wearing. She had on black lingerie, the top was something he had never seen before and she was wearing what Jake could only imagine was a lace thong, since the fabric was so small and dainty. He felt all the blood rush to his groin, even though he was seething mad at her.

Then a thought occurred to him, why was she wearing such an outfit? It sure as hell wasn't for him, since she wasn't ready to have sex with him, but it looked like she was ready to have sex with someone. He felt his fists curl at his sides and his breathing grow heavy at the thought of another guy seeing Lexi in her current get-up. He watched her put her hands on her hips, as if what she was wearing wasn't the sexiest thing he had ever seen. Her stomach rippled with muscles and her toned legs were completely bare, giving Jake a mouth-watering view. She lifted her chin at him in defiance.

"What the hell are you doing here?"

"Why the hell are you wearing that?" He pointed at her outfit, while ignoring her question.

Lexi looked down at herself and then answered, "That's none of your business."

"The hell it's not. Last time I checked, you were my girlfriend and I have the right to know why the fuck you're wearing…that," he said, while pointing up and down at her body.

"Oh, is that right? Then how come you didn't give your girlfriend the courtesy of letting her know you were okay yesterday?" Her voice caught in her throat. He couldn't deal with her right now if she decided to cry. When she cried, it completely tore apart his tough exterior and broke him down to absolute mush.

"Oh, you mean you actually wanted to know how I was? You didn't have other things to do? You weren't too busy to care?"

"How dare you?" she asked, while charging toward him. She pushed his chest, but he stood still, not budging an inch. "I can't believe you didn't call me…out of spite."

"It wasn't out of spite."

"Yeah, right. You're a fucking bastard. I was worried sick about you, wondering if you were going to be able to walk and instead of easing my worry, you decided to use that moment to get back at me? What the hell is wrong with you? Why would you do that?" A tear ran down her face, but she quickly wiped it away.

Jake didn't intentionally handle the situation with malice, but now that he thought about it, his subconscious might have helped him in some of his decision-making.

"That was not my intention. But it does suck, doesn't it? When you care about someone and they won't talk to you. Now you know how I felt all last week."

Lexi turned around and paced the room. When he looked down at her perfect, round ass he confirmed that, in fact, she was wearing a thong. Jake couldn't help but stare at her tight little bubble butt. God, even though he was furious with her, he wanted her so bad.

"I can't believe you," she let her tears flow now. "I was genuinely scared, Jake. I was scared I wouldn't be able to talk to you again and you decided not to talk to me because of what happened last week?"

"How do you think I felt all last week? Worrying about you and what was going on, wondering if you were going to break up with me because you wouldn't let me close enough to help."

"So you go and punish me?"

"No! That wasn't intentional." They were both screaming at each other, most likely putting on a good show for her neighbors.

"Sure it wasn't, Jake." She threw her hands up in anger.

"And like yours wasn't intentional. You're the whole reason I got hit, because I was worried about you."

She charged after him. "How dare you blame that on me?" She was still crying, but screaming at him at the same time. He tried not to focus on how the swell of her breasts jiggled ever so slightly when she yelled at him.

"Well, it's the truth. Let's just get it all out in the open, Lexi…are you cheating on me?"

"No!"

"Then what is it?!" He yelled back.

"My dad beat the shit out of my mom and I was housing her last week; I didn't want you to have to get involved, you ass!"

Devastation wrapped around Jake's heart as Lexi went into the bathroom and slammed the door shut. Jake felt all the wind in his chest get knocked out of his lungs, leaving him breathless. He was a gigantic ass, but what he didn't understand was, why she didn't just tell him? He would have helped her through it. That's what being in a relationship was about, being there for each other and taking care of each other when they needed it the most.

While she was in the bathroom, he ran his hands through his hair and paced her room, trying to figure out how to handle the situation before him. He heard her blow her nose and wished he could just go in there and pull her into a hug. He stared at the picture he first saw of her and her parents that was displayed on her desk. They all looked so happy in the picture. Who knew behind those smiles was a world of pain and despair? Jake's heart ripped in two for Lexi. He didn't have his parents anymore in his life, but when they were alive, his dad treated his mom like a queen and his dad would always tell Jake that he needed to treat his woman the same way when he was older.

His dad was right. Lexi was his woman, the one he wanted to be with, the one he loved. The last statement hit him like a ton of bricks. He loved her. He fucking loved her more than anything. He needed to take his father's advice and treat Lexi like she deserved to be treated, like a queen.

He went to the bathroom door and knocked on it. She didn't answer, so he twisted the knob, praying she didn't lock him out before he got the chance to enter the small space. Thankfully, she didn't. He pushed the door open and found her sitting on the counter with her head in her hands. He pushed her legs open and wrapped them around his waist. He tilted her chin up and wiped away the tears that were streaking down her face with his thumbs. He kissed her forehead and pulled her in for a hug.

"I'm so sorry, baby…about everything. I'm so damn sorry."

She cried into his chest and squeezed him tight. "I'm sorry too. I should have told you about my mom, but I was so ashamed."

"I don't want you to think you can't tell me things. I'm here for you, no matter what."

He bent down and kissed her lips, they tasted like Lexi with a hint of salt from her tears. She wrapped her arms around his neck and deepened their kiss right before she said, "Take me to bed, Jake."

He stepped back and looked at her. "What?"

"Take me to bed, Jake." She hopped off the counter, grabbed his hand and walked him toward her bed. She put her hands under his shirt, grabbed the hem and lifted it over his head, exposing his bare chest that she explored with her dainty hands. Her gentle touches were making his senses run wild. He felt himself growing hard at a rapid pace in his southern region at every stroke and caress she played against his body. She took notice of his growth and pulled his pants and socks off, leaving him only in his boxer briefs covering up his very noticeable erection.

"I've missed you," she whispered, as she kissed her way up his chest.

"I've missed you so much, baby."

He lifted her up on the bed and settled between her legs, taking her lips with his. She met each stroke with his and he felt his entire body go numb as she moved her hands in tiny circles down his chest as they kissed. He didn't know if she realized what she did to him with her hands, but she drove him crazy. He placed his hands on her waist, relishing in the feel of her bare skin. She moaned into his mouth making him grow harder.

He stopped what he was doing and leaned his head against hers. "Shit, I don't have protection with me."

"I thought ahead," she said with a wink and then leaned back on the bed, inviting him on top of her. Thanking the Lord for his well-prepared girlfriend, he straddled her little body and rested his hand on her ribcage.

"You look so fucking gorgeous, babe"

She brought his head back down and started kissing him at an alarming rate. He slid his hand to the front of her bra and started undoing the four clasps that held the frilly fabric together. With every pop of the clasp he felt himself get even harder. On the last one, he looked down as he watched her bare, tanned breasts spill out from the top.

He gulped. "Do you tan naked?"

She smirked at him and that was all the evidence he needed. What a vixen! He took one of her breasts in his hand and felt the weight she had to offer. He brought his head down to her breast and took her nipple in with his lips. Lexi threw her head back on the bed and moaned as he circled her nipple with his tongue, turning it into a hard little peak. He went to the other breast and conducted the same routine, causing more moans to fly from Lexi's mouth.

"Jake…that feels so good."

Jake slid the bra completely off Lexi and tossed it to the ground. He kissed his way down to her panties and shucked those was well, revealing a perfectly waxed area. God, she was full of surprises. He moved his way back up to her lips and whispered to her.

"You are so damn beautiful."

Lexi moved her hands down to the waist of his boxer briefs and started to pull them down. Jake allowed her to push them down and he helped her take them fully off when she couldn't reach them anymore. They both stared at each other for a second before Jake climbed on top of her again, placing his forearms on either side of her head as he stroked her hair. He gently brought his head down and kissed her ever so gently. He wanted to savor this moment, the moment where they felt flesh on flesh for the first time. He was so lucky to have her, to be able to love her. He wasn't ever going to forget this moment for as long as he lived.

She kissed him back being just as gentle as he was. The light touches, caresses and kisses drove him to the edge. He spread her legs and quickly remembered he needed a condom.

She knew what he needed and said hastily, "Nightstand."

Jake reached in the drawer, ripped the condom open and rolled it on. She just stared at him, licking her lips. He spread her legs again, grabbed her hands and linked them with his over her head. He stared her in the eyes as he entered her. He watched as her eyes widened at his size and her little mouth formed an "O" shape.

"Am I hurting you?" he asked.

She shook her head no and moved her hips to encourage him to go deeper. Once he was fully inside her, he started rocking back and forth, forcing Lexi to throw her head back in pleasure.

"Oh God, Jake. Yes."

Jake never thought Lexi would be much of a communicator in bed, but he liked it. He also liked how, even though she had a strong personality and did things a lot of the time her way, she let him have control in bed.

He bent his head down and started kissing her deeper than before. He slid his tongue in her mouth and she met him with hers. They tangled themselves up as Jake continued to thrust. He felt the pressure in his body start to build up with every thrust of his hips and thrust of his tongue. All his senses were on fire and he didn't know how much more he would be able to hold on.

Jake left Lexi's lips and headed down her neck trailing his touch with kisses while still holding her hands above her head. He found his way to her plump breasts and sucked in one of her nipples. At that moment, Lexi cried out and her inner walls constricted around him. She screamed out in pleasure and Jake followed right after her. His whole body went numb as he released himself into the woman of his dreams.

Lexi continued to move her hips around, sucking out every last pleasure point, reveling in the pleasure. He felt like he was floating on a cloud. Never in his life had sex ever been so powerful. Yes, it had felt good before, but sex with Lexi was on a whole new and different level. He had the biggest orgasm of his life and it was all because of his brilliant little blue-eyed blonde.

He pulled himself out of her, grabbed a tissue from her night stand to clean up and then pulled her in close to him, wrapping his limbs around her. He buried his face in her hair and kissed her head.

"Mmm…" she said, while wiggling to get closer to him, arousing him once again…and so quickly too.

"I love you, Lexi."

His confession caused her to separate herself from their joining and turn around to face him. One of his hands was on her bare hip and the other was propping his head up.

"What did you say?" she said with shock. Normally he would have thought he would be terrified at this moment, the moment he confessed his love for a woman for the first time, but he wasn't. He didn't care if she didn't say the same three little words back. He loved her and he wanted her to know.

"I said I love you, more than anything, babe."

Lexi put her hand on Jake's cheek and stroked his face. She kissed him lightly on the lips. "I love you too, Jake."

Jake pulled her in at the hip so they were face to face with an inch separating them from touching. He stroked her hair as she snuggled into his arm.

"Best thing I've heard in a long time," he said. "I'm sorry about everything."

"Me too, but let's forget about it and enjoy this moment."

Jake kissed her nose and then her mouth which turned into more frantic kisses and more touching. As Jake found his way inside her core again, he thought to himself how life couldn't be any better than this. As long as he had Lexi by his side, he could do anything.

Lexi

Lexi turned over in bed to snuggle up closer to Jake, but found nothing but sheets and blankets. Disappointment washed through her body as she opened her eyes and didn't see Jake lying next to her. Last night, she'd turned off her alarm so she could sleep in and spend more time with Jake, but it was pointless since he wasn't in bed with her. She'd skipped her morning class, which she had never done before, but Jake was nowhere to be found.

Panic instantly hit her. They finally had sex for the first time last night and now he was gone in the morning. Did he get what he wanted and bolt? She shook her head no, not possible. He told her he loved her last night. Jake Taylor loved her. She still felt like she was floating on a cloud from hearing those words come from his mouth. He completely caught her off-guard with his declaration, but it was one of the best things she had heard in a while. It felt great to be loved, to be wanted by another person, to be cared for.

Lexi sat up and stretched as the sheets fell off her body, exposing her bare breasts. She flushed thinking about all the ways Jake pleasured her last night by just touching her breasts. He declared in the heat of the moment that her breasts were by far the most amazing ones he had ever seen. Lexi laughed to herself, thinking about how heavy his voice sounded when he said it.

She hopped out of bed and grabbed a long shirt to slip over her head. When she stuck her arms through the sleeves, she heard a huge crash in the kitchen. She quickly left her bedroom and looked over the kitchen bar to see Jake holding a bunch of pots and pans. He was only wearing his sweats leaving his chest bare and available to stare at. She sighed at the sight and went over to help him.

"What are you doing?" She helped him with the pots and shoved them back in the drawer. He had one pan in his hand and placed it on the stove.

"I'm making you breakfast, short stack." He leaned over and gave her a quick peck on the lips. "How do you like your eggs?"

She gave him a skeptical look. "You know how to cook?" She crossed her arms over her chest.

"I know how to cook eggs. Place your order babe or you're getting whatever I serve up."

She leaned in and gave his butt a squeeze. "Surprise me, big guy."

He playfully squealed like a girl when she squeezed his butt and swatted at her hand. "If you don't mind, Ma'am, no playing around with the help."

"Hey, if you're my help, I can do whatever I want with you." She leaned in and placed her hands on his chest.

He wrapped his arms around her, bringing her in closer. "Is that right? Well then, do with me what you will."

She pulled him down so she could plant her lips on his. She was almost touching his mouth with hers when she said, "Omelet with veggies and cheese."

She broke their embrace and sauntered over to the counter, where she hoisted herself up and sat down. She crossed her legs and planted her hands behind her so he got a great view of her shirt against her breasts. He walked over to her with hunger in his eyes and not the kind of hunger that could be fixed by a veggie omelet. She stopped him with her foot on his chest before he could get too close.

"What do you think you're doing?"

He groaned. "Babe, you can't sit like that and expect me to back off."

"Check your libido at the door mister, you have breakfast to make."

He shook his head. "You're such a cock tease. You know that?"

She just smiled at him and watched him slump his shoulders while he formed a pouty lip. He grabbed the eggs that were on the counter and started whipping them. She was mesmerized by the way his forearm muscles rippled with each swish of the fork against the eggs.

"Cheer up whipping boy; if you do a good job, I might reward you after breakfast."

He perked up at the sound of her mentioning a reward. "You know, I live for your rewards."

Lexi watched Jake move around her kitchen, as if it was home to him. She had a great view of his backside as he made her an omelet. She observed how his back muscles flexed when he was chopping up peppers sending her to distract herself because she was getting all hot and bothered.

Sex had never been something she needed, probably because she was never with someone like Jake. With Jake, after finally giving herself over to him, it was all she wanted. They fooled around all night in bed, sleeping for a little then waking each other up wanting more. Lexi was sore from her head to her toes, but in a good way.

When they sat down at the table to eat their breakfast, Lexi couldn't help but think about all the women Jake had been with and how she had only been with one other guy. She wondered if Jake was so good at what he did because he had so much experience. Was she his best? Or was she just subpar?

"Is your omelet not good?" Jake asked, interrupting her thoughts.

She noticed she was just pushing it around on her plate and not eating it. She took a big bite and shook her head. "No, it's great. Thank you."

Jake took his finger and pressed it between her eyes to smooth out her frown. "Then what has you all worried."

She blew out a breath. "Just being a girl."

"Tell me. Remember we're going to be open with each other. That's what being in a relationship is all about, being there for each other?"

Jake was right, they had a long conversation last night after they tired from sex. They talked about Lexi's mom and dad and what Lexi could do to help them. She told him how it all started when she was in high school and how her dad didn't start abusing her mom until she left for college, which relieved him a little. Jake was nervous Lexi's dad struck her when she was still living at home, but that was never the case. She wondered if her dad was always abusive toward her mom but she just never took notice.

Lexi and Jake talked until they fell asleep. It felt good to get everything off her chest and out in the open. Jake couldn't have been more understanding about everything she revealed to him. He just held her in his warm embrace while she let everything out. If she didn't already love him, she would have fallen in love with him last night.

She looked up at Jake and made a hesitant smile. "I was just wondering about, you know how I was."

"How you were?" he asked with a cute quizzical look that made her want to jump on his lap and devour him.

"You know…in bed."

Jake threw his head back and laughed out loud, causing Lexi to turn a dangerous shade of red. She swatted his chest. "It's not funny. I'm not as experienced as most girls you've been with. I'm self-conscious about it."

"Babe, you're serious?"

"Yes." She wanted to stomp her foot like a child.

He grabbed her hand and kissed the back of it. "You are, by far, the best I've ever had."

She lifted an eyebrow at him. "I find that hard to believe. I've seen the women you've been with. Marissa on the soccer team, she's got to have some tricks up her sleeve. And what about Darci on the swim team, she looks flexible. And then there's…"

Jake placed his hand over her mouth to stop her from talking. "Let's not go down the list. They were nice, but they were nothing compared to you. You're sexy as sin, beautiful and passionate. You do this thing with your hands that drives me crazy and I am so far in love with you that when we connect intimately, it feels like I will never come back down from heaven." He pulled her on his lap and she placed a hand on his chest, slowly drawing circles with her finger. He kissed her lightly on the lips and said, "That's exactly what I'm talking about."

"What?" she asked.

"What you do with your hands. Can't you feel how fast you made me hard?"

She shifted on his lap and felt the evidence of her finger on his chest. Her eyes widened. "Well, aren't you a strapping young lad?"

"I can't get enough of you," he said, while burying his head in the crook of her neck and kissing her until she felt her toes curl. "I love you Lexi, and I don't want you thinking poorly about yourself where I'm concerned. You are the most amazing, beautiful, funny girl I have ever met and there is no way I will ever get enough of you." He emphasized each word with a kiss.

She leaned her head to the side, granting him more access to work his magic. "I love you too, big guy."

He swept her up into his arms and carried her off to her bed. She reveled in the feel of being handled so delicately by him. She always had her guard up and had to be the leader most of her life, but it was nice to have someone else do the leading. It was nice to finally be the protected instead of the protector.

CHAPTER TWELVE

Lexi

Winter break flew by way too fast. Lexi and Jake spent every waking moment together. They mostly trained, Lexi for her upcoming season and Jake for the Scouting Combine and championships. Lexi had to admit, Jake was much faster than her and obviously lifted more than her. Even though his endurance exceeded hers, she was still able to keep up. She enjoyed being in a relationship with someone who had the same goals in mind.

During their break, they went to the beach for a weekend and didn't think about working out once. They just laid around and enjoyed each other. Jake told her all about his parents' accident and Lexi went into more detail about her family's past and when everything really started to turn south. She, in some ways, blamed herself because it wasn't until she left for college that her dad became physically abusive with her mom. Jake helped her through the guilt she was feeling and told her it wasn't her fault; it was her dad's. They left the beach house a stronger couple than they were before. They knew information about each other they would never tell another living soul. They told each other about their weaknesses, strengths, and guilty pleasures.

That was when Lexi found out Jake had a huge crush on Britney Spears when he was younger. They swore to each other that what they talked about at the beach house stayed at the beach house, but Lexi was dying to let out Jake's dirty little secret about how he had every album Britney Spears ever made . Although, if she did say something, she knew Jake would expose her love for the *Teletubbies* and she knew her secret would be more damaging to her reputation then the satisfaction of exposing Jake for being able to recite the lyrics to "Baby One More Time" without any music.

During their time at the beach house, Lexi almost split a gut when one morning she played "Baby One More Time" on her laptop to provoke Jake, but instead, her plan backfired because he got up and started dancing around the room doing the infamous moves from the music video without any shame.

When they returned from their trip, Jake helped move some of Lexi's stuff to his place, just so she'd be able to stay at his place and not have to go back to her apartment for clothes as often. When students started coming back to school, Lexi felt sad that her little love break was over because she knew an uninterrupted opportunity to get to know each other wouldn't come around again. Once they graduated, she and Jake would be off to their next adventure. They talked about what cities they preferred to live in. Jake teased her about living in Kansas and Lexi thought New York might be fun, but then Jake reminded her that winter out there was an actual winter full of snow and cold weather.

Lexi hadn't spent Christmas with her parents, which she felt bad about, but she didn't want to expose Jake to their dysfunction and, frankly, didn't feel like dealing with her parents fighting, literally. It wasn't until after Christmas that Lexi found out her mom had permanently walked out on her dad and started seeking medical attention both mentally and physically. Lexi could not have been prouder of her mom. Of course her dad was begging her mom to come back, stating he was a changed man, but every abusive man said that when he finally lost his punching bag. Her mom was staying strong with her decision and getting her life back on track, which made Lexi very proud. Her mom had never had a career of her own. She had always had her husband to support her, so starting a new life was proving to be quite difficult. Her mom was tenacious, though, and kept working at building a new life for herself.

Margo and Parker seemed to start to get along again. She was actually meeting them both for coffee the day before classes started up again. Lexi threw on her yoga pants and sweater to stay warm in the chilly weather. It was cold in California, at least to her it was cold; she knew it was nothing compared to the twenty degree temperature people in the northeast were experiencing, but still chilly for her bones.

When she walked up to the coffee house, she saw Margo and Parker already seated at a table with a cup waiting for her. She realized that, even though she had a fantastic break with Jake, she missed her friends; she didn't realize it until she saw them again. She realized that since she and Jake were so consumed with themselves, she had forgotten to be a friend.

"Hey you guys!" She gave them both a hug and sat down at the table that looked out onto the bustling street. "Thank you for the coffee."

"Not a problem." Parker waved a hand at her. "I'm sorry if this is offensive, but damn Lex, you look amazing. I didn't think it was possible for you to be any more toned."

Margo agreed. "Yeah, I was going to say the same thing. Did you spend your whole break on the treadmill?"

Lexi smirked at both of them. "Did you ever read that study about how having sex can burn a great deal of calories?"

Margo and Parker both laughed. "Look at you, you vixen," Parker said. "Love looks good on you, kid."

"Thanks, I'm partial to it myself."

Margo just looked at her friend and shook her head. "Never in a million years did I ever think I would see you like this. It's like you found your happy place. You are able to be with a man, while at the same time, perfect your workout routine and concentrate on your sport. I'm impressed."

"Well, thank you. Now enough about me. Parker how is Sierra?"

"Done—zo."

"What?" Lexi asked. "When did this happen?" Lexi took a quick glance at Margo when she asked the question to gauge her friend's reaction, but Margo was stone-faced. Damn, she thought. She would have loved to see a real reaction from Margo when she found out Parker was done with Sierra.

"She was starting to be kind of a bitch and, frankly, I didn't want to deal with it. I'm kind of jealous of you and Jake, but I don't have time for a real relationship right now. The season is obviously upon us and I really need to concentrate on that if I want to go any further with my career."

"That's smart," Margo said. Lexi whipped her head around to look at her friend, who was shocking the hell out of her. Lexi wondered if Margo went to a yoga retreat or something of that essence during her winter break because Margo was cool, calm, and collected. It was rather frightening.

"Yeah, so I guess I'm single and by no means mingling. It's time to buckle down. Are you girls ready for the season? Where do you go first?"

Margo answered for the both of them. "We're going to Texas for a tournament. Hopefully, we're ready. I know I am."

They chatted about the season and what they expected from the freshmen who were just recruited. Parker had little to say about the freshmen's talents on his team, but both Lexi and Margo were confident that they had a good batch on their team, with some promising talent to contribute to the team.

Margo changed the subject abruptly, "So, I had an internship over break, well more like I did some volunteer work, but it was so rewarding." Parker and Lexi both looked at their friend with stunned expressions. "Don't look at me like that, as if I just told you I was pregnant with twins."

"I wouldn't be shocked by that announcement," Lexi joked.

"Ha, ha. You pick up that sarcasm over break?"

Lexi chuckled. "Sorry, I just never knew you to do volunteer work."

"Well, I felt like I needed to give back and figure out what I was going to do with my life."

"Good for you," Parker said. "So, tell us about it."

"I volunteered at an animal shelter this winter and fell in love with all the animals. I talked to the director of the shelter and asked about future employment and maybe also bragged about how I was friends with two potential sports superstars whom could be pursued for good publicity. Well, long story short, it looks like when I graduate, I will be the new Development Coordinator for the San Diego Animals in Need Shelter."

Lexi was stunned. She didn't think her friend would come back to school with this kind of news. She felt so incredibly proud of Margo, but also sad because her friend was moving on and without Lexi. Lexi fought back the jealousy that was coiling deep down in her stomach and remembered that she had Jake. He was going to take them places and take care of her. She had nothing to worry about.

Lexi leaned over and hugged her friend. "That's amazing, Margo. Congratulations."

"Yeah, Margo that's quite an accomplishment. So what exactly will you be doing?"

"Raising money for those amazing animals. I was the lead on the Christmas fundraiser and brought in five thousand more dollars than any other year they had the fundraiser, as well as tripled the amount of donations and I did it in three weeks, which was what sealed the deal for the director. I will be doing some light projects here and there until I graduate, but after that, I'll be setting up office downtown. The pay is not as much as I would have hoped, but it's an opportunity I don't want to pass up."

"That's amazing." Parker leaned over and gave Margo a hug. Lexi watched how Margo buried her head in Parker's shoulder and closed her eyes as if it was the last time she was going to see him.

Parker turned to Lexi and kicked her foot under the table. "That leaves you, kid. What do you plan on doing after you graduate?"

The dreaded question…she hated that question more than anything. She smiled at her friends and said, "I will be traveling with Jake." Parker motioned his hand, as if telling her to continue with her statement. "That's all." At least she hoped she would be traveling with Jake. They had never really talked about it.

Parker and Margo both exchanged worried glances. "But what are you going to do?" Margo asked, concern dripping from her mouth.

"Be with Jake." Her answer felt stupid, but they didn't understand; they didn't need to understand. She and Jake needed each other. "I can help him train and be there for him at events. Plus, if he gets a big enough contract, he could fly me to some of the away games so I can still be with him."

Completely talking out of her ass, Lexi wished she could turn the conversation away from herself because sweat started to build up at the base of her neck.

Parker shook his head at her. "Jeeze, Lex, seems like you're giving up your life for a guy."

Rage started to fester in her body, but she tamped it down before she let loose on Parker and Margo. These were her friends; they were just concerned about her. She took a sip of her coffee and wiped her mouth with a napkin. "I'm not giving up my life, Parker. I want to be with Jake. This is what I want."

"It seems like it's what Jake wants," Margo intervened, not really knowing that Lexi really hadn't had a conversation with Jake about their future. "What are you going to do if this doesn't work out? Being with a soon-to-be-superstar can only cause trouble and possible heartbreak. What will you do if that happens? You're going to need something to fall back on. You need a career."

Lexi now was seething and her cheeks felt hot from the anger that boiled inside of her. "We are not going to break up. We love each other."

Parker placed his hand on hers as a calming gesture. "Lex,

we're not trying to be mean. We're just watching out for you. We want to make sure you're going to be okay. We don't want to see you get lost in Jake."

Lexi slapped her hand on the table. "Why does everyone keep saying that? I'm not going to get lost in Jake. That is ridiculous. What does it even mean anyway? I am fine!"

Then, as if all their talk conjured up the man in question, Jake came through the doors of the coffee house and headed straight for their table. He looked amazing, as usual. His eyes twinkled when he made eye contact with Lexi and his smiled stretched from ear to ear.

"Hey, baby. I was just going to call you. Do you want to help me run some fifties on the indoor track?"

Lexi was happy for the escape from an infuriating conversation that had once been pleasant. She grabbed her purse and coffee, which was, thankfully, in a to-go cup. "Sure. Sorry guys but I have to cut this short," she said to Margo and Parker. She gave Margo a hug and said another congratulations in her ear. When she gave Parker a hug, he whispered in her ear.

"This is what I'm talking about, kid. You can't drop everything, including your friends for him. Don't forget who you are. I love you and don't want to see you get hurt."

Lexi took his advice with a grain of salt and nodded. She waved goodbye and linked her hand with the one Jake was holding out to her. He felt so warm and safe, exactly what she needed. Anything out in the real world was too scary. Jake had turned into her home and her protection. She wasn't getting lost in him like everyone thought. She was becoming one with him. They were forming an unbreakable bond.

Jake pulled her in close and kissed her on the head as they walked toward her car. "Mason dropped me off, so you don't mind driving do you?"

"Not at all." She smiled up at him and gave her a quick kiss on the nose.

"What did Parker say to you? I saw he was whispering to you

in your ear. He wasn't trying to tear you away from me, was he?" Jake used a joking tone. Lexi shook her head and tried to come up with something to say, but couldn't think of anything on the spot. He stopped her and lifted her chin up so they were looking each other in the eyes. "Everything okay?"

"Of course." She wrapped her arms around him and pulled him down for a kiss. She felt the tension he had built up in his body from her uneasiness float right out of his body. He met her kiss with his more powerful one. She felt her body tingle from his touch and the magic his lips made when they were on hers.

He pulled away and opened her door for her. "You're amazing."

"I know," she said with a smile. He swatted her ass before she got in the car, causing her to squeal like a little girl. She pointed at him. "Don't get fresh with me or I might have to punish you."

He waggled his eyebrows at her. "I like your punishments. I wouldn't mind getting tied up again." He shut her door and climbed in the passenger seat. She laughed at his comment and remembered how incredibly hard he got when she tortured him with a feather.

"Oh no, we are not talking about feather time."

He swept her hair to the side and started kissing her neck. She leaned her head to the side to grant him more access. "But I liked feather time," he said in between kisses.

She felt her breath start to kick up from the way his mouth skimmed across her bare skin. "Then it's not much of a punishment is it? I'm talking about you running one hundred yard sprints while I get a tan in that itty bitty red bikini I have."

He stopped kissing her and looked her in the eyes. "That's not a punishment, that's torture."

She laughed and put the car in drive. "Then you better be on your best behavior, Taylor."

"Yes, Coach," he said, while placing his hand on her thigh, slightly rubbing the inner side with his thumb. She was in heaven and she didn't care what her friends said. They didn't understand the dynamic between her and Jake and no one had to. All that mattered was they were together.

Margo

Margo and Parker watched in shock as Lexi quickly excused herself from their little gathering and took off with Jake. She didn't even give them a second thought when Jake asked for help, as if he trained her to be his little puppy that jumped at his call. Margo shook her head in bewilderment and looked at Parker. He was still staring after Lexi's wake with his mouth open.

"That was kind of crazy," Margo said, breaking the silence between the both of them.

"Kind of?" Parker shook his head and downed the last drops of his coffee, tossing the empty cup in the trash can behind him. "That was scary. We've known Lexi for a while now and have you ever seen her listen to a man like that before, or anyone for that matter?"

Margo thought about the last three years and how strong-willed, hard-headed and stubborn Lexi had been. No one ever told her what to do besides her coach and she didn't take crap from anyone, but when Jake came into the coffee house and snapped his fingers, it was like she was hypnotized. She instantly got up and left whatever she was engaging in and went to Jake's side. It was a little nauseating to watch.

"I feel a little baffled. I don't know what to say. It makes me nervous."

Parker nodded. "I agree. It's not like her to not have a plan for after college, she always has a plan and a goal to accomplish."

"Do you think Jake is pressuring her, you know, controlling her life?"

Parker took a second to think about her question. Margo tried to ignore how sexy he looked while pondering his thoughts. She was still extremely attracted to him, but knew their physical paths would never cross. They were strictly in the friendship zone, which, over break, she came to terms with. Working at the shelter had opened her eyes to a whole new world. Petty things like crushes and long-legged blondes seemed so juvenile compared to the thousands of animals that needed help in the area. She found a place to be a part of, something that was bigger than her. She had never felt so good in her life. Especially after the rumor-filled semester she had just lived through.

Parker interrupted her thoughts. "I truly don't think Jake is like that. He supports Lexi, you can tell. I think Lexi is terrified about graduation and is taking the easy way out by tagging along with Jake."

Margo concurred with his statement. Lexi was panicking about graduation and what to do with her life, but Margo never thought she would see her independent friend saddle up with a guy and live his life, not her own. It was so strange.

"What should we do?" she asked Parker.

He shrugged his shoulders. "I don't think there is much that we can do. If we push her on the subject, it's very unlikely that we will change her mind and she'll only grow to resent us. I think we need to just sit back and watch her make her own mistakes. And hey, you never know, this might be the best thing that ever happened to her."

Margo finished her drink and Parker took her trash from her. "Thanks. I just wish she had a back-up plan you know. I wish she had something for herself because I'm afraid once Jake starts traveling and she realizes how lonely life is going to be, she's going to lose her mind and, Lord knows, that's never good."

They walked out of the coffee house and toward the parking lot where their respective cars were parked. Margo felt his arm around her shoulder, a friendly gesture, something he always did with her and Lexi. His arm felt so strong and so protective; she was going to miss him, terribly.

When they got to Margo's car, Parker turned toward her. "I've missed this, you know."

"Missed what?"

"Our friendship. Last semester, it seemed like we really drifted apart."

Margo felt guilty; that was her fault, but she also blamed the leggy blonde basketball player. "I know, I'm sorry."

"Did I do something wrong?"

Yeah, go out with the blonde bitch from hell, Margo wanted to say but she refrained from letting the words loose from her mouth. "No, it was all me, but I'm over it."

"Do I get to know what it was?"

Margo felt herself turn beet red. Parker nudged her shoulder and egged her on.

"Fine, you might not want to hear this, but I had a crazy idea that we would…you know, be something of a fling."

Margo watched pure and utter shock cross his face. She didn't think she would catch him so off-guard. She thought he'd picked up a little on her slight flirting, but according to the look he was giving her, he'd picked up on no such thing.

"Jeeze, don't look so shocked. I'm not a cow or anything."

Parker smiled and shook his head. Rubbing the back of his neck with his hand, he looked down at her still with astonishment. "You are definitely not a cow. I just, wow. I guess I never knew."

He just stared at her, making her uncomfortable, so she decided to make her escape before things turned even worse.

"Well, that's over now, so no worries." She gave him a quick hug and got into her car. She pulled out into the road and watched him stare her down in her rear-view mirror. She tried not to recall the look he gave her when she announced her most embarrassing declaration. What was she thinking? What he must think of her. Oh well, she thought, that didn't matter anymore. She had more important things to focus on and they had four legs, not two and the potential to be a major league baseball player.

CHAPTER THIRTEEN

Lexi

"Stop fidgeting, babe; you look amazing."

Lexi tried to smooth out the blue dress she'd worn the first time she ever went out with Jake. She didn't want to wear it because it was full of bad memories, plus she had already worn it to a fancy occasion of Jake's. She didn't want to double dip her clothing, but Jake insisted she wear it again. He pointed out the fact that he didn't get to take full advantage of the slit the first time she wore it.

Things had been a whirlwind for them. Jake had led the football team to another championship season, winning the final game by two touchdowns. Jake was able to score field passes for Lexi, Margo and Parker, which made Parker's life, he said. Lexi had never seen him so excited before when she held the passes in front of his face.

Lexi was so beyond proud of Jake and his accomplishments. After the game, he talked about how it felt so nostalgic to be done with his last college game. He stayed on the field for a while after their last game, soaking in the sights and smells of the stadium he said he grew up on. Lexi sat next to him while he laid on the grass and looked up to the stars. She thought about how her last game was going to feel and how she wouldn't be able to keep it together as much as Jake was. Then again, he had a future in his sport and she didn't.

After the game, Jake was named MVP, which was no big surprise; he deserved it. He brought his team a championship trophy three years in a row. It wasn't the perfect season he wanted, but it was perfect enough, his eyes told her. The school newspaper had a field day covering the games and Jake's success. They approached Lexi and Jake about doing a piece about them and their relationship. Lexi didn't really want to participate, but Jake was so excited, she couldn't let him down.

They were depicted in the newspaper as the king and queen of campus. It was all rather embarrassing for Lexi; all the attention was something she was not used to but it wasn't a deal breaker when it came to her relationship with Jake. After the football season was over, Lexi found herself squeezing in parties and social gatherings they were invited to by either professors or alumni. She didn't know Jake's life was so political, but she stood by his side at every event she could manage to attend, given her busy upcoming schedule.

She made sure all the outings didn't interfere with her playing and school, she told Jake if she felt herself start to slip, she would have to skip some occasions. She only missed one of Jake's events, which was impressive, she thought.

When she was at the different outings, she made sure to put on a bright smile, make friendly chit chat and stand by her man, whom she was so incredibly proud of. She didn't think she could actually feel such pride for another human, but she did. When she watched Jake talk to people and sign autographs, she thought about how proud and lucky she was to be in his life.

Now they were at, hopefully, their last outing of the season…the end of the year football banquet. She wasn't into the heavy part of her season yet, so squeezing the night in wasn't too difficult.

Life was so much more enjoyable now that they spent equal time at each other's places. They would wake up in the morning at whoever's apartment they were at, workout together and then grab a smoothie from Jamba Juice. Being with Jake became routine; it became so right. She helped him train and get ready for the Scouting Combine that was taking place in February and he helped her prepare for her upcoming season. They mainly focused on Jake's training though, because if he had a good showing at the Combine, it was a fast-track ticket into the NFL, which was Jake's dream and now Lexi's.

She fixed her dress and looked up at Jake. He was wearing a slate-gray suit, navy blue shirt to go with her dress, and a black tie. He looked so sharp and sexy, Lexi almost felt inferior to be with him. He smiled down at her and offered her his arm.

"Come on, I want to show off my hot girlfriend to everyone."

"Are you sure I should have worn this dress?"

"Positive. You look sexy as hell. I have to keep my eyes from looking at your slit or I might have an embarrassing problem when I receive my award."

Lexi giggled and placed a kiss on his cheek. "I'm so proud of you, you know."

"I know, babe. Thank you. Let's have some fun tonight."

Lexi agreed and let him walk her into the ballroom where their banquet was being held. The room looked magnificent and it was hard for Lexi not to look around with her mouth open. She was amazed at how much the school and alumni spent on such events like the end of the year football banquet. Her softball banquet at the end of the year was in the gym and there was pizza to eat for food…Not your choice of steak or salmon.

Luckily, their seats were at the same table as Mason and Brooke, who looked fantastic as always.

"Lexi! Wow you look fabulous," Brooke said, while placing a kiss on her cheek.

Lexi looked Brooke up and down and said, "So do you, I envy your long legs." Brooke was wearing a short dress that made her legs look a mile long.

Jake squeezed her waist and whispered in her ear. "I love your legs, short stack."

Lexi rolled her eyes at him and sat down next to Brooke to catch up. They talked about the championship game, of course, and how amazing it was, as well as Brooke's vacation she took with Mason over break. For Christmas, he got them tickets to go to Cancun. Lexi was instantly jealous, but then thought about the beach house and the little world she was in with Jake during winter break. They'd stayed in town, trained and then spent a weekend the beach house. It wasn't elaborate, but Lexi couldn't have imagined doing anything else with the man she loved. As long as they were together, that was all that mattered to her.

The night seemed like it was going rather quickly. The speeches from the alumni were boring as sin, but thankfully Lexi made it through them. After going to multiple events with Jake, Lexi decided if she was ever asked to give a speech at a banquet, she would make sure to be lively in her dialogue and make the speech relevant to what the event was about. The speeches she listened to were wretched and usually about what the speaker accomplished in their life and had nothing to do with why they were gathered.

Finally, it was time to hand out the award for Most Valuable Player. Lexi squeezed Jake's leg under the table and when they called him up to receive his award, he gave her a kiss on the lips and walked up to the podium. Lexi was amazed by how graceful and gracious he looked up at the podium. The speech he gave was wonderful, reflecting over his past three years and how he didn't get to where he was today by himself. Lexi felt herself start to tear up, but gained control of her emotions before embarrassing herself.

So many people loved Jake and she couldn't blame them. He so easily was able to capture someone's heart…even when they wanted nothing to do with him. It was impressive to watch and she knew that he would go on to capture many more hearts in his future.

The awards were over, but Jake stayed up on the stage to take pictures with random people. It was his duty, so Lexi didn't think much of it. Instead, she applied some more lip gloss and watched her man in action.

"Lexi, right?"

"Lexi looked up and saw Professor Lyon." She felt embarrassed because the last time she spoke to him was when she was retrieving her cell phone from his office, thanks to Jake. She inwardly smiled about that day. She was so furious with Jake, but little did she know, it was probably one of the moments that made her fall in love with him.

"Yes. Hello Professor Lyon. How are you tonight?"

"I'm great, what a nice ceremony." Lexi nodded in agreement. "I'm glad to see you two are still together. He's a good guy."

Lexi watched Jake and agreed with her former professor. "Yes, he really is. So what brings you here tonight?"

He shrugged his shoulders. "Good friend of the coach, big supporter of the team. I also do some media coverage occasionally."

"You do?"

"Yes, just on occasion. Say, I was looking at some random DVDs, trying to clear out my office, and I ran across your audition tape."

A shade of crimson red ran from her toes to her head. She put her hand over her mouth. "Oh my God. I'm so sorry you had to be subjected to that hideous recording."

Professor Lyon looked shock. "Hideous? I thought it was great."

"Are we talking about the same audition tape?"

He thought about it for a second and then nodded his head. "Yes, you were interviewing Parker Hill on the baseball team. I thought it was great."

She laughed. "Well, thanks, I guess. It was just for the project for your class."

"Well, you should consider sending it out to different stations."

She waved her hand in dismissal. "No, but thank you. I don't think that's what I want to do."

"What do you want to do?" he asked, with a raised eyebrow as he crossed his arms over his chest.

Lexi wanted to groan out loud and slam her head against the table. She always got the dreaded question, "What do you want to do?" If she knew what she wanted to do, she would tell everyone, but she had absolutely no clue. All her friends knew what they were doing and, for the first time in her life, she actually was ashamed of herself. She felt so lost when it came to thinking about graduating, except when she was in Jake's arms. When she was with Jake, she saw a future; she saw herself not alone and lost in the world. She had a place with Jake. But did he have a place for her? The thought made her break out into a cold sweat.

She shrugged. "Not sure."

He patted her shoulder. "Well, you better figure something out. What are you going to do when Jake gets drafted? Follow him around?"

That was the plan, but she'd never really voiced it to Jake. Holy crap, what if he didn't want to be with her? What was she going to do? She, all of a sudden, got an extremely sick feeling in her stomach. What if he was drafted to a team far away from San Diego? Would he ask her to go with him? She just always assumed they would be in San Diego together, or go away together wherever he was drafted. How naïve of her to think that. The comfort she was feeling a few minutes ago vanished and in its place was dread and panic.

"I guess I don't know."

"A pretty, smart girl like yourself will land on her feet. Just make sure you do something for yourself and don't get lost in Jake's shadow." With those words of advice he patted her shoulder again and got up from the table.

Get lost in Jake's shadow? She wasn't doing that, was she?

She was merely standing by his side like any girlfriend would do, right?

She looked over at Jake and made eye contact with him. He smiled at her and winked, sending chills up her spine. What if, when he was drafted, he left her? What would she do then? The future she was relying on would be completely gone, leaving her to have to return to her abusive home.

Completely devastated, she spent the rest of the night sitting at the table alone, while Jake took pictures with people. Girls were hanging all over him, caressing his chest and pressing themselves against him. Lexi didn't care for the multiple sluts that were at the banquet, especially since everyone knew she and Jake were an item. It was a scary thing to watch from a distance how Jake reacted to their come-ons. He just smiled, put an arm around them and took a picture. By the time the event was over, Lexi was feeling neglected, angry, and full of panic for her future…a lethal combination.

Jake

Jake knew Lexi was upset with him. If her silence in the car wasn't any indication she was mad, then her blatant attempt to not hold his hand on the way home, was. He just didn't know what was bothering her. He thought they had a nice night. They danced, kissed and celebrated a great season. Yes, toward the end he had to take a lot of pictures, but he had warned her about that happening.

They pulled up to her apartment and she practically sprinted out of his Jeep. He turned off his car and quickly followed Lexi into her apartment before she could slam the door in his face. She stormed into her bedroom and he followed every mad step of hers.

"Do you mind telling me what's wrong, or are you going to act like a child all night?"

She turned around and glared at him. If looks could kill, she'd just obliterated him.

"Excuse me?" The way she said the two words was almost frightening. He never knew Lexi could speak with such malice in her voice.

He didn't want to blow up whatever it was that was bothering her to be any bigger than it was, so he used a more even tone in his voice. "I just want to know what's going on. You were so quiet all the way home and wouldn't hold my hand."

"Do you enjoy embarrassing me, Jake?" She unzipped her dress, tore it off and tossed it on the ground. She was wearing a strapless bra that framed her breasts in the most exquisite way possible and she had a matching thong to go with it. Jake had to remind himself to focus on what they were talking about, not the amazingly hot girl standing right in front of him. He took off his jacket, tie and shirt, since things were getting heated up.

"How did I embarrass you?"

She got in his face and poked his chest. "How do you think I felt watching girls throw themselves at you tonight and you not even bothering to shake them off?"

Jake rolled his eyes. "Oh come on, Lex, are we seriously back to this?"

"Don't you dare roll your eyes at me."

She went to push him, but he stopped her with his hands. "How many times do I have to tell you, I don't care about the other girls?"

"It sure didn't seem like it. While you were laughing it up with the female population, I was sitting alone at our table, once again."

"What was I supposed to do? Ignore all of them? That would have been rude."

"Oh, but it's okay to ignore your date? You're an ass."

She stalked off to her bathroom and started undoing her hair. He watched as her blonde locks fell past her shoulders and framed her face.

"How could you even think I would be interested in anyone else? Look at you."

She looked in the mirror and then at him. "You're right. Look at me." Jake took the free moment she gave him to thoroughly check her out and what he saw only made him hard and wanting. "I could get any guy I wanted and for some odd reason I choose to stick with an inconsiderate prick."

Jake felt rage starting to boil inside of him. "Is that how you see me?"

This time she looked him up and down and nodded her head. She pushed past him and went to her dresser drawer. She pulled out a tank top and a pair of boy shorts.

"If the shoe fits, Jake."

He grabbed her arms and stopped them from the busy work she was doing in her drawer. He turned her around to face him head on. "What happened tonight that is turning you into such a raving bitch?"

Her mouth dropped open and she slapped him across the face. His cheek burned from her hand and he rubbed the sore spot to loosen up the tightness that formed.

She pointed to the door and said, "Get out! I don't want to see you." She was screaming, they both were, something they did very well with each other. Her neighbors must really love sharing a wall with the king and queen of the campus.

He stood in place, not making a move to follow her demand. "I'm not going anywhere. Unlike you, I actually want to work this out."

"There's nothing to work out. You're a selfish prick who only thinks about himself and is leaving soon anyway, so just leave now and spare me the trouble."

"Leave? What are you talking about? Are you trying to break up with me?"

She looked up at the sky as if trying to solve one of the world's hardest equations, then looked him square in the face. "I guess I am."

That caused him to lose it. "What the fuck is wrong with you?" He knew he needed to take a more sensitive approach, but he couldn't; it took all the energy in his body not to throw her up against the wall and shake some sense into her. "I'm not going anywhere, so you can deal with it."

She went to push him once again, but he stopped her, pulling her closer. She tried to get out of his grip and strike his chest with her tiny fists, but he wouldn't let up. "Let go of me, you son of a bitch."

"Not until you tell me why you're trying to leave me."

"I don't want to leave you," she screamed, as a tear fell from her face. Jake was so confused he didn't know what to do. She wiggled out of his grasp and flung herself on her bed, burying her head in her pillows. Jake tried to ignore the fact that she looked like a dream laying on the plush comforter exposing her almost-bare ass. Down boy, now was not the time, he thought.

He went up behind her, laid on the bed and pulled her close into his chest. She instantly pulled away and curled herself in the corner, while sitting up. He had never seen her like this. If he was going to get anywhere with the conversation, he was going to have to suck up his pride, use calming tones, and see what was really bothering her.

"Babe, please come here." She just shook her head, so he crowded her little corner and pulled her into him.

"Let go of me," she said, while weakly pushing him away.

"I swear to God Lexi, if you push at me one more time, you are not going to like what happens," he said through gritted teeth. "Now tell me what has you upset. It can't just be the pictures. You haven't had a problem with that in a while."

She looked up at him with tears flooding her eyes. She blinked and he watched two drops stretch down her cheeks. He wiped away the runaway tears with his thumbs. She took a deep breath and then looked him square in the eyes. The blue of her eyes was so startling, it almost hurt to look at her.

"This isn't going to work, Jake…us, we're not going to work."

Jake tried to control the anger boiling deep in his stomach. "Why's that?"

"I can't do a long-distance relationship, especially since

women will be throwing themselves at you all the time. It's just not going to work."

Jake ran his hand over his face. "Who said anything about a long-distance relationship?"

"Jake, what are the odds you would be drafted by the San Diego Thunder? Slim to none."

"I know that."

He watched her eyes produce more tears. "See, I knew I was right."

Jake blew out an exasperated breath and tried to ignore the couple of tears that dropped onto her swelling breasts. His fingers and lips itched to caress her, but he wouldn't. Instead, he focused on the task at hand.

"What were you right about?"

"You're going to leave me when we graduate." She buried her head into her hands and started crying hysterically. What the hell?

He pulled her in closer and this time she didn't give him a hard time. He rubbed her back and avoided the clasp to her bra. All he wanted to do was unhook it and make love to her, to show her how much he loved her and didn't want to be away from her…ever.

When her breathing steadied, he tilted her chin up so they were looking each other in the eyes. "Baby, I'm not going to break up with you. I could never do that. I want to take you with me, wherever I go."

Lexi looked stunned, as if the possibility of them still being together after they graduated was the strangest thing she had ever heard.

She wiped at her face. "You mean you would really take me with you?"

He couldn't help but laugh at her innocence. "Of course." He kissed her on the lips. "I've been planning on taking you wherever I go for a while now."

"Oh." She looked down at her hands that were twisting in

her lap. "I don't know what to say."

He kissed her again. "Say you'll go with me. Say you'll be by my side."

He watched how a smile lit up her face and took over any fears she might have been feeling. He felt bad that he'd never actually told her his plans, but he assumed she was thinking the same thing.

"Of course I will be by your side." She wrapped her arms around him and straddled his lap, giving him no room to be a gentleman. He enclosed his arms around her and snapped the clasp of her bra, letting her breasts fall. She pressed up against his chest so he could feel her hardened nipples on his bare skin. She moved her tongue inside his mouth and started stroking him gently in his mouth. The movement combined with the circular motions she was making with her fingers on his neck drove him to the edge.

He pulled away, out of breath. "You really thought I was just going to leave you?"

"Yeah, sort of. I had a weird conversation with Professor Lyon. He worried me about your move and told me not to fall into your shadow."

A frown crept over his face as he thought about what the professor said. "You won't get lost in my shadow. You're my number one fan, my personal cheerleader. I need you by my side."

"I like the thought of that." She wiggled on his lap, causing him to groan out loud. He was so hard, the slight friction from his pants made her wiggling extremely uncomfortable.

"Babe, can you do something about my probing issue?" He looked as her lips, while he gently thrust his hips up. She giggled and then got off the bed. He watched her breasts move about with her movements and he thought he was going to explode. She was so hot that it almost hurt. He would never get tired of looking at her tight little body.

She pulled him to the edge of the bed and unbuckled his pants. She pulled them down, along with his boxer briefs, springing his erection free. She pushed him back on the bed so his feet were dangling off the edge and the back of his head rested on the mattress. She kissed his lips and then worked her way down his chest until she was hovering right over his hardening center.

He propped himself up on his elbows so he could see what she was doing. Her hair fell on either side of her face, tickling him. The sensation made him even harder than he thought he could be. She kissed the tip of his penis and he felt his gut tighten.

"Babe, you don't have to do that."

"Shh…" She gripped the base of his cock, put her mouth over the tip and then sucked him all the way in. He threw his head back and reveled in the pleasure Lexi gave him. She smiled at him and continued to work the length of his rigid cock. The slight rub of her nipples on his legs when she moved up and down caused him to start to let go of all the tension in his body. His legs started to go numb and his body glistened with slick sweat as she worked him like a fucking lollipop. He couldn't take it anymore.

"Lexi please, let me be inside of you." She gave him one last kiss on his tip and then grabbed a condom from the nightstand. She expertly rolled it on and then straddled his lap, sinking her wet heat onto him. "Oh fuck, baby, that feels so good."

Lexi moved herself up and down and rode Jake like he was a bucking bronco. He watched in ecstasy how her breasts moved about and her face contorted with pleasure from the friction they were causing. Her hips moved back and forth as her hands rested on his chest. The sight of her was so incredibly erotic; he knew the image of Lexi on top of him would rest in his mind for a very long time.

He felt her tightening around him and listened as soft cries erupted from her mouth. He joined in on their movement and pushed his hips up to meet her movements. She continued to place her hands on his chest as she met his mouth with hers. When their tongues met in the middle, they both groaned in each other's mouths and came at the same time.

Pure bliss rolled through Jake's body as she practically sucked him dry with her constricted center. Their bodies slid together as they soaked up every tremor from their lovemaking.

After they fully satisfied themselves, Lexi planted herself on top of him. Her head was on his chest and her hand was making circles on his bare skin.

"I'm sorry," she softly said. "I don't handle unplanned situations very well and I was scared, scared about what was going to happen to us."

He kissed her head, losing himself in the scent of her hair. "It's okay, baby, but next time, can we try to act like rational adults?"

She giggled into his chest. "But then we wouldn't be able to have amazing make up sex."

He laughed. "We don't need to get in a fight to have amazing sex and you know that."

She playfully swatted his chest. "Are you implying I am a bit of a slut, Mr. Taylor?"

"No, not at all," he said, while tickling her sides. She squealed and lifted off his chest. He instantly missed her warmth. "Hey, where are you going? I was comfortable."

She sashayed over to the bathroom and said, "I feel like taking a shower." She winked at him over her shoulder and turned on the shower. He shot out of bed, grabbed another condom, and followed the love of his life into the shower…where they made love again. Jake thought afterwards when he was holding Lexi in his arms about how he was going to propose to her. It had only been a couple of months for them, but being with her had been the best couple of months of his life.

He wasn't going to propose right away, no he would propose as a graduation present. Until then, he would soak up every last bit of Lexi and remember the free moments they had together because, once he was drafted, he knew he was going to be away from her more than he wanted. But, since they would be a couple, he knew everything would be alright.

Lexi

Lexi popped out of the shower and put on her boxer shorts and a tank top. She threw her hair up in a towel and put some lotion on her face. She had run Jake into the ground today at the indoor track. She joined him for about seventy five percent of his workout, but then held back, since her season was beginning and she didn't want to wear herself out.

She had Jake do timed fifties and in between he ran through ladders, small hurdles and hoops, so he could work on improving his footwork, something that saved him while trying to find a receiver to pass to. After the workout, they both went to their separate apartments to get ready for the school week. Lexi felt empty not having Jake around, but knew it was good to have some time apart. Margo was tucked away in her room, most likely getting ready for the school week as well. They had a lot to do before their trip to Texas.

Luckily, Lexi was able to get a jump start on her classes during the break, like she always did before the season. If she started ahead of time, it was hard for her to fall behind during the season because she was already a step in front of her classmates.

Lexi pulled off her towel, ran mousse through her hair and then twisted it up into a messy bun. Her hair would be in perfect waves in the morning. She brushed her teeth and went to get in bed when she stopped in her tracks and raised her hand to her chest.

"Jesus, Jake you scared me."

Jake was lying on her bed, wearing his gym shorts and T-shirt with his hair wet, clearly from a shower. She could smell his soap from where she stood and it was intoxicating as hell. It was like it radiated off his body, wrapped itself around her and pulled her in.

"Sorry, babe." He held out his hand for her to come to him. She reached out and he pulled her down on the bed.

"I thought we were going our separate ways tonight."

"That was a stupid plan," he said, while nuzzling her neck, sending chills down her legs. "So, I made an executive decision and came here. Do you mind?"

He was so cute; he looked so concerned, it tore at her heart. "Of course I don't mind. This is a lovely surprise. Did you get all you needed to get done, though?"

The Scouting Combine was in a week, while she was in Texas, of course, and they'd both worked hard at getting ready and making sure the classes they were missing were being recorded for them.

"Everything is done, except for one thing."

She pushed at his chest so they were sitting up on her bed. She put some space between them. "Jake, we said we would get our stuff done tonight. What did you need to get done?" She felt like his mother, but she didn't care; she was trying to take care of him.

He smiled at her and pulled something out from under her covers. "The last thing I had to do was give this to you." He handed her a velvet box.

She looked up at him in shock to meet his face which was grinning like a gorilla. "Jake, what is this?"

"Open it and find out." He wrapped his arms around her and pulled her back into his chest so he was looking over her shoulder while she opened the gift.

She tore the ribbon off that was wrapped around the special box you could only get at a jeweler's and opened it slowly. She knew it wasn't a ring because the box was too big and also because that would be crazy. Too crazy, but she thought about how her answer would be yes, an instant yes. She didn't even have to think about it. She had known for a while now that she would marry Jake. One day she would be Mrs. Lexi Taylor. She liked how is sounded.

She opened the top of the box and saw a brilliant diamond heart necklace in the box. She choked on her words. She didn't know what to say. The necklace was white gold and the heart had individualized baguette diamonds layering on the inner part of the heart, making the light reflect beautifully off the piece of jewelry.

She covered her mouth with her hand and shook her head.

"Jake, I don't know what to say."

He took the heart out of the box and put it around her neck. "Say you like it."

"Jake, I love it and I love you." He clasped the necklace together and kissed the side of her neck. She grabbed his head from behind and brought his lips to hers while she leaned back into his chest. She lost herself in his lips, relishing in the fact that she had an amazing man who cared for her and cared enough to buy her such a precious gift.

When their lips parted for a second he said, "I love you too, baby. Now, when we're apart, you will still have my heart with you."

Lexi touched the necklace and looked into his eyes, his beautiful green eyes. "Thank you so much. This means so much to me."

He leaned in and stole another kiss. "I'm glad. You better not forget about me now when you're on your long trips away from me."

Lexi laughed and spun around so she was straddling his lap. "I could never forget about you."

"I hope that's the truth." He pulled her tighter against his body and they lost themselves in each other. They spent the rest of the night, not relaxing like they told each other they were going to do…No, they spent the rest of the night burning off more calories than ever…A skill they'd perfected masterfully together.

CHAPTER FOURTEEN

Jake

"You all ready to go?" Mason asked Jake when Jake let Mason in his apartment.

Jake surveyed his bags and let out a long breath. "I think so."

"Did Lexi take off already?"

"Yeah, she's on a plane right now headed to Texas. I was clocking her the other day around the bases and she had some of the best times of her career. She's ready for the season."

Mason grabbed one of Jake's bags and headed out to his car. Jake followed right behind him, while locking up his apartment.

"When is she not ready for the season? You've never seen her play before, have you?"

Jake shook his head in shame. He hated how he never knew Lexi until their last year in college. He was mad at himself for being so self-absorbed and for not attending any other games, outside of basketball. He should have been going to track meets, soccer games, and everything else. Instead, when he wasn't practicing, he was partying; no wonder he never really ran into Lexi. Her work ethic was completely different than his, up until this year. She rubbed off on him and made him work harder than he ever had before. He knew he was ready for the Scouting Combine because of her and Mason, of course.

"I've never seen her play. It kills me that I've been such a bastard the past three years."

They threw his gear in Mason's trunk and got in the car. When Mason turned on his car, the newest Pitbull song came blaring through the speakers. Mason quickly turned down the music and turned to Jake. "That's embarrassing."

Jake just laughed and shook his head. "Pitbull? Really?"

Mason shrugged and pulled out of the parking space. "What? He's worldwide, he gets me pumped up."

"Maybe try some Queen or classic rock."

"Oh please, you can't tell me you don't like listening to Pitbull, especially at the bars when you're dancing with hot chicks."

"I'm only dancing with one hot chick these days."

Mason nodded in agreement. "And she is one hot chick. I didn't know the girl could get any more toned until I came back from break. Does she have a twelve pack or something?"

Normally, Jake would punch Mason's lights out for talking about Lexi's body, but Jake was distracted by the thought of her being naked in his arms. She was toned, but also curvy in all the right areas. Her stomach was flat and chiseled, as well as her arms, but her ass was a perfect little bubble and her breasts were amazingly plump for her size. Jake felt himself get aroused just from the thought of her.

"Earth to Jake." Jake shook his head and tried to forget about Lexi being naked, since he didn't want to embarrass himself. "Dude, you're so gone with her."

Jake agreed. "I am. I can't help it. I'm going to ask her to marry me." Mason almost crashed the car on the side of the road at Jake's proclamation. "Watch it man. I would like to make it to the airport in one piece."

"Are you really? You're going to ask Lexi to marry you?"

"Yes."

"When?" Mason's voice went an octave higher when he asked the question. It was as if he was the one doing the proposing, not

Jake.

"You know you're not the one doing the asking, right?"

"No shit, dumbass. It's just a very big step. I'm not even there with Brooke, yet. Close but not there."

"Why not?"

Mason ran his hand through his hair. "I'm just not ready for that kind of commitment. I mean, I love her, more than anything, but I'm not ready to tie the knot." Mason paused for a moment and drove in silence. Then he spoke up, "Plus, we haven't been as close as we used to be. She's been acting weird lately. I don't know if it's because of graduation or what, but she's been distant lately."

Jake did notice that Mason had been hanging out solo a lot more than he used to. The last couple of nights it had been him, Lexi, and their third wheel Mason. They didn't mind, but Jake and Lexi had to start setting boundaries if their nights were going to continue the way they had been. Jake enjoyed Mason's company, but he enjoyed Lexi's a lot more and he enjoyed Lexi's "special" attention a whole lot more, which she couldn't give Jake when Mason was around.

"Don't let it get to you, man. I'm sure it's just graduation getting to her."

"Probably. So, back to you. When are you planning on giving up your manhood and strapping yourself to a lady for the rest of your life?"

"Real pleasant, you are," Jake said sarcastically. "I want to propose after graduation. I have everything planned, I just need to get a ring. I want to get her a good one, but clearly I can't afford one right now…well, not until I sign with someone."

"Maybe you can do an I.O.U."

"That is so lame. I'm not even going to think about how you just suggested I do that."

"Just trying to help." They pulled up to the airport and they both got out of the car, pulling Jake's bags out of the trunk. They set them on the curb and faced each other. Mason held out his hand and pulled Jake in for a hug. "You are going to do awesome man. Go bury some dicks."

Jake chuckled. "Will do. Thanks for the lift."

"No problem. Let me know when you get there."

"Okay, Mom."

Mason playfully punched Jake's arm. "Don't you sass me, boy."

Before Jake left, he eyed Mason, trying to gauge his feelings. Mason should be going to the Combine with Jake, but didn't quite make the cut. It didn't mean the end of the road for him when it came to playing professionally, but he would have to work at it.

"Dude, I'm sorry…"

Mason cut him off. "Don't, this is your time, enjoy it. I already have Coach working with me. I'm going to make it. I won't have the same paycheck as you," he said with a smile, "But I will be giving your sorry ass a run for its money out on the field.

Nodding his head, Jake grabbed his bags. He tipped his head at Mason and went into the airport. He was going to miss Mason when they separated. For the past four years, they had been attached at the hip and made football history at Cal U. He couldn't imagine having to pass to someone else on the field or talk about his life issues in the locker room with another guy. It almost felt like he would be cheating.

Getting through security was a breeze and he boarded the plane in record time. When they were waiting to take off, Jake thought about Lexi and whether she'd made it to Texas safely. He hadn't been apart from her in quite a long time, but it was something he would have to get used to, especially during the season. He would be gone a lot and, unfortunately, she wouldn't be able to go everywhere he was going.

An older lady boarded the plane at the last minute and took the seat next to Jake's. She smelled like roses and had a headful of curly short white hair. Jake wanted to touch it out of curiosity, but refrained from molesting the old lady's head. She buckled her seat belt with shaky hands and then turned toward Jake.

"My goodness, you are a big boy. I bet you drank your milk

like a good little boy when you were young." She pinched Jake's cheek, then patted it, while she pulled out a butterscotch candy. "Would you like one?"

Jake held up his hand. "No, thank you. That's very kind of you."

"Oooo, a polite little guy you are. If I weren't the age of your grandma, I would snatch you up all for myself. Does a nice man like yourself have a lady friend?"

Jake chuckled to himself. "Yes, I do."

"I bet you do." She winked at him. "She is one lucky lady."

"No, I'm the lucky one when it comes to her."

"Oh, steal my heart." She started fanning her face. "It's getting hot in here." She turned to the lady across the aisle and said, "Do you see this man over here, don't you just want to bite into him?" His seat companion started giggling and Jake wondered if she was either bat-shit crazy or drunk. The lady across the aisle sized Jake up and agreed with the lady. "Where you off to sonny?"

Jake didn't want to make a big deal out of where he was going, since where he was going was just that, a big deal. "Uh, Indiana." He wasn't very good at thinking on his feet, while the old lady stared into his soul and licked her lips.

"A big, strong guy like you must own a farm." She grabbed his bicep and squealed. "That's rock hard!"

Jake was starting to feel uncomfortable now. She was a nice old lady, but a little too touchy-feely for his liking. She licked her lips again and, as she was finishing the last stroke with her tongue, her dentures almost popped out of her mouth.

"Oh dear," she said in a muffled tone, while slipping them back in place. "These bloody things never want to stay put. I told the dentist they were too big for my mouth, but he didn't listen. Now they fall out of my mouth all the time." She pulled them out completely and grabbed her denture cream from her bag. She applied a thick application and then shoved her teeth back in her mouth. Jake tried to not look revolted at watching someone adjust their teeth in their mouth.

"There all better. Now, where were we?" she said, while wrapping her bony hands around his bicep again.

Jake leaned his head against the headrest and exhaled. This was going to be an extremely long flight, he thought.

Lexi

Lexi was sitting next to her coach on the bus that picked her team up from the airport. Lexi was called to the front by her coach and was now waiting for her to get off the phone to talk about whatever was on her coach's mind. They usually re-hashed the games and talked about what needed to be improved on or what went well.

They took second in the tournament, which was pretty good, since they were down a pitcher due to an injury. Marissa had a sore back and instead of coach pitching her, they gave her a break, so she would be ready for the season. It was a smart move because the tournaments they went to were only pre-season games. They needed to make sure everyone was healthy for their conference games, which were of the highest importance. Conference games were what counted toward making the championship tournament.

Personally, Lexi had never played better than she did at the tournament they just played. She made a couple of game-saving catches in the outfield and went twelve for sixteen during the tournament with two walks. She also stole three bases, which led her team to score some winning runs. She had never felt better after a tournament, especially since she was able to talk to Jake before they boarded their plane. He told her the Combine went great and he was able to push himself enough to make a great impression on the scouts. He also thought his in-person interview went well.

Everyone knew he would be playing in the NFL come fall, but what kind of contract he was going to sign was in question. He also talked about how a little old lady hit on him the entire flight to Indiana. Lexi thought it was quite amusing, but apparently Jake thought otherwise.

Her coach hung up her phone and turned toward Lexi. "Great showing this weekend, kid. I don't think I've ever seen you play so well."

"Thanks Coach, I've been working hard this season."

"It shows." Her coach sat back in her seat and crossed one of her legs. "So I want to talk to you about what's going to happen once the season ends."

Not burying her head in her hands and groaning out loud, she held back her obvious dislike for the conversation that was about to take place. She thought they were going to talk about the season, but apparently not. She didn't want to discuss life after college, at least not with anyone other than Jake. Her hands started to get clammy and she felt anxiety start to roll through her body. Her coach was a tough lady and she could easily crush someone only using her words…Lexi was not ready to be that someone.

Her coach continued. "I just got off the phone with the head coach over at Texas University." Her coach paused for effect and Lexi wondered where her coach was going with this. "She wanted to know what your plans were for after graduation."

Lexi groaned out loud and then covered her mouth. Her coach raised an eyebrow at her and Lexi apologized. "Sorry Coach, I just don't understand why people are so worried about my life after college."

"They're not worried over at Texas, they want to offer you an assistant coaching job when you graduate."

Shock was not a good enough word to describe what encompassed Lexi at that moment. Texas wanted her to be an assistant coach? They'd only seen her play a couple of times, since her team wasn't in their conference. They only played each other during pre-season, so why they would offer her a job was beyond her.

"They want you to move right after graduation and go to scouting tournaments with them this summer. I told them I would talk to you and see what you said. I think this would be a great opportunity for you."

Lexi was so stunned, she didn't know what to do. Her immediate thoughts went straight to Jake. If she worked in Texas, what were the chances that he would get drafted to a team in Texas? Slim to none, she couldn't risk not being near Jake. They planned on living together and, if she was in Texas and he was somewhere else in the country, they would never see each other, especially if she was off at recruiting tournaments. She knew how demanding the tournaments could be because she lived through them. Some days she and her travel ball team would play six games and the college scouts would sit through all of them.

Her coach poked her in the shoulder. "Lexi, you would be stupid not to seize this opportunity." Great, Lexi thought, here it comes, her coach's so highly-regarded opinion. "Tell me this, what do you plan on doing after college?"

Lexi bit her bottom lip and contemplated lying to her coach. She knew her coach would never agree with Lexi's decision to be with Jake, but she couldn't bear to lie right to her coach's face, especially since her coach had always been so supportive and honest with her.

"Uh, I planned on moving in with Jake."

Fury laced her coach's eyes. "Jake Taylor?" Lexi just nodded. Her coach slapped her hand on the seat in front of her. "You have got to be kidding me. Lexi, please tell me you are not giving up your future for a guy."

Her coach's voice was louder than Lexi wished. She didn't want the whole team hearing their conversation. "Coach, I'm not giving up my life. I'm making a new one."

"That's bullshit and you know it. So you're going to play house with him, is that what you plan on doing?"

"Well, no. I was going to find a job wherever he gets drafted."

"Why do you need to find a job when you have one already lined up for you? Lexi, listen to me, you need to take this. You have plenty of time in your life to be in love. If what you have with Jake is meant to be, then your relationship will survive a little separation."

Lexi spoke softly, she almost couldn't hear herself. "But I don't want to be separated."

Her coach ran a hand over her face. "Jesus. What happened to the tough independent girl I recruited three years ago? Your game might be at its peak right now, but you have lost yourself." Her coach leaned in so only Lexi could hear her. "Do you want to turn out like your mom, who lost herself in a man and wound up in an abusive relationship? I don't mean to be harsh, but don't repeat history."

Lexi almost fell out of her chair at her coach's words. The only reason her coach knew about her family situation was because her sophomore year, Lexi asked her coach to extend her stay in the dorms over winter break because she didn't want to go home. Lexi had to give her coach a reason why and Lexi had to tell her the truth. Never in her life did Lexi expect her coach to throw her family life back in her face.

Speaking in a firm tone, trying to avoid a hitch in her voice so she didn't show any weakness, Lexi said. "Jake would never act like my father."

Her coach just shrugged. "I bet your mom thought the same thing." Lexi was so mad, she stood up and started to walk away. Her coach grabbed her arm and said, "Sit down Knox or sit out the rest of the season."

Because softball was extremely important to her, Lexi quickly took the seat next to her coach, but avoided eye contact. She didn't want to look at the witch that was sitting next to her. Her coach could be harsh and tell it like it was, but Lexi believed her coach had overstepped her boundaries this time.

"Listen, I'm sorry if what I said offended you." Wow, an apology, Lexi never thought she would ever hear such a thing come out of her coach's mouth. "But I care about you and I want to see you reach your potential and shacking up with a guy right out of college is not meeting your potential. You are smart and a leader; you need to take those traits and make something of yourself.

Don't sit in someone else's shadow."

Lexi was about to explode. She was so angry, her entire body felt like it was being attacked by fire ants. She was itchy, fidgety, and ready to pop her coach in the mouth. She took a deep breath and said, "I'm so sick of people telling me not to live in someone else's shadow. What is so wrong with wanting to be in a relationship with someone and supporting them while they accomplish their dreams?"

"There's nothing wrong with that, but what about your dreams, Lexi? What do you want?"

Lexi opened her mouth to answer, but nothing came out because she couldn't think of what her dreams were. All she ever wanted was to play softball at one of the highest levels and, since softball was no longer an Olympic sport, college was as far as she was going to go. She had no other goals or dreams.

How pathetic. Lexi shook her head in disappointment. She was ashamed of herself for not wanting anything for herself. What if she had never fallen in love with Jake? What would she be doing? Would she be heading back home to a broken family? Lexi felt tears starting to well up in her eyes and she took deep breaths to hold them at bay. She didn't want to cry in front of her coach.

Deep green eyes, a sculpted jawline and an adorable chin cleft came into her mind, making her feel instantly at ease. Thank God for Jake, she thought. If it wasn't for him, she would have nowhere to go; she would be nothing. At least with Jake, she was a part of something, something big. She wasn't living in his shadow like everyone said, no she was his main source of support. She took great pride in being his number one fan.

"Lexi? Are you going to answer me?"

Lexi put her brave face on and turned toward her coach. "Please tell Texas thank you for the opportunity, but I have already committed myself to Jake. I'm sorry if that's not what you want to hear, Coach, but it's what I want."

With that, she left her coach and went back to her seat on the bus. Once Lexi sat down, she watched her coach bury her head in her hands and rub out the tension that must have built up during their conversation.

Lexi tore her gaze away from the disappointment she'd instilled in her coach and checked her phone. She had a text message from Jake.

Jake: Meet you at your place, baby. I love you and can't wait to see your fine ass.

Lexi grinned and sent a quick text message back to him to let him know she would see him soon. Why on earth would she give up such a sweet man for a job that was so uncertain? She was doing the right thing. She and Jake were going to have a fantastic life together and they were going to show everyone how wrong they were.

Jake

Jake opened the door to Lexi's apartment and watched his little blonde goddess run up to him and throw herself into his arms. He wrapped himself around her, grabbed her bag with his spare hand and dragged her in the apartment. He plastered her against the closed door and took ahold of her lips. She was so soft and sweet, he couldn't get enough of her. She weaved her hands through his hair and opened her mouth to him, so he could explore the sweetest thing he had ever laid his tongue on. He would never get enough of her.

She pressed her body against his and moaned quietly into his mouth. He felt himself go instantly hard and was about to pull her shirt off, when she separated their embrace. She looked up at him with water-filled eyes. He cupped her face and gently stroked her jaw with his thumbs.

"Hey, what's wrong?" She shook her head and laid her forehead on his chest. He brought her chin up with his hand and asked again. "Baby, what's wrong?"

She let out a sigh. "I just missed you."

"I missed you, too." He wrapped his arms around her and pulled her in even closer. "That can't be why you're going to cry, though. Tell me." He led her to the couch where he sat down and pulled her onto his lap. She snuggled in close, causing his heart to melt.

"I just had a rough conversation with Coach on the way home from the airport. She was mad that I turned down a job to be with you."

Job? When did that happen? Jake had to shake his head in confusion.

"Wait, what?"

"Texas University offered me a coaching job, but I said I didn't want it because I was going to be with you. Coach didn't agree with that decision and gave me a hard time. When I saw you at the door just now, it just brought that conversation back to mind."

Jake didn't know what to say. She turned down a job to be with him. He never even thought of Lexi getting a job, he just assumed he would support her. He didn't really want her working anyway, he wanted her to be able to relax and enjoy herself.

"Do you want a job?" Jake asked, a little hesitant to hear the answer.

She looked at him. "Well, I guess wherever you end up, I'll try to find something."

"But, do you want to work? You know you don't have to."

"Jake, I need a job. How else am I going to afford anything?"

Jake laughed at the absurdity of her comment. "Babe, I'll have plenty of money to cover whatever you need."

She was genuinely shocked by his statement, which made him love her even more. She wasn't expecting to be supported by him like any other woman would have. She actually thought she was going to get a job so she could earn her keep. He laughed again.

"I'm not just going to be a freeloader." She crossed her arms in defiance.

"You're not a freeloader, you're my girlfriend and I want to support you. I don't want you to have to work. I want you at my side, cheering me on and visiting me while I'm on the road. Now how are you going to do that if you're working a nine to five job? No, you're all mine, my personal assistant."

Lexi smiled and lined his jaw with her finger. "And what exactly are the job requirements as your personal assistant?"

Jake looked up to the ceiling and thought about her question for a second before answering. "Well, I guess you would be required to sleep naked, with me of course, provide me pleasure when I need it and allow me to touch you whenever I need to. Of course, the occasional shared shower and rub-down would be necessary."

She playfully swatted his chest and got off his lap. "You're disgusting. I'm not going to be your sex slave."

"I didn't say anything about sex." He said with a grin.

She shot him a look that said, "Nice try buddy."

"Can I at least get the sleeping naked thing?"

Undressing, she ripped off her shirt and pants, exposing her cute ass and amazing breasts and walked toward the bathroom. "I'll give you occasional shared showers, which starts now, so you better cash in."

As he chased her into the bathroom, he thought about how grateful he was that they were both on the same page when it came to their future and she wasn't getting swayed by her overbearing coach. If Lexi ever changed her mind about what their plans were for after graduation, Jake wouldn't know what to do. He had the ring all picked out for her and was already planning how he was going to propose. Everything just needed to go as planned so he could secure the future he never knew he wanted, but now knew he couldn't live without.

Lexi

Lexi woke up to knocking on her bedroom door. She lifted

her head and looked over at Jake, who was sound asleep. She hated how he was such a heavy sleeper, but she loved how he looked when he was sleeping. His jaw was lined with some morning stubble and his hair was all askew in a bad-boy kind of way. His bare chest was screaming for her to touch it, but instead, she reluctantly got out of bed to answer her door. She threw her robe on so she didn't flash whoever was asking for entrance and opened the door. Margo stood in the doorway, her hair half in a ponytail, half not and she had sleepy eyes.

"You have a visitor," came a groggy morning voice.

Over Margo's shoulder, Lexi saw her mother sitting on the couch. Panic instantly set in and Lexi didn't know what to do.

She leaned into Margo and asked, "What is she doing here, how did she get in?"

Margo leaned in ever further. "I was making coffee and she knocked on the front door. I thought it was okay to let her in, since she is your mother. Now stop being ridiculous and go give her a hug; she looks good."

Margo was right; her mom did look good. Lexi tightened her robe and packed on the courage she needed to face her mother. It's not that she didn't want to see her mom, it was she didn't want to see her mom if she'd decided to go back to her dad. Lexi couldn't handle it if her mom was here to tell her she was back with her dad. Also, she wasn't quite ready for her mom to meet Jake.

"Hey Mom, what a surprise. What are you doing here?"

"Can't I come to see my daughter without being questioned?" She pulled Lexi into a hug and held on longer than usual.

"You look good, Mom, have you lost weight?"

Her mom did a little spin in the middle of the room, while plastering a big smile on her face. "I've lost fifteen pounds and counting, thank you for noticing."

"Wow, that's great." There was an awkward moment of silence between them because Lexi wanted to ask what she was really doing here, but couldn't muster the courage. She wanted to know if her mom was going back to her dad. Instead of being a grown up, Lexi just looked down at the floor and played with the carpet with her foot.

"I'm not going back to him." As if her mom could read Lexi's mind. Lexi shot her head straight up to look at her mom. She was completely genuine with her statement, which made Lexi want to jump for joy.

"You sure, Mom?"

Her mom nodded. "Yes, I came here to celebrate."

"Celebrate what?" The question came from a low sexy male voice. Both Lexi and her mom turned around to see Jake bare chested, wearing a pair of sweats and rubbing his eyes. Lexi turned to face her mom, who looked as startled as a mother could be when they saw an almost naked man walk out of their daughter's bedroom in the morning.

Completely oblivious for a second, Jake finally took in the situation and processed who Lexi's early morning visitor was. He smiled, walked over to Lexi and wrapped an arm around her waist, while holding out his other hand.

"You must be Mrs. Knox. Now I know where Lexi gets her good looks."

Lexi's mom blushed, actually blushed and shook Jake's hand. "Please call me Maria and you are?"

Hurt flashed through Jake's face, but he quickly recovered. "I'm Jake Taylor and awfully fond of your daughter here." He gave her a gentle squeeze. Lexi's mom looked at her with confusion and slight disapproval. Lexi could tell she didn't quite approve because her mom always had a crease between her eyes when she wasn't on the same boat as Lexi. Completely uncomfortable, Lexi shifted in place trying to avoid her mom's gaze.

"Nice to meet you, Jake."

The air was much too tense for Lexi's liking, so she tried to break the tension by bringing the conversation back to why her mom was in her apartment. She cleared her throat. "So, Mom, what are we celebrating?"

Her mom looked between the two of them and grabbed her

purse that was on the couch. "I can see that I interrupted something here; I can come back later when you two are more…decent."

Lexi had never felt more embarrassed in her life. "Mom, please don't go. Uh, Jake was just getting ready to leave." She elbowed him in the ribs and said, "Weren't you?"

"No, I wasn't actually." Lexi felt her mouth drop to the ground. Where was the easygoing Jake that she knew and loved, why was he trying to make things more difficult for her? She tried to give Jake her evil eye, but he wasn't having any of it. "I actually want to know what we're celebrating. Maria, please sit down and tell us what brought you here."

Maria eyed Jake for what seemed like forever and then finally took a seat in a chair opposite of the sofa so Jake and Lexi could sit together. Lexi took a seat and tried to put some distance between her and Jake, but he wasn't having any of that. Instead, he scooted closer to her and put his hand on her thigh. Heat radiated up her leg from his light touch and she felt herself go red. She tried to casually shake his hand off, but it was as if he glued his hand to the inside of her leg.

Her mom was fixated on Jake's hand and that was when Lexi realized she was wearing a short robe, so she tried to cover up what she might have been showing. She was mortified, not only was Jake in the apartment in the morning, but he was making a huge production of them being together in front of her mom. Her mom had never seen Lexi with a guy, so this was a new experience for everyone.

Jake cut through the silence. "So, you were going to tell us what we're celebrating this morning."

Maria shifted her gaze back up to Lexi, stuck her chin up and said, "This may seem strange to you…Jake, but I filed for divorce today." She looked at Lexi. "I'm moving on."

Finally, her mom was freeing herself from a terrible past. Lexi felt like shooting to the roof to do a happy dance. Lexi was about to say something when Jake cut her off. "Maria, that's great." He got up and scooped her up in a big bear hug. "Good for you."

"I beg your pardon?" Maria said. She shot daggers at Lexi. "You told him?" Lexi twisted her hands in her lap and tried to avoid eye contact with her mother. "I don't even know this boy and you tell him about your family secrets? I can't believe you would go and tell some nobody about my life. How dare you?" By now, Jake had let go of Lexi's mom and was standing to the side watching Maria attack Lexi.

Lexi could barely move, she felt so paralyzed. She stole a quick glance at Jake, who had hurt written all over his face and then looked at her mom, who was fuming with fury. This was not the morning she envisioned. A beep went off in the kitchen, which beckoned Margo into the room. Margo stopped mid-stride and looked at the extremely uncomfortable situation playing out in the living room.

"Uh, coffee anyone?" Margo asked, trying to ease the tension. Jake went over to the kitchen, grabbed a mug and poured himself a giant cup.

"Look at me, Lexi," Maria said. Lexi looked up at her mom and wondered when she became so tough. "Were you going to tell me about how you're a floozy and sleeping with random men?"

Mortification was not a good enough word for what Lexi was feeling at the moment. Anger steeped her body. She was angry at Margo for letting her mom in the apartment in the first place. She was angry at Jake for not going with her lead and leaving her alone with her mom and she was angry at her mom for talking so poorly about her and Jake. Lexi finally found her words and snapped.

"Just one man, Mom. I'm not the floozy you might think I am. I've been seeing Jake for months now and we're in love. I didn't tell you because, frankly, I didn't want him to meet you. Not when you walk around with bruises and black eyes as if nothing is wrong. Didn't you wonder why I never came home?"

"Lexi..." her mom said in a tight voice, but Lexi didn't stop.

"I'm happy for you, Mom, I really am. I'm glad you've finally faced your demons and left Dad, but don't you dare come into my home and start calling me names and making my friend and boyfriend uncomfortable because you're insecure."

Lexi glanced over at Margo and Jake, who were both leaning against the counter in the kitchen with coffee mugs perched against their mouths and their eyes practically bulging out of their sockets.

Her mom looked at Jake and Margo and then Lexi. She put her head in her hand and said, "I'm sorry. I didn't mean to be so insulting." She gestured toward Jake and Margo. "Please, come sit down. I want to get to know you."

Margo grabbed a box of doughnuts off the counter and Jake poured two more mugs of coffee and they spent the morning talking to Lexi's mom. Jake told her all about football and the Scouting Combine; Maria looked impressed that Lexi could land such a man. Margo talked about her animal shelter and the fund raiser she was currently working on, part-time, of course. Lexi just sat back and watched her two lives mesh into one. After Lexi's outburst, Maria calmed down and intently listened to all their stories.

Finally, Jake looked at the clock and grimaced. He turned to Lexi. "I have to go. I have a meeting with my coach."

"On a Sunday?" Lexi asked.

"Yeah, sorry." He gave her a quick peck on the lips and got up to grab his stuff from her bedroom. Margo picked up the coffee mugs and the empty box of doughnuts.

"I have to go to. I need to get in the shower and then head down to the shelter. Maria, it was good to see you again." Margo gave her a quick hug and vanished into her room.

Jake appeared back in the living room, this time wearing a shirt and he had his backpack strapped to his back. Lexi sighed as she watched him approach her. She could never get enough of this man. He waved goodbye to Maria, as Lexi walked him to the door. She blocked off her mom so Lexi could have a semi-private moment with Jake before he left.

"When will you be back?" she asked, while grabbing at his shirt.

He stepped away and said, "Uh, don't know. I might just stay at my place because I have a lot of things I need to catch up on."

Lexi felt her gut twist. He was pulling away. She spoke to him in a low whisper. She didn't want her mom seeing her getting in some kind of tiff with her boyfriend.

"Jake, are you mad at me?"

Jake ran his hand over his face. "Now's not the time, Lexi."

A cold wind passed between them. Jake had never acted so cold toward her; she didn't know how to react, so she turned into a blubbering girl.

She grabbed his arm and pulled him closer. "I'm sorry if I upset you. Please don't be angry."

He reclaimed his arm and pulled out his car keys from his pocket. "I got to go, I'll call you later. Let your mom know I had a nice time."

Lexi felt tears start to well up in her eyes, so she went after him into the parking lot.

"Jake, wait." He stopped in his tracks, but did not turn around. "Please don't be mad. I'm sorry."

He turned toward her. "Do you even know what you're sorry for?" Lexi felt her mouth go dry. She couldn't even answer because she was so taken back by the hurt that was pouring out of him. "That's what I thought." He opened his car door and got in. Before he shut the door, he said, "Go back inside; you're practically naked." Then he slammed the door and drove off, without a good bye kiss or even a hug. Lexi had never felt so torn before in her life. She knew why Jake was mad; he was mad because her mom had no clue who he was. They were planning on living together after college and she had never even mentioned him to her parents.

Lexi quickly wiped away the tears from her face so her mom wouldn't see her at such a weak state and walked quickly back to her apartment, so no one saw her in her robe that kept blowing open in the breeze.

When Lexi got back to her apartment, her mom was standing right next to the door. She had most likely watched the entire encounter with Jake. When Lexi shut the door and faced her mom, she knew her mom had heard everything from the look on her face.

"Lexi, I need to talk to you."

"Not now, Mom."

Her mom had a tone in her voice that Lexi had never heard before, it was strong and demanding. "Now, Lexi. Sit down."

Lexi took a seat on the couch and her mom sat next to her. Lexi wished it was Jake again who was sitting next to her.

"Lexi, tell me what you plan on doing after you graduate."

Completely exasperated, she should have expected such a question. It was the million dollar question these days. Lexi didn't want to be having this conversation right now; she wanted to be chasing after Jake and making sure everything was okay between them.

"I don't want to talk about this right now." She tried to get up, but her mom stopped her.

"Well, you're going to, young lady. You need to have a future."

"I do!" Lexi shouted. "But that future just walked out of here pissed at me because I was too ashamed to bring him home and tell you about him."

Lexi saw the hurt flash through her mom's eyes, but instead of backing off, her mom rolled with Lexi's punches. "So Jake is your future?"

"Yes, of course, Mom. I love him."

"Well, of course you do, dear." Her mom was talking in a soothing voice now that made Lexi remember the days when she was a little girl and her mom would tell her stories about princesses being rescued by their handsome prince when she was braiding her hair. "But when Jake is off playing football, what are you going to do?"

Lexi shrugged. "I don't know. I'll find something. Jake doesn't really want me working. He said he wants me to be able to relax and he is going to support us."

Lexi's mom patted her hand and shook her head. "Don't do it sweetie. Don't do what I did at your age."

"And what is that, Mom?"

"Don't fall for a man who is promising you the world. That's what I did." Lexi was about to interrupt her, but her mom held up her hand. "Please let me finish. I'm sure Jake is a great guy and would never do what your father has done to me, but that is beside the point. I let your father take over my life; I let him decide what I was going to do and it left me with nothing. I'm fifty five and just starting to gain work experience. Don't let that be you. Don't make the same mistakes I did. You need to find yourself first before you attach yourself to such a strong alpha of a male."

"But Jake would never leave me."

"Honey, I know it may seem like that and you might be right. He might never leave you, but what if he did? Where would you be? You would end up exactly where I am, working an entry level job, living with a friend, just trying to make ends meet. Make something of yourself first, sweetie. If Jake loves you the way I think he does, then he will let you find your way. And if he is a decent man at all, he will help you find the path you're meant to take. Don't settle for being a trophy wife; you're better than that. You're stronger than I ever was and there is a future out there for you, a bright one. Go out and seize it."

Maria pulled Lexi in for a big hug and then got up, leaving Lexi on the couch trying to process everything her mom just said to her. Her mom walked toward the door and turned around.

"Thank you for letting me in and for being there for me when I needed you the most. It seems like you have a wonderful life here and wonderful people around you. Just remember, you're meant to do something big and standing in a man's shadow is not in your future. Don't be me, learn from me. I love you, sweetie. Call me if you need anything."

Once her mom was completely gone, tears instantly fell down Lexi's face. Was her mom right? Was Lexi following in her mom's footsteps? Lexi never gave thought to what might happen if she and Jake ever broke up or if Jake got sick of her and tested the waters with other women when he was out on the road. That would be a typical move that her father would do. Would Jake turn into her father? She always heard that women chose to fall in love with men who resembled their fathers. Was she one of those women? Jake had never been physical with her and he always supported her; no, he couldn't be like her dad.

Although, he was quite demanding when it came to her not having a job. He only wanted her to be there for him, nothing else. Was he trying to control her? She shook her head, no. He loved her and just wanted her to be with him at all times, like she wanted to be with him.

She thought about Jake and how he'd left her, without the slightest bit of love radiating from him. She didn't like the way he looked at her this morning. Was that a sign of things to come? She felt so confused, she didn't know what to do so she walked into her room, shut the door and buried her head in her pillow so she could cry her eyes out. One thing was for sure, she didn't like how she left things with Jake this morning and, if that wasn't an indication that she loved him and wanted to be with him, then she didn't know what was. Everything would be fine; she needed to stop letting people spook her about being with Jake and their plans for after college.

She needed to forget all the negative comments and nay-sayers and move forward. She needed to work on letting Jake know how much she loved him and how sorry she was about not telling her parents about him. She needed to make it up to him because she couldn't bear to think about not having him in her life. That was not an option. She needed him. He was her future.

CHAPTER FIFTEEN

Lexi

Lexi paced back and forth in her bedroom, worrying frantically about Jake. She had not heard from him since he left her place earlier in the morning. She called him too many times to count and sent way too many nagging-girlfriend text messages. She even resorted to trying to get in contact with Mason, but he didn't answer his phone either.

Lexi stole a glance at the clock on her cell phone and noticed it was almost midnight. This was not like Jake. He should have come over by now, or at least contacted her. She felt a heavy knot form in her stomach. She knew she was wrong for not mentioning Jake to her family, but she didn't think that it would be so big of a deal that he wouldn't talk to her. She thought they actually had a semi-pleasant morning with her mom, after they got past all the initial awkwardness of the situation.

Margo berated Lexi later on in the day about keeping Jake a secret. She was disappointed and Lexi was disappointed in herself as well, but it wasn't like she was keeping him a secret; she just failed to mention she was in a serious relationship with the next possible NFL star.

Rubbing her eyes, she decided to hell with it, she was going over to his place. She should have done that a while ago. She grabbed her keys and purse and headed out into the breezy night. The walk to Jake's apartment wasn't very long, but she didn't like the eerie feeling the night air carried. Shadows played with her mind as she walked through the buildings, causing her to quicken her pace.

Loud music was blaring from one of the apartments and, when she got to Jake's place, she realized the music was coming out of his place. Confused, she pulled out her key and let herself in. She instantly was smacked in the face with cigar smoke and the blasting music. Jake, Mason and a couple other guys from the football team were sitting around the dining room table playing poker. Jake glanced up at her and then looked back down at his cards. He didn't even give her the time of day. She had never been so shocked in her life.

Lexi just stood in the entryway of his apartment and watched Jake push all his chips to the center. One of the guys, Dex, she thought was his name, was already out of chips and was smoking a cigar, watching the guys interact. All the other players put their chips in and revealed their cards. Jake smirked and announced his hand of three queens. The other guys threw up their hands and pulled away from the table.

Not a single guy acknowledged her as she stood in the entryway of Jake's apartment. Jake must have told them some story to make them be so turned off by her presence. The only person that truly made eye contact with her was Mason, as guilt flashed across his face. She was about to walk up to Jake and pull him in his room when a girl popped out of his bedroom wearing one of the skimpiest dresses she had ever seen. She slipped on her heels and gave each guy in the room a peck on the cheek. She folded up a wad of ones and said, "Thanks boys. You all have been lovely."

They waved goodbye and Dex got up to walk her to the door. The girl looked Lexi up and down and smiled at her as they walked past her. Lexi felt like she just swallowed a glass of one hundred proof alcohol; her throat burned with fury, while she tried to hold back her anger and tears.

"Jake?" Her voice squeaked out, as she turned down the music.

The guys all looked at each other and got the picture; they gathered their items and gave Jake a pat on the back as they all walked out of his apartment, leaving only Jake and Lexi in the room.

"What are you doing here?" he asked, while he picked up the chips from the table and stacked them back in the silver case they came in.

"What am I doing here?" Lexi asked, rage boiling over. "I wanted to see if you were okay, since I haven't heard anything from you since you walked out on me this morning." She gestured around the apartment. "Apparently, you're just fine." She got in his face and shoved his chest. "Who the fuck was that girl?"

Jake shrugged. "Just a little entertainment."

Lexi could not believe what she was hearing. "You hired a stripper? What, am I not good enough for you? You have to go somewhere else to get your jollies?"

"Dex brought her," was all he said.

"Oh okay, so that makes everything fine then. Did you watch her as she took her clothes off?"

"Well, I sure as hell wasn't going to tuck my tail between my legs and wait in my room until she was done."

Lexi slapped him across his face so hard that she thought her hand would never recover from the sting that was radiating up her arm. "You're a fucking bastard, you know that?"

He grabbed her wrist and held her tightly. "Hit me again and you won't want to see what happens next. "

"Is that a threat? Maybe my mom was right, maybe you are just like my dad."

That comment brought out the anger in Jake's eyes. She thought she might have seen hurt cross that beautiful face of his, but only for a second because all that was steaming off him right now was pure anger. She tried to pull away, but he didn't let go.

He gritted out. "Don't compare me to that ass-hat of a man

you call dad. I am nothing like him and never will be." He let her hands go and strode toward his kitchen where he threw empty beer bottles in his sink. She watched as some of them broke and shards of glass flew in the air. "How would your mom even know what I was like anyway? She had no clue I even existed." Jake put his hands on the counter and looked down into the sink.

Lexi was mad at Jake, but a part of her heart tore at the sight of him. He looked so incredibly sad that she neglected to tell her family about him. But did that give him the right to ignore her all day and have a drinking party with a stripper? No, it didn't.

"I didn't want you to be exposed to my family. I'm sorry I never told them, but frankly, I didn't care if they knew because I don't really talk to them much."

"Do you know how lucky you are that your parents are actually around? I would give anything to have my parents see me right now," Jake screamed. "Yeah, your family life sucks, but your mom's not too bad and you could have least told her that you were practically living with me. Do you know how embarrassed I was that she had no clue who the hell I am?"

"You don't understand," Lexi said under her breath.

"You're damn right I don't understand. Are you ashamed of me?"

Still standing in the middle of his living room, she felt incredibly awkward while he stood in the kitchen dabbing at something with a paper towel, most likely beer from the bottles in the sink.

"I'm not ashamed of you; I'm ashamed of them. If I told them about you, they were going to want to meet you and I didn't want you to meet them and then leave me because it was too much to deal with. I didn't want to lose you." Lexi tried to keep her voice at a normal level and not shout, like they always did, but it was hard when she kept envisioning Jake watching that girl strip. She ran her hand through her hair and said, "I can't do this. I need to leave."

"Perfect," he screamed. "I'm the one who is hurt and you turn the situation around so you're the victim. Fucking perfect."

"You watched another woman get naked tonight and ignored me all day. For all I know, you went back to your wild ways and fucked her on the same bed we made love in the other night." Lexi's voice was no longer at normal conversation decimals. It had risen to shouting level.

Jake covered the distance between them in the matter of seconds. He got right in her face. "You know I would never cheat on you, so don't make me out like I would."

"But you did. Looking at another naked woman is cheating, Jake."

He ran his hand through his hair and that was when she noticed his hand was bleeding, a lot. Shocked, she ran to the kitchen, grabbed some paper towels and tried to soak up the blood that was coming out of his forearm. He tried to pull away, but she wouldn't let him.

"Let go of me," he growled.

"You're fucking bleeding, you lunatic. Let me at least apply pressure."

He ripped his arm away from her along with the paper towel. "Like you care."

"I do care, you ass. For some godforsaken reason, I actually care about you." She paced in front of him and sucked up her pride. "Listen, I'm sorry about my parents. I was wrong. I should have told them and I'm truly sorry that I hurt you."

The frown that was on his face ever since she walked in his apartment and spotted him playing poker with his buddies started to fade. The tension that was bunching up his shoulders had eased. He pulled her onto his lap and nuzzled her neck.

"Jesus. I'm sorry, Lexi."

Lexi felt her toes start to curl from the way his lips were making pathways up and down her neck.

"What are you sorry for?" she asked, while she gave him more access to her neck. Their relationship had always been like a very old shower; one minute they were incredibly hot and then the next moment they were cold and bitter.

"For ignoring you today. I was an idiot for worrying you. I just wanted you to feel as bad as I did."

Lexi went stiff on his lap and pulled away so he couldn't do magical things on her neck anymore. She got off his lap and sat next to him on the couch. He reached out for her, but she didn't let him hold her.

"Is that why you had a stripper here? To get back at me? Is that what our life is going to be like? I don't know if I can trust you, Jake, to not cheat on me if you're going to turn to the next pair of sloppy tits to get back at me."

Jake placed his hand over her mouth to shut her up. "I didn't invite her here, Dex did and I didn't watch. Mason and I actually went to grab more beer when she did her routine. It wasn't right to sit there and watch."

Lexi stared at him in disbelief. She had never been more furious with him in her life. "So you decided to torture me with the thought of me wondering if you liked her better naked?" Lexi got off the couch and grabbed her items, taking off for the door. She opened it up, but in seconds, it was instantly slammed shut by Jake's hand over her shoulder. "Let me out," she screamed.

He pulled her in tight and she fought him until she had no more fight left in her. She just stood there with her arms in between their chests as he held her so close she had no room to move. She sobbed into his chest and he rubbed her back with his strong hands.

"Christ, I'm sorry baby. I was just so mad at you, but I swear I didn't watch her. Why would I want to watch her when I have the hottest, sexiest woman in my arms every night?"

Tears continued to fall down her face as held her. She didn't know when it happened, but she found herself lying in Jake's bed, wrapped up in his arms. He no longer was wearing a shirt, probably because she drenched the one he was wearing with her tears. She finally pulled herself together and looked up at him.

"Are you okay?" he asked.

"Yeah." She wiped her nose with the back of her hand and

Jake handed her a tissue.

"Want to talk about it?"

"Haven't we done enough talking for tonight, or at least shouting?" She rubbed her cheek against his bare chest and he brought her in even closer. "I hate fighting with you, Jake."

"I hate fighting with you too, baby."

"I feel like we're either having sex or fighting."

Jake chuckled and she felt his chest rise and fall against her cheek, making her feel at home. Jake was her home.

"Well that's because after we fight, we always have makeup sex. Speaking of which…" He looked at a fake watch on his wrist. "It's about sex o'clock right now and we are due for some mind blowing orgasms."

Lexi playfully swatted his chest and looked up into his eyes. "I love you, Jake, and I'm so sorry about earlier."

"I'm sorry too, baby." He cupped her face and brought his lips to hers. "I love you so damn much."

"Enough to never look at another woman's naked body?"

Jake groaned and grabbed the ticklish spot above her knee, causing her to squeal and lean back. He took advantage of her position and covered her body with his. He now had his arms on either side of her face and was stroking her hair.

"You are so damn beautiful, why would I want to look at another woman?"

He kissed the tip of her nose and stared into her eyes as he laid there as if he was searching for something.

"What is it?" she asked.

He shook his head. "I just can't imagine what life would be like if I'd never approached you at that football party."

"There would be a lot less fighting in our lives," she said with a smirk.

"Where's the fun in that?" He kissed her forehead. "Do you ever think about our future?"

"What do you mean? Of course I do, we're going to live together wherever you get drafted."

He continued to stroke the hair that framed her face as he talked to her. He hovered over her so he didn't apply any pressure on her body. That was when she realized he had been bleeding. She sat him up and looked at his forearm. There was a small gash from where pieces of glass must have nicked him. The blood that was coming out of him before was now dried up. She pulled him to his feet.

"We should clean this up."

He stopped her. "Lex, do you ever think of our future past moving in together."

She just shrugged her shoulders because she didn't want to talk about how she already had a Pinterest board set up online with ideas for her dream wedding with Jake.

"Do you want a future with me?" he said, in almost a whisper. He seemed so fragile and little when he uttered the words.

She grabbed his head with her hands and looked straight into his eyes. "Of course I want a future with you. You're it for me."

"You're it for me too." He brought his lips down onto hers and pulled her in close. He had one hand on her lower back and the other one traveled south, cupping her ass. From his firm squeeze, she let out a little whimper and melted into his body. He was practically holding her up on his own while he took control of her mouth, something he so expertly did. He made her feel light, like she could be floating on clouds.

When he finally pulled away, she instantly missed him. She wished they could make out for life. She would need a lot of Chap Stick, but she knew she would die a happy woman if that was all they did. She grabbed the hem of her shirt and lifted it over her head and then un-did her bra. Jake's gaze turned into passion as he took her in her naked body as if he was trying to commit the sight in front of him to memory.

"God, you're gorgeous. How did I get so lucky?"

She pulled off his shirt and pressed her bare chest against his so she could feel skin on skin. It felt so erotic, so right that she needed him right then and there.

"Take me, Jake, please take me to bed."

He didn't need any more asking then that. Even though their relationship ran hot and cold and seemed like an almost terrifying roller coaster, she would never give it up. There was a thrill in knowing they could scream at each other, but then the next moment be so utterly connected, like nothing ever happened. She lived for the moments where it was just her and Jake and the connection of their bodies.

"Tell me what you want, baby," he said, while pulling off her pants.

"You, Jake. I want you."

Jake

Home. That was all he could think of when he looked at Lexi. She was his home, his safe place. He was a giant dick for not talking to her throughout the day after he left her apartment, but he was so damn mad, he didn't think he could talk to her.

But now, all that petty crap didn't matter because he was holding his girl in his arms, looking down at her beautiful face that was full of love for him and only him. He was so damn lucky it was almost incomprehensible for him to understand how he was able to snag such a woman.

As she lay in his arms, she wiggled under him, trying to urge him on, but he wasn't giving in. He wanted to take his time, he wanted to show her how much he truly loved her.

"Jake, please…"

"Shh, baby. Let me take my time."

"I don't want you to take your time." She reached down and grabbed his erection, making him buck his hips away.

"Hey, watch it, lady."

"Take your pants off."

"So demanding." He shook his head as he took his clothes off, leaving him completely bare to her. He was kneeling before her, giving her a great view of everything he had to offer. She put her hands behind her head and looked him up and down, while biting her bottom lip. Her pose made him almost explode on the spot.

"You're hot," she said, while staring at his erection.

"Right back at ya."

She giggled while he came down on her and pulled her in close. Her skin was so incredibly soft and intoxicating, it was hard not to get lost in her body. His lips met hers in a passionate kiss that sent shivers down Jake's spine. Her tongue was demanding as it begged for entrance into his mouth.

Not being able to hold back from giving her anything she wanted, he opened his mouth for her and met each stroke she threw his way. Making out with Lexi, was almost as good as having sex with her…almost.

His hand traveled down her body as he continued to make out with her. He gripped her round breast and ran his thumb over her taught nipple. The movement and friction made her disconnect their mouths and moan out loud as she threw her head back. Her hips jutted forward as she sought release for the pleasure that was starting to build up in her body.

Seeing her react to his touches was intoxicating, which only spurred him on even further. He felt his heart pounding in his chest, as well as a slight pounding sensation spreading down through his legs as his cock jutted against Lexi's perfect legs.

Fuck, he didn't think he was going to last very long. It was a common occurrence he found himself battling when he was with Lexi. She made him beyond turned on so quickly, that he spent most of their time together trying not to go too early.

Her hand traveled down his chest as they continued to kiss. She traced the lines of his abs all the way down to the V of his stomach that led straight to his crotch. He was massaging her breast while she gripped the length of his cock and started stroking him as if it was the last time she was ever going to touch him. The pleasure that spread through his body from her simple touch had him backing away from her mouth so he could rest his forehead on hers.

They looked at each other as she continued to stroke him with an extremely impressive pressure that had him begging for more. He moved his hand down to her slick folds and smiled when he felt how extremely wet she was for him. He did that to her, he made her excited, he made her want him. It was an overpowering thought to know that he could turn on a woman like Lexi.

"Shit, babe. That feels so damn good."

"Jake…oh God. I need you inside me."

He slipped two fingers inside of her as his thumb stroked her clit. Her head shot back and she moaned his name as he continued to stroke and thrust inside of her at the same time.

"Fuck, Jake…please." Her arm flew out to the side as it fumbled around with the nightstand drawer, looking for a condom. Jake took pity on her and helped her out.

After he rolled on the condom, he positioned himself over Lexi and was about to enter her when she shot up and pushed him down on his back. He was so caught off-guard, he fell over like a leaf being blown around by a fall wind.

"I'm taking charge now. You've fucked around too much."

She gripped his cock in her hand and guided it right into her moist center as she completely sat on top of him.

"Motherfucker," Jake exclaimed, as he threw his head back from the pressure she put around his cock.

Lexi placed both of her hands on his chest as she moved her hips up and down, stroking him for everything he had. Every time her ass dropped down on his legs, his balls seized from the pleasure that rocketed through his body.

"Babe, I'm going to fucking come any second."

"Me too, big guy."

Once the words slipped from her luscious lips, her head flew back in ecstasy as she screamed his name and pounded her hips up and down.

The sight in front of him of Lexi's magnificent tits bouncing up and down, her tight body moving up and down, sent Jake straight over the edge as he joined her in finishing off. His legs went completely numb as all he felt was the sweet release of him emptying his seed into Lexi's center. He pounded into her until he didn't think he could move again.

Lexi flopped her spent body on top of him as he gripped her closely. Her blonde locks spread across her back and her breathing was just as erratic as his. He rubbed her back gently with his fingers as she snuggled into the crook of his neck.

"I love you so fucking much," Jake whispered into her ear.

He felt her smile against his chest as she nuzzled even closer. They were still connected in the most erotic way possible and there was no way Jake wanted to leave that connection anytime soon, so he pulled the blankets over them and held his girl in his arms until they drifted off to sleep.

Love had never been on his radar, but Lexi had changed that in every way possible. He was truly happier than he ever thought he would be. As long as he had Lexi in his life, he knew that he was going to be okay. She was his new home, his new haven. She was the one thing that could make him…or break him.

Jake

March flew by. It was hard to believe that Jake would be heading off to the NFL draft in two days. His future crept up on him faster than he realized. He felt like everything was too good to be true right now. He was in top contention to be the number one draft pick; his career was set for him and he had the most amazingly beautiful girl attached to his hip.

"Come on, man, stop daydreaming and let's get out of here," Mason called over his shoulder, while he packed up his backpack. They both had been keeping up on their workouts and hit the gym hard today. Now, they were heading over to Lexi's for dinner.

Jake didn't really want to have Mason and Brooke over for dinner, since he was leaving soon for the draft. He just wanted to spend time with Lexi, especially since he would be away from her for his birthday. Jake pulled a white polo over his head and put on his favorite pair of faded blue jeans.

"Shit," Mason said, while digging through his backpack.

"What's wrong?"

"I left my wallet at the football house. Can we stop there on the way to Lexi's? I need my ID to pick up a package at the bookstore tomorrow and won't have time in the morning to grab it."

"Sure. We're taking my Jeep, I'm assuming?"

"Do you mind?" Mason asked, while slightly cringing.

"No, I'm sure you want to drive home with Brooke later anyway. Are things better with you two?"

"Yeah, I guess so. She jumped my bones last night. I was caught off-guard since, you know, we haven't really done much recently." They headed out to Jake's Jeep. "I was just sitting on the couch and she came strolling in completely naked and straddled me. It was fucking hot."

Jake chuckled. "Sounds like it."

"Does Lexi ever surprise you like that?"

Jake thought about how they made love the other night. They didn't have sex, they made love. It was like Lexi was his instrument and he took pleasure in stroking all the right cords and making her sing his name. Watching her fall apart in his arms was the most pleasurable experience he had ever had in his life and he would never trade it in for anything. She owned him, mind, body and soul.

Jake just shrugged. Lexi had her moments. She never just walked in naked and straddled him, but she was a temptress in her own ways.

They pulled up to the football house and Mason hopped out of the Jeep. "Hey, why don't we pick up those bags of footballs the guys needed to transfer to the field house while we're here? I can help you carry them in, in the morning."

This little rendezvous of Mason's was taking Jake longer then he wanted; he wasn't going to fight with his friend, though. He didn't have much time left with Mason either, so whatever time he had left, he was making sure they were having a good time, not getting all bent out of shape because he was making Jake late for dinner with his girl.

Jake opened the door to the football house; it was completely dark, so he reached for the light switch and turned on the hall light.

"SURPRISE!!!" Yelled what seemed like the entire athletic department. Jake nearly fell over from the voices that trailed through the house. He looked at the crowd in front of him and standing dead center was the love of his life wearing an incredibly short denim skirt, cowboy boots and a cut-off flannel shirt that was tied above her belly button, showing off an incredible amount of toned skin.

His mouth watered at the sight in front of him. He was instantly turned on and wanted to put a sheet over his girl so no one else could look at her. She came running up to him and gave him a huge hug and kiss while the crowd hooted and hollered their appreciation for the very public display of affection.

"Happy Birthday, big guy," she said, while cupping his face. "Are you surprised?"

The people around him were dressed in western gear as Jake surveyed the crowd. "Uh, yeah. I can't believe you did this."

She grinned up at him, extremely pleased with herself. She shouted to the crowd. "We surprised him!" Everyone cheered and started going in different directions, grabbing beer and food. Country music started to blare from the speakers around the house and people patted Jake on the back while they went their different ways.

He looked down at Lexi, who was still smiling. Her hair was wavy, just the way he liked it; he couldn't believe she was all his. He leaned down and whispered in her ear. "You look fucking hot, babe. Like…I might have to go to the bathroom, kind of hot."

Lexi rubbed her body up against his and puffed her chest out displaying an immense amount of cleavage. Jake felt himself gulp. "Baby, please. Unless you plan on leaving now so I can take you to bed, you might want to lay off."

She continued to grin and then pulled him to the back of the house where they normally hung out at the football house. It was usually quieter, but not tonight. Tonight there was a mechanical bull set up in the back and everyone was surrounding the ring.

She kissed his chin and tore her hand from his. She hopped over the fence to the mechanical bull, as someone tossed her a hat. She straddled the bull and winked at Jake.

"Oh, hell no," he muttered.

Mason came up from behind him and gripped his shoulders. "Get ready to have to excuse yourself after you watch this. Brooke told me she's been practicing and let's just say, she's good…too good."

The bull Lexi was straddling started to move as Jake stared at her and never took his eyes off of his hot girlfriend. She moved her hips with the motion of the bull, which caused Jake's mouth to go dry as everyone around him started cheering her on. Her denim skirt rode up her thighs, barely covering any kind of under garments. She had one hand gripping the bull and the other was in the air, causing her shirt to ride up just below her boobs. Jake wanted to punch every guy's lights out for staring at her, but he couldn't move. He was mesmerized.

The slow movement of her hips on the bull made him think of her riding him and he felt himself go hard. This needed to end. The speed of the bull picked up and she rode the bull for what seemed like half an hour, but was really only a couple of minutes until she was knocked off. Everyone cheered for her as she got up. She took a bow, showing off more cleavage then he would have liked. She ran to Jake and threw herself into his arms, laughing and smiling.

"Did you like that?" she asked.

Jake swallowed hard and just nodded. She laughed and pulled him over to the corner they normally sat in where there was a cold beer waiting for him. He sat down and she sat on his lap. He wrapped one hand around her waist and grabbed his beer with the other. She squirmed on his lap, feeling the evidence of how much he enjoyed watching her on the bull.

She whispered in his ear. "Were you picturing me on top of you while I rode the bull? Because I was picturing myself straddling you."

Coughing uncontrollably, Jake nearly choked on the swig of beer he took. Lexi just laughed and rubbed his back. What the hell had gotten into his little blonde angel? She was a vixen tonight, not that he minded. He actually was enjoying the naughty little girl side of her. He made a vow to punish her when they got back to her place.

Mason and Brooke joined them in their little seating arrangement. Lexi played with the hair on the back of his neck and all he wanted to do was get lost in her touch, but he knew he had to converse with people, since it was a party for him.

Jake nodded toward Mason. "You knew about his?" Mason grinned, took a sip of his beer and nodded. "What happened to bros sticking together, asshole?"

"Where's the fun in that? I enjoyed watching you nearly shit your pants in front of the entire athletic department."

Jake took another sip of his beer, while Lexi continued to play sensual mind games with him. He mumbled, "I wasn't going to shit my pants."

"Well I sure as hell wasn't going to clean you up if you did," Mason countered.

Brooke took a swig of Mason's beer and giggled. "You looked terrified when we yelled surprise. It was actually quite priceless." She acted out his reaction and they all laughed, except Jake. Mason made a farting sound with his mouth and acted out Jake's shock while squealing like a girl. They all were laughing, too hard.

Jake punched Mason in the arm. "I didn't squeal like a girl."

Lexi brushed his hair with her hand and said, "You did put your hand over your heart, though, as if you were in the midst of an attack." She acted out the motion and started laughing some more.

Jake finished off the rest of his beer, while his friends and girlfriend continued to make fun of him. He squeezed Lexi's waist causing her to squeal, actually squeal, not squeal like everyone thought he did when they surprised him.

He whispered in her ear. "Keep laughing at me, babe, and I'm going to have to punish you when we get home."

There was a twinkle in her eyes when she said, "Is that a promise?"

Oh hell.

Lexi

Lexi was in the kitchen getting Jake another beer when Darren on the Lacrosse team came up to her. She hadn't seen Darren in an incredibly long time, which was her fault because she had been so consumed with Jake and training that she blocked everyone else off from her life. He smiled at her, so she gave him a hug.

"Hey, Darren. I haven't seen you in a long time."

"I know," he said, while slightly swaying. His eyes were glassy and Lexi could tell he'd had one too many beers. "You're always with Jake these days."

"I know I've been a bad friend. How is your season so far?"

Lexi hated that their seasons were at the same time because she never really got a chance to watch the lacrosse team play. When she wasn't at one of her games, she was either practicing or trying to catch Parker and the baseball team play. The softball team kind of had a loyalty to the baseball team, leaving no time to catch any lacrosse games.

"We're doing pretty shitty this year."

"Oh no, really?"

"Yeah. We lost a couple of our good players during that whole rumor situation with Margo. The guys deserved what was coming to them because of the way they treated Margo, but some of us suffered because of their choices."

Lexi knew that some of the guys left the team, but she didn't know it was because of the rumors about Margo. Everyone thought it was because they had bad grades and couldn't keep their scholarships. It was kind of nice knowing that their coach wouldn't take any kind of bullshit from his players.

She placed a hand on Darren's arm. "'I'm so sorry. I hate that it's your senior year and you're having such a bad season." He just shrugged. "At least you have, uh, what's her name, Darla?"

"Debra," Darren corrected her. He took a sip from his cup, which smelled like toxic chemicals. Lexi wondered what the hell he was drinking that smelled so terrible. "Debra is alright."

"Just alright? She's so pretty."

He shrugged, passing off her comment. "She's not you."

Lexi froze in place. She knew that Darren was always touchy-feely and close to her, but she didn't really think it was because he had feelings. He came toward her and cornered her in the kitchen. Lexi felt her body start to get incredibly uncomfortable. She liked Darren, he was her friend, but she didn't want to see him get himself in trouble. Especially if Jake saw what Darren was doing at the moment.

"Darren, what are you doing?"

"I don't know." He swayed again and took another sip of his drink before setting it on the counter behind her and pinning her between his arms. His face was mere inches from hers. She tried to shove him away, but just like every other male in the athletic department, he was stronger than she was.

"Darren, I think you should back off. You're drunk and you don't know what you're doing."

He leaned in closer instead of listening to her advice. She could smell the toxic fumes on his breath. If she continued to stay this close to him, she was bound to get drunk just from the fumes blazing from his mouth.

"I know exactly what I'm doing. I'm taking what should have been mine at the beginning of the year, when Jake dropped you for some other girl at the Alumni party."

Darren leaned forward some more and Lexi closed her eyes,

turning her head. She didn't want Darren to kiss her. She didn't want him near her. All of sudden, there was a burst of wind and a loud crack. She looked up and saw Jake standing over Darren, who was now on the ground with a bloody face. She looked at Jake and he was shaking out his hand.

Lexi gasped and lunged at Jake when he went to throw some more punches at Darren. She wrapped her entire body around Jake, straddling his hips. She wrapped her arms around his neck and looked him in the eyes. The fury that was in his eyes disappeared when he looked at her. She wriggled on him and kissed his mouth with all her might. When she pulled away, he grinned at her, that boyish grin that stole her heart every time she saw his dimples appear.

"What are you doing, baby?"

"Let's go home," she said, while smiling back at him.

"I'm not finished here."

Lexi looked down at Darren, who grabbed a paper towel from one of the girls at the party. He was applying pressure to the cut on his face. "I think you're done." He ran his hands up her side and nodded.

They decided to go to his place so they would have more privacy…he started to take off his shirt. She stared in awe at the perfect male specimen in front of her. He was so incredibly good looking it took her breath away. His muscles were more defined than when she first met him, due to his intense workout regimen and every last bit of his body was chiseled. Muscles rippled when he took off his pants and pulled her closer to him. When she grabbed his hand, she noticed it had swelled up from where he punched Darren.

"Jake," she gasped. She went to go get ice, but he stopped her. "I need to get you ice."

"I'm fine," he said with a growl.

"Jake, you can't afford to mess up your hand, especially over some drunken idiot. Let me get you some ice."

"I don't care if I broke my hand on that fucker's face."

"Jake, he was drunk; he was harmless."

He pulled her in tightly, so close she felt his bare skin on her exposed skin. It made her nipples go hard, which she knew Jake could feel through her shirt.

"No one," he said in a territorial voice, "I mean, no one gets that close to my girl. You're mine, Lexi. When I walked in and saw him pinning you against the counter, I lost it. No one gets to be that close to you besides me. You hear me?"

Lexi should have been insulted by his blatant display of machismo, but she was, instead, turned on. What was wrong with her?

She pulled his head close to hers and kissed him, letting him know she understood. She threaded her hands through his hair as his hands made their way up her stomach, just below her breasts. His touch made her tremble in her boots and all she wanted to do was get naked with him. She pulled away from him and shimmied out of her skirt, leaving her boots on. Then she grabbed the front tie of her shirt and undid it. She watched Jake's eyes widen at the display of the itty bitty red lace bra and panties she was wearing. She watched his chest heave and could see the almost animal instincts running through his eyes.

She gave him a little twirl and flipped her hair over her shoulder. "What do you think?"

Jake swallowed, hard. "I think I'm the luckiest son of a bitch this side of the Mississippi," Jake said with a twang. Lexi giggled and ran into his room, throwing herself on his bed. She started to take off her boots, but he stopped her. "Leave them on."

Lexi grinned and slowly sank into his warm inviting bed. She was the luckiest little lady this side of the Mississippi, she thought, as Jake slid his boxers down, revealing how turned on he was. Yes, she was extremely lucky indeed.

CHAPTER SIXTEEN

Lexi

Lexi sat in the home dugout before the game retying her cleats. Excitement bubbled through her body. She'd received one of the best phone calls from Jake last night. He was drafted by the San Diego Thunder. She couldn't believe it when she heard the news. She wasn't able to watch the draft on TV because she was playing a double-header against their ever-present rival. Luckily, they won both games, making the day that more glorious. Jake was trying to catch a flight home so they could celebrate, but he wasn't sure exactly when he would get back.

Lexi had the hardest time going to sleep last night. She thought about where they could live, how she would be close to Margo and not have to leave the hometown she loved so much, plus she got to stay close to the beach, which was always a major plus for her. She talked to Jake for hours on the phone, discussing parts of town they wanted to live in and how they were going to go furniture shopping. He told her anything she wanted, she could have. She felt at ease. She didn't have to worry about life, she was taken care of by Jake.

Even though she knew her life was set now, a little voice in the back of her head kept nagging her. Ever since she talked to her mom, she got the feeling that her mom was right. Lexi wondered constantly if she was doing the right thing, if being by Jake's side was what she needed in life. When she talked to Jake about the new chapter coming up in their lives, he kept saying how she could stay at home and relax, make him dinner, be the little housewife he always wanted. Even though that sounded like heaven, it made her feel a little restless…like, if she settled for that life, she would always feel like something was missing.

She pushed the negative thoughts to the back of her head and, instead, surveyed the field. The grass had never looked greener. If they won this game today, they would be one step closer to a spot in the championship tournament, something she and her teammates had worked so incredibly hard for. She watched the grounds crew put their final touches of chalk around the pitching circle and wheel their chalk cart off the field, making sure to avoid any pristine lines they'd already made.

"You ready for this?" her coach asked, while standing next to her.

"Always, Coach."

"Good, I wanted to make sure your head was in the game."

"Why wouldn't it be?"

"Well after such news about your boyfriend last night, I for sure thought your head would be out of it."

Lexi frowned at the suggestion. Except for the beginning of the year, her head had always been in the game, especially when it mattered. She prided herself on being able to close off the rest of the world when she was on the field.

"No worries, Coach. I'm here to play."

"Good." Her coach paused for a second and then let out a long breath. "I'm assuming you're still going to stick to your original plan and stay with him?" Her coach had an annoyed tone to her voice. Lexi just nodded, not being able to look at the disappointment in her coach's eyes. "Well, I hope everything works out for you. It's a shame, though." With that, her coach walked away, making the nagging voice come back in full force.

To avoid punching the cinderblock wall of the dugout out of

frustration, Lexi grabbed her bat and went to hit a couple more balls off the tee before the game started.

It was the third inning and Lexi had already hit a double in the first that spiked a little hitting sequence in her team, giving them a two-run lead. She was feeling really good today, even though there was an emotional war going on in her head. The opposing pitcher was warming up while Lexi was waiting on deck, loosening her back with her overdramatic swing. Warm-up music was playing, but was instantly faded out and replaced with chanting. What the hell was that?

She looked around and spotted ten incredibly ripped men wearing jeans with their shirts off walking in a line over to the field. There were hoots and hollers from the crowd and the line of men took up residence against the fence. They all had a letter painted on their chests. They scrambled and stood in formation. Across their chests spelled out, "Let's Go Lexi." They were cheering her name and making a huge production, so much that the opposing team stopped warming up and just stared. Lexi shook her head and knew Jake was behind this. He couldn't be there to support her in person, so he sent his guys in his place.

Margo leaned over and, in her ear said, "Uh, how am I supposed to concentrate now?"

Lexi laughed. "I have no clue. Let me know if you find out."

The number nine batter, Mary, got on base with a surprise bunt. She was a lefty slapper just like Lexi and coach was hoping she would be the lead off next year. Lexi had been working with her all season and Mary had showed a lot of improvement.

Lexi stood up at the plate and the football players let out a huge whoop, causing a scene once again. Lexi blocked them out and went through her routine before she got in the batter's box. She watched her coach as she ran through a bunch of different hand signals, giving Lexi the sign to execute a hit and run, one of Lexi's favorite things to do. Lexi patted the top of her helmet, then the middle of her bat and stepped in the back of the batter's box, giving herself plenty of room to slap the ball.

As the pitcher started her motion, Lexi started to move her feet and instantly made contact with the ball, sending it flying over the right fielder's head. Lexi was off, sprinting around the bases; she watched as Mary rounded third, giving Lexi the open base. She made eye contact with her coach as she waved Lexi to get down and slide. Lexi hit the dirt, reveling in the feeling of sliding in the dirt, as her hands gripped the white base in front of her. After she touched the base, she felt the third baseman touch her back with her glove, but she was too late; Lexi was already safe.

Her coach called time-out as Lexi stood up and shook the dirt off of her. Her coach patted her on the head, showing her satisfaction in Lexi's execution.

Her coach leaned over and said, "A single would have been just fine, but I'll take a triple any day."

Lexi chuckled and settled herself back on the base.

The announcer cut in before the next pitch was thrown. "Excuse me ladies and gentlemen. I would like to announce that Lexi Knox just surpassed the leader in all-time hits for college softball. Please join me in congratulating her." Everyone stood up and gave her a cheer. The pitcher threw the ball Lexi had just hit to her coach, which her coach pocketed, letting Lexi know her record breaking ball would be safe with her until after the game.

There was a loud cheer and a whooping that caught Lexi's attention. She looked over and saw Jake running up to the field with an exclamation point painted on his chest. He looked mouthwateringly good. He winked at her and everyone took notice. More cheers erupted from the stands that almost blew Lexi over. She had never felt so much love, but then she noticed no one was looking at her. They were all looking at Jake, who stood there waving at the crowd.

"Ladies and Gentlemen. What a surprise," the announcer chimed in. "Our very own Jake Taylor is here at the stadium today. For those of you who might be living in the dark, he was just drafted to our home team the San Diego Thunder. We could not be prouder of you Jake and will be cheering you on as you move forward in your professional career. Let's give Jake a round of applause for his accomplishments."

Lexi watched as Jake stood there and shook peoples' hands, signing autographs and soaking up the limelight that had been instantly taken away from her. Lexi tried not to let the pain that was festering in the pit of her stomach take over, but it was. She had just broken a national record and received two seconds of praise before Jake came waltzing in.

Her coach turned to Lexi and whispered in her ear. "Get your head back in the game, Knox. I see those wheels turning; wait to break down afterwards." Her coach gave her a hard squeeze with her hand and then went back to her coach's box to give the next batter her usual signals of swing away. No squeeze bunt, Lexi thought. Probably because her coach knew Lexi needed a second to regain her composure.

They ended up winning the game, putting them one step closer to the playoffs. Lexi ended the game going four for four and was a homerun away from hitting a cycle. She had only hit one homerun in her college career; it was very rare since she was slapper. Lexi cheered with her team, but didn't feel the excitement everyone else did. Instead, she felt empty.

The school sports reporter came in the dugout and pulled out his recorder. It was the usual bit they went through after every game. "Hey Lexi, got a second?"

"Of course," Lexi said to Harry, who had a huge head of curly hair on him. His parent's named him right, he was hairy for sure.

"Great, thanks. Good game today. Tell me how excited you are that Jake was drafted by the San Diego Thunder, how did you find out?"

Lexi almost stumbled backward. Not the question she thought he was going to ask. What happened to, how does it feel knowing you are almost headed to the playoffs or how about that record breaking hit you had? Lexi looked over Harry's shoulder and saw the school photographer taking a picture of Jake with his guys. Harry followed her gaze and smiled.

"We want to do a whole story on Jake and how, even though he just got drafted, he still came to the softball field to cheer the girls on."

Girls? Lexi refrained from punching Harry in the face. Jake was here for one girl and that was her, not that she really wanted to welcome him home right now. He was soaking up the limelight like it was his job. She always knew he had to put on a good face, but the Jake she was seeing right now was different. It was as if he came back as a different person. She shook her head; she was being too sensitive.

She went back to answering his question. "I'm very excited for Jake. He called me last night to let me know who drafted him. Since we were playing a double header, I was unable to watch everything go down, but I know he is extremely excited to stay in his hometown. That was the ideal situation he wanted."

"That's great," Harry said. "Do you think he is going to stick with number eight and carry on the tradition?"

Lexi had to mask her face at the ridiculous question. "Uh, I'm sure if it's available, he'll want to snatch it up. It's his go-to number."

"Did you pick number seventeen because it added up to Jake's number?"

Okay, this was getting absurd. She crossed her arms over her chest and sat back to enjoy the Jake ride. "No, I didn't know Jake when I first came here. We just started dating this year."

"Oh, I didn't know if you switched your number."

Lexi was burning with fury. "What do you think, I'm some lovesick puppy that my world revolves around the man I'm dating? Well, it doesn't. I've been able to take care of myself and make decisions on my own since way before Jake came around. I don't need him convincing me which godforsaken number to slap on my back."

"But, I heard you had a job opportunity to work as an assistant coach with Texas, but dropped the offer because you would rather be by Jake's side."

Lexi was inches away from slapping the idiotic reporter in the face. Instead she grabbed her bat bag and said over her shoulder. "We'll see about that." Then she stormed off, using the back exit to avoid Jake and the crowd that had formed. She wasn't quite ready to face him yet.

Jake

The softball field was completely empty. Jake looked around, but didn't spot Lexi anywhere. He knew he had to stay longer at the game to accommodate all the well-wishers, but he thought after she was done talking to the reporter, she would sidle up next to him and be by his side, like she always did. When he went back to the parking lot, her car was nowhere in sight. Frowning, he pulled out his cell phone to find out where Lexi went.

Jake: Babe, where are you?

He went to the locker room and took a quick shower to wash off the paint from his chest. His plan to surprise her was well executed and he was happy he had the chance to catch her record-breaking hit. He could not have been more proud of his girl. His phone chimed back.

Lexi: At home, in bed. Have a terrible headache.

Jake threw his clothes on as quickly as possible after drying off from the shower and went out to his Jeep to drive to her apartment. He felt like an ass that he stayed longer with his fans when Lexi wasn't feeling well. He asked if she wanted him to pick anything up while he was out, she said no. She must have been feeling really bad because her text messages were short and lacking any kind of emotion. It was so not like her.

He pulled up to her apartment and let himself in with his key. Her door was shut and he saw no light coming from underneath.

Slowly he opened the door and went to her bed. She was lying still, so he assumed she was asleep. He closed the door quietly and tore his shirt off. He pulled back the covers of the bed and slipped in next to her, while wrapping his arms around the sole reason he was able to function.

He must have startled her because she stiffened in his grasp.

"It's just me, baby." He kissed the side of her head and pulled her in closely. "How are you feeling?"

"Fine," she squeaked out with a nasal like tone. Maybe she was coming down with something.

"Do you need anything?"

"No, I'm just going to sleep."

"Okay." He pulled her in closer and lifted the back of her shirt so her skin was touching his. He always felt so at home when they were touching so intimately.

"Good game, by the way, baby. You were amazing."

She must have drifted off to sleep because she didn't say anything to him. He snuggled in closer and buried his head in her hair, while closing his eyes. This was perfect, he thought; he had the girl, he had the NFL contract, he got to stay in his hometown, nothing could be sweeter.

Lexi

Lexi lay stiff in her bed while Jake held onto her tight. She quickly wiped away her tears when she heard Jake come into her room. She couldn't let him see her crying; he would instantly want to know what was going on and she wasn't ready to dive down into her feelings just yet. She'd faked a headache, hoping Jake wouldn't come over, but she should have known better. She knew he would want to make sure she was okay.

Being okay was the farthest thing from her feelings right now. She wasn't okay at all. Today was like a huge slap in her face. She knew Jake was the center of this school's attention, but she couldn't get past the fact that she was doing what everyone told her she was…living in his shadow. She tried to deny it, but everyone was right and she finally saw the ugly truth today. While she had made a huge accomplishment in her life, it was overshadowed by Jake's presence. Not that she needed a parade, but a little acknowledgement was all she was looking for and it wasn't like Jake helped. He could have stopped everyone and reminded them of why he was at the game and who he was cheering for, but he didn't. What did that say about him?

He wanted her to be his little sidekick, be at his beck and call and she didn't think she could do that, especially after witnessing what happened today. He didn't even realize she was gone until he was done with his fans. He didn't text her until a half hour after she got back to her place. The thought made her sick to her stomach.

She heard his heavy breathing and knew he had fallen asleep. She didn't want to be held by him right now; she wanted to be by herself so she could think everything through. Could she really live the life Jake was handed? Would he soon forget she even existed? The thought of him ignoring her again like he did today made tears fall from her eyes. Maybe today was a blessing. Maybe today was the rude awakening she needed, the swift kick in the ass her coach and others were trying to give her.

Could she really give up Jake and all the certainty she was looking forward to? With Jake, she knew she would be taken care of and she wouldn't have to fend for herself. She could rely on Jake for everything. But did she want that? Would he actually be there for her like she needed him to? Because he wasn't there today. The minute he had all the attention, he completely forgot about her. It would only get worse, she thought. The attention would only get stronger; he would be hounded by more women trying to throw themselves at him while he was on away trips and she would sit at home, alone, with nothing to do but plan out the next meal to serve him when he got home.

Where had she gone wrong? She shook her head as more tears fell. She let herself get so wrapped up in a man that she lost herself. Not that she ever knew who she really was, but Jake should have tried to help her establish that definition. Instead, he hindered her ability to focus on herself and made her into his little tag-a-long.

He rubbed the bare side of her belly and snuggled even closer, if that was possible. Lexi silently cried herself to sleep, wondering how she was going to even begin to talk about her feelings with Jake and if he would even care about the emotional battle her brain was currently going through.

Jake

Feeling amazing, Jake walked into the locker room. He'd slipped out of bed as quietly as possible so he wouldn't disturb Lexi, in case she still had a headache. Now that his future was set, he was going to propose to Lexi. He had the ring picked out, now he just needed to go pay for it.

He couldn't believe his luck when the Thunder drafted him. It was his number one pick and apparently he was theirs. He wished he had his parents with him to celebrate; they would be so proud, but he had a great support system in place and he had Lexi. That was all that mattered.

Thinking about his parents, Jake knew they would have loved Lexi; they would have loved everything about her from her spirit to her sweetness to her ability to put him in his place when he was being a smartass. He was upset they never got to meet her, but he knew they would approve of his hopefully soon-to-be wife.

Jake was going to take Lexi out tonight to celebrate their new life, since they didn't get a chance yesterday. He felt bad that she wasn't feeling well; it made his stomach twist in a knot when she wasn't her normal self. He thrived on her ability to lighten the room whenever she was around him. He thought about proposing tonight, but he really wanted the ring when he did it. He didn't want to give her an I.O.U.

Jake was tying up his sneakers when Mason walked in the room and stopped dead in his tracks and gave Jake a painful look. Jake sat up and asked, "What's wrong with you?"

There should be no painful look on Mason's face, especially since he was drafted by the Denver Stallions. It was sad that they were no longer going to be playing with each other, but Jake was damn proud of his friend. Mason was going to have to work hard to earn his spot on the team, but Jake had no doubt in his mind that Mason was going to make an impact on the Stallion's offense.

Mason pulled out a rolled up newspaper. "Read the headline today?"

"Does it look like I'm a fifty-year-old man who wakes up at the crack of dawn to read the newspaper? No, I barely rolled out of bed and kissed my girl goodbye before getting here."

"You might want to read it." Mason tossed him the rolled up newspaper that fell right in front of Jake and unfolded, revealing a very disturbing headline and picture. The major headline of the paper was a picture of Jake signing autographs at Lexi's game and a broken down picture of Lexi after the game. She was sitting in the dugout with her head between her hands. The headline read, "We will see…"

"What the fuck is this?" Jake asked.

"Just read it, man." Mason went off to the bathroom as Jake sat back in his locker and read the article.

"We will see…"

Jake Taylor, quarterback and center of every girl's dream at Cal U might be single and ready to mingle in the upcoming days. This past weekend, Jake was drafted by our very own San Diego Thunder, something the school is incredibly proud of, but not everyone is happy about our home-grown hero's success. After being approached after a victorious three-game series against Cal U's rival, Lexi Knox was less than thrilled about her famous boyfriend's new career path.

When asked if she watched the draft she simply stated, "I was unable to watch everything go down." While every other girl was holding her breath as Jake sat patiently to see which team would pick him up, she was busy playing softball. Can't hold that against her, but the enthusiasm dripping from her words was less than satisfying.

We briefly discussed the similarities in their numbers and what kind of connection it meant, Jake being eight and Lexi being seventeen, but she set us straight in our assumptions.

"What, do you think I'm some lovesick puppy that my world revolves around the man I'm dating? Well, it doesn't. I've been able to take care of myself and make decisions on my own since way before Jake came around. I don't need him convincing me which godforsaken number to slap on my back." Lexi spat back at us.

It seems like the lovey-dovey act the superstar and his girl have been putting on has all been a façade. When asked to comment about their relationship, all their friends declined interviews saying Jake and Lexi's relationship was between them and only them. A typical response whenever asked, but now doesn't it seem a little strange, especially since the tension between the two has been thick enough to cut with a knife?

Lexi was offered a job with Texas as an assistant coach. It was assumed she would be shacking up with Jake after graduation and proposal rumors have also been flying around for the two lovebirds, but when we told her we knew she would be living with Jake after graduation her exact words were, "We will see about that." Then she stormed off.

Ladies, go get your hair done and your waxes taken care of because Jake Taylor is soon to be free and will need a warm body to fill his cold, cold bed.

**Since the Women's Softball team won the three games series this past weekend, they are one step closer to clinching a spot in the playoffs. Lexi Knox also surpassed the record for all-time collegiate hits in the nation.*

Jake sat at his locker staring at the paper when Mason came back into the locker room and sat next to him. They didn't say anything to each other; they just sat there quietly. The interviewer had to have jumbled her words. There was no way Lexi was turning back on her promise to be with him after college. They loved each other. Jake stood up and tore the newspaper in half.

"Jake, calm down; there has to be a reasonable explanation for all this."

Jake didn't even look at Mason, he grabbed his keys and headed for his Jeep. He needed to see Lexi. He needed to clear the air. There was no way he could function knowing she might not want to be with him.

When he reached Lexi's apartment, he tore through the doors and noticed she was still in bed. That was odd. She was never in bed this late. He went over to her and that was when he saw her tear-stained face. He rolled her over and pulled her into his arms. He sat there and held her until she calmed down from the sobs that were pouring from her mouth.

"Shhh, what's wrong baby?" She shook her head and didn't say anything. "Baby, please talk to me. I'm scared. I read something in the newspaper this morning and it made me really nervous." She stiffened in his arms and pulled away.

She frantically wiped away at her face and backed herself up into the corner of her bed. "You read Harry's article?"

Jake was confused. "When did you read it?"

"I didn't."

"Then how do you know what it says?" Jake's stomach was so twisted up in knots, he felt like he was going to puke any second.

"I know what I said," she whispered.

Completely deflated, he realized at that moment that she wasn't taken out of context in the article, all the things she was quoted for were true. She actually said them. He just stared at her. He didn't know what to say. She pulled her knees up to her chest and hugged herself. She didn't say anything either. The silence between them was deafening.

"Lexi…"

"Please, Jake, don't say anything."

"Well, one of us has to say something; we just can't sit here in silence. Talk to me."

Lexi twisted her hair on her finger, a tendency Jake noticed she did when she was feeling nervous or anxious.

"We need to talk."

Oh, hell no.

"Lexi, please don't." She held up her hand.

"Jake, I can't do this."

Jake's heart felt like it was going to pop out of his chest. "Can't do what? This conversation? It's okay baby, we can just go grab breakfast…" He tried to get closer, but she held out her hand as if she'd put up a force field.

"No, Jake. I can't do us."

She might as well have ripped his heart out of his chest and tossed it to opposing linemen to do what they want with it. This could not be happening. Jake felt his throat close up and he lost all ability to speak.

Lexi got out of the bed and paced her room with her hand to her head. She was wearing one of his T-shirts and that was it. The sight of her in front of him squeezed out every last bit of his heart. He couldn't take the sight of her when she uttered such foul words about their relationship.

"What are you saying, Lex?" he was able to barely whisper.

"I can't make you happy the way you want me to. I can't be that perfect little wife that waits around for you while you are off playing games. I need to make something of myself Jake; I don't want to be like my mom who depended on her man. Look what happened to her."

Jake stood up in anger and pointed his finger at her. "What did I tell you about comparing me to your dad? I am nowhere even close to that man."

"You might not be him, but the way you try to control my life is what he did to my mom."

Jake ran his hand over his face in anger and shouted. "How the hell am I controlling your life?"

Lexi looked at him as if he was stupid. "You don't want me to work; you just want me to stay home and be at your beck and call."

"I never said I wanted you at my beck and call. I want to be able to provide for you and for you to relax, enjoy life."

"I don't need to relax," she shouted back. "I want to be my own person. I don't want to live in your shadow."

"Is that how you see it? That's a lovely shade of green on you, Lex."

"Fuck you." She pushed at his chest, but he didn't move. "Did you even know I broke a huge fucking record yesterday? I made a huge accomplishment yesterday and once you showed up at the field, no one gave two shits about what I did."

"How is that my fault?"

Jake tried to ignore how Lexi's shirt kept lifting up and down, giving him peeks at her underwear when she was flailing her arms about in anger.

"It's your fault because you should have redirected the attention back to me, at least for a second. I know what you did was greater than what I will ever be able to accomplish sports-wise, but for once Jake, you should have let me have the spotlight. If you loved me, you would have redirected everyone's attention back to what was happening on the field, not off."

Damn it, she was right. He hated admitting it, but she was so God damn right, it tore even harder at his chest. How could he have been so naïve? She didn't get to go on playing the sport she loved like he did. Instead, she had a couple of games left and every moment in those games mattered and he stole one of the biggest moments of her softball career.

He ran his hand through his hair and blew out an exhausted breath. "Jesus, Lex you're right. I'm so sorry. I got carried away yesterday and I took something from you I didn't have the right to take."

He must have surprised her because Lexi stood there and just stared at him, as if she wasn't expecting him to concede.

"Will you forgive me?" he asked, hoping and praying she would soon fly into his arms and they could move past all this.

She nodded and he felt like crying. He went over to wrap her in his arms, but she stopped him. He gave her a questioning glare and she said, "I still can't do this, Jake."

"Wait, what? But I said I was sorry."

"I know, but I can't be with you. I need to find myself and, if you're with me, then I won't be able to do that."

"I can help you," he said with a pathetic pleading tone.

"No Jake, you will only be a hindrance."

Never in his life was he ever mentioned as being a hindrance. The cruel tone she used was like a slap to the face. He would have actually preferred Lexi's tiny hand connecting with his face like it had in the past. She wasn't even yelling at him now; she just looked deflated, hurt and sad. Did he really do this to her? Did he take away all her independence? He thought back to when he first met her and remembered how independent she was, but that was just because there really was no one to watch over her, except for Parker. Did Parker say something to her?

"Is this Parker's idea?" Jake had to ask, even though he knew the question might start up World War three, four and five.

"Are you fucking kidding me right now?"

Yup, wrong time to ask that question, he thought. She was yelling again. At least he could deal with the yelling Lexi, the deflated Lexi he had no clue how to handle.

"You're such dick, you know that? I don't need a man telling me how to live my life."

He let out a frustrated growl. "I shouldn't have said that, I'm sorry. I'm just so frazzled right now. I don't know what to do. I can't lose you Lexi, you're my everything, and you make me who I am."

"No Jake, you made yourself. I had nothing to do with who you are."

"How can you even say that?" He tried to hold her hands, but she rejected his touch. He had never seen her like this, so turned off by him, except for the first night they met, but even then, he saw a little sparkle in her eyes. "Lexi, I've changed so much this year and in a good way. You make me want to be a better man. How can you say you didn't have any part in that? Please, let's just sit down and talk this out. We can figure out what you want to do. I'll help you."

She just shook her head. She wasn't even giving him a chance. "No, Jake. I need to do this myself and I can't have you around when I try to figure things out. I'm sorry."

He finally was able to take her hands and he put them up to his beating heart; he felt tears prick his eyes. "Please Lex, please don't do this to me. I need you."

She looked away from him as tears fell down her cheeks. "I'm so sorry."

"No, baby."

She pulled her hands out of his grasp and cried into them. "Please go."

"I can't. I need to make everything okay."

"Jake, GO!" she shouted. "I don't love you anymore, okay? Don't make this harder than it is."

Jake's heart stopped beating from the heinous words that flew out of her mouth. His entire body went numb and anything he was feeling completely vanished. There was nothing anyone could say to him now that could hurt worse. It was as if her words instantly removed his soul.

"You don't mean that."

She looked him dead in the eyes and said, "Yes, I do. Now leave!"

Jake took a step back from the venom that was pouring out of her eyes. This was not the Lexi he loved; this was a confused Lexi that was trying to salvage a life she thought she wanted and nothing he did was going to change that. Jake took one more step back and then turned for her door. He looked over his shoulder as she crumpled to the floor and sobbed. He wanted to go over there and console her, but he knew it wouldn't help anything. Instead, he walked out of her door and out of her life like she wanted.

CHAPTER SEVENTEEN

Margo

Screams vibrated through the apartment as Margo sat in her room and listened to Jake and Lexi yell at each other. Normally, listening to them fighting wouldn't be such a big deal; they had at least one major fight a week, so hearing screaming coming from Lexi's room didn't faze Margo. What made Margo nervous was how closed off Lexi was when she got home from the game; how she left Jake without celebrating with him and how she didn't get out of bed this morning to go train like she always did. Something was wrong…something was very wrong.

She went out to the kitchen to grab the bagel she toasted and put some peanut butter on it right when she heard Lexi scream at Jake to leave. Margo cringed from the hateful tone Lexi used. She didn't want to get caught eavesdropping, so she quickly put the peanut butter away and went to grab a drink from the fridge, but that was when Jake left Lexi's room and made eye contact with Margo.

Never had she ever seen such hurt and dejection in his eyes. Margo wanted to reach out to him and make him feel better, but she knew she had to be there for Lexi. They just stared at each other and the only reason Margo broke the stare was because she heard Lexi sobbing from her room.

Margo went toward Lexi's room, leaving her bagel and drink behind. When she passed Jake she squeezed his arm and he bent down and whispered, "Take care of her for me, Margo."

The tightness in his voice from not wanting to cry nearly brought Margo to her knees. Jake was always the strong, hero-type guy that everyone could rely on. He was everyone's rock when they needed him. To see him so helpless killed Margo.

"What's going on?" she asked as quietly as possible, so Lexi wouldn't hear her conversing with who Margo now assumed was the enemy.

Jake shook his head and squeezed the bridge of his nose then rubbed his eyes. He sucked in a huge gulp of air and slumped his shoulders. "I have no fucking clue. She broke up with me because I control her life, apparently."

Margo stopped listening after he said she broke up with him. She shook her head in disbelief. "She what?" Margo practically hissed.

He put his head down and shook it. "She broke up with me."

Margo pulled him into a hug and shook her head. "No, she didn't mean it. I will fix this, Jake."

Jake pulled away. "No, I don't think you can. I've never seen her like this. She doesn't want to be with me. She called me a hindrance to her life. It's over, Margo."

With that, he pulled his keys out of his pants pocket and left their apartment. Margo just stood in the middle of the living room watching Jake leave. Lexi broke up with him? What was wrong with her? She was so in love with him; they were going to live together. He was going to propose. He told Margo all about it…it was the sweetest thing. There must be something seriously bothering Lexi for her to leave Jake and Margo intended to find out what that was.

She grabbed a tissue box off the coffee table and headed toward Lexi's door. Margo's heart broke from the sniffles and hurt radiating from Lexi's room. Lexi had always been a strong girl and took care of Margo, even during her worst. It was time Margo returned the favor. She needed to make everything okay, if not for Lexi, then for Jake. She might not have been on board with Jake taking her into his world and Lexi following him around, but she sure as hell didn't want them to break up.

Margo instantly felt an enormous amount of guilt settle on her chest. Was she one of the reasons why Lexi pulled away from Jake? Were her and Parker's comments the reason why Lexi broke everything off with Jake? Margo quickly grabbed her phone from her room before heading into Lexi's. She sent a text message to Parker.

Margo: Help! Lexi broke up with Jake just now. She is sobbing in her room.

Margo paced back and forth for what seemed like forever to receive a message back from Parker, but in reality, it only took him a couple of seconds to respond.

Parker: WHAT?!? I'm on my way!

Margo: Door is unlocked. I will be with Lexi.

Margo took a deep breath and entered Lexi's room. The curtains were drawn and there were no lights on. The only reason Margo was able to see Lexi as a heap of human on the floor was because there was light beaming through the creases of her window. Margo slowly walked over and sat down next to Lexi who was curled up like a ball on the floor. She gently placed her hand on Lexi's back and Lexi jumped at the touch. She didn't even realize Margo had walked in the room.

Her friend cried her heart out as Margo rubbed her back in silence. Margo lowered herself on the ground and pulled Lexi into her embrace, so she was spooning her.

"Shh…" Margo whispered in her ear. "I got you Lex."

Margo didn't know how long they laid there like that because, next thing she knew, Parker was bursting through the door wearing sweats and a T-shirt with his hair sticking sporadically out of his head. If Lexi wasn't so upset, Margo would have taken the time to really soak in Parker's I-just-got-out-of-bed look.

He bent down and picked Lexi up, pulled her close to his chest, and sat on her bed. Margo instantly felt a twinge of jealousy, but quickly stored it away because Lexi needed Parker. He would be able to help her. Parker nodded toward the window, so Margo went over and opened the curtains. The light was almost blinding, since she had been lying in the dark with Lexi for so long. Lexi buried her head in Parker's chest, trying to avoid the light. He didn't let her.

"Lexi," he said in a soothing tone. "You need to talk to us." He looked up at Margo. "Can you get her some water?" Margo nodded and left the room. She heard Parker whispering things to Lexi in her ear, but couldn't make out what he was saying. She wished she was in Lexi's place. How weird was that?

When she came back in the room, Lexi had her face pulled away from Parker's chest and was wiping away tears. Her face looked swollen and red and her eyes were completely bloodshot. Margo's heart went out to her friend. Why was she doing this to herself? If she was in this much pain, why did she break up with Jake in the first place?

"Lexi, tell us what happened," Parker said.

Lexi sat up a little taller, but still in Parker's lap. "I broke up with Jake."

"We gathered that," Margo said. Parker kicked her with his foot. "What? It's obvious." Parker just scowled at her.

He directed his attention back to Lexi. "Why did you break up with him, kiddo?"

"You guys were right." Crap, Margo thought, they did have a hand in this. "I was living in Jake's shadow; I kind of lost who I was and I finally realized it. It took me a while, but I realized it. I need to find out who I am and what I'm going to do with my life. Not ride around on Jake's coattails."

"You were never riding his coattails," Margo said, while

rubbing Lexi's arm. "You were helping him achieve his goal, but we just wanted to see you have goals for yourself as well. You didn't have to break up with him."

"Yes, I did," she said, while getting off Parker's lap and standing up, looking more sure of herself now than she was a couple of seconds ago. "If I stay with him, there is no chance I will be able to figure out what I want to do with my life."

"But, don't you love him?" Margo asked, not trying to drive a stake through Lexi's heart, but just trying to figure out her reasoning.

Lexi put her head down and grasped it with her hands. "I do. I love him so much."

Parker got up and pulled her into a hug. "Lex, you don't have to let him go. You guys can work at this together."

"No." She pushed away. "I have to do this on my own. I need to."

Parker and Margo both nodded. "You can stay with me," Margo said. "I have an apartment lined up for after we graduate. It will be small, but you can stay with me so you don't have to go back home."

Lexi looked up at Margo with a tear-stained face. Lexi flung her arms around Margo and squeezed her so tight Margo was afraid her head was going to pop off her neck.

"Margo, I can't even tell you how much that means to me. I know I want to do this by myself, but I can't do it back home. Thank you."

"Of course, sweetie. It's okay to ask for help, you know. You're not alone here."

"I know. Thank you." She grabbed Parker's hand and Margo's in hers and looked between the both of them. "You two are the most amazing friends. Thank you for everything."

Parker placed a kiss on her head. "You're welcome, but are you sure you want to break up with Jake?"

Lexi nodded her head. "If we are meant to be, then we will find our way back together."

Margo hoped so because she had never seen Lexi so happy in her life as when she was in Jake's arms. Margo only wished she had that kind of relationship with someone. She glanced over at Parker, who grinned at her. He would be leaving soon. Rumors were he would be going to the Atlanta farm system, but those were just rumors. The thought of him being so far away killed Margo. It was a whole other time zone.

Pushing the thoughts of Parker out of her head, she focused on her future. She had a fundraiser to take care of and a job to get ready for. She was going to be starting a new chapter in her life soon and, unfortunately for her heart, Parker was not involved.

Jake

Darkness surrounded him as Jake sat on his bed. He didn't know how long he had been there; he didn't even really know what day it was. All he knew was, Lexi ripped his heart out of his chest and stomped all over it. He didn't believe what she said. He didn't believe that she didn't love him. If she didn't love him, then there was no way she would have been as upset as she was when he left. No, she loved him. She was just pushing him away, which hurt. They were supposed to support each other. He didn't understand why that concept kept fleeing from her mind.

There were many times in their relationship where she didn't trust him to help. Jake thought he showed Lexi how much he wanted to be a part of her life, how much he wanted to be there for her and how much he wanted to walk through life together. Why was she shutting him out now?

There was a knock at his front door. Jake ignored it. He didn't want to talk to anyone. The brief thought that it might be Lexi crossed his mind, but he pushed that thought back. She wouldn't be at his place, not after the things she said to him. He fell back on his bed then heard another knock but this was more of a banging that kept rapping at his door. Jake let out a frustrated growl and charged toward his door.

He whipped it open and yelled, "WHAT!"

In front of him stood Parker with a depressingly sorry look on his face. Jake didn't want his pity, so he went to slam the door shut, but Parker pushed his way through.

"Jake, I want to talk to you."

"Well, I don't want to fucking talk to you."

"You might want to."

What the hell did that mean? Jake gripped Parker's shirt and pushed him up against the wall of his entryway. "What the fuck did you do?" He pushed him harder. "Was this your idea? I swear to God I will rip your balls off and use them as a hood ornament if it was."

"Jesus," Parker said, while trying to break Jake's clasp. "I didn't even know Lexi was upset." Parker tried to fight Jake off, but even though they were evenly matched in size, Jake had rage coursing through his body, giving him the edge.

Finally, Jake let up on Parker's shirt and walked toward his living room while running his hand through his hair. He heard Parker following him, so he turned around and shot Parker a warning glare.

"Why are you here?"

"I wanted to see how you were."

"You come to laugh? Gloat? See how I've completely fallen to rock bottom after Lexi ripped my heart out. I know you've always pined after her. I'm sure you're enjoying this."

Parker shook his head. "I'm really not. Watching Lexi cry her eyes out is not at the top of my list of fun things to watch and there is nothing I can do about it. Lexi and I are friends, that's it Jake. When are you going to get that through your thick skull?"

Jake sank down on his couch, put his elbows on his knees, and his head in his hands. Then he remembered what Parker said, Lexi was crying…a lot. He shot his head up. "So, you saw her?"

Parker took up residence in the chair across from Jake. "Yeah, and she's a fucking mess, man."

"What the hell? Why is she doing this?"

"That's why I came over. I thought I would give you a little insight. She still loves you; she told me just now." The vise that was closing off the breath to Jake's lungs loosened at Parker's words. She still loved him. He knew it. He knew she didn't mean any of the words she said.

Needing to be with her, Jake shot out of his chair and grabbed his keys. The only reason he didn't make it out the door was because Parker stopped him.

"Where are you going, man?"

"I'm going to get my girl. Now get the fuck off of me."

"You can't do that."

Jake spat back, "And why the hell not?!"

"She needs time. You need to give her time. If you crowd her now, you're going to ruin everything. She needs to find her path, man."

Jake shoved Parker to the side. "I'm her path. You have no clue. You haven't been around lately. I'm what she needs."

Parker shook his head. "I might not have been around lately, but I've been there for the past three and a half years and I'm telling you, if you go over there now, you're going to ruin any chance you have of getting her back. Please listen to me when I tell you, she needs to do this on her own. She is stubborn as shit and when she says she needs to find her way, let her." Jake loosened the grip on the doorknob he was planning to rip off the door in order to get to his Jeep. "Give her some space."

Jake dropped his head. "I don't want to give her space."

"I know, but you have to."

Unfortunately, Jake understood what Parker was saying. Lexi was one of the most stubborn women he knew and when she had her heart set on something, she went all out, hence the reason she just broke the all-time hits record. He had to let her go, even though he didn't want to. If he didn't let her go, he might never get her back. Jake threw his keys on the ground and slid to the floor so his back was against the door. He didn't like looking like a pansy in front of Parker, but right now he didn't care too much.

"Christ, this is so fucked up," Jake muttered, while rubbing his eyes with the palm of his hands. Parker slid down next to him.

"I agree, but all you have to remember is that she loves you. She loves you so much."

"I don't understand why she is doing this if she loves me."

Parker was silent, contemplating his words, but then broke the silence. "Don't you see, man? She's trying to separate you from her father."

Jake felt the rage boil back up inside of his body. "How many fucking times do I have to tell her? I am not like that bastard of a father she has."

"You can't tell her, you have to show her," Parker said quickly. Jake didn't interrupt Parker, he let him continue. "She needs her independence. Her mom warned Lexi about becoming her. Lexi watched her mom become so dependent upon her dad that she swore she would never be like her mom and when her mom tried to get away and stick up for herself, find her own way, her dad just beat the shit out of her. As if he was trying to show her she belonged to him. I know you are nowhere near her father, but Lexi is testing you. She saw herself becoming her mom and now she is trying to become the independent woman she once was. She is testing you to see if you will let her."

It all clicked in Jake's head. "Well, Jesus. I can help her, for fuck's sake."

"She doesn't want your help."

Jake blew out a frustrated breath. "That's what being in a relationship is all about, helping each other, being there, and taking care of each other."

"Yes, you're right, but there's a fine line between helping her out and running her life."

Jake shot Parker a warning glare. "I was not running her life. She could fucking choose whatever she wanted to do."

Parker held up his hands in defense. "I know, but you have to put yourself in her shoes. She has seen the extremes of what a guy can do, so if she senses any kind of control you're taking away from her, she's going to push it to the extreme."

Shit. Parker was right. He didn't want Parker to be right, but he was. Lexi was so sensitive when it came to her family and if he reminded her of any negative aspects of her family, then he could understand why she needed to separate herself and re-group. It didn't make sense in the real world, but it made sense in Lexi's world and he had to accept that.

Finals were right around the corner and then he would be heading off to start training with the Thunder's trainers. His life would soon be fully consumed by football and he hated knowing that the last free weeks he would have would not be shared with Lexi. But, if he thought about it, what were a few weeks compared to a lifetime without her? He needed to give her some space and time to figure things out.

"Alright," Jake said in a defeated tone.

"Alright?" Parker asked, confused.

"I'm going to give her the space she wants. I don't like it, but I don't want to lose her either."

"Smart," was all Parker said.

CHAPTER EIGHTEEN

Lexi

Lexi stood in the dugout waiting for her name to be called. She'd just played her last game and her emotions were out of control. They lost in the second round of playoffs, but at least they were able to lose at home where all her friends were, her family not so much. Her mom was the only one present; her dad lost the privilege to watch her play when he started beating the hell out of her mom.

It had been a couple of weeks since she last spoke to Jake. She missed him terribly, but she wasn't going to go back to him. She couldn't. She couldn't end up like her mom, who completely relied on her husband. Her mom now struggled to pay the bills on a tiny apartment, while she worked like a dog just to stay afloat. Lexi tried convincing her mom to ask for alimony during the divorce filings, but her mom refused to take anything else from her dad. Lexi admired her mom for her decision, even though it was slowly putting her mom in an early grave. Watching her mom fight for herself inspired Lexi even more to land on her feet after college.

Texas once again approached her, but Lexi declined and, this time, it had nothing to do with Jake. She didn't really want to be a coach, even though softball had been her whole life. That was the sole reason why she didn't accept the offer. She needed to separate herself from the sport that had run her entire life ever since she could remember. She had applied to a couple of odd jobs, but didn't really get any bites and there was nothing that really called out to her. She would be nervous if it wasn't for Margo. She hooked Lexi up with a temp job at the animal shelter until she got a real job. Lexi had to be able to pay the bills somehow. She wasn't too worried, she knew she was going to find her way and at least she would be providing for herself. Things were going to be tight, but she would be finding her way.

Lexi looked out on the field and took in all the sights, sounds and smells. Before the game, she put some of the dirt from the infield in a bottle for a keepsake and laid out in the outfield with Margo, looking up at the sky like they did their freshman year, marveling at the fact that they were going to play softball for Cal U.

The last four years had been a dream come true, especially the past year. Finding a man that loved her was something she would never let fall from her mind. She loved Jake, she truly did, but she just couldn't be with him right now.

Lexi was knocked out of her thoughts when the announcer said, "Number seventeen, Lexi Knox!" Lexi was escorted out to the field by her mom, where she met her coach in the pitcher's circle. It wasn't until the game ended and she got out to the pitcher's circle that she noticed the crowd in the stands and around the fence. It was completely packed and the cheering from the supporters nearly bowled her over.

The right field fence was taken up completely by the football and baseball teams, most likely Jake and Parker's doing and the stands were filled with future Cal U softball players. There were signs with her name plastered on them and chants filling the air. Never in her life had she ever experienced something so wonderful. Her mom was crying next to her and it took all the energy in her body not to break down.

She was finally getting the recognition for her past four years of dedication to her school that she deserved. She soaked up the moment and committed it to memory. The way the warm breeze crossed her face as she looked out at her adoring fans was something she would remember forever. Margo, the only other senior on the team, joined her and they held each other while basking in the cheers.

Margo leaned over and whispered in her ear. "Remember this, girl. This is all for you."

"You too," Lexi said, while looking up at her.

Margo pointed to a tall, handsome figure standing front and center in the stands and said, "No this is all for you. He did this all for you."

The man standing in front of her made Lexi's heart beat so fast that she thought it was going to pop right out of her chest. The photographer made Lexi and Margo stand together while looking out at the field as he took pictures of their backs, as well as their fronts with the crowd. It was a moment she definitely wanted captured. She turned and looked over at Jake who was cheering and smiling at her. Damn him, Lexi thought. Her heart was already weak; she didn't need him doing such amazingly sweet things for her.

Once the crowd died down and she hugged pretty much everyone she came across, Lexi took once last look at the field that all her blood, sweat and tears were shed on and stepped out of the dugout. She was startled when she saw Jake leaning up against the outside wall, waiting for her.

"Hey," he said.

"Hey." Lexi didn't want him here, she wasn't strong enough.

"I'm sorry you lost." Lexi just shrugged and fidgeted with her cleats in her hand. She always put on her slip-on sandals after games. "Are you going to the athlete party later this week?" he asked.

"Don't know yet." Lexi felt so awkward. He started to come toward her and she froze; she knew she needed to move away, but she couldn't. The draw to him was too powerful.

He wrapped his hands around her waist and pulled her in

close to him. "Damn. I miss you so much." Lexi didn't know what to say, so she stayed silent. He gave her a big hug and kissed the top of her head. She didn't respond, but she didn't pull away either. "Please say something," Jake said.

Lexi looked up at him; his eyes were full of hope and she knew she was leading him on. She let him hold her and touch her and that was wrong. She pulled away and said, "Jake, I can't do this. You know that. I'm sorry."

She started to walk away, but he stopped her. "Lexi, please talk to me. I want to fix this."

"That's the problem. Jake. You always want to be the solution. Well I don't want that. I want to do this on my own."

Jake ran a hand over his face. "But being in a relationship means helping each other out. Please Lexi, let me help you."

Lexi shook her head. "No, Jake." She continued to walk away from him, but turned around quickly and spread her arms out. "Thank you for everything today. It was truly magical." He looked so sad and depressed. "I'm sorry, Jake. I'm sorry I'm being so awful to you. You deserve better and I'm sure you will find that special person someday."

"I already did," he said, while she was walking away. "And she keeps choosing to walk away from me. This isn't over Lexi, not by a long shot."

Lexi didn't stop to listen to the rest of his speech, she kept propelling her legs forward, as far away from Jake as possible. She was way too weak where Jake was concerned. He was perfect in every way, but that was not what she needed. In order to even be good enough for Jake, she needed to find out who she was first, then if he already wasn't with someone, then she could fully give herself over to Jake: mind, body and soul.

Margo

Margo pulled on her short denim skirt and paired it with a deep blue halter top and strappy wedges. It was the last party of the year and Margo wanted to go out in style. Some people had been drinking all day, starting at nine in the morning and were still at it. Margo wanted to stay classy, so she waited until the party. She talked to Lexi all week about going to the party, but kept getting turned down.

They had moved into their new place, well Margo's new place where Lexi was a temporary guest. Margo didn't mind having Lexi stay with her; it was actually kind of nice, since Lexi could help Margo ease into a new place. Starting next week, they both would be reporting to the shelter to start work, Margo more on the business side and Lexi on the day-to-day operations. Margo wasn't sure how happy Lexi actually was about the whole job situation, but she did know she was grateful for the opportunity.

Jake called Margo a couple of times during the week, asking if Lexi was going to be at the party. Sadly, she had to keep telling him no. He was going to start training soon with the Thunder, so he wouldn't be seeing Lexi around campus anymore; Margo felt awful. She didn't know what to do; she wanted to help Jake and snap Lexi out of the funk she was in, but she also didn't want to push Lexi too much. She was determined and Margo didn't really want to get in the way of that.

There was a knock on her door that had Margo turning around to see that Parker had let himself in. He looked way too good; he should be illegal. He wore tight-fitting jeans, a button-up grey shirt and black vest, as if he'd just jumped out of a Justin Timberlake video. Margo tried not to stare, but she couldn't help herself; he was gorgeous.

"Hey, beautiful." Parker leaned down and kissed Margo on the cheek. She inhaled the sweet scent of his cologne and committed it to memory. He was going to Atlanta for baseball and he would be leaving soon to get settled, even though the baseball season just started. Everything was changing and Margo wasn't sure if she would be able to handle it.

The horribly embarrassing moment they shared outside the coffee house, where Margo confessed her feelings for Parker was never brought up again. Margo was grateful because she didn't know how she would react if Parker asked her about her confession. Her confession was put to rest, thankfully.

"Hey, Parker. You look good," she said with a smile.

"Speak for yourself. I'm going to need to behave myself."

Margo giggled and thought to herself if only he wouldn't behave himself, this one time. She grabbed her purse, threw some lip gloss in it, as well as her camera and phone and turned toward Parker.

"You ready?" she asked. Parker was giving her a ride, so she didn't have to get a taxi later. Parker said he would be the designated driver, since he was trying to prepare for his upcoming move.

"Where's Lexi?" Parker asked, looking around the living room when they were heading for the front door. Margo peeked around the apartment and saw no traces of Lexi anywhere.

"I have no clue where she is."

Parker wiggled his eyebrows. "Oh, I might know where she is. I bet she's with Jake right now, making up for lost time." Parker was grinning like a fool.

"No, that's not going to happen. Believe me. I don't know where she is. Let me send her a text to make sure she's okay."

Margo: Hey, where are you?

Parker led Margo out the door by placing his hand at the small of her back. The feel of his strong grip against her skin made Margo's toes curl. Why did she have to be so attracted to Parker? It wasn't fair. Margo's phone beeped, startling her. She looked at the text she'd received from Lexi.

Lexi: At the party, you and Parker ever going to make it?

Margo stared at her phone, confused and then looked up at Parker who was matching her confusion. "She's already at the party, which is so weird because I don't even remember hearing her get ready."

Parker shrugged and pulled the car door open for Margo. "Maybe she really did end up going with Jake."

"I guess there's only one way to find out."

Parker closed her door and walked around the back to his side. Margo would miss this, the precious time she spent alone with Parker. Even though Lexi was acting weird, Margo was not going to let Lexi get to her and ruin this night. No, Lexi drama was going to be nonexistent and Margo was going to enjoy the time she had with Parker, what little time she had left.

When Parker pulled up to the infamous football house for their last party, Margo felt more than nostalgic. The football house was where she first met Parker. Lexi was already friends with him from one of her classes, but introduced Parker to Margo at the football house. It was one of the only parties Lexi actually attended her freshman year. After the catastrophe in the kitchen with beer spilling down the front of Lexi's shirt, Lexi wasn't too keen on going to parties after that. Margo couldn't blame her.

They both got out of Parker's car and walked to the back porch, as usual. Margo instantly spotted Jake and he didn't look happy at all. He actually looked like steam was coming out of his ears and he was about to murder someone. The grip he had on his beer could possibly break the bottle if he held on to it any tighter.

Margo nudged him with her hip and asked, "Hey, what's going on?"

Jake looked up at her and frowned. He took a sip from his beer and nodded over where the beer pong tables were. Margo could hardly believe what she was seeing. Lexi was at the party, playing beer pong with Marcus from the baseball team. Margo couldn't help but notice how good looking Marcus was. He was the right fielder and was also graduating, but he didn't have ambitions of going pro like Parker; he had a job lined up in advertising with some big firm in San Diego. Margo watched Lexi smiling as if she didn't have a care in the world. She had no clue what was going on.

Was Lexi trying to make Jake smash Marcus' head into a brick wall?

Parker just came back from getting beers and asked, "What are we looking at?" He must have spotted Lexi because he muttered, "Oh shit," under his breath.

Margo took a seat next to Jake and pulled his attention away from the game that was going on. "Jake, don't look over there."

"How can I not?" He nearly spit all over Margo from pure rage. "That's my girl over there playing with another guy. How the hell am I supposed to look away from that?"

Margo let out a deep sigh. "She's not your girl anymore, Jake."

Wrong sentence, Margo thought instantly because the fire pouring out of Jake's eyes nearly singed off every last hair on her body.

He pointed his finger and beer at Margo while he spoke. "Don't you dare fucking tell me she's not my girl." Jake ran his hand over his face and, this time, when Margo looked at him, he didn't look pissed; he looked defeated, sad, as if he was giving up on life. "I just don't get it," he said. "What did I do that was so wrong? I wanted to take care of her. I wanted to provide anything for her that she wanted. Any girl would want that…except the one girl I can't have."

Margo's heart ripped apart for him; she felt so terrible. She hated seeing Jake like this. He was always the fun, outgoing guy at parties, not the depressed guy who sat in the corner sulking while everyone else had fun.

Margo grabbed Jake's hand and squeezed it. "Listen, you did nothing wrong, not really, at least. She just needs to show her independence; you can thank her parents for that. Give her time, Jake."

Jake shook his head. "I don't know if I can." Lexi took that moment to let out a burst of laughter that snapped Jake's head up and brought back the fury Margo saw when she first sat down. She didn't like how this night was already starting out and she knew it wasn't about to get any better. She just hoped that Marcus would be able to walk out of the party alive.

Jake

Jake couldn't be outside anymore, that was why he found himself staring into a fridge full of beer and not making a move to grab one. He was letting the cold air cool down his raging temper. How could she do this to him? What was she trying to prove by showing up with someone else? Whatever she was doing, she was doing a good job at hitting Jake right where it hurt.

He didn't think when he begged and pleaded to have Margo bring Lexi to the party that Lexi would show up with another guy. Margo and Parker seemed just as surprised as he was, which was a relief. At least they didn't know about Lexi being with another guy and were hiding it behind his back. That would have felt even worse. Jake thought he earned a sense of loyalty with Margo and Parker. Yes, their loyalty shifted a little more toward Lexi, but at least they both had been very honest with him during the whole catastrophe of his break up with Lexi.

A small hand started climbing up Jake's back under his shirt and he snapped straight up and slammed the door shut. He turned around hoping to see his favorite set of blue eyes, but instead fell short on a pair of brown ones. One of the freshmen from the basketball team was trying to get close to him, too close. He couldn't remember her name; she'd hit on him a couple of times, but once news broke out that he and Lexi were a couple, she backed off. Apparently, she was back on the prowl.

"Come be my partner at the beer pong table…please."

She made a pouty lip that always made Jake angry. Why did women think they could look like a child and get whatever they wanted? Jake was in no mood to play around with the slut in front of him, but then again, who was she planning on playing beer pong against?

"Who's playing?"

A huge grin broke out across her face. "Oh you know, Lexi and Marcus."

Just as he suspected. Jake didn't want to play with this girl, but playing with her meant being able to get closer to Lexi without looking like a stalker. All he wanted was to find out what was going on with her and Marcus.

"Sure," he replied. "Let me grab a beer and I'll meet you out there."

The girl grinned and sashayed herself out to the back of the house. Jake reached in the fridge and grabbed a beer. He popped off the top and took a very long swig. If he was going to get through the next couple of minutes, he was going to need some liquid encouragement.

When he made his way out back, he saw Marcus, Lexi, Margo and Parker all talking, waiting on him to show up. Jake knew Lexi had no clue he was partners with the basketball slut because the look on her face when he sidled up next to his partner was priceless.

Marcus looked up and frowned. "Uh, hey. Didn't know you two were partners, Jess." That's right, her name was Jess, Jake thought.

Jess wrapped her arm around Jake's waste and squeezed tightly while planting a kiss on his cheek. It took all of Jake's energy not to wipe the kiss off in front of everyone. He needed to act like he wanted to be there, not like he wanted to punt the annoying Jess across the yard.

"It was a surprise to me too," she said, "But here we are, aren't we baby?"

She was putting on a show. Jake glanced over at Lexi, who was now frowning at him. What was her deal? She was the one who was hanging out with another guy. Out of spite, Jake wrapped an arm around Jess and pulled her in tight, causing Lexi to turn away.

Margo piped up. "Hey, why don't we take this game and give you two a break?" Margo said to Lexi and Marcus.

Marcus looked down at Lexi and whispered something in her ear. She shook her head and he said something else. Jake was seconds away from throwing the table to the side and ripping Marcus' whispering lips right off his face.

"Uh, we're going to play," Lexi said to Margo.

"Are you sure?" Lexi just nodded. "Alright, Parker and I are just going to stand here and watch then."

Jake knew Margo and Parker had people they wanted to talk to and hang out with, but they knew better than to leave Jake alone with lover boy and Lexi.

After many rounds of shooting ping pong balls into plastic cups, slugging beer and staring Marcus down, each team was down to their final cup. It was Jake's turn to shoot; if he made this, then he would win. Jake wanted to make the shot, not only to win the damn game, but to show how he was better than Marcus, in so many ways. Jake knew it was stupid because it was a beer pong game, but if he could make this shot, then, in his mind, it would seal the deal on all the reasons why he was better than Marcus.

Jake took a deep breath and shot the ball. He watched as it landed safely in the cup and he threw his hands up in celebration. Marcus rolled his eyes and Lexi just looked down at the cup in disbelief. Next thing he knew, Jess had both legs wrapped around his waist and his head in her hands. She planted a huge kiss on his mouth and then started cheering. Jake was so stunned he didn't know what to do. He glanced over Jess' shoulder and saw Lexi look at him with the most hurtful look he had ever seen and then she walked away.

Panic wrapped his heart as Jake instantly shimmied Jess off of him and chased after Lexi. He heard Jess scream something at him, but he didn't care what it was; he was going after Lexi. He caught up to her right outside the front yard while she was reaching for her phone. He spun her around and was struck in the heart when he saw tears rolling down her beautiful face.

"Don't," she said and started walking away again. What was her problem? She was the one who started all this.

"Don't what? Come after you because I'm worried about you?"

She spun around and jabbed her finger in his chest. Even though he knew jabbing his chest was a mad tendency of hers, it was almost reassuring because it was part of the Lexi he knew and loved.

"You don't care about me. If you did you wouldn't have been squeezing that chick's ass all night and letting her kiss you all over."

"I was not squeezing her ass!" Lexi gave him a "get real" look and Jake conceded. "Okay, maybe once, but it was only because that ass-fuck had his hands all over you."

"That wasn't my choice. He was the one making the moves, not me."

"Why were you with him in the first place?"

"It doesn't matter Jake because we aren't together."

Jake wanted to punch a wall. He didn't need her or anyone else reminding him of the fact that they were no longer a couple.

"You don't think I know that? You are slowly killing me each day, Lexi, by not being with me. I don't understand why you're doing this. Clearly you were upset when I was with the other girl, so why don't you give up the charade and come back to me."

Anger lit up Lexi's blue eyes. "Did you do all that to prove a point?" She pushed Jake in the chest. "God, you're such a dick. Why would I ever go back to someone who would play mind games with me? Just so you know, I came here tonight to have one last night with my friends. I got here before everyone else and, when Marcus asked me to play, I decided to go for it, have a little fun since it would be one of the last times we would all be together. Simple, innocent fun. But you had to take everything to another level by rubbing your little basketball player in my face. I would never do something like that to you, Jake."

"But you did," Jake shouted. "By playing with that ass-hat, you hurt me."

"Oh, so am I not allowed to ever talk to another member of the opposite sex ever again? Grow up Jake, I wasn't doing anything wrong and you know it. You were the one who took it up a notch because you're a jealous bastard. Well, I hope you're happy because after tonight, you completely destroyed any chance of ever getting back together with me. I don't want to be with someone who would purposely try to hurt me with someone else."

Jake felt his stomach sink to the ground. She didn't mean what she said. Jake tried to get closer to her, but she wouldn't let him, she kept backing away.

"Please, Lexi. I'm sorry. I was an idiot. I just didn't know how to react when I saw you with Marcus. I'm sorry I hurt you. Can we please talk about this?"

"No, Jake. Clearly, you didn't get it when I said I needed some time. Instead, you tried to hurt me and make me jealous. Well, you're an ass and I don't ever want to see you again. Good luck with your professional career; I'm sure you're going to be fully satisfied, especially by all the women who will be knocking at your door."

With that, Lexi turned around and ran off toward a cab that she must have called when Jake was chasing after her. Jake didn't know what to do. He felt completely numb. Did he really just blow his last chance at ever getting back together with the love of his life? There was no way he was going to let that happen. He wouldn't be able to go on if he knew she wouldn't ever speak to him again.

Jake turned toward the house to go back in, but decided to go to take a long walk instead, where he could think about what he did tonight and how he had possibly destroyed his future, the only future he really wanted.

CHAPTER NINETEEN

Lexi

Lexi pulled her graduation cap off her head and shook her hair loose. She never understood why the graduation caps had to be so hideous, but she made it look as good as possible. Her mom showed up to her graduation, but her dad stayed away, which was a good call on his part because Lexi would not have been happy to see him. She was still bitter toward her dad and Lexi wasn't sure when that feeling was ever going to leave.

She felt tired and not excited to be graduating. Life for all her friends was changing all around her and she felt like her life was at a standstill. The other night at the football party, Lexi thought she would have fun; never did she think she was going to see Jake hanging all over another girl right in front of her. The whole night made her physically sick, just thinking about it now twisted her stomach into a knot. She knew she was the one who broke things off with Jake, but never did she think he would move ahead with someone else so fast.

When she left that night, she went straight to the apartment she was sharing with Margo and cried herself to sleep. Luckily, by the time Margo arrived back home, Lexi was done crying, so she didn't have to deal with a million questions from Margo. Margo tried to bring up the party the next morning, but Lexi refused to talk about it.

Lexi started her job at the shelter on Monday and she wasn't really excited at all about the prospect of picking up dog crap and answering phones. This was not what she planned for her life. She had higher hopes for herself, but she washed them away. Lexi occasionally thought what life would be like if she hadn't broken up with Jake. She sure as hell wouldn't have the awful nagging pain in her heart that she had to deal with on a daily basis. She would be taken care of and probably in some nice apartment overlooking the ocean, instead of sleeping on her friend's couch.

Sometimes when Lexi looked at the decisions she made, she considered herself an idiot, but then she would talk to her mom and realize why she broke up with Jake; she needed to be independent. She needed to find her own way before she could live a life with Jake, that's if they even had a chance now. She blew up at him the other night and the look on his face was something Lexi would never forget. She had never seen Jake look so defeated, except for when she told him she didn't love him. Why did she ever say that? It wasn't the truth. She loved Jake, more than anything and she didn't think she would ever stop loving him.

"Lex, take a picture with me," Margo said, jarring Lexi out of her thoughts.

Lexi plastered on another fake smile so she could get through the day and just get home. She didn't even want to walk in her graduation, but her mom made her. Lexi would have been just fine with receiving her diploma in the mail.

Ha, her diploma, much good that was doing her. No employer wanted to touch her with a ten foot pole. That was what she got for spending her whole life focusing on softball and then her senior year focusing on helping someone else accomplish his goals, rather than thinking about her own future.

"Can I get a picture too?" Parker walked up next to Lexi and pulled her into a hug. "You look good, kid. So do you, Margo."

"Thanks," Margo beamed.

Lexi felt bad for Margo because Parker would be leaving

for Atlanta shortly and Margo would never get the chance to act on the feelings she harbored for Parker. She wished there was something she could do for her friend, but she knew there was nothing. Parker and Margo were going their separate ways; maybe someday they would meet up again, who knew?

"What are you girls doing after this?"

"Going out with our parents to eat," Lexi chimed in.

"Look out!!!!! Incoming graduate!" Mason nearly knocked Parker over with a tackle. Margo laughed and Lexi, once again, plastered on a fake smile.

"Dude, what are you doing?" Parker asked, trying to catch his balance.

"Celebrating!" Mason threw his cap in the air and cheered.

"Don't mind him; he's drunk." The-all-too familiar male voice came up from behind them. Lexi didn't have to turn around to know who it was.

Jake.

"Let's all get a picture together," Margo said.

She handed her camera to Lexi's mom and then grabbed Lexi's waist to pull her in. Jake stood on the other side of Lexi and wrapped his arm around her shoulders as well as Mason's who was doing the can-can while holding onto Jake.

"Say, go Bears!" Lexi's mom said.

"GO BEARS!!!" They all said, while Mason shouted.

Jake leaned down into Lexi's ear and said, "Congrats, Lex."

His breath caressed her cheek and all Lexi wanted to do was lean her head into Jake's chest to seek comfort, comfort she had been missing for a while. Instead, she just looked up at him and smiled.

"I want to get a picture of just you and Jake," Lexi's mom said.

Traitor. Lexi glared at her mom, trying to silently ask her what the hell she was doing, but her mom didn't care. She kept waving her hands together gesturing for Jake and Lexi to get closer. Jake took the lead and wrapped both his arms around her from behind and rested his head on hers. Her mom counted off and Lexi smiled for what she thought could be the last time because she was going to lose it any second.

Before letting go, Jake pulled her in for a huge hug and kissed the top of her head. When he pulled away, he tilted her chin up and said, "What happened the other night was a huge mistake. I want to let you know that, no matter what, I will always love you and I will wait. I will wait for you to find yourself and I will wait for you to come back to me because you are mine, Lexi. You and I are meant to be together and if that means I need to wait one, two or even five years for you to come back to me, I will. You hear me? I'm waiting for you and only you."

He pulled her closer and placed a soft kiss on her lips before letting go and grabbing Mason by the shirt. They walked away, holding each other by the shoulders. Lexi felt tears trickle down her face. How was she supposed to react to that?

A soft arm pulled her in for a hug. "Shh, it's going to be okay, baby girl," her mom whispered in her ear. Lexi just shook her head. "It is." Her mom pulled her head down and caressed the back of her hair with her hand. "Time will heal all wounds."

"What was I thinking, Mom?"

Lexi's mom gripped the side of Lexi's head with her hands and made Lexi look her in the eyes. "Believe me, baby girl, it's hard now, but it will get better. You made the right choice. He's a good man and if he means what he said to you, then he will wait. What you need to do right now is focus on yourself. Find who you want to be."

"I don't know what that is."

"Well, you have a world to discover, so go out and discover it." Lexi's mom slipped a piece of paper into Lexi's hand.

"What's this, Mom?"

"Open it, sweetheart"

Lexi looked down and saw a check for an inappropriate amount of money in her hand. Why was her mom giving her this?

"Mom, where did you get this money?"

"It's from your father."

Lexi shoved it back at her mom. "I don't want his money."

"He doesn't know about it. He owes us both and I want you to take this and go explore the world. Come back when you're ready, but you need to go explore."

"But Mom, you need the money more than I do…"

"Hush. I don't want your father's money and I don't need it. Do this for us, go explore, baby girl."

Lexi didn't know what to say. She looked up at her mom, who was smiling and all Lexi could do was nod her head and then hug her.

Go explore? By herself? This was a once-in-a-lifetime opportunity and she was going to take advantage of it. This was just what she needed. She was going to clear her mind and find her new path.

A man standing behind Lexi and her mom cleared his throat. "Pardon me, Lexi, I wanted to talk to you for a second."

Professor Lyon was standing next to her with a huge smile on his face. Lexi excused herself from her mom's embrace and walked over to a secluded area with her old professor.

"Sorry to bother you, but this will only take a minute. I kind of overheard your conversation with your mom. Are you going to go travel after this?"

"I guess so," Lexi responded, nearly blown away by her own response.

"Well good for you, but I want to let you know, if you're interested, I have a job for you. A real job that does not require you to pick up dog poop."

"A job, really?"

"Yes, when you get back, I'll give you all the details, but you have to make sure to be back by September." Lexi gave him a quizzical look. He laughed. "I'll give you all the details later, but just so you know, it pays well and the employers are extremely excited about having you on board."

"Why so secretive?" Lexi asked, wondering why he wouldn't

just tell her about the job.

"Because I want you to go out and enjoy yourself. Experience the world for what it has to offer." He handed her a business card. "Contact me when you get back. Have fun, Lexi."

Lexi shook her head in astonishment and waved goodbye to the man who might have just possibly saved her life. Lexi looked down at the check again that had her father's name on it. She was going to take full advantage of this opportunity and then, when she got back to San Diego, she was going to start her new life.

Margo

Margo was waiting in the coffee shop for Parker so they could have their last coffee together before he went off to Atlanta. Margo didn't really want to meet Parker because that meant that Parker was, in fact, really leaving. They'd made no plans to see each other at a later date, so it seemed like Margo had to say goodbye forever. She was dreading the meeting and almost thought about not showing up; she thought it might have been easier to just not have that awkward last goodbye, but she couldn't do that to him.

She looked down at her cell phone to check the time, he was fifteen minutes late. That was strange for him. She took a sip of her drink and thought about the trip Lexi was taking. Margo just dropped her off at the airport before she came to the coffee shop. Margo was so jealous. Lexi's dead beat dad was at least good for something. Lexi planned a month in Europe, followed by a month in Australia and then she was headed off to Hawaii and some other tropical islands. It seemed like a dream.

Lexi didn't even act like she was scared. She was more eager than anything. More power to her, Margo thought. There was no way Margo would be able to travel around the world by herself, she would be too scared. They made sure to pack her a Taser and some pepper spray, so she could be somewhat safe when she was alone. Lexi was saving money by staying with some host families, so at least she wouldn't be alone all the time.

"This seat taken?" Margo looked up and saw Jake standing in front of her. Lexi was an idiot for breaking up with him, he was a god wrapped in muscle.

"No, please sit down," Margo responded.

"So, how's it going?" Margo knew he was just being pleasant. He most likely wanted to know how Lexi was doing. Poor guy. He used to have a spark in his eyes, but now he looked sullen all the time. Lexi was breaking his heart and all Margo wanted to do was fix it, but she knew she couldn't pressure Lexi…that would be the worst thing to do. What a stubborn best friend she had.

"It's going alright. What about you? You don't look so great."

Jake leaned back in his chair and blew out a long breath. "No, not doing so well. My training is kicking my ass and a little blue-eyed blonde is kicking my heart. God, I know you must be sick of hearing it, but I miss her so damn much. I don't understand. I thought after graduation she would have called or something. It's been a week and a half and I haven't heard anything."

"You mean she didn't contact you before she left?"

Jake sat up straight in his chair as concern crossed his eyes. "Left? Where the hell did she go?"

Oops, Margo thought, her and her big mouth.

"Uhh…"

"Margo, where did she go?" Jake said through gritted teeth.

Margo fiddled with her cup in front of her and Jake stopped her hands. Margo looked up at him and caved. "She went to Europe."

"Europe?" Jake nearly screamed. "What the hell for? Please God, don't tell me she's moving there."

"No, no, she's just visiting."

"Jesus, I thought I almost just had a heart attack. For how long?"

Margo shrugged her shoulders. "I don't really know."

"What do you mean you don't know? She must have a return flight."

"Well she does have another flight, but it's not back here."

Jake slammed his fist on the table they shared, startling the crap out of Margo. "For fuck's sake Margo, just tell me what the hell is going on."

Margo didn't really think Lexi would have wanted Jake to know where she was, but then again, Margo couldn't sit across from Jake with such hurt on his face and not tell him.

"She got a bunch of money for graduation and decided to travel the world. I don't know when she'll be back. All I know is, she's alone. She is traveling to multiple points in the world and has enough money to do so."

Jake leaned back in his chair again. "She's alone? What if something happens to her?" Jake rubbed his chest where his heart was and if Margo didn't know he was one of the healthiest guys she ever met, she would have assumed he was about to have a heart attack. "I don't know how I'm going to get through this."

"Get through what?" Parker stood next to their table looking down at the both of them with a huge grin on his face and a green tea in his hand.

"Did you know about Lexi leaving town and traveling?" Jake asked

Parker slightly cringed and then nodded. Jake swore under his breath. "Sorry man, I thought she would have told you."

"Well, she didn't!" Jake jumped out of his chair. "Did she tell you when she would be back?"

Parker shook his head. "No, sorry man. She didn't know when she would be back."

"Jesus. Thanks. See you later." Jake shook Parker's hand. "Good luck in Atlanta, man."

"Thanks." Parker took Jake's seat and they both watched Jake stalk out of the coffee house with one thing on his mind, Lexi.

"Man, I feel bad for the guy." Parker looked over at Margo and smiled. "Sorry I'm late, I was on the phone with my agent. How weird is that? I have an agent."

"You're all grown up," Margo said in a teasing tone. "When do you leave?"

"Shortly, I just came in to say goodbye to you; I can't stay long."

Figures, Margo thought. It was all for the best though, she didn't want to make saying goodbye to Parker a long drawn-out process. She just wanted to get it over with.

"Well thank you for squeezing me into your busy schedule." Margo meant for her comment to be a joke, but it came off more as a snide remark and Parker picked up on it. He reached across the table and grabbed her hand in his.

"You know I'll always make time for you. You're one of my best friends."

"Alright." Margo couldn't look at him or say anything else because she was going to break down if she did.

"You're like a sister to me, Margo. I could never not make time for you."

Ouch! Like a dagger to her heart. A sister? Wow, she thought, if only he knew the very un-sisterly like thoughts she had about him. That solidified her future with Parker. They were friends and would never be more. Margo didn't really think anything would change between them, but she always wondered if there was a possibility. After Parker's sister comment…that squashed all thoughts of being romantically involved with him.

He looked at his watch. "I hate to cut this short, but I do have to go. Come give me a hug, kid."

Margo got up from her seat and settled into Parker's warm embrace. She laid her head on his chest and reveled in the strong muscles that tickled her cheek. She soaked up every last moment she had with him. This was it, she probably wouldn't see him again.

He lifted her chin up and made her look him in the eyes. "I'm going to miss you."

"I'm going to miss you too," she croaked out, holding back her tears.

"Take care and don't forget to stay in touch."

"You too!" That was the last thing she said to him as he walked out the door, right out of her life.

Jake

It had been three months since Jake found out Lexi had left the country. He'd tried contacting her many times through e-mail, phone, and text…any possible communication he could think of, but he never heard anything back from her. Every day of silence from her was like she was slowly jabbing a knife through his heart, pulling it out and repeating the process. He had never felt so broken and numb in his life. Instead of pining after Lexi and wallowing in his bed, he put all his energy toward football.

At least during the days he focused on football; at night, all he could think about was Lexi's soft curves up against his hard body, the way she giggled when he kissed her neck and the way she played crazy seductive tricks, just using her fingers.

He had many sleepless nights with thoughts and images of Lexi running through his head. He started taking some holistic sleeping pills just to get a couple hours of rest. He kept telling himself that the pain would get better, that he wouldn't feel like his heart was nonexistent, but it didn't. Life didn't get easier. He had many opportunities to move on with other women, especially since Adidas signed him on as their new spokesperson, but he wasn't interested in other women.

Women practically threw themselves at him, but he wanted nothing to do with them. He only wanted one girl and, ironically, she wanted nothing to do with him. She had completely removed him from her life.

His phone chimed as he put on his jersey. He quickly grabbed his phone to look to see if it was Lexi, sure she wouldn't miss his big day.

Margo: Good luck today, Jake! I will be rooting for you.

Jake had stayed in contact with Margo during the summer and she was the only reason why Jake knew Lexi wasn't dead. Margo would occasionally slip Lexi into their conversations, something Jake appreciated greatly.

Jake: Thanks.

Jake wasn't really in the mood for conversation, so he put his phone down. Margo was the last person, besides Lexi, he expected a text message from for good luck. Mason, Parker and a couple other guys from the team had wished him luck, even a couple of professors. But nothing from Lexi.

It was his first game with the San Diego Thunder and he was able to prove himself all through the summer workouts and training camp to earn the starting quarterback position. He was well-respected amongst his teammates and had a good rapport with his coach. Everything seemed to be going great in his life, except for his love life, which was nonexistent.

"You ready, rookie?" Bear, the center asked. The guys all called him Bear because he literally looked and acted like a bear. He was extremely hairy, big, and one hell of a center. Jake was easily able to tell the difference between the level of play in the NFL and college.

"More ready than I'll ever be."

"That's what I like to hear. Go get 'em, kid."

"Thanks." Jake really liked his team.

When Jake first came onto the team, he expected to get ridiculed and segregated because there was a lot of hype around him, but the team embraced him instead and helped him grow into a player that he never thought he could be. He was at a level of play now that, if he did everything right, he could easily land himself in the Football Hall of Fame.

Jake grabbed his helmet and walked out of the locker room to go warm up on the field. There were press people swarming the hallways as the PR guru for the Thunder approached him.

"Jake, I need you for a pre-game interview. Do you have a moment?" Marci asked.

"Anything for you, Marci." She was an older lady and had seen her fair share of players walk the hallways, but she was still on top of her game for her age. She could diffuse any situation in a matter of minutes.

"Great, we're going to conduct the interview out on the field." She guided him out onto the field, where there was a camera set up and a woman with blonde hair cut to her shoulders reading over some cue cards. "Okay, this is our new on-field correspondent. She'll cover interviews before and after the games. Be sure to look for her at all times when we want to get an interview, okay?

Jake nodded his head and walked up to the girl whose back was to him. She turned around and whipped off her sunglasses. Jake felt like his heart exploded into a thousand pieces.

Lexi was standing in front of him, with a new haircut, tight skirt, blazer and her make-up was camera-ready. Jake felt like he'd swallowed his tongue; he couldn't find any words to speak.

Marci grabbed Lexi and brought her over. "Jake, this is Lexi Knox, our new on-field correspondent. She will be at every home game and maybe some away games, so you two will get to know each other pretty well." Lexi just smiled up at him with that gorgeous smile of hers. Her eyes were bluer than he remembered and sparkled with delight. She didn't look shocked at all or uncomfortable, probably because she knew where Jake was all this time.

"Lexi, I have to take off. Can you handle this?" Marci asked.

"Of course," Lexi said with a smile. The sound of her voice was like music to his ears. Lexi watched Marci walk away, but Jake kept his eyes on Lexi the whole time.

Now that she was in front of him, he didn't want to lose track of her again. He must be dreaming because there was no way she was standing in front of him, let alone working for the same team that he was playing for.

"Lexi?" Jake asked, as more of a question to see if he was living in real life or if he was in one of his fantasy lands.

"Hello, Jake." She still smiled at him, but turned her head.

"What, why, I mean…what are you doing here?"

Lexi twisted her hair, that nervous tic she had which made Jake want to grab her and run off to the locker room to show her how much he missed her.

"I, uh, hope this is okay…you know…that I'm working here. Professor Lyon helped me land the job and I couldn't refuse."

"Of course it's okay." Jake ran his hand over his hair and just stared in disbelief. "I thought you were out of the country."

Lexi looked at her watch and frowned. "I'm sorry, Jake. I would love to catch up, but I really have to get this sound bite from you before the game."

Jake shook his head and went back into starting quarterback mode. Now was not the time to get caught up in his emotions and personal life.

"Of course. Where do you want me to stand?"

Lexi shifted him so he was standing in front of the camera, then she talked to the cameraman about her questions. Occasionally, she would look up at Jake and smile. Those little glances were slowly taping his heart back together. Jake knew at that moment, that everything was going to be okay. Things between him and Lexi were going to be okay.

Jake cruised through the interview with Lexi and treated her like any other reporter and she did the same with him. It proved that they could still do their jobs, even though they had a past and even, hopefully, a future. Jake thanked Lexi for the interview and before he put his helmet on to jog out to the field, she grabbed his hand and gave it a squeeze.

"Good luck, big guy. Make me proud."

Jake did just that, he went through all four quarters of his first game as a professional football player, making Lexi proud. Jake had a great game. He led his team to their first victory of the season and couldn't wait to celebrate. There was one person he wanted to celebrate with and he was looking for her after the game, but she was nowhere to be found. He thought Lexi was supposed to do the after the game interviews as well, but he couldn't find her. Marci came up to him and started directing him toward the press conference.

"Uh, we aren't doing any on-field interviews?" Jake asked, trying to sound casual and not like he was wishing he could get another glimpse of the hot new on-field correspondent.

"We usually do, but we're going straight to the press conference this time since it's the first game. Follow me."

Jake was able to stop off in the locker room quickly to change into a clean shirt and made sure to grab his phone before he entered the press conference. He wanted to see if Lexi had tried to contact him. When he looked at his phone there was nothing, except congratulations from everyone else. Jake's heart dropped once again. Maybe his mind was playing tricks with him. Maybe Lexi was just trying to be nice earlier and she didn't really want anything to do with him.

Still, he needed to know, so he sent her a text message before he went into the press conference.

Jake: Hey, where are you? I want to see you again. I have a press conference, so I will call you after.

Jake sat through what seemed like a million questions about his transition into the NFL, the win, and how he was adjusting to his new receivers, which he had proved today that he was adjusting quite nicely. It felt weird not passing to Mason out on the field, but he was able to form a new bond with the guys on his team. Half an hour later, Jake was heading out of the room with a bottle of water. He called Lexi, but still no answer.

Damn it, he thought. He went back to the locker room and took a hot shower. What should be one of the most amazing nights of his life was turning into another night of anger and disappointment. When was he ever going to learn to let her go?

All the guys invited him out to dinner, but he turned them down, saying he was tired and just wanted to get some rest. He was called a few pansy names, but then left alone. Jake threw on a pair of nice jeans and a button-up shirt. Thankfully, the dress code after games wasn't strict, so he could walk out of the locker room feeling like a normal human and not like a suit.

He grabbed his keys and headed out to the parking lot. He was checking his phone when he heard someone clear their throat. He looked up and saw his blonde goddess leaning up against a pole. She was still wearing her sexy interviewer outfit and he just realized she was sporting some of the sexiest heels he had ever seen. His mouth watered at the sight of her, but he kept his distance. He didn't know how to react. She had ignored him so many times, he didn't know if he could take one last rejection.

Lexi

Lexi stared at Jake and was mentally kicking herself in the ass. How long had she denied herself of him when she could have had him all along? She wasn't going to wait for him after the game, but after receiving his text message, she decided to wait. She'd watched the entire game with a knot in her stomach because all she wanted was for Jake to do well. She'd watched him from a distance all summer. She only traveled for a couple of weeks, but then went back home. It didn't feel right to explore the world alone. She didn't want to do it alone.

When she got back to San Diego, she contacted Professor Lyon and he told her about the job with the Thunder. Apparently, he'd kept her video resume they did in his class and given it to his friend who worked for the Thunder. They liked her so much, they hired her. Lexi couldn't believe it. It was like fate was telling her she belonged in San Diego and she belonged with Jake, cheering him on like he always wanted, but also while she did her own thing. She spent the whole summer working with Professor Lyon, honing her interview skills and feeling more comfortable in front of the camera. The executives loved her so much that she was instantly put on the field for the first game. All they did was change her clothing and hair and she was good to go.

She didn't expect her first interview to be with Jake, but she was glad it was; it felt right. She made sure to tell her boss about her relationship with Jake and he didn't seem to care. He said as long as she did her job and didn't show any bias, then she was fine. That was easy enough, Lexi thought because there were plenty of times where she had put Jake in his place.

Speaking of Jake, he looked so mouth wateringly good in his jeans and button up shirt. His smile was big enough where she got a great view of his dimples and she couldn't help but melt into a puddle. She missed him. She missed him so damn much.

"Good game, big guy," she said, breaking the tension that was forming between them.

She knew she was the one who put the tension there, but she had to in order to get to where she was today. The only reason she was able to be as good as she was right now at her job was because she set Jake aside and really focused on her skills. Lexi also thought that was the reason why Jake improved to a status no other rookie quarterback could reach. They put their relationship on hold and both focused on themselves.

"Thanks." He walked toward her, but she could tell he was hesitant. She didn't blame him. She didn't have a proven track record lately of staying around. "Uh, what are you doing here?"

"Waiting for you." His smile got even bigger. Lexi held back the I-love-you sigh that wanted so desperately to come out of her mouth.

"For me?" he asked, while pointing at his chest and moving closer to her. They were only about a foot apart now and Lexi could smell the soap he used in the shower mixed with his cologne. The scents sent her desire for him skyrocketing. "You waited for little, old me?"

Lexi looked him up and down and said, "There is nothing little about you, Jake Taylor."

"You would know, babe." He closed the distance between them even more and rested his hands on her hips.

She looked down at his hands and then back at his face.

"What are you up to, Taylor?"

Jake looked down at their hips that were touching now and he thought about her question for a second. "I would say about eight to nine inches."

Lexi laughed and swatted him. "God, you haven't changed."

He chuckled and started making a circular pattern on her hips with his thumbs. Her mouth went dry as her knees started to wobble.

"I've missed you," he said very quietly. Lexi's heart broke in half. She couldn't believe Jake still wanted to talk to her after the way she treated him. She didn't deserve him, but she was a selfish woman and didn't feel like giving him up, not now.

"I've missed you too, Jake. I don't deserve your kindness or affection. I've been awful to you the past couple of months. You should be walking away right now and telling me to go to hell."

Jake shook his head. "Never. I told you I was going to wait and I did. The question is, are you going to stay this time or keep running?"

Lexi knew the answer instantly. "I'm staying."

Jake lifted her chin so she had to look him in the eyes. "I'm proud of you, baby. You made a name for yourself. It was hell on me, but I understand why you did it and I'm glad I gave you the time to think about what you wanted to do because you were amazing today. All the guys kept talking about the new on-field correspondent and it took all my energy to not knock their heads into a wall."

Lexi giggled. "Glad to see your temper hasn't changed.

"When it comes to you, nothing has changed. In my heart you are still mine and I'm going to make sure it stays that way. I told you I was going to wait and I did. I need you to tell me if I can stop waiting."

Lexi hooked her arms around Jake's neck and pulled him down so their foreheads were touching. His arms were wrapped around her waist and he pulled her in tighter.

"No more waiting Jake. I'm here and I want to be with

you. I can't live another day not being held by you, touched by you, or kissed by you. I'm so sorry I put us through hell, but I'm not sorry about the growth we both made." She lightly kissed him on the lips and then looked into his eyes again. "I love you and I want to be with you, now and forever."

Jake let out a breath he must have been holding in since he'd asked her if he still needed to wait. "Baby, you have no idea how amazing that sounds to me. God, I love you."

He pushed her up against the pole and linked their hands together as he took over her mouth with his. She felt all her limbs go numb from the pleasure he was shooting through her body. She missed this man, the man who taught her to love and who gave her the time to find herself in the messed up world she was living in.

They pulled apart and both looked at each other. "Where you headed?" he asked.

She shrugged and said, "I think I was kicked out of Margo's place today; I guess I started putting lumps in her couch. I found a place downtown that I'm thinking about renting…" Jake put his fingers against her lips to stop her from talking.

"Don't even think about it. You're coming home with me. You won't be leaving my sight unless absolutely necessary."

Lexi was hoping he was going to say that. "My bags are packed; lead the way handsome.

Jake

Jake made her close her eyes all the way to his house. He wanted his residence to be a surprise. He couldn't believe his life was fully complete now. He had his girl and there was no way in hell he was going to lose her now.

He parked in the driveway and cut the engine of his new Land Rover. He couldn't help himself; he loved his Jeep, but he wanted a little upgrade. Lexi seemed to like it a lot because when she slipped into the passenger seat she gave him a look that was full of lust. Yes, his night got ten times better.

When he pulled into the driveway, he put the car in park, ran around to the passenger side and opened the door for her. "Keep your eyes closed."

"Jake, I don't understand why this is such a big deal."

He didn't answer her, but instead, pulled her in front of the house. He stood behind her and held onto her shoulders. He leaned down so his lips were pressed against her ear, making her shiver. "Okay, baby. Open those beautiful baby blues of yours."

Jake knew the moment she opened her eyes because he heard her gasp as her hands went directly to her mouth. She spun around in his arms and looked at him in shock. Tears were welling up in her eyes. She shook her head and then kissed him, gently.

"Jake, you bought the beach house."

He gripped her hand and brought her into the house that now felt like home, since she was with him. "Yes, I did. It held too many amazing memories not to have it in my life, just like you."

She just kept shaking her head in astonishment. "I can't believe you bought it." She walked out the sliding glass doors that spanned the whole back wall and opened them up. The sea breeze filled the air and all the memories they had together over their winter break flowed through his mind all over again.

He slid up next to her and wrapped his arms around her. They both looked out at the ocean and soaked up the atmosphere that once was their winter haven, but now would forever be their home.

"This is so amazing." He kissed her temple and twirled her around in his arms so she was facing him.

"You're amazing. The most amazing person I've ever met." He kissed her on her nose and smiled brightly at her. "I love you so much, Lexi, and want nothing more than to spend the rest of my life with you, making more memories in this house. You're moving in with me, right?"

Her bright smile eclipsed his heart. "I couldn't imagine living anywhere else. This is seriously the most romantic thing ever." She playfully swatted his shoulder. "You're scoring major points, big guy."

Laughing, Jake placed a gentle kiss on her forehead. "I just want to make you happy."

"You do, every damn day of my life." She kissed him again and whispered in his ear. "I love you so much, Jake."

"Music to my ears, babe."

In that moment, Jake didn't think he could be any happier. He had the life he always wanted, a successful career, and the girl of his dreams. He was waiting for someone to pinch him because he wasn't sure if it was all real.

Lexi led him into the house, pulled off her blouse and threw it on the floor. Yes, he was the luckiest man in the world. Life didn't get better than this.

She wiggled her little finger at him and said, "I have a couple of months to make up to you for treating you so terribly and I have a couple of ways how to do so in mind. Follow me, big guy." She sauntered off to the bedroom and Jake quickly followed her, while pulling each article of clothing off his body as he trailed after her. He was so damn lucky.

EPILOGUE

Mason

He was engaged. He couldn't believe he actually did it. He pulled the trigger and finally gave himself over to one woman, the woman of his dreams. Mason looked up at Brooke as she straddled his lap and worked him up and down. She was gorgeous with her brown locks flowing over her shoulders, green eyes piercing his soul and slight body that starred in his sexual fantasies. She pretty much rocked his world.

Never did he think he would be ready for marriage, but after she worked with him all through the summer after graduation, gave him massages and helped him reach his dreams of becoming a starting wide receiver for the Denver Stallions, he knew it was time to make her his…for life.

Asking Brooke's dad for permission to marry his daughter was beyond nerve-racking, but the rich fucker didn't seem to mind too much that Mason wanted to whisk his daughter away. The man was a massive prick, but also could give two fucks about what really went on with his daughter, as long as she was happy and supported.

Mason was now making a decent paycheck, so he was able to get them an amazing apartment looking over the Denver skyline and it was close to the stadium, which was convenient for Mason.

He was starting a new life and he'd just made sure Brooke was a part of it, by asking her to marry him.

She continued to gyrate her hips up and down, driving him crazy. Sex had always been amazing with Brooke. She was conservative on the outside, thanks to her rich upbringing, but she was crazy in bed. She did shit to Mason that he didn't think women ever wanted to do, which was another reason to tie her down. She loved to please her man.

"Fuck, babe. That feels good."

"I'm going to fucking come, Mase."

She was also very expressive in bed, which Mason appreciated. He liked to know he was doing a good job, well…she was doing all the work at the moment, but still, it was his dick that was applying the pressure.

Brooke gripped his chest, dug her fingernails into his skin and threw her head back in ecstasy. Her inner walls contracted around Mason's cock as she continued to slam down on him. His balls tightened from the sensation pouring through him and he finally found his release. He felt every last drop he had to offer explode into Brooke's center. She was on birth control, so using a condom never crossed his mind and he was grateful for it because he couldn't get over the feeling of being wrapped up without any barrier in her sweet, moist center. It was amazing.

"You are so damn good," Brooke said, as she rested her head on his chest. "Plus, you're damn fine."

"Thanks, babe. I would also like to say that I'm an attached man." He kissed her ring finger to remind her of their impending nuptials. "When do you want to get married?"

She didn't respond right away, so he thought that she might have drifted off to sleep until she lifted her head and stared down at him.

"I don't know. We're in no hurry."

What woman wasn't in a hurry to get married? Now that he thought about it, he would have thought she would have already set a date, booked a venue and already picked out a wedding dress.

Her lack of excitement was a bit concerning.

"You want to get married, right Brooke?"

She sat up, but still straddled him. "Of course. Mrs. Brooke Dashel. Has a good ring to it, don't you think?"

Smiling up at her, he agreed. "I think so. You sound good with my name attached to yours."

She shrugged her shoulders and then got off of him to go to the bathroom. He watched her beautiful ass sway back and forth as she sauntered off to the connecting bathroom.

Their room was made up of plush carpets, neutral tones and a massive four-poster bed in the middle. Brooke loved being tied up and Mason loved doing it at the same time. They were making a home for each other and Mason had to laugh at himself because he never thought he would see the day when he would be shacking up with a girl, proposing and thinking about actually starting a family.

Brooke came out of the bathroom, fully clothed and hair brushed to perfection. She put on her shoes and grabbed her purse.

"I'm heading out to hang with some friends. I'll catch you later, Mase."

"Wait? What?" Mason sat up in bed, completely confused about what the hell just happened.

"I promised some friends I would meet up with them."

Friends? When the hell did she make friends?

"Okay, but I thought we were going to hang out all night. I was kind of looking forward to tying you up and then banging the fuck out of you."

She walked over to him, patted his face gently and said, "Don't wait up." She kissed his lips gently and then left him alone in their bed.

What the fuck? Her nonchalant attitude was a little frightening.

He wanted it all; the job, the wife, the family…everything. He wanted it all with Brooke; he wanted a life with her and a family. She was it for him, even though she might currently be acting a little strange.

The minute he saw Brooke for the first time, he knew he wouldn't be able to shake her. She was a bit of an addiction for him and, even though recently she had been acting strangely, he loved her. He loved her so damn much that he would be lost without her. Asking her to marry him was one of the best decisions he ever made.

Or so he thought…

Book Two in The Love and Sports Series
Double Coverage
Available Now

Thank you for reading Fair Catch! I hope you enjoyed it. If you did, please help other readers find this book:

1. This book is lendable, so send it to a friend who you think might like it so she can discover me, too.
2. Help other people find this book by writing a review.
3. Come like my Facebook page: Author Meghan Quinn
4. Find me on Goodreads
5. Don't forget to visit my website: www.authormeghanquinn.com

ABOUT THE AUTHOR

I grew up in Southern California where I was involved in sports my whole life. I was lucky to go to college in New York where I met the love of my life and got married. We currently have five, four-legged children and live in beautiful Colorado Springs, CO.

You can either find my head buried in my Kindle, listening to inspiring heart ripping music or typing away on the computer twisting and turning the lives of my characters while driving my readers crazy with anticipation.

Made in United States
Troutdale, OR
11/05/2024

24471694R00186